The Glooming

Wrath of the Old Gods Book I

John Triptych

For my grandmother. Thanks for always being there for me.

Author's note:

Dear reader, I would like to thank you for purchasing this book. As a self-published author, I incur all the costs of producing this novel so your feedback means a lot to me. If you wouldn't mind, could you please take a few minutes and post a review of this online and let others know what you think of it?

As I'm sure you're aware, the more reviews I get, the better my future sales would be and therefore my financial incentive to produce more books for your enjoyment increases. I am very happy to read any comments and questions and I am willing to respond to you personally as quickly as I can. My email is jtriptych@gmail.com if you wish to contact me directly. Again, thank you and I hope you enjoy reading this book as much as I enjoyed writing it!

Please join my exclusive VIP mailing list! You will get the latest news on my upcoming works and special discounts. Subscription is FREE and you get lots of FREE books! Just copy and paste this link to your browser: http://eepurl.com/bK-xGn

For the Gods we know not of, who give us our daily breath,
We know they are cruel as love or life, and lovely as death.
O Gods dethroned and deceased, cast forth, wiped out in a day
From your wrath is the world released, redeemed from your chains, men say.
New Gods are crowned in the city; their flowers have broken your rods;
They are merciful, clothed with pity, the young compassionate Gods.
But for me their new device is barren, the days are bare;
Things long past over suffice, and men forgotten that were.
Time and the Gods are at strife; ye dwell in the midst thereof,
Draining a little life from the barren breasts of love.

Thou hast conquered, O pale Galilean; the world has grown grey from thy breath;
We have drunken of things Lethean, and fed on the fullness of death.

All ye as a wind shall go by, as a fire shall ye pass and be past;
Ye are Gods, and behold, ye shall die, and the waves be upon you at last.
In the darkness of time, in the deeps of the years, in the changes of things,
Ye shall sleep as a slain man sleeps, and the world shall forget you for kings.
Though the feet of thine high priests tread where thy lords and our forefathers trod,
Though these that were Gods are dead, and thou being dead art a God,
Though before thee the throned Cytherean be fallen, and hidden her head,
Yet thy kingdom shall pass, Galilean, thy dead shall go down to thee dead.

-Algernon Charles Swinburne, "*Hymn to Proserpine*"

1.Intruders in the Dust

When he finally opened his eyes and sat up, Gyle found himself staring at a glaring, afternoon sun hung in a blood red sky. After stretching his back, Gyle's bare feet touched the cold tile floor of the bedroom and he stood up, his massive six-foot four-inch frame still sore from last night's excursions. Gyle kept looking down at the geometric patterns on the floor as he walked gingerly to the bathroom, his sore ankles protesting. He kept thinking there was maybe some sort of hidden message in the way the different colored lines in the tiles bent and curved in and out of themselves. Since Muslim art forbade idolatry, their architects instead focused their skills on intricate geometric patterns of lines, circles, squares and stars, a form of mathematics he could barely understand, but found fascinating.

As the sink started filling up with tepid water, Gyle stared at himself in the mirror. He had just turned forty-two, and the bags around his tired blue eyes were getting deeper and more wrinkly every time he looked at them. He figured it was time to call it quits when his contract ended in a few months. His body was starting to break down and he couldn't stand it anymore. Dipping the disposable razor in the water, Gyle started shaving the top of his head, not too fine but just enough to prevent the itchiness on his scalp every time he needed to wear those bulky ballistic helmets with their night vision goggles. He had a two-inch long, reddish-brown beard that was starting to

1

turn grey, another reason to retire from all this.

Glancing at the side of the bathroom mirror, he noticed there was a half-inch small picture of a young Iraqi girl pasted near the bottom of the frame. When he had come into the house last night, he hadn't noticed it, but now it was glaringly obvious. It was held in place by a piece of Scotch tape at the back and he peeled the picture out and looked at it closely. The girl in the portrait was well-dressed, it looked like she was posing for some sort of religious ceremony, probably the daughter of the previous owner of this house, a former general in the Iraqi Army, who was now probably dead somewhere out there.

Gyle sighed as he put the picture back in place. Looking at it reminded him of Marie and his twin daughters back home. When he told her he got an offer from the CIA to go back into Iraq four years ago, she just put her head down and cried. She had thought that his last deployment was the end of it and he would be living back in Dallas to be with her and the kids. But the thrill of being back in the front lines, even now as a CIA advisor, was just too enticing. Gyle just couldn't picture himself working in a nine-to-five job back in Texas, he still had an itch to scratch. But now, with his aches and pains, he figured it was time. After this operation he would finally call it quits.

After putting his gear on, Gyle hefted the M4 carbine from the side of his bed and slung it over his shoulder before going downstairs for breakfast in the afternoon. His full name was Patrick Gyle, but everyone who was familiar with him just called him G, his nickname since his Marine BRC training days. As he walked down the stairs, he noticed his partner Matt was already eating from an MRE packet on the dusty kitchen counter.

Gyle unslung his weapon and placed it on the counter, right beside the Falcon III tactical radio that was still squawking. "What's the sitrep?"

Matt Walker was a younger guy in his late twenties, thick black hair and beard. He had been recruited by the CIA right out of college because of his language skills. Gyle didn't really get along with Matt because he never served in the military. He barely knew the kid, they had been assigned to each other just a few days ago. "Same old, same old, they want us to recon ahead to Mosul since there's been no resistance," Matt said.

Gyle frowned as he tore open a packet containing maple sausage from the MRE box on the counter and started eating. Mosul was at the heart of the IS insurgency. The Islamic State, used to be nothing more than a fringe terror group that believed in a radical vision of Islam. It was the incompetence and corruption of the Iraqi government combined with American carelessness and naivety that had allowed it to grow into an international movement. The Sunni extremists had joined up with former Iraqi soldiers and cronies of the late dictator Saddam Hussein. Within a span of a few months, they were able to capture huge swaths of the Iraqi countryside as well as parts of Syrian territory because of the civil war occurring over there.

However, there seemed to be a new development within the past two days as a raging sandstorm from an unknown source struck Mosul and the surrounding areas. When Iraqi army troops at the front lines began to report surrendering IS units that were fleeing to the government controlled south, both the Iraqis, the Kurdish Peshmerga in the north, and the US military decided to launch an offensive to ascertain what was happening and to take advantage of the recent turn of events. Only two days into the operation and Gyle's advance team, which was part of the US 4th Infantry Division, had already gone past Al-Shirqat and were now less than forty miles from the outskirts of Mosul. Just last night, the Iraqi army had reported they had already recaptured Hawija to the east without a fight.

Gyle opened a plastic bottle and started sipping the water in it. "Okay, let's saddle up then, you good to go?"

"Affirmative," Matt said as he began to pack things up.

Gyle walked out through the front door. There were several sand-colored Humvees and MRAP armored vehicles parked along the side of the dusty street. A few American soldiers were standing around nearby. Bravo Company had hunkered down in this little town on the outskirts of the main highway to Mosul just a few hours ago. The low visibility from the sandstorm made it too dangerous for them to proceed. Even though Gyle could have overridden that order from Captain Ron Kelly, the company commander, he chose not to since he knew everyone needed a break from the almost relentless forty-eight hour push north. He found Kelly and Lieutenant Ed Zwelinski in the adjoining house, they were with a couple of sergeants and were poring over a map spread out on top of a dining room table.

"Any new developments, Captain?" Gyle said as he walked into the room and stood in front of them.

Captain Kelly was clearly exhausted, but he was smiling. "Peshmerga units from the north of Mosul report unmanned IS checkpoints and no enemy patrols whatsoever. We're coordinating with them and will do a combined assault from two sides into the city sometime this evening. If all goes well, IS in Iraq could cease to exist by tonight."

Gyle scratched his beard. Something seemed off. IS were normally fanatical fighters, but within the last two days, none of the enemy was putting up a fight. The few prisoners they took had been in hysterics as they were led away to the rear, nothing coherent came from their interrogations. "Any intel from Mosul at all?"

Kelly shook his head. "Still nothing. It's almost as if every Daesh combatant in the whole region just decided to turn tail and give up. I've never seen anything like it."

"What about from the air?" Gyle said.

"No intel either," Lieutenant Zwelinski said. "The sandstorm means we can't bring drones or gunships in for a closer look. We have close air support, but we're gonna need to paint the targets with laser rangefinders because visibility in that sandstorm is close to zero."

"It's funny, I've never heard of a sandstorm lasting this many days over a city," Gyle said.

"Whatever it is, I'm just thankful it's making the enemy surrender. The way IS troops have been acting, it's almost like a sign from God. It's as if he somehow told them they're following the wrong religion," Kelly said.

Gyle looked at him. "Are you religious, Captain?"

"Evangelical and proud of it," Kelly said. "This is surely an act of the one true Christian God, our Lord Jesus Christ."

Gyle smiled. "Whatever it is, I'm thankful it's nearly over. What time do we begin?"

"At twenty-one hundred hours, G," Kelly said. That made it less than two hours away. "Let's see how long this miracle can last."

Gyle walked out of the house and back into the street. He could see Matt on the other side of the road loading his gear into the Humvee as he stared out into the highway to the north. From the corner of his eye, he could see the sun had begun to set and there were wisps of dust devils out ahead of them. A brownish wall of floating sand could be seen miles away, almost like a mythical mountain range made up of swirling dust and dirt, just beckoning at them. He had read some bedtime stories to the girls when he went on leave last year, and this reminded him of one story in which a young prince would make his way to a dark castle to find a princess being guarded by an evil witch. It scared the girls silly when he read it to them one night—they begged to sleep with him and Marie in the master bedroom. Gyle had that sort of feeling his kids had now, even though he was never scared by the enemy combatants, he felt that there was something else out there, something powerful and terrifying. But as to what it was, he just couldn't figure out.

"Uh, G?" a voice behind him said.

Gyle turned around. It was Sergeant Winston, a huge black guy from Tennessee. He remembered doing a recon with Winston's squad on the first day of operations. "What is it, Sergeant?" Gyle said.

Winston took off his helmet and sheepishly rubbed his forehead. "I dunno if I should be saying this, sir, but I saw something last night. I tried telling the captain and the lieutenant about it, but they said I was just seeing things."

"You don't have to call me sir, Sergeant. I'm attached to the CIA, remember? That means I'm technically a civilian so just call me G. Go ahead and say what's on your mind. What did you see?"

"G, something weird happened when we passed through Al-Shirqat last night, sir."

"What happened?"

"Remember those old ruins? I think they told us it was some sort of a temple before those IS ragheads blew them up or something."

"It's called Assur. It's an Assyrian archaeological site."

"Yeah, that one, sir. Anyway, when my two MRAP vehicles passed alongside of it, my driver, Specialist Carruthers said he thought he saw some sort of weird lights around one of the ruins, you know," Winston said.

"Lights? What sort of lights?"

"I dunno, sir. I was on the top of my MRAP as gunner on the Browning Ma Deuce, so I swung it around because you never know if any of those ragheads might try to sneak one by us you know."

"And? What did you see?"

"I saw something alright, I'm not sure if it was lights or maybe my eyes were playing tricks on me or something, but it seemed like one of the ruins was like, glowing, sir."

"Glowing?"

"Yes, sir. Like some sort of glowing lights on it like you know, when there's smoke effects on the dance lights when you go to a club or something," Winston said.

"You sure it wasn't a reflection from our vehicle lights?"

"I don't think so, sir. It had a different color and it was glowing."

Gyle stared blankly at him. "Glowing lights, huh?"

Winston shook his head. "I know you must think I'm on drugs or something, but I swear everyone in my MRAP saw it! I tried telling the Captain, but he said maybe we we're just seeing things."

"Who knows, maybe you did see something, I can't figure out what these IS combatants are doing. Maybe they saw it too before they ran away."

"There was one other thing, sir."

Gyle pretended he was still listening. "Yeah? Go ahead."

"I think I might have seen something moving near the lights, but only for a second."

Gyle frowned. What was this guy playing at? "Moving? Like men?"

"No sir, it seemed bigger than a man."

Gyle was slightly confused. Was this guy playing a joke on him? "What then? A vehicle? A car maybe?"

"No, sir, it looked like an animal."

"A mule or donkey then."

Winston was agitated. He could tell that Gyle didn't believe him either, just like his commanders. "No, sir, it was bigger, it looked like a big cow or a buffalo or something, but at least twice as big."

"Well, there are cows here in this country so I guess that would be normal."

"I don't think it was a cow, sir. It was way bigger and dark skinned and it looked like it had wings."

Gyle's eyebrows furrowed. "A giant black cow with wings?"

Winston looked down. "I'm sorry if it sounds like a joke, sir, but I'm serious, I really think I saw it."

Gyle crossed his arms and snorted. "Okay, Sergeant, maybe it was a mutant cow from the hidden Iraqi chemical weapons stash that we've been looking for all these years."

"I knew you wouldn't believe me, sir."

Gyle looked away. "Anything else, Sergeant?"

"I think it might have had a weird looking head, sir, like a human head, only bigger. Just wanted to add that, sir. I saw it for a few seconds and then it was gone. Okay, I think I need to go back to my squad now, sir."

Gyle thanked him and walked towards his Humvee, shaking his head. Matt was already in the driver's seat. The windshield was caked with dust and there wasn't any time or sufficient water to clean it. The upholstery smelled of sweat and there was assorted gear strewn around at the back. But Gyle was thankful they had a vehicle to themselves, he hated it every time he had to travel with a fully loaded Humvee. He could see the other soldiers getting into their vehicles; Bravo Company needed to move now if they were going to hit the outskirts of Mosul by the start time of the offensive.

Matt started up the engine. "What was that convo you were having back there?"

Gyle just shrugged as he put his helmet on. "One of the sergeants just told me he saw a giant buffalo with wings last night when we passed by Al-Shirqat."

Matt started laughing. "Holy fuck. Do you think the NCOs in this unit are on drugs or what?"

"Well, it's either that or the Apocalypse has already started."

The lone highway to the city of Mosul was pretty much deserted. They hadn't seen any civilians either on the road or on foot. The one time Gyle did see anyone was when they started their breakthrough two days before. A gaggle of refugees running south from the front lines turned into a full scale exodus. Since Matt spoke the language, he had interrogated a number of them, but nobody could give any specifics other than hysterical whispers about something terrible happening in Mosul. There were no more living souls within the city. The few IS combatants they had been able to capture told them the same thing—their leaders had disappeared and that any group that attempted to go north into the city were never heard from again. Matt had wanted to stay and question the refugees further, but the orders had come directly from the embassy in Baghdad to join in with Bravo Company for the push up north. Their mission was to report on the ground once Mosul had been recaptured.

As the convoy started towards the city in a single line, Matt drove the Humvee so it was just behind the lead vehicle. Just ahead of them was an MRAP, otherwise known as a Mine Resistant Ambush Protected armored vehicle driven by Sergeant Morris. So far, the only mines or booby traps they had encountered happened right when they broke through the IS front lines just north of Baiji, where there was an improvised explosive device at the side of the road just after the abandoned IS checkpoint. The mine blew up the lead MRAP, but thankfully nobody was seriously hurt. Captain Kelly quickly got a replacement vehicle and kept his unit going.

The only illumination now came from the vehicle headlights of the convoy as night had finally descended. For an hour, the MRAPs and Humvees kept the pace as visibility started to get worse. Gyle was reminded of his training in night diving when he was still with Force Recon, the utter blackness of the deep ocean around you with the only thing you could see was wherever your flashlight pointed at. As they kept advancing, the convoy was now immersed in a swirling dust of sand.

Sergeant Morris's voice on the radio cut through the silence as the lead vehicle slowed down. "Visibility down to just a few feet. Can't see for shit now."

"Continue your advance, just take it slow," Captain Kelly answered on the radio. "Any contact?"

"No contact, sir. Nothing. Not a goddamned thing. Not even any animals," Morris said through the radio as the static interference began to build.

Gyle turned to Matt. "Are we still in contact with the embassy?"

"Let me check," Matt said as he flipped the switch on the backpack radio beside him. He tried to call in, but all he got was static. "Negative."

Gyle activated the vehicle radio to talk to the convoy. "Captain, we lost contact with the embassy, are you still in touch with division HQ?"

There as a lot of static in the reply. "G … can … bare … hear … we … push … on.…"

"Goddamn it," Gyle said as he turned to look at Matt once again. "Do we still have GPS coordinates?"

Matt was pushing the button on the console near the dashboard. "No, I've been sending out the signal for the past half hour, but as soon as we entered the sandstorm … nothing's come back."

"Is it working?"

"Yes, it's working, I'm still able to turn it on."

At that moment, a loud thump on the passenger side window startled both men. Gyle pulled out his pistol and turned to his right, but was instantly relieved to see Lieutenant Zwelinski outside banging on the window with his palm.

As Gyle rolled down the window, he noticed the pace of the convoy had slowed to a crawl. "What's going on?"

"We're gonna stop, CO's orders!" Zwelinski shouted to him as he ran forward to try and get the lead vehicle's attention. The lieutenant succeeded and the whole convoy was now stopped. Gyle got out of his vehicle after putting on his goggles and wrapping a bandana over his nose and mouth. The sand storm was unexpectedly mild as only a fine curtain of particles hung in the air. In fact, it seemed to be more like a fog than a massive dust devil, but visibility was still only a few feet. As Gyle turned to his right, he could only see the faint white headlights of the vehicles behind him.

"Wait here, I'm gonna talk to the captain," Gyle said to Matt as he turned and started running down the convoy line. As he passed about a half dozen vehicles, he noticed the captain's MRAP with its extra antenna and he ran over to the side passenger door.

Captain Kelly noticed him, opened the door and got out. "I'm ordering Bravo Company to hold here. We have no visibility and we've lost communications with Division HQ. If we encounter anything ahead of us, we can't call in any air support. We've got to wait until this storm clears or we regain communications. I'm not risking my men till I know what's out there."

Gyle thought about it for a minute. "Understood, Captain. Matt and I will be going ahead. My orders are to find out what the situation in the city is."

"Are you sure about that? If you go too far ahead, we may not be able to offer you support. You'll be on your own."

"Understood, but so far we've encountered no resistance whatsoever. If anything goes wrong, we'll try to make it back here."

"Well, you're not part of my command so there's not much I can do to stop you. I'm ordering my men to set up a perimeter around this convoy. If you find yourself in any kind of trouble, try and make your way back here."

"Roger that," Gyle said and then he turned and started running back to his vehicle.

As he got back in the Humvee's front seat, he noticed Matt was still trying to get the GPS locator to work. "Damned thing just isn't getting a signal back," he said.

Gyle grabbed his carbine from the backseat and placed it on his lap as he pulled the bandana down to his neck. "Bravo Company is holding up here and setting up a perimeter. I told Captain Kelly that we're going ahead."

Matt looked at him. "Are you sure about this?"

Gyle looked at his watch. "We've been on the highway for almost three hours now. We should be close to the outskirts of the city. Since we encountered no resistance, I don't think we're in any danger."

"Famous last words, but the Lord hates a coward," Matt said as he twisted the steering wheel and stepped on the accelerator so that the Humvee started to bypass the lead MRAP. Zwelinski saw what was happening and looked confused. Gyle waved goodbye to him as the Humvee got ahead of the convoy and continued on slowly past it. Within minutes, the vehicle was surrounded by a cloudy darkness, with only the first few feet ahead of it illuminated by the light truck's headlights as they continued on the deserted highway. It felt like they were in a misty dream.

Both men kept quiet as the vehicle drove on. Within half an hour, they came upon on what seemed to be a few dozen stationary cars facing south. The vehicles were all partially covered with sand. Matt didn't notice any movement as he stopped the Humvee in front of them.

Gyle checked to see if there was a chambered round in his carbine. There was. He put his bandana and goggles back on and then pulled out a flashlight. "Stay here, I'm going to check it out."

Matt grabbed his own rifle from the backseat and chambered a round. "You want me to get on the turret?" The top of their vehicle had a ball turret with an MK-19 grenade launcher mounted on it.

"No, stay on the wheel. If things get hairy, give me some time to run back in the car, okay?"

"Wilco."

Gyle got out of the Humvee and started walking slowly to the line of cars ahead of him. Even though his vehicle had its headlights on full power right behind him, he could only see the faint outlines of the other cars. The lead car looked like a light truck with an improvised recoilless rifle mounted at the back. As Gyle looked inside, he noticed two corpses on the driver and front seats. The bodies had no clothes on and looked mummified, drained of all body fluids with their mouths open in silent agony, it looked like they were flash burned alive. As he went to the second vehicle, he saw it was a minivan packed with corpses that looked just like the ones in the previous car. Examining the vehicle more closely, he noticed that whatever burned the occupants miraculously hadn't affected the cars themselves, other than the dust that caked the van. Looking down at the wheels, Gyle noticed that all the tires had no rubber on them.

Shining his flashlight further down the road, he could see at least a dozen fainter outlines of cars ahead, with no end in sight. It looked like this convoy was on its way south from the city, as if they were all fleeing from something.

As he turned to face the Humvee and started walking back to it, Gyle saw hazy flashes of lights and heard the sound of gunfire and explosions towards the south of the road. Quickly breaking into a run, he realized the light show and the noise must have been coming from Bravo Company's perimeter. They were under attack.

"Go, go, go!" Gyle said as he got in and slammed the door shut.

Matt heard the sounds too as he quickly made a U-turn and started to accelerate southwards before slowing down again due to the minimal visibility ahead. "I'm sorry, I can't go any faster. I'm afraid we might collide with another vehicle if I go faster than this."

Gyle said nothing as he merely nodded and then climbed in the back of the vehicle, stood up, and opened the turret hatch. The automatic grenade launcher was caked with sand as he wiped some of it off the barrel, then he racked the massive bolts on both sides to ready it for firing. Gyle pulled at the lever near the turret ring to rotate it. Although it traversed slowly because of the fine sand seeping into its ball bearings, the turret could still rotate a full circle. Gyle adjusted the sights as the sounds of fighting got closer.

Within a few minutes, they had arrived to the edge of the security perimeter.

It looked like a scene from Hell. Gyle could see that the desert plains at the sides of the highway were glowing with some sort of illumination, it was as if the sand of the surrounding desert was on fire. He could see a smashed MRAP, it was as if some giant hand of God had grabbed it and tossed it on its side by the road. A few soldiers were outside of their burning vehicles and shooting wildly in all directions, their faces contorted in fear and hysterics.

As he traversed the turret to the right flank, Gyle noticed some sort of movement at a nearby sand dune. He quickly zeroed in on the sights of the grenade launcher and was ready to fire when his target finally came into view.

For the first time in his life, Gyle finally saw what it was they were fighting against.

He screamed in terror even as he pushed the trigger.

2. Strength of Stones

England

"And as Joseph Campbell said, 'Tear off the mask of God and you will find man.' The myths we dismiss as fiction these days had very profound meanings in ancient times and still shape our lives even today. There is substantial evidence there may have been indeed a Trojan War and it wasn't just an invention by Homer to amuse the Greek youngsters. He may have, in fact, been retelling an age-old oral tradition, and while he may have embellished a few things here and there, much of these oral myths have a basis in historical fact. Even the myth of the Gorgon, you know the hideous woman whose face could turn people into stone, may have been in fact, a proto-Greek matriarchal religious cult that was conquered by the Mycenaean tribes and then later was incorporated into their own myths and legends. Don't believe me? The Gorgon aspect of the hideous face with bulging eyes, fanged teeth, and outstretched tongue has been recorded in other cultures of the world. It is a universal symbol of fear and dread to the point where some cultures used that power as a form of protection rather than intimidation...."

Dr. Paul Dane, Professor of Anthropology and world renowned mythologist, was in the middle of his lecture as a special guest of the University College of London's Institute of Archeology at their main auditorium. There was much publicity about Professor Dane's latest speaking tour across Europe for the past several weeks, and this was his final stop before heading back to Harvard, where he was an emeritus of their Anthropology Department. In academic circles Paul was treated as a sort of celebrity, he had appeared in numerous TV shows and documentaries and was hailed as the successor to the late, great Joseph Campbell. The audience was composed of not just students, but fellow academics, media people, and even some celebrities who wanted to bask in Paul's popularity and charisma.

There were several reasons for Paul's popularity with the masses. As a writer, he had runaway successes with several bestsellers in both the New Age and self help sections in bookstores. His brand of blending in ancient myths with pertinent advice for today's world drew a following among people who were disillusioned with their traditional religious values, and those seeking a new meaning in spirituality by going back to ancient folklore and legends. With his salt-and-pepper-colored beard, steel-rimmed glasses, and eloquent speaking voice, Paul was a constant fixture on cable TV and internet documentaries on just about anything that had to do with ancient history.

"There were depictions of Gorgons in the Minoan palaces at Knossos. Even the Humbaba, a mythical monster that was described in the Sumerian epic of Gilgamesh was said to have such a hideous face, its gaze would kill anyone who dared to look at it. The Gorgon myth may be very well related to the evil eye, the superstition that if one looks at another in a malevolent manner, it would then bestow a curse upon its victim. An evil stare was considered to be so powerful that many cultures all across the world have their own variations of charms and spells to protect themselves from it. Even animals that stare back at human beings, like cats, owls, and goats, were considered to be cursed beasts, or familiars to witches and sorcerers and sadly many of these poor creatures were killed because of it. These myths can be found in practically every human culture all over the world...."

Paul Dane made a short pause. It usually happened during these times, when he was right in the middle of a lecture, in front of an audience and the heat of the spotlight was on him, was when he thought of Elizabeth, his wife of thirty-three years. They first met when they were undergraduate students in Harvard. They both liked the same things: ancient history, the study of dead languages, and a fondness for pistachio ice cream. The first time he laid eyes on her was right after their anthropology class when they ran into each other in the library. Both had attempted to grab the same book and when their eyes met, it was nothing but bliss. Although they had similar tastes, he was the more "laid-back," "down to earth" kind of guy and she was the passionate romantic, their debates about the origins of the Sea Peoples had kept them awake for weeks at a time, and they both wrote completely opposite theses on it for their postgraduate studies. Paul was given tenure first and Elizabeth, not to be outdone, went over to get her tenure at MIT after what she believed was an unfair decision by the Harvard faculty in choosing Paul over her. Ultimately, they patched things up and got married, but she never forgave him for it. Every time they disagreed (which wasn't often), she would bring up the point she was passed over because she was a woman. Paul would have none of it even though he knew it was all in jest. Although they never had any children, they soon became renowned experts in folklore and mythology because they would frequently contradict each other in public, even though they remained deeply in love in private. All that time, they taught and lectured, traveled the world, and enriched their experiences to further hone their talents. It was only in their thirty-second year of marriage when tragedy finally struck: Elizabeth had been diagnosed with stomach cancer. She bravely fought on, but the sickness had spread and she died within the year. Grief-stricken, Paul quit the faculty and remained in seclusion for a number of years before turning out his latest bestseller, *The Myths in All of Us*, which rocketed to the top of the bestseller lists for months. Although he felt like he was only half a man now, Paul dedicated his life back to his work, in memory of his wife. As he had paused but a few short seconds ago, Paul feigned a cough and sipped on a glass of water before continuing once again.

"In conclusion, I must say that everyone has a myth to tell. Everyone has a myth to experience. Why should we put any importance to these old legends at all? Because these myths are what keep us grounded in this world, without these age-old stories, our very existence would be relegated to acquiring nothing but material possessions. It also proves that myths are universal and it shows that there are more similarities to all cultures and ethnicities than there are differences. Myths provide meaning to both our history, and to our future. Thank you."

With that, the audience rose up and applauded loudly. Some whoops and cheers were shouted out and there was even a short chant, but Paul would have none of it as he cheerfully waved them away and just smiled before walking down the stage.

A small crowd of well-wishers, fans, and friends gathered in front of him as most of the audience began to file out. Megan Abramson, his graduate assistant, introduced two students from the university with copies of his latest book.

Paul smiled as he signed them with his autograph and posed for pictures. He sighed with exhaustion after the students thanked him and left. "I hope that was it. I am bushed and I'd like to go back to the hotel soon," he said to her.

Megan had been with him for three years now and knew his exact itinerary. "I'd like to introduce you to two more people," she said as an old man in a tweed suit stepped up to shake his hand. "This is Sir Wilfred Pyles, Professor of Anthropology here at UCL."

Paul smiled as he shook the old man's hand. "How do you do, Professor Pyles?"

"I must say that was a splendid lecture you gave, I was absolutely entertained for three hours, better than going to a concert with some strange bands that you don't even know what kind of music they play nowadays," Sir Wilfred said, smiling.

Paul laughed. "Thank you, Sir Wilfred."

"And this is Brian Farrar, from the Associated Press," Megan said as a younger man in a dark suit stepped up from beside Sir Wilfred and offered his own hand.

"Mr. Farrar, how are you?" Paul said as he shook his hand.

"I'm doing well, thanks." Brian said. "Can I get any comments from you on the situation here in Europe, Professor Dane?"

Paul arched his eyebrows. "What situation are you referring to?"

"The refugee crisis," Brian said. "My sources tell me the blockade against the refugees that are trying to pour into the Eurozone from both Syria and Iraq has been ineffective due to the fact that the number of displaced persons coming over to the shores of Greece and Italy have more than quadrupled in the past few weeks, they say. There's also large scale rioting occurring in Turkey."

Paul shrugged. "I think you're asking the wrong person about this. I'm a professor of anthropology. Shouldn't you be asking the EU ministers instead?"

Brian smirked. "Well, as a matter of fact, my sources tell me that the refugees are fleeing some sort of new cult that has arisen from that region, and that this new religion seems not to be Muslim in nature but is in fact ancient Babylonian."

Paul was shocked. "What?"

Even Sir Wilfred was surprised. "Excuse me, Brian, but did you just say that there is a new faction in the civil war over there and that they worship Babylonian gods? Surely this must be some sort of joke."

"I'm afraid it's serious, Sir Wilfred," Brian said. "I have a colleague in Iraq and I just got this piece of information a few hours ago. I've been told the US military has lost contact with an entire division of its own troops near Tikrit. Both Baghdad and Washington are on high-alert and they are putting a muzzle on all media personnel down there. There's a massive sandstorm that's blanketed the entire region as well, and this new cult is sweeping everything before it."

"I heard some rumblings about it on the internet earlier today, but nothing's confirmed, it's all just rumors, CGI and conspiracy theories," Megan said.

Paul shook his head. "That's impossible. A religion takes years, even decades to convert people into their cause. The Muslim conquests of that region took over four hundred years to complete. You're saying that this new religious group just came out of nowhere, swept the Islamic insurgency away and is now threatening the whole country in just a matter of days? I just can't believe it."

"It's not just that region," Brian said. "There have been reports of large scale riots in both China and in India. The Chinese have been arresting every foreign journalist in the country and their own government controlled news agencies are in complete denial mode. Something is happening all over the world and it's happening fast."

As the four of them were talking in the now nearly empty auditorium, they didn't notice a dour-faced, grey-haired man in a dark grey suit flanked by two armed policemen by his side walk up to them. The man cleared his throat and the four of them stopped talking and turned to face him.

"My name is Malcolm Pryce and I'm with the MOD," he said before looking at Sir Wilfred. "Are you Professor Pyles?"

Sir Wilfred looked at him with equal astonishment. "I am indeed. What can I do for you?"

Malcolm remained impassive. "Will you come with me, please."

Paul arched his eyebrows. "MOD?"

"Ministry of Defence," Brian said before turning to Malcolm. "May I ask what this is about, Mr. Pryce?"

Malcolm looked at him with cold, grey eyes. "No, you may not. This is a D-Notice affair so I must kindly ask you to leave, Brian."

"But, this is absurd!" Brian protested.

"Now," Malcolm said.

Seeing he wasn't going to win, Brian swallowed his pride and walked out of the room in a huff. Malcolm watched him silently until he was gone.

Paul frowned. "D-Notice? Ministry of Defence? What's going on?"

"A D-Notice means there's a government news blackout," Megan said to him before looking at Malcolm. "Do you want us to leave as well, Mr. Pryce?"

"Not just yet," Malcolm said to her before turning to Paul. "I understand you are an expert in anthropology and folklore, Professor Dane?"

"I have had some experience in researching it and I wrote a few books about it," Paul said. "But I don't even know what you want."

"Yes," Sir Wilfred said. "What is it you want with us?"

Malcolm's face remained impassive. "Professor Pyles, I understand you have been at the forefront of ongoing research on Stonehenge, is that true?"

"Yes, but I'm afraid I don't see how this relates to a D-Notice, or to you," Sir Wilfred said.

"You will need to come along with me to the site right now," Malcolm said before turning to Paul and Megan. "You two are American citizens, so I cannot compel you to join us, but I would like to request you do because we may need your additional expertise, Professor Dane."

Paul looked at Sir Wilfred, who merely rolled his eyes, before answering. "I have no idea what this is about, but from everything I've just heard in the last few minutes, this is far more interesting than having a bubble bath back in the hotel."

The drive from the heart of London towards Amesbury was less than a hundred miles and would take a couple of hours on the road, they estimated. Paul sat with Sir Wilfred in the backseat of the sedan while Megan took the front passenger chair beside the driver, who was a uniformed policeman named Steve. Malcolm was riding in another police car ahead of them. The small convoy was using their sirens to get ahead of the busy London traffic. It was early evening and the city seemed calm. The weather was a different matter. When Paul began his speaking tour a few weeks ago, most of Europe had been experiencing strange weather phenomena. There were cloudy days and almost daily rain showers and blankets of fog across entire regions, the meteorologists were divided as to what the causes were. The economic effect of the rains and storms was devastating as many airlines had at first rescheduled and then later on cancelled flights due to the danger. Meanwhile, international trade between countries was also disrupted as ships mostly stayed in port.

Sir Wilfred sighed as he adjusted his seatbelt. "And here I was, thinking this would be a quiet day in the United Kingdom...."

"London seems pleasant enough," Paul said.

Sir Wilfred smiled at him. "When did you arrive, Professor Dane?"

Paul smiled back. "About two days ago, why?"

"I guess you missed the news then," Sir Wilfred said. "In the past few weeks, all the major cities in the country have been gripped by spontaneous rioting and looting, mostly caused by young people, but their motives remain unknown and hundreds, possibly thousands, have been detained. The last few days were the exception since all police units are now on high alert."

"I'm sorry, I haven't been watching the news much since I started my tour," Paul said. He started to feel guilty about not watching or reading the news in the hotel rooms where he stayed the last two weeks, preferring instead to concentrate on his writing and lecture notes. "I did hear about the same things when I was in both Germany and France as well."

"I was keeping up with the news for you, Dr. Dane," Megan chimed in. "It seems to be happening all across the EU and nobody has any idea as to why."

"Happening in Eastern Europe as well, ma'am," Steve the police driver said as he kept his eyes on the road.

Paul leaned forward. "Excuse me, what?"

"We've been getting reports there's massive rioting in the East like Russia, Hungary, Poland, and in others as well, sir," Steve said nonchalantly.

Paul sat back into the seat cushion. "Oh my god, what is happening?"

Sir Wilfred put his hands up and wriggled his fingers. "The end of the world."

Megan couldn't help but laugh. Steve glanced at her briefly with an approving smile.

Paul turned to Sir Wilfred again. "Professor Pyles, could you give me a short briefing about Stonehenge? I've only been to that site once before and I was just a tourist then. Since Malcolm mentioned it, I'm beginning to wonder if there's a connection with all of this."

"You can call me Will or Willy when there isn't an audience around, Paul." Sir Wilfred winked at him. "As far as Stonehenge goes, it's really just a circle of stones. Radiocarbon dating estimates that the building of the site started around three thousand BC. We know there were three major building phases that occurred around that time, but the whole area was already being developed even long before that, people may have been using the site for well over ten thousand years."

"It was a druidic ceremonial site, was it not?"

"That is the common belief, but it may not be true," Sir Wilfred said. "The druidic cults as we know them started around three hundred BC, but we know full well the site is a lot older than that. The Neolithic people that inhabited the area did not have any written records so it's all just mostly guesswork, I'm afraid. What we do know is that it was some sort of burial site and people from all over Europe have ended up there. We unearthed the remains of a teenage boy dating back from fifteen hundred BC, and based on isotope analysis, it seems he was raised near the Mediterranean Sea while other remains were found to have originated in France and even Germany."

"Amazing," Paul said. "But the druidic influence is pretty strong these days when it comes to talking about Stonehenge, right?"

"Quite right, quite right," Sir Wilfred said. "Everybody who thinks of Stonehenge these days immediately thinks Druids! The disruption caused by the Neo-Druids these past few months has been nothing short of staggering."

"I'm sorry, Neo-Druids?"

Sir Wilfred chuckled. "Yes, it's one of these New Age, Neo-Pagan religions that have sprung up ever since Stonehenge was discovered by the world, so to speak. There had been a few nutters like Morgannwg who claimed, back during the time of the eighteenth century, that he was some sort of descendant of the last line of Druids, or whatever that means, and he soon gained some followers. Anyway, this movement really has no connection with the actual Druids who lived during Julius Caesar's time, if you ask me. It's all chanting and New Age pish-posh and all that. There isn't even a set dogma or belief system between the different groups."

Megan turned around. "I have a few New Age friends back at the university and they seem pretty mellow, what kinds of problems have these Neo-Druids been causing?"

"We didn't have too much of a problem with them before, other than the occasional disruption at the Stonehenge site when they demanded access to it for one of their annual ceremonies," Sir Wilfred said. "The authorities would naturally not allow anyone without special permission to touch the stones nowadays in order to prevent vandalism and erosion, but they recently relaxed this during the summer solstice months in the past few years so the pagans could do their ceremonies. However, these past few months have been a nightmare. Hundreds of them have been camping out near the site and have demanded all-year, full access and the authorities are not giving in on that demand, with good reason."

"Interesting," Paul said. "What's changed to make them do this now?"

Sir Wilfred shrugged. "I'm afraid I haven't the faintest idea."

"We're almost at the site now," Steve said as the car made the roundabout turn out of Amesbury.

Everyone gasped as they started towards the area. The circle of stones was visible from a mile away, but there were huge numbers of people all over the Salisbury plain. There was a traffic jam within the last mile before the turn due to the fact that massive crowds had been standing on the highway.

Steve cursed as the car slowed down and they were surrounded by a crowd of Neo-Pagan worshippers. Megan shrieked when the mass of people started thumping at the windows, shouting some sort of indelible chant. Some of them pressed their faces on the car windows and the whole scene was like watching a live Hieronymus Bosch painting close up. Paul made sure the doors were locked as Sir Wilfred just sat back and calmly faced forward.

The lead car kept the loud wail of its siren and even started honking its car horns, but the crowd was still too large to be controlled. All of a sudden, dozens of riot policemen with plastic shields formed a wedge and made their way to where the two cars had floundered until there was a sufficient lane for them to go through. The small convoy finally made it just inside the knee-high, single-rope fence where a police HQ had been set up using a cluster of small tents.

As Paul got out of the car, he could see Malcolm Pryce talking to the police commander. Megan was still in shock as Steve helped her out of the vehicle. Sir Wilfred took out his cane and gingerly walked over to get beside Paul. He could see no more than a few hundred police constables who were doing their best to hold back the huge crowds of thousands that were trying to get into the stone circle of Stonehenge.

"What in the hell is going on?" Paul said to know one in particular.

"I-I have no idea," Sir Wilfred said. "Every Neo-Pagan in Europe must either be here, or they made new converts from the crowds gathered around us."

Paul surveyed the crowd. They all seemed to be of varying ages though he saw only a few children. About half of them wore white sheets over their clothes. They all seemed to be chanting or just swaying back and forth as if waiting for something. Some of them even stared back at him, doing nothing but grinning ear to ear and looking like live, human gargoyles. There were a couple of news crews staying well at the fringes while a police helicopter flew overhead, occasionally putting a spotlight on parts of the crowd.

"Can you understand what it is they're chanting?" Paul asked.

Sir Wilfred pursed his lips. "I'm not sure, it seems to be Old Celtic with a sprinkling of Latin, I believe."

Megan walked over and joined them. Paul turned and gave her a hug. "Are you alright?"

"Yeah, I'm fine, Dr. Dane. I just got a little frightened for a minute there."

Paul smiled at her. "I'm sorry I put you through this. I'll ask if one of the cops can take you back to the hotel."

Megan shook her head and smiled back. "It's okay, Doc. I think I'll stay with you. Anyway it doesn't look like they can spare anybody."

Paul tuned to Sir Wilfred. "Can you make out what it is they're chanting?"

Sir Wilfred squinted as he strained to listen. "I'm not quite sure, they seem to be chanting about a man in the woods over and over again."

"That doesn't make any sense."

"It must be a form of mass hysteria or something to that extent, thank goodness this hasn't turned violent," Sir Wilfred said.

Steve had put on his black policeman's cap and walked over to them. "Mr. Pryce would like you all to join him in the command tent, if you please," he said as he pointed to the biggest tent just beside the monument.

As the four of them ventured inside, Steve went ahead and joined the other constables to help man the perimeter. The command tent was the size of a small room, with a folding table in the middle. There was a topographical map of the area laid out on top. Malcolm stood there waiting for them, along with police Commander David Tennyson and two other constables who stayed near the entrance flap of the tent.

"I apologize to the three of you for the delay in getting you here, but we do have a situation," Commander Tennyson said. "My men cannot hold this perimeter. We fear something may happen and things could get dicey very quickly."

"Which is why I've sent for the Army," Malcolm said as he pored over the map. "They should be here in about an hour so all we have to do is hold on."

Sir Wilfred frowned. "What's all this hubbub about anyway? What kind of situation are you expecting that you need to call in the military?"

"Her Majesty's government has reason to believe that what happened in Iraq may very well happen here, and could threaten the entire country," Malcolm said dryly.

Paul shook his head. "I don't get what you're saying, you're telling me the British government fears that some sort of religious conversion might just happen here? Right now?"

"Ridiculous," Sir Wilfred said. "The Neo-Druid Pagans have never been known to use violence, most of them can't even figure out their own dogma. This whole event seems to be nothing more than a case of collective delusion."

Paul turned to Commander Tennyson. "How did this situation start?"

Tennyson rubbed his forehead. "We received a call from local units stationed here that massive crowds had begun to gather this afternoon. Even though the Commissioner has brought in every available constable, the mass of people has kept growing until they now outnumber us at least ten to one. Although no one has attempted to trespass past the fence yet, I can feel the situation is getting worse by the minute."

"This can't be spontaneous, there must be something causing it," Paul said.

Malcolm kept looking at the map. "What I'm about to tell you is to be held in strictest confidence. A similar situation in France happened just yesterday."

Everyone's eyes locked in on him. Nobody else said anything.

Malcolm continued, "Carnac, in Brittany. I'm sure you three are familiar with that site because it happens to be very similar to Stonehenge. While not arranged in a circle like the stones we have here, the menhirs in Carnac are of the same age as the stones in this site. Last night, the French government reported seeing huge groups of people just like these over in Carnac, and they immediately sent in all available police units to the area."

"Go on," Sir Wilfred said.

"Sometime close to midnight, the authorities lost contact with their police units that had been sent to the area, and observers from several miles away reported seeing strange lights emanating from the Carnac site that reached up into the sky. A heavy fog soon settled into the area and there were no reports of anyone coming out. Additional police units were sent in, but none of them came back or reported in, and now the French government is enacting a state of emergency over the entire province as well as a media blackout," Malcolm said.

"Good god," Sir Wilfred said. "Why wasn't this in the news earlier then?"

"There were media personnel in the Carnac site that went in with the police, but their own news organizations have lost contact with them as well," Malcolm said. "The French government has seized all their video and audio recordings before the time of the incident in order to prevent widespread panic, while their military units have set up a perimeter just outside the affected zone."

"A-are we in any danger?" Megan said.

"I believe that once we get in additional reinforcements, we can disperse this crowd and all will be well," Malcolm said calmly.

Paul crossed his arms. "You can't be sure of that. And how do you even know that whatever caused the incident in Carnac was caused by the crowds of people?"

Malcolm looked at him with bored resignation. "The whole incident in Carnac happened only after the crowds were already there, so logic suggests that whatever caused it was certainly triggered by the masses of people. If we can just get these hippy tossers out of—"

His words were interrupted by a loud crash as well as shouts coming from outside. As everyone rushed out of the tent, they realized the crowds had begun to rush the perimeter to try to reach the circle of stones. The constables tried their best, but there was just too many of them as huge numbers of laughing and screaming people began to get through. Megan gasped.

"We've got to get out of here!" Paul shouted at Sir Wilfred as he grabbed a hold of Megan's arm and the three of them started running towards the nearest police car. The old man could barely keep up as he hobbled along with his walking stick.

The crowd surged into them like a swarm of ants. Megan screamed as Paul lost his grip on her arm. Sir Wilfred tried to swing his walking stick, but the people just started running over him as he fell over. Paul couldn't withstand the crush either as he was pushed to the ground, just as people were trying to go past him in their relentless quest to reach the inner ring of stones. As someone stepped on his ribcage, Paul let out a yell. A split second later, someone grabbed hold of his arm and started to pull him up.

It was Constable Steve. His uniform was torn and he had a gash on his forehead, but he was able to get both Paul and Sir Wilfred upright as there seemed to be a gap in the surge. "You both go on, I'll try to get Megan and bring her out of here, sir."

Paul clapped him tightly on the shoulder for a brief second before taking Sir Wilfred by the arm and getting to the car. As they got inside, he noticed the people around them had thinned as most of the crowd was already at the inner ring of Stonehenge. The masses were heaped on top of each other like a stack of squirming, white-sheeted ghosts as they clambered into the inner circle. Megan was nowhere to be seen.

Sir Wilfred was able to get his car door closed just as Paul started up the engine. "Good god," the old man said.

As the police car started on down the road, Paul noticed more people coming up from the highway. There must have been tens of thousands of them and more on the way. He quickly turned and started driving through the farmlands towards the south, hoping he wouldn't have to hit anyone along the way. As he kept driving, he noticed a flash of light in his rearview mirror.

"Oh my god," Sir Wilfred said as he turned around to see what was happening while Paul kept one eye in front and another at the rearview mirror.

It had seemed the Neolithic stones in the circle had begun to glow with a pale green radiance. Within seconds, a gigantic column of light shot up from the center of the ring and into the night sky. Then a massive wave of blinding energy began to radiate outwards with a gargantuan shockwave that hit the rear of the police car and sent it tumbling forward like a piece of paper caught in the wind.

Paul let out a curse while gripping the steering wheel as the car overturned. The last thing he heard was Sir Wilfred's scream.

3. Pampered Pets

Sandra McLeod and Jennifer Haggard were always a pair. Even when they were just children, they attended the same schools, became part of the same cheerleading squad in high school, and married husbands with very similar outlooks back in the 1980's. Both couples never had any children because Sandra's husband Donald was diagnosed with a low sperm count, while Jennifer's husband Joshua just didn't want any. Since both women needed companionship at home while their spouses were at work, they both became very proud and very particular pet owners and that's where they differed, because Sandra liked dogs and Jennifer preferred cats. So when Sandra called Jennifer up and asked her to come by her house that afternoon to see her new pet Chihuahua, Jennifer asked if it was safe to bring along her beloved Siamese cat Oodles. Sandra said it wouldn't be a problem and so the date was set.

As Sandra pulled her sedan into the driveway, she hoped Jennifer hadn't come too soon and had possibly left after she saw the house was empty. That was because Sandra just had to get her hair and nails done at the salon over at the nearby strip-mall. But that got delayed by over an hour because her beloved manicurist was out sick with a headache, and the receptionist had assigned a Vietnamese woman to do her nails that day. Naturally, Sandra had protested and didn't want the hands of an "oriental refugee" touching hers and so demanded they get somebody else to do it. The manager sighed and then asked another manicurist to take over, but Sandra wouldn't have it either since the replacement was a full-blooded Navajo, so she just sat on the black leather salon chair and waited with a sneer. The manager finally drove over to her personal manicurist's apartment to pick her up from her sick bed and bring her back.

Sandra looked at her perfectly manicured hands just before opening the front door to her house. Her lacquered red nails had a nice crimson sheen to them and she was sure the other two were supposed to replace her personal stylist would have certainly botched the job. She had been going to that salon for years and they owed her the best service they could give, since she was obviously their best costumer.

As she closed the door behind her, Sandra immediately went into the kitchen and placed her handbag on the marble countertop before checking that the little sandwiches she had made for Jennifer were ready in the fridge. The cucumbers were crisp and the bread wasn't soggy yet, so she took the tray out and placed it on the counter. With the snacks ready, she immediately started to look for her beloved pet. She needed to make sure the dog was still properly groomed since she took it to the pet salon only yesterday.

"Bibsy, where are you? Bibsy!" Sandra shouted across the house as she tried to imitate a puppy voice. Her beloved beagle Snoopers had died just under two weeks ago after being faithfully by her side for fifteen years. For a few days after that, she was inconsolable to the point where she wouldn't see anybody, not even Jennifer, and stayed in the house and didn't leave her bedroom for over a week. Donald had to take time off from his corporate law practice just to bring takeout food to her.

Right on cue, the little brown-furred Chihuahua came running over to her. It had large, bat-like ears, an apple-shaped head and slightly bulging eyes. Its coat was cut very short because Sandra told the groomers to please keep it as short as possible. Summer days tended to get hot in Scottsdale and she didn't want the poor little thing to die of heatstroke. As Sandra picked it up, she gave it a little kiss on its nose and examined its body. Everything looked great except the smidgen of excrement on its butt.

"Oh, you dirty little dog!" Sandra said as she took her pet to the bathroom and unrolled a few sheets of scented toilet paper and wiped the dog's backside. As she flushed her handiwork down the toilet, the doorbell rang. Sandra immediately yelped for joy as she took Bibsy in her left arm and hid the dog behind her while walking towards the door.

"Good afternoon, beautiful!" Jennifer said as she held out her left arm for a hug as they met at the open door. Both middle-aged women gave each other a kiss on the cheek.

"How are you, Jen?" Sandra grinned as she noticed Jennifer was carrying her Siamese cat in a carrier bag with her right arm. "Come on in!"

Both women walked into the living room after Sandra closed the front door behind them. It was a good thing Bibsy stayed quiet so she could surprise her best friend with it.

Jennifer put down the pet carrier near the rug as she looked around. "Oh my, I love what you've done with the place, Sandy! Your new living room is gorgeous!"

Sandra laughed. "Why thank you, Jen. Guess what else I've got?" she said as she pulled out Bibsy.

"Oh, how cute! What a cute little puppy!" Jennifer exclaimed as she massaged Bibsy's head.

Sandra laughed. "Actually he's not a puppy. The breeder I bought him from said he was already two years old, in dog years that makes him fourteen."

"But he looks so small! It is a he, right?"

"Yes, he is," Sandra said as she gave Jennifer the dog before heading to the kitchen. "Hang on to him, I'm going to get the coffee and sandwiches I made."

Jennifer liked her coffee with just a little milk in it so that's exactly what she received as both women sat down on the new white leather sofa Sandra's husband got her as an anniversary present.

"Have you been watching the news lately?" Jennifer said as she nibbled on a cucumber sandwich.

Sandra had Bibsy on her lap and was stroking its head. "Not today, I've been soo busy! Can you believe the beauty parlor actually replaced my manicurist with a gook today? It was just horrible. I don't think I'll ever go to that place again … they're hiring way too many foreigners and aliens. Where do you go to have your nails and hair done these days?"

"Over at Eden Hair and Nails, near the airport. I'll give you the address. I know the owner and she only hires whites."

Sandra sat back on the couch. "Oh, that's a relief. This country is going to the dogs. Did I tell you that the third house across the street a Latino family moved into? I was in shock! I can't believe those wetbacks can afford to live in this neighborhood."

"They're drug dealers, I bet. It's the only way Mexicans can make money; they just don't have the intelligence to be doctors or lawyers like your husband is. Josh told me he booked a beaner dealer the other day after a drug sting and the thug tried to bite him! Can you believe that?"

"Oh those people are animals. I hope he's okay."

Jennifer laughed. "Oh, Josh is fine. My husband is the toughest man I know. Naturally he beat up the guy so badly, the criminal had to be taken to the hospital, but Joe's partner covered for him so there won't be an investigation. They just said he tried to resist arrest during the raid."

Sandra nodded. "Good for him, I hope they deport that thug. Or even better send him to death row. There're so many wetbacks coming across the border now and that stupid president of ours won't even call the National Guard to help us."

"Oh, tell me about it. Since you didn't hear the news today, I'll go ahead and bring you up to date. The latest reports say that the number of people trying to cross our borders has gone up over five times in the past few weeks. It's a deluge of brown crap heading straight for us!"

Sandra put her hand over her mouth. "That's terrible, Jen! And still nothing doing from our president?"

"Not a damned word. But then again, you know what they say, he himself is a Muslim alien who wasn't even born here. With the way he's acting, I definitely believe it. I think he wants to bring the illegals in so he can get a third term."

"I believe that too. Also, the news did give us an update on the multiple airline crashes on the radio when I was on my way to the salon. That scared me to death, Jen."

Jennifer's eyes widened. "Oh? I must have missed that since I was just keeping up with the illegal alien news. What happened last night? You said six airliners crashed?"

"Seven, actually. There was another unconfirmed airline crash last night, it was a red eye from Seattle and it disappeared over the Pacific. The news said that the FAA might be planning to ground all commercial air travel in the country until they find out what happened."

"Oh my god!" Jennifer said. "That's hundreds of people dead! How awful."

"Yes, it must be those Muslim terrorists again." Sandra said. "I just can't believe we don't just arrest every single raghead and put them in camps or something. They want to kill anyone who isn't one of their own. Our Muslim president just lets them do whatever they want. Donald told me if he was president, he would have used nuclear weapons against the entire Middle East the moment he got sworn in. Turn the whole region to ash and be done with it."

Jennifer nodded. "If Donald runs for office he has my vote. It's those leftists and the liberals. It's their fault alright. They're the ones who want to let in all the illegals, plus they want gay marriage and they want all those black criminals released from jail. And those fags are truly disgusting and it's against the Bible. I tell you Sandy, they'll destroy this country if we don't stand up to them and right now. They're race traitors and communists, that's what Josh told me and I think he's right."

The Chihuahua seemed restless so Sandra let go of it. The dog immediately leaped off the couch and began sniffing at the pet carrier that Jennifer left on the floor. Sandra looked at her dog with obvious pride. "Isn't he so cute? Look, he's not even barking at Oodles. I think they'll be great friends."

Jennifer looked down at them and smiled. "Let's give them a few more minutes before I let Oodles out, she may start a fight and run all over the place. If that happens, we'll be here all day and night trying to get her back in the carrier. Where did you buy that dog anyway?"

"Oh, I got it from a breeder over at Flagstaff when Donald and I visited there a few weeks back after Snoopers died. The breeder said that this particular dog was from a litter he got at the Navajo Nations reservation. I don't normally take in pets raised by those redskins, but when I looked at him and he looked at me with those lovely big eyes I just couldn't resist," Sandra said as she winked and blew a kiss at the dog.

"I agree, I hate those Indians too. They're nothing but welfare addicts and drunks. They did nothing at all but drag this country down when it was the whites that built everything. They're no different than the blacks but at least they don't riot, that's the only good thing I can say about them."

Sandra looked at her approvingly. "You're right, those blacks are another problem. Did you see the riots on TV last night? Those coons are choking the life out of all the big cities all over the country. Thank the Lord there aren't a whole lot of Negroes here. They should all be shipped back to Africa where they belong. That reminds me, will you be going to the anti-immigration rally next week?"

"I don't know if I can, Josh might have a hearing he has to attend because he beat up two drunken Indians last year near the reservation, so he's under investigation by Internal Affairs again, so if I go join that rally, those liberals might use it against him. It's too bad though, I really want to go," Jennifer said.

"If someone ought to be exiled from these lands then it should be the two of you along with your evil husbands, you bigoted old hags," a tiny voice said.

Jennifer shrieked and dropped her half empty cup onto the mahogany coffee table, its lukewarm contents spraying the rug underneath it. Sandra nearly choked on her sandwich as she too dropped bits of cucumber, mayonnaise, and bread on the couch. For a long minute both women just stared at each other.

It was Jennifer who first started talking. Her eyes had widened like saucers. "D-did you hear that?"

Sandra's mouth was open, but she didn't say anything, she merely nodded.

"Wh-what was that?" Jennifer said. Her voice carried a touch of fear and hysteria.

Sandra immediately got up and started examining the couch and the nearby furniture. "I think Donald must have left an open mobile phone here somewhere, it must be some kind of trick."

"The only trick is how monsters like you two can have everything you've ever wanted and yet still hate those that are different, no wonder the gods are displeased," the voice said.

Jennifer grabbed at her curly bleach blonde hair and screamed as Sandra frantically looked around. From the proximity of the sound, the voice came from within the living room, in fact, it seemed like it was right next to them.

Sandra looked at Jennifer with a growing fear in her eyes. "Who's saying that?"

Jennifer said nothing as her mouth was agape, drops of saliva drooling down from it. Her shaking index finger was pointed near the edge of the rug.

Sandra turned and looked down, but all she could see was Jennifer's pet carrier on the carpet and her dog sitting on its hind legs right beside it. "Where?"

Jennifer was stammering. It was clear she was starting to lose it. "I-it's your dog!"

Sandra looked at her in disbelief before facing Bibsy again. "Are you crazy? Dogs can't talk. He's just an animal. God decreed that only mankind can talk."

"Wrong again, you big stupid, white hairless monkey. Why don't you stick another sandwich in your big fat mouth and just shut up," the dog said to them.

It was all just too much for them. Jennifer started to wail, grabbed a small throw pillow on the couch, and tried to shield her face with it. Sandra took a small ceramic leprechaun that was adorning the coffee table and got ready to throw it at Bibsy. The dog tilted its head slightly to the side.

"You wanna play catch now?" the dog said while Jennifer kept on screaming.

Sandra's hand was shaking. She couldn't believe what was happening. "Get out of my house, you spawn of Satan! The Lord is my shepherd and I shall not want, let him deliver me from your evil!"

"Oh come now," Bibsy said. "You didn't even get half of that verse right, you bimbo. By the way, you're definitely not a Christian. You can call yourself one, but that doesn't make it true."

Jennifer's screams continued. Sandra tried throwing the ornament at her dog but missed wildly as it shattered on the living room floor. Then she remembered that Donald had a gun in the bedroom. There was an unholy thing in her house and it was her Christian duty to destroy it.

"Hang on, Jennifer, I'm going to get Donald's gun!" Sandra said as she started to make her way towards the master bedroom.

"Aah, don't leave me with that thing!" Jennifer bawled as she got up and sprinted after her.

Both women ran into the master bedroom. Jennifer was crying her eyes out, her tears were streaming down her cheeks and had melted her makeup, making her look like some grotesque cabaret performer with raccoon eyes. Sandra desperately opened Donald's nightstand drawer and began to frantically rummage through the piles of papers, pens, and assorted bric-a-brac until her fingers felt the cold, bluish steel of Donald's .38 caliber snub-nosed revolver.

Her husband had taught her how to use it years before when she went with him to a gun range for the first time. Sandra was hesitant at first but realized she needed to know how to use it in case the blacks or the Latinos ever attempted to rob them in their house so she would have a credible means of defense. She never realized that she would now have to use it to kill her demon-possessed pet Chihuahua, but it needed to be done.

As she held the gun in her hands, Sandra pulled back the revolver's hammer with both thumbs and started to walk slowly out into the corridor towards the living room. Jennifer followed close behind, still sobbing with fear.

When both women got to the living room, Bibsy was still there, sitting quietly on his hind legs. The two of them slowly walked to the edge of the living room, right beside the stone mantelpiece of the fireplace.

Sandra's hands were shaking as she aimed the gun at the dog. "I'm sending you back to Hell, Satan!"

Bibsy looked at them with wide-eyed curiosity. "My friend that's sitting on top of the fireplace might have something to say about that."

Both women turned. Jennifer's pet cat was sitting on top of the mantelpiece just a few feet above them. Oodles instantly leapt onto Jennifer's face and began to bite and claw at her as they both fell on the carpeted floor. Jennifer screamed while trying to grab her cat, but Oodles kept at it, raking its claws on her face with the ferocity of a small tiger.

Sandra screamed as well and aimed at the cat before pulling the trigger. The sound of the gunshot was louder than she had anticipated, and the revolver flew out of her hands and landed on the carpet as she panicked. Oodles had somehow leapt away just as she fired and Jennifer took the bullet right between her eyes. Sandra started to sob as she knelt down beside her dying best friend.

4. The Flayed

New York City

Instead of checking her phone, Detective Valerie "Val" Mendoza looked at her watch. Cell signals had been erratic in the past few days due to storms and floods. Rolling power blackouts had begun to sweep many parts of the country. Huge slowdowns of the internet had begun to occur as major gateways across countries were rapidly being lost, while service providers were doing their best to reroute data on the few still functioning servers still out there. It didn't help matters much that there were two more airline crashes that were reported as evening fell, and that the FAA was ordering a ban on all commercial flights by midnight until they could find the true causes. The media and conspiracy websites were rife with all sorts of rumors, ranging from Muslim terrorist groups having developed a new kind of EMP weapon system that could disrupt everything, to religious zealots on the news proclaiming that the Apocalypse was about to begin, and for everyone to repent all their sins to the true god before all hell broke loose.

Valerie sighed as she leaned back and stretched her arms upwards. She sat in the front seat of the unmarked police cruiser. The only sounds inside the car came from the two-way police radio and the pitter patter of water droplets on the windshield from the rain outside. It was only her third year as an NYPD detective and already she found the job to be too monotonous. She was short and compact, with dark brown hair and olive skin. Valerie's dad was a Puerto Rican mestizo who came over from San Juan back in the Groovy Seventies, met her mother Josefina, a young Mexican girl who worked as a nanny, and after their marriage she gave birth to almost a dozen children. Valerie was the second youngest and the only one to finish high school. The two eldest brothers in the family were dead, one from getting knifed in jail and the other from AIDS complications because he used dirty needles for his heroin habit. Three other brothers were languishing in prison. Mama Josefina endured those painful losses with a quiet stoicism she was able to instill in Valerie and her sisters. While her sisters eventually ended up in menial jobs like seamstresses and fast food workers before they got their own husbands and became traditional wives, Valerie had higher ambitions as she willed her way to finish school and get accepted into the police academy. Even though her mother had hoped she would find a husband and bear her some grandchildren, Valerie refused to get into relationships with men who were interested in her, preferring instead to single-mindedly focus on her job as a cop. Her dedication paid off after she was finally promoted to full detective. But at this point in her life, Valerie had begun to experience the slight pangs of regret. She had turned down numerous opportunities for love and a relationship. In these past few months, she had begun to realize just how empty her life was outside of her job.

The driver's side door opened and Myron Jones sat down behind the wheel. "Here you go, Val," he said as he placed a cardboard tray with two Styrofoam cups between them before closing the car door so the rain wouldn't keep hitting him. "The one with the letter S is yours. No cream, only sugar."

Valerie took one of the cups and sniffed at the brewed coffee aroma. "Thanks."

Myron took the remaining cup, tore off the plastic lid and started sipping. "This situation is getting worse by the day."

"Which one? The non-stop rain, all the rioting in the city as well the rest of the world? Or the one where no planes can fly and we're about to lose all our phones and the internet?"

"All of them," Myron said. He was almost six feet three inches when standing fully upright and was a former all-star defensive end back in his high school days, before he tore up his knee. Myron Jones came from a God-fearing, traditional black family. Brooklyn born and bred, he was a twenty-year veteran and detective first-grade, a position that belonged to the most experienced and best paid investigators the city had to offer. They had been partners ever since Valerie made it to detective. Myron was both a mentor and second father to her.

Valerie sipped at her coffee. The squawk on the police radio was incessant. Riots continued to flare up all over the city and the entire New York Police Department was working double shifts. Many of them hadn't even been paid overtime yet because the city was already in a cash crunch when the disruptions started happening. And it was getting worse by the day. Thousands were now being detained in overcrowded holding cells, police and city psychologists could not identify the cause of the rioting other than to say there was a mass hysteria occurring. A few days ago, thousands of seemingly normal people, both the old and the young, inexplicably began to rampage through the streets and would start fires and physically attack anyone who attempted to intervene. Even when under lock and key, many of them continued their bizarre behavior and would only speak in gibberish when questioned. Firefighters and emergency crews were at their breaking point. The city was ready to explode.

Valerie hissed as she kept adjusting the controls of her handheld radio. "This stupid thing keeps losing the signal. I don't think I can communicate with Central if I'm outside of the car."

Myron checked his own handheld. "What about your cell phone?"

"Same thing, sometimes the signal goes out too. They're saying we could lose the entire cell grid within the next few days if the situation doesn't improve."

Myron sighed. "We could lose more than just that, Val. They suspended trading on the NYSE this morning because the market couldn't keep taking losses like it has in the past few days. All the other stock markets in the world will be doing the same thing. And they say the weird weather all over the country is killing the electrical grid. Looks like our Lord Jesus is on his way back and he's gonna be here soon."

Valerie smirked. She really wasn't religious. She just didn't have the time to even think about it. "You really believe that, Myron?"

"I dunno what to believe anymore, Val. I'm supposed to be two months from retirement and there's still no word on Kevin either," he said softly. Myron's only son Kevin was in the US Army and he was stationed in Iraq. Then the unthinkable happened as a strange sandstorm had blanketed the entire region. The US military refused to admit on national TV they had lost communications with several thousand American troops in the region. Now people were starting to lose faith in the government's ability to handle this new, terrifying crisis. Not even an hour-long appearance by the president on every single news outlet could assure everyone that the situation was under control.

Valerie turned away and looked down. "I'm so sorry, Myron. I shouldn't have brought it up."

Myron placed a reassuring hand on her left arm and smiled slightly. "Hey, I was the one who brought it up so don't worry about it."

The squawk on the police radio got louder. "Thirty-two Delta, two down, possible knife assault at seventy-two Baruch Drive."

Valerie grabbed the microphone as Myron started the car. "Thirty-two Delta responding. Can we get backup?"

"Be advised, no backup available at this time," Central said over the radio.

"Ten-four. En route to location," Valerie said on the microphone before putting it back on the side of the radio.

"Shit," Myron said as he activated the dashboard siren while pressing on the accelerator. The rain came down harder as it pelted the windshield of the speeding car.

Valerie grabbed the microphone again. "Thirty-two Delta to Central, any word on the victim's conditions? Is a medical team on the way?"

"No other information, Thirty-two Delta. A civilian called it in. Said there were two men on the ground with stab wounds, both black. We're trying to get emergency crews to you as soon as we can."

"That means the paramedics will get there in a few hours," Myron said as he made a left turn into West Houston Street and sped on. They would be in the Lower East Side in a few minutes and then make the final turn into Baruch Drive. There were very few cars left on the streets because people were fearfully staying in their homes as many businesses stayed closed earlier during the day, while schools were suspended indefinitely.

It was the largest low-income housing project in Manhattan. Baruch Houses covered almost thirty acres and the two thousand apartments that were spread out in seventeen seven-story high-rise apartments that were built in the tail end of the fifties. By the twenty-first century, most of the residents were comprised of Hispanics and blacks who needed government subsidies in order to live in Manhattan. Both Myron and Valerie knew the area well, they had been called over there numerous times back when they were still rank and file police officers.

Baruch Drive was a residential street that cut directly into the heart of the area. As the car slowed and made its way to the crime scene, the squawk on the police radio had begun to lose reception, as the constant updates from the dispatchers were interrupted by static white noise. Both detectives noticed that only one or two streetlights were working, huge parts of the street and the surrounding apartment buildings were covered in an eerie darkness. Unpicked trash and debris littered the sides of the lane. Myron cursed again.

As the car made its way to the scene, both detectives noticed that there were three of them. Two men on the ground and another man kneeling over them. Valerie couldn't make out their faces, as the only illumination came from their car's headlights. Myron maneuvered the car so that its front was facing the three men before coming to a full stop. Both detectives grabbed flashlights and buttoned up their coats as they got out of the vehicle.

"Hey, over here!" the man who was kneeling down said as he waved to them. The rain had died down somewhat, but it was still enough to partially obscure everything. The sidewalk where the three men were was strewn with trash. There was a knee-high fence behind them with some open square spaces that used to have some grass growing on it. Now they were used as garbage dumps since the breakdown of waste collection services in the city. The towering apartment blocks of Baruch Houses were spaced about thirty yards apart and loomed over them.

Myron pointed his flashlight at the man's face while his other hand gripped his Smith and Wesson M5906 that still lay snug on his side holster. "NYPD, can I see your hands, sir."

"I'm the one who called it in, officers," the black man said calmly as he raised his hands. He was bald and had a grayish beard. Valerie noticed that he had on a clerical collar.

"I'm Detective Jones and my partner, Detective Mendoza. Reverend Beekman? Is that you?" Myron said as he walked over to them while putting on his blue plastic gloves. While the gloves were normally used for forensics work, they could double as medical gloves too. "What happened?"

Reverend Beekman knelt down beside the two other black men as Valerie put on her own gloves. Both men were barely conscious and breathing heavily. They were cut up bad. Open gashes, cuts, and stab wounds on their arms, legs, and torsos. Myron saw that their hands were torn up the most, probably defensive wounds in an attempt to block the edged weapons their attacker used. Both detectives noticed that there were pieces of green glass strewn about. Valerie ran back to the car and grabbed the first aid kit, as the Reverend and Myron used their handkerchiefs to staunch the deepest wounds on the two wounded men.

"I was at the nearby church and I heard some screams out here so I ran over," Reverend Beekman said as he pointed to the church no more than thirty paces away. "I didn't see who it was that attacked them."

Myron looked at the men while trying to apply pressure on a serrated chest wound. "I know these two, they're local gang members. Two of the Bloc Boys."

Reverend Beekman nodded. "Yes, Detective. Believe it or not, these boys have been behaving themselves lately. They even started to attend my church just a few days ago, ever since the worldwide troubles started. I had hoped that the rumors about demons running loose in the world would bring these boys back in the fold of God. But now I see that it's come to affect us all. When is the ambulance coming?"

"It should be on its way," Valerie said as she started putting tourniquets on the men's arms. "You sure you didn't see or hear anything?"

"I didn't see anything because I was inside the church, but I did hear screams and some foreign language I didn't understand," Reverend Beekman said.

"Reverend, you know Spanish, right? Are you sure it wasn't that?" Myron said. Hispanics were the largest ethnic group in these tenements.

Reverend Beekman shook his head. "I know the language, and it wasn't Spanish I heard it. The only two words I remember from the shouting sounded like 'quihahuit' or 'quinnaquilook' or something like that."

Valerie turned to him with a surprised look on her face. "What? Are you sure those were the words that were shouted during the attack?"

"I think so, I think there were more words spoken, but that's all I could remember," Reverend Beekman said.

"You know those words, Val?" Myron said to her as he tried his handheld radio, all he got was static.

"The reverend is right, those words aren't Spanish. They're actually Nahuatl, the language of the Aztec," Valerie said as sounds of thunder roared above them. "Quihahuitl means rain and quinnanquilique means they were answered."

"For real?" Myron said. "How'd you know how to speak Aztec, Val?"

"My mother taught me," Valerie said as she subconsciously rubbed at the jade and obsidian necklace underneath her blouse once again. It had been a childhood gift from her mother and she wore it at all times. "She's Mexican, but she always claimed to be full-blooded Aztec."

At that moment they heard shouts. All three turned to see a figure that waved at them in front of the fire exit at one of the apartment blocks. It looked like an old Hispanic woman who could barely stand.

"We'll be right back," Myron said to the reverend as both he and Valerie ran over to the old lady. As they got to the front of the apartment block, the old woman slumped down at the edge of the red-painted fire door.

"Help me," Myron said as they both took the woman by her arms and set her down by the base of the stairs. The entrance to the fire exit was pretty much just a small foyer and stairs leading up. The overhead fluorescent light was flickering and it provided only the dimmest illumination. Nobody else seemed to be around.

44

"Are you okay?" Valerie said as she knelt down beside her. The old woman had a wet knitted shawl over her shoulders. She had swollen bare feet and had a tattered old black dress on. Her white hair was matted down from the rain and drops of water had soaked the wrinkles of her face. "Estas bien?" she repeated in Spanish.

The old woman's voice was hardly a croak. "Los ninos, que tienen los ninos."

"What's she saying?" Myron said.

"She said they took the children," Valerie said to him before turning back to the old woman. "Que ha llevado a los ninos? Who took them?"

The old woman's eyes had a white glaze over them. It was clear she had cataracts. The one word she said was tinged with fear. "Tlaloc."

"Oh my god," Valerie said to Myron as she pulled out her Glock and started going up the stairs. "We need backup now! Stay here with her, Myron!"

"Val, what in the hell are you doing?" Myron said. "Don't go up there, we don't have backup yet!"

But Valerie was already on her way up. She tried the second and third floor fire doors, but they were locked tight. She ran up one more flight as Myron kept shouting at her to go back down. She noticed that the fire door on this floor was propped open and a darkened corridor lay within. Valerie turned on her flashlight with her left hand while keeping the gun close to her body as she went inside.

The corridor felt like a tomb. The lights in the whole block were apparently out due to the incessant storms and the neglect of the city, since the more affluent neighborhoods were clamoring to get their own power restored first. There were pieces of trash all along the corridor while the adjoining doors seemed to be locked up tight. Valerie could hear the crunch of glass on her shoes as she stepped forward. As she tried knocking on a few of the doors with her flashlight there was no answer from any of them. The handheld radio that was attached to her belt continued to squawk intermittent bursts of static.

As she got to the other side to where the main stairwell was, Valerie could see some illumination on the murky glass windows outside, but it wasn't enough, her only means of visibility was now the flashlight. Putting her gun back in its side holster, Valerie tried once again with her handheld radio, but she got nothing and there were no signal bars on her cell phone either. Whoever attacked the two gangbangers was still on the loose, and might just be in the building with her.

After putting her cell phone back in her coat pocket, Valerie pulled out the Glock once more. If there was one thing cops feared more than a gunfight, it was going up against a blade-wielding assailant, while a wound from a gun was quick, a knife attack was far more terrifying, they said. While a gun was definitely the superior weapon because of its range, a darkened building afforded the perpetrator a number of advantages, namely surprise, and the chance to get in close before the gun wielder knew where to fire at.

While peering at the adjoining corridors and seeing nothing, Valerie once more aimed the flashlight down on the floor and saw the pieces of green glass, this time she knelt down and looked closer. The stuff on the floor wasn't just ordinary glass; it was green obsidian, a volcanic glass that was used in the manufacture of Aztec weapons like knives and the dreaded macuahuitl, a wooden sword which was studded with sharp obsidian blades on its sides. As she kept looking at the shards on the floor she heard the sound of breaking glass behind her.

Valerie turned as she kept both the flashlight and her pistol level while preparing to open fire.

"Whoa!" Myron said as he held up the side of his gun so it wasn't pointed at her. "Take it easy."

Valerie let out a sigh of relief. "Jesus, Myron! I could've killed you!"

Myron grinned sheepishly. "Sorry, I didn't mean to creep up on you like that. The paramedics arrived and they're treating the two men. I brought the old lady over to them and Reverend Beekman is there too. So now I got your back once more."

As Valerie smiled back at him, she noticed there was a silhouette of something behind Myron. Something oddly shaped and she noticed the flash of green. "Myron, look out!" she said as she tried to aim.

Myron turned as the obsidian knife slashed at his arm. He cried out and fell over sideways as he tried to hold on to his gun. Valerie could now clearly see a man who seemed to be wearing the skin of an animal of some sort, like a tiger costume. He had on a feathered headdress and an obsidian knife in both hands. She instantly fired three times, hitting him twice in the torso. The man went down.

Valerie ran over and knelt down beside Myron, who was clutching his arm with his other hand after dropping his flashlight. It was a vicious gash, but it didn't look too deep. Myron was lucky when he reacted so the assailant missed with putting a whole lot of force on the blow. As she kept the gun aimed at the perpetrator lying on the ground, she placed the flashlight down so it kept pointing at the outer corridor, and then took out an embroidered handkerchief from her coat pocket and gave it to Myron.

"Goddamn, that hurts!" Myron said through clenched teeth as he applied pressure on the wound with Valerie's handkerchief. "It cut so quickly. Tore right through my jacket."

The assailant wasn't moving as Valerie took up the flashlight once more and walked closer to it. "I think he's still alive, but he's bleeding out," she said as she looked at the bullet wounds. The animal skin the man was wearing looked like the hide of a jaguar. The suspect was clearly South American, with a beaklike nose and deep brown skin. He looked like a young man in his twenties. As Valerie aimed the flashlight at the man's face, she let out a gasp.

"What is it?" Myron said as he tied down the handkerchief on his arm.

"His head," Valerie said slowly as she was starting to feel sick. "It's misshaped, his forehead is flattened and the rear part of his head is elongated. I know the Mayans did things like this to their children, but not the Aztecs."

Myron stood up and recovered his flashlight. He contemplated shifting his gun to his left hand, but he never practiced shooting that way, so he decided to keep it in his right. Shooting with a wounded arm might be painful, but he would have more accuracy over an arm he didn't favor. "Oh my god, what in the hell are we dealing with here?"

At that moment, they both heard a scream coming from upstairs. It was clearly a child's voice. Both of them started running to the main stairway, flashlights and guns at the ready.

As they reached the fifth floor landing, Myron almost slipped as the floor was wet. Valerie was able to grab his elbow and steady him just in time. There was a pungent, metallic stench in the air.

"What in the hell is that smell?" Myron said as he pointed the flashlight down at the wet floor and gasped.

"What is it?" Valerie said as she too looked down. It was then she saw it and then bent forward as she vomited a little bit of her coffee. The floor was wet with blood. Now it was Myron's turn to steady her. For a minute, they both just stood there as Valerie caught her breath.

Myron looked at her. "What made you go nuts down at the fire door? That old lady said only one word, and you went wild."

Valerie wiped the last of the vomit from her mouth with her coat sleeve. "She said Tlaloc. That's the name of an Aztec rain god. When she said they have the children, I knew we had to save them."

"Save the children? From what?" Myron said as they started checking the corridors.

"I think the children of this housing project are in great danger. The rain god demands sacrifices, like what happened to the Bloc brothers."

"Sacrifices? Human sacrifices?"

"Child sacrifices," Valerie said softly.

As they rounded the next corner they saw her. She was a small black girl, probably no more than six years old. And she was just sitting in the middle of the corridor, with bits of obsidian and blood strewn all around her. She wore nothing but a bloody nightgown and she clutched a small teddy bear. She had been whimpering in the dark.

They ran over to her. As Valerie knelt down and examined her, Myron kept shining his flashlight at the end of the corridor and let out a yell. Valerie looked up and almost fell over with fright. The end of the corridor was much shorter than the ones found on the other floors. But that was because there was a newly added barrier right in the middle of this particular passageway.

It was a mound made of dead flesh and dripping blood. There must have been dozens of them stacked up as the heap covered it from floor to ceiling.

Bodies of naked men, women, and children, their skins had been torn away to reveal their blood-soaked musculature, organs, bones, and deathly naked eyes. That was where the blood on the floor had come from.

As if on cue, the little child started screaming again. Suddenly, all the doors along the corridor opened and dozens of bloodstained men and women ran out, each one of them howling like wolves and wielding green, crystalline obsidian knives, a hint of death and madness in their eyes.

Both detectives reacted and instantly began firing, but there were too many of them and they were way too close. Valerie felt a crippling pain in her arm as someone sliced it open and she dropped her gun. Almost at the same time, she felt a sharp sting that started from her forehead, then to her nose and finally down to her chin as somebody slashed a crystal dagger at her face.

The last thing she sensed was the child's incessant screaming.

5. The Interlopers

They called him Bucktooth Billy Ray Rockwell, or just Buck for short. He had received the name because of his protruding front teeth he couldn't hide, no matter how hard he would push his bottom lip forward. It didn't help that Buck didn't have much of a chin either so they had been making fun of him from kindergarten all the way to his sophomore year at the local high school when he finally dropped out. When his parents kicked him out of their house a year later, he tried to work in an auto repair shop but quit a few months after because they were making fun of him there too. After that, he joined in with some childhood friends and made a living burglarizing houses and stealing cars, until he finally got caught and spent eight years in prison for it. Having just been released a few weeks ago on probation, he was staying at a friend's house when all hell broke loose.

There were very few channels left that were still broadcasting, so Buck just kept flipping through them on the remote control. He sat slumped in the torn-up couch of his friend's living room while trying to pass the time. Although he heard on the news that the electrical grid was shutting down, the power was still going here, so he kept all the lights on in the house as he waited till his friends got back. The little bit of money that they gave him upon his release was already spent on booze, cigarettes, and a little bit of blow. Empty beer cans were lying around his dirty bare feet, along with crushed plastic wrappers on the dingy carpet. His friend really didn't seem to care much about cleaning. He had his scalp shaved every morning, just like the skinhead gang he was a part of in prison. Buck didn't have a whole lot of clothes when he was let go, so he was wearing the sleeveless plaid shirt that once belonged to his friend's ex-girlfriend. He kept the old, torn up denim jeans he took in with him when he got arrested all those years ago.

It was now early afternoon and just as he was thinking of throwing the remote control at the television set to see if it would shatter the monitor, he heard his friend's pickup truck going into the front driveway. Quickly turning off the TV, Buck looked around and found a pair of old tennis shoes which he started putting on his feet.

"Buck, what have you been doin' there, you ol' possum!" his friend Mark Gooch said as he opened the screen door and strode in, carrying several semi-automatic rifles slung on his back that he then placed on top of the grimy coffee table beside the couch. Mark was about a shade taller than Buck and more heavyset, his hair was deep black and curly but he had a neatly trimmed beard. They had met while in jail and became friends ever since.

"Holy sheeiit," Buck said as he picked up one of the rifles and started examining it. The weapon was an AR-15, one of the most common types of semi-automatic rifles being sold to civilians in the country and it looked brand new. He noticed that there was a custom made forward grip on it as he checked whether the red dot sight that was attached to the upper rail of the carrying handle was fully operational or not. It was.

Mark put his hands into a black plastic trash bag that he was carrying and took out two handguns, one was a Glock and the other was a chromed .357 Magnum revolver and threw them on top of the couch as he started laughing. "I tell you, boy, we hit the mother lode!"

"Where'd you git all of this?" Buck said as he locked back the AR-15's collapsible stock and began sighting it.

Mark racked the slide of a 1911 Les Baer .45 pistol before thumbing the safety and holstering it on his hip. "Remember that gun store over at Midland? Well, we waited till the owner had boarded it up and left, then we just came in with bolt cutters and opened her up like a cardboard box. I tell ya, it was easy as pie!"

Mark's hulking cousin Lance Gooch came through the door pushing a dolly that was stacked with several boxes. "Where in the hell do I put all of this, Mark?"

"Right behind the kitchen counter, if ya please," Mark said as he picked up another AR-15 from the table and started to examine it. He was wearing desert camouflaged cargo pants and a grey-colored tactical vest that he took from the accessories section of the gun store, they were so new the price tags were still on them.

"Yessiree," Lance said as he wheeled in the boxes and began to stack them on the kitchen floor. At six foot two, he was the tallest and most heavily built of the three, with dark brown hair in a crew cut and similarly-colored short beard. A former cop, Lance had been fired two years ago after he had beaten up and shot a couple of black men he had seen loitering in a Dallas alleyway. One of the men had died and the family sued. Although Lance's partner and the police union had stood behind him, the media firestorm that erupted over the whole affair forced the police chief to terminate him although he was able to avoid any criminal liability. At that point Lance began to harbor a smoldering resentment against anyone in the media as well as all types of liberal politicians.

Buck had a quizzical look on his face. "What in the hell are in those boxes?"

Lance had finished stacking them and opened up the top of one of the boxes. "Ammo, boy, ammo! We got at least several thousand rounds of ammo here for all the guns we got. And I've got some molds and a swag press too so we can even make our own bullets."

Buck nodded. Lance was the smartest. "Did y'all take everything?"

Mark shook his head and smiled. "Nah, there were some others that were with us and they helped themselves too. With the world as broken as it is, we figured it's gonna be every man for himself now."

Lance laughed. "Things got a bit dicey when the owner of that store and his son came back just as we were about finished."

Buck scratched his forehead. "What happened then?"

"Oh some of the other guys just shot 'em," Mark said nonchalantly.

Lance nodded. "Shot his son too."

Buck had slung the rifle over his shoulder and looked at them. "They dead?"

Lance just shrugged. "Probably. They were bleedin' out by the time the other boys were done with 'em."

Buck started walking around the room with the slung rifle to see how it felt. "This rifle mine?"

"Sure thing, Buck," Mark said and pointed to the couch. "Take one of them pistols too, you're gonna need a backup weapon just in case."

"Yessir," Buck said as he picked up the revolver and tried to stick it into his jeans, but the barrel was too big to fit in properly.

"Take a look at him," Mark said to Lance as he started chuckling. "Tryin' to Mexican carry that big 'ol Magnum, he looks like a crazy Jethro hillbilly!"

Buck stopped what he was doing and just held the pistol in his hand as the other two were laughing at him. "Shut the hell up, Mark, or I'm gonna shoot ya."

Mark kept laughing as he put the rifle down and drew the 1911 and pointed it at Buck. "How you gonna shoot me when yer guns aren't even loaded, boy?"

Buck started to grimace as he moved over to where the ammunition boxes were and started to dig through them to find the right caliber for his gun. Lance got his meaty arms on him and pushed him away. Buck nearly fell as he stumbled backwards a few feet.

"Alright, that's enough joking around," Lance said. Like his cousin, he too was wearing civilian tactical gear, although they from his days in the police force. "We're gonna need each other and we need to work as a team. That means no more fightin' among ourselves."

"I was just jokin' around," Mark said as he holstered the pistol. "We need to train Buck here on the use of these weapons so that we can properly defend ourselves."

Buck sat back down on the sofa, his burst of sudden anger evaporated. "Before I got sent in, I had a pistol and then when they let me out they said I can't have guns no more."

Lance stood in the kitchen behind them as he continued to unwrap several assault rifle magazines from one of the boxes. "Don't you worry, Bucky. The law ain't around anymore so you just hang on to that AR and just make sure you don't shoot me or Mark, okay?"

"I ain't got a problem with that," Buck said as he sighted the revolver. "I'll shoot just about anybody else though."

"Now that's a great idea!" Mark said as he slumped down beside Buck. "We can go after anybody and get whatever we need. We got the firepower now."

Buck placed the pistol on his lap and looked at Mark. "You wanna go get that ex-girlfriend of yours back here? We can just shoot her dad and take her, now that we got the guns."

Mark laughed. "Nah, fuck that bitch. I am done with her, but you have a good idea, Buck. I say we just drive around and look for a house with some women in it and we take them back here and choose our wives."

Buck frowned. "Ah, that's too bad then."

"Too bad about what?" Mark said to him before he started chuckling again. "Oh, so you wanted to screw her too, didn't you? You horny armadillo. I thought all that prison sex must have made you queer or something."

"I never had any kind of sex when I was inside," Buck hissed. "Screw you."

Lance walked over and sat on an old armchair facing them as he placed two fully-loaded assault rifle magazines into the ammo pouch on his tactical vest. "Calm down, boys. I think we may need some target practice just to cool both your heads off. Let's think about this for a minute. What kind of live targets can we practice on?"

"Let's go drive around in your pickup and find us some niggers to shoot," Buck said.

"I know a few buddies of mine that's been doing that since yesterday," Lance said. "I don't know if there's any blacks still in Odessa. From what I heard, a lot of them started moving up north when a lot of the cops started quitting."

Buck thought about it for a minute before he answered. "Let's go shoot some wetbacks then. A couple of them beaners came at me with a shank while

I was in the joint. I got a long scar on my belly and I need some payback."

"Whoa, I think he's onto something here," Mark said. "Remember the news last night? I dunno if you watched this in your house, Lance, but last night the reporters said that several million Mexican refugees were now in El Paso and the Border Patrol and the National Guard couldn't even stop them."

Lance nodded. "Yeah, it was something like ten million I think. Too many wetbacks for the authorities to shoot and that traitor president of ours probably let them in anyway."

"The news weren't sure of what's driving them up north," Buck said. "I didn't understand what that anchorman was sayin'."

"I was on the internet in my house just before it got slow two days ago," Lance said. "Some reports said it was packs of chupacabras that was killing 'em down there, but then I saw some of those videos they posted from the survivors who made it here, and those things looked more like vampires or zombies."

"What's a chupacabra?" Buck said.

"Some sort of monster dog or bear or something like that," Mark said. "Stupid Mexicans and their dumbass religious crap."

"Whatever is causing it shouldn't be our problem. It's theirs and they should be dealing with it," Lance said. "Those goddamned Mexicans have flooded into our border states. Before it was just a few hundred thousand and now its millions of them brown-skinned scumbags, we gotta do something."

"Sounds like a good idea," Mark said before turning his head to look at Buck. "You cool with shooting a few hundred wetbacks today?"

Buck grinned. His yellow teeth were crooked and it made him look like cartoon character so he didn't smile much except for special occasions. "I got no problem with it."

Lance got up and took out his mobile phone as he went to the kitchen. "Hang on, since I can still get a cell signal, lemme call up a friend of mine. He personally knows Obediah Smith."

"Obediah Smith? The chairman for AFAF?" Mark said.

Lance waved at them from the kitchen as he started talking to someone on his hand phone. "Yeah, that's him. Hold on…."

Buck leaned over to Mark. "What's AFAF?"

"America for Americans Foundation," Mark said. "They are one of the biggest anti-immigration groups in the country. Obediah Smith's their chairman and a local boy from Houston. He's been on TV a lot of times and a regular commentator on XOX News."

"I think I might have seen him once or twice when I was in the hole," Buck said.

"Obediah's a good man. If he ran for president, I would vote for him in a heartbeat. The only good times this country had was when a Texan was president," Mark said.

"Okay," Lance said as he walked back over to them with a smile. "I just talked to one of his assistants. There's huge numbers of Mexicans trying to cross the border and ICE is pretty shorthanded. Since we're in Odessa, they could use some volunteers over at Fort Hancock, that's only a few hours away. They said there's already a small group of citizens over there defending the place and they need more. Obediah is also on his way over there so we can meet him in person."

Mark grinned. "That's mighty fine! How much ammo do we bring?"

"My friend said that Obediah will be bringing in a truckload of ammo, but let's bring at least ten full mags each," Lance said. "That way we still have a reserve in case their supplies run out."

"That's gonna be at least three hundred rounds for each of us," Mark said as he got up and headed to the boxes by the kitchen.

Buck was now grinning ear to ear as he also stood up from the couch to join Mark in loading his guns, this was the best day of his life since he got out of prison a few weeks ago. While most of the news reports were saying that the world was turning into Hell, he never felt better.

The drive south towards Fort Hancock took almost three hours. Traffic was pretty light since most people were trying to flee northwards instead of going down to the southern border. Mark drove the pickup truck while Lance was in the front seat. Buck was riding shotgun in the back along with a few boxes of extra ammunition for their rifles. He was so excited, he started firing a few shots at a group of Mexicans that were trying to thumb a ride north on the other side of the road. Mark kept the gas on the pedal as Lance opened the truck's rear window and told him in no uncertain terms to stop shooting until they got to the border. Buck complied and sat back down on the rear bed of the pickup, as he was scared of Lance and he hoped they wouldn't leave him behind. Anyway, he didn't think he hit any of those Mexicans since the truck was at a high speed and he saw them diving to the ground as soon as he pointed the AR-15 at them. Buck was still somewhat keyed up as he took some ammunition out of one of the boxes and reloaded his spent magazine. The sun was out and it looked to be a beautiful, hot afternoon.

As the truck drove into the town's gas station just under a mile from the border, they noticed a few other cars there with other people readying their own guns. Fort Hancock was really nothing more than a crossroads with a few dilapidated buildings nearby, the rest of the place was desert scrub and farmland. Buck immediately jumped off the back of the pickup and stretched his back. Lance got out of the front seat and saw someone he recognized, an old man wearing a Stetson and carrying an old Remington bolt-action hunting rifle that had a brand new scope attached to it.

Lance put his wraparound sunglasses on the top of his baseball cap then he walked up to the old man and shook his hand. "Hey, Lamar, how you doin'?"

"Lance, it's been a long time since I saw you, I'm doing well, sir," the old man said. He had a white moustache and wore a brown leather vest on his chest. "You here to help defend our nation's borders too?"

"Yes, we are," Lance said as Mark and Buck joined them. "My cousin Mark, and our friend Buck."

Lamar shook both their hands. "Welcome to our makeshift citizen's border patrol, gentlemen."

Mark adjusted his tan baseball cap. "How long have you guys been here?"

"Oh, we just got here ourselves," Lamar said. "We're all just waiting for Obediah Smith, he should be coming any minute now."

Mark tapped Buck's shoulder and started walking to the station desk. "I'll be right back, I'm gonna buy some gas for the ride home. Come on, Buck."

As the other two men walked away Lance put his hands on his hips. "So what's the situation out here then?"

"Well, sir, the locals have been asking the government for help for the past week now," Lamar said as he looked down on the sun-bleached pavement. "They've been saying that more and more Mexicans have been crossing the border right here. A month ago, it was just a trickle and now it's a goddamned flood of 'em just wading across the Rio Grande. You know that in this juncture the river is nothing more than a stream, so even their kids won't have a problem crossing it since most of 'em don't even know how to swim anyway."

Lance just nodded. He didn't know how to swim either, but he wasn't about to say it out loud.

Lamar slung his rifle over his shoulder. "So the citizens of this town keep asking for help and what does the gubmint do? Nothin.' It's an absolute disgrace to our forefathers, the ones who built this country with their bare hands. Yessiree, it's a disgrace. So the townsfolk, many of 'em already left, but the few that are still around are gonna make sure this piece of land remains a part of America. I got a call from Obediah just yesterday so me and my wife been gettin' over here as fast as we can."

Right after the old man said that, the sound of firecrackers could be heard in the distance. It wasn't too close, but it didn't feel too far either. Everyone knew that the shooting only meant that the Mexicans were trying to cross in force again.

Lance looked around. "Is the sheriff still here?"

"Yessir, he and his deputies are just to the right of us, over there," the old man said as he pointed his finger towards the southwest boundaries of the town. "He's coordinating the defense on the southern edge of the town. Some of our boys here are gonna join 'em."

Just as the old man finished his sentence, a small convoy of cars pulled up into the gas station's driveway. The lead car was a white Ford SUV and a heavyset man with a silvery beard got out of the front seat. Everyone immediately recognized him as Obediah Smith, the famous anti-immigration advocate. A few people went forward and shook his hands, but he immediately waved them back as he took out a bullhorn from the backseat of the vehicle.

"Everyone, good afternoon to y'all," Obediah said as he amplified his voice using the bullhorn. "I'm sorry about the lack of decorum right now, but we need to get into position right away. I got a call on my mobile phone from the sheriff of this town on my way here, and he needs volunteers to man the front lines immediately. We're gonna need about ten volunteers over to where he is, which is down there," Obediah pointed towards the southwest, just like Lamar did. "The rest of you boys could follow me in my car. We need to position ourselves on the northern edge of town. The ones headin' over to the sheriff's side needn't worry about ammo since he's got a supply with him, and the ones going with me will be given a few hundred rounds each, depending on what type of weapon you got. Does anyone have any questions before we get going?"

One man with an AK-47 raised his hand. "How long do you expect us to be here, sir?"

Obediah smiled. "You can stay as long as you want. I'm gonna be here for a few days at least to assess the situation. The sheriff has told me there are some houses nearby with beds that some of the citizens will allow you boys to sleep in, but I'm sure some of you brought sleeping bags so camping isn't a problem. My lovely wife Sara has brought along enough chili to feed a hundred people for tonight's dinner, and I've made arrangements with the local eateries here so the volunteers that wish to stay can have some free meals. I hope most of you boys would be willing to stay for a few days, at least."

Some in the crowd murmured while others cheered. Mark frowned and looked at Lance as he forgot to think about bringing any sleeping bags, or a tent. Buck cheered along with the others since the thought of free food and several days of live target practice just about sounded like the best thing he ever heard.

Another man raised his hand. He looked to be middle-aged and was evidently from out of state from the looks of his clothes. "Mr. Smith, will there be any possible liabilities if we … you know, end up shooting and maybe killing somebody?"

Obediah nodded as if he was expecting that question to come up. "I've talked with my people in Homeland Security and I can tell you the Border Patrol is stretched thin, most of their agents have quit. The section chief hinted to me that we can pretty much do anything we want as long as no American citizen gets hurt. So you boys can shoot, but make sure that the person you shoot at ain't an American citizen is all. If any of you boys get hurt, then I'm sorry, but I can't help you other than to give you a few bandages that I brought along." A couple of chuckles erupted from the crowd. "Now I'm gonna remind y'all again, if you end up hurtin' an American citizen, you're on your own, but if it's anybody else, then I would say you don't have to worry 'bout anything, ya hear?"

Loud cheering erupted from the crowd as Obediah waved at them and started to shake hands with the more insistent ones before getting back in his car.

Mark turned to Lance. "Which group are we a part of?"

Lance smiled. "Let's go with Obediah's group. Get back in the truck now and let's go."

It was late afternoon by the time they got into position. Mark had wanted to park the car on the side of the highway, but Lance convinced him to drive over the barren field and leave the pickup right at the edge of the gully facing the Rio Grande, so that they wouldn't have to walk far if they needed more ammunition or a ride back. While the sun still shined on their side of the border, Buck could see a massive storm front to the south, the entire sky was practically opaque, with grey clouds like a giant wall of haze that had blotted out the southern horizon. The three of them could see sheets of yellow lightning strike down several miles away.

"Good lord, I've never seen anything like it," Lance said. From their position, they would cover around several hundred yards of open ground around the river. A few hundred yards to their right was Obediah's main camp.

Mark walked over to a small boulder and sat down on it as he pulled out a pair of binoculars and began to scan the border. "I can see about two dozen wetbacks heading towards the river. They ought to be here in about fifteen minutes."

"Okay," Lance said as he crouched down behind a dried out shrub. "Everybody get into position, a few yards apart."

Buck nodded as he walked to the right of them for a few yards and dutifully sat down. Almost immediately, he stood up again as he had just sat down on a small cactus. Cussing, he kicked at the plant as he pulled at the back of his jeans to get the spikes out of his buttocks. This time he carefully chose a spot that was just bare sand and knelt down on it until he too was behind a desert shrub. The other two were busy sighting their rifles so they didn't notice what had happened.

Mark kept looking through the binoculars. "They're almost to the riverbank. Do we fire a warning shot?"

"I'll do it," Lance said as he flipped off the safety to his AR-15 while sighting with the red dot optical scope. He fired a few rounds near a Mexican leading a woman wearing a dusty old dress down the bank. The Mexican looked around at first as if he was confused, but then started to pull the woman to the water of the Rio Grande.

"Stupid wetback didn't get the message," Mark said as he started to sight his rifle.

"Open fire once they get to the other side," Lance said tersely.

Buck forgot about the pain in his buttocks and started to chuckle as he tried to get a bead on them using his red dot sight. The Mexican couple looked like middle-aged farmers with their brown and wrinkly skin, but they looked determined to make it as both waded in the water for a bit until the man finally grabbed onto a small rock on the other side of the river and began to pull the woman to him. Mark and Lance both fired almost at the same time. The man took a few rounds in his chest and he fell back into the swirling water. Buck could see the woman was terrified as she tried to grab at the man's hand so he fired at her, but he kept missing as his shots started making small puffs of smoke along the sandy bank or just harmlessly hit the water; on his last shot he finally hit her square in the forehead and she too fell into river.

Buck whooped. "I got her! I got that brown bitch right in the head! Yeehaw!"

"Yeah, but only after you emptied your mag, dingleberry." Mark chuckled. "You're gonna be outta ammo before we even get started, boy."

"Shut the hell up," Buck said as he dropped the magazine and slapped in a fresh one before he whacked the bolt release. "That was my first time shootin' this here rifle."

"Alright, knock it off you two," Lance said as he stayed in position. "Buck, just work on your aim, center the target on your optic sight before firing again."

"Here come more of 'em," Mark said. "Looks like a whole train load this time, boys."

Buck began to sight his scope again. Mark wasn't kidding. This time there looked to be about close to thirty Mexicans making their way towards the riverbank on their right. They evidently didn't see what had happened to the couple just a few minutes ago, the bend in the river obscuring their vantage point. Most of this group were young men though there were a few women and two small children being carried along. Buck was tired of waiting so he just started firing as soon as they started making their way down to the riverbank on the other side. Buck fired the full load on his magazine and hit about three men. The rest of the crowd stood in shock for a minute and then began to panic and scatter in all directions.

Mark snorted. "Buck you idiot, why didn't you wait until they were on the other side?"

Buck reloaded, sighted a woman who was just standing there screaming, and finally hit her in the chest on his third try. "Who cares, they're just a bunch of wetbacks anyway."

"He's right, nobody is gonna care either way now," Lance said as he too started to fire. "Open fire once any target is in sight."

All three men started to fire on anyone they saw on the other side of the border now. Lance was able to gun down three men while Mark got one man and a woman who stopped running momentarily as she tried to pick up a small child. Buck shot the little girl in the stomach on his second try as she stood there crying over the woman that Mark got. As they kept shooting, the three of them didn't realize that the setting sun on their side of the border had finally been obscured by a massive cloud front sweeping in from the north.

"Jesus, Buck, that was a goddamned kid you shot!" Mark said.

"Who cares, they're all wetbacks anyway," Lance said nonchalantly as Buck giggled with delight.

It was then that the sky suddenly turned dark as it plunged the entire area into a grey twilight. All three men stood up in surprise as they finally noticed the massive overcast right above them.

Mark's mouth was open as he looked up at the sky. He had never seen anything like it. "What in the hell is going on?"

Lance's eyes opened wide as he pointed at something in the northern horizon that was coming right at them. "What in blazes is that?"

It was then that they saw a glimpse of it. Although it was partially obscured by the low hanging grey clouds, they could see its monstrous outline. It was the size of a small building as it uttered a shrill scream, then dived down on them with solid black wings that echoed the sound of rolling thunder, the force was so powerful, its shockwave blew the desert sand around them into the air. Almost instinctively, all three men began to panic fire at it as it swooped down and pounced, but it didn't seem to affect it as the sharp, deafening thunderclap that followed it drowned out their dying screams.

6. The Northern Lights

Lapland

It was late afternoon and they still hadn't arrived. Anders stood outside the Kiruna police station and smoked a cigarette. He had come in just last week, right before things started to get strange.

First, it was the animals that seemingly began to migrate south by passing right through the urban areas. In his first night on the town, he saw herds of reindeer and quite a few moose in the streets as they continued to move out of the region. Anders had laughed at first because he had never seen it before and found it quite amusing, until he saw that even the wolves had come out and started moving south. The police and the townspeople were on the ready as small packs of wolves descended into town and also followed the reindeer herds southwards. It was then that Anders heard the townspeople talking and mentioning that the wolves looked tired and starving, but they showed no signs of aggressiveness, in fact it looked like they were afraid of something as they passed through. Then the smaller animals like snow lynxes and even the owls started flying through the town. By the third night, about a dozen bears had entered into the city streets; the police were ready, but even these powerful animals largely ignored the people who were observing them. The only time there was a conflict was when one particularly large bear was shot and killed by local hunters as it wandered into the street near the church. The other bears didn't even stop to rummage and eat in any of the trash cans in the nearby park, they just kept going as well.

The fourth night was even worse. Even though the northern lights, the aurora borealis, was regularly seen around the evenings, the lights themselves began to act strangely, no longer did they streak across the night in wavy lines but instead started to fall, like shooting stars, driving their streaks of light into the earth as seen from the far horizon. It was then that the snow began to fall. The next evening, all the dogs in town began howling all night, no amount of love or harsh discipline could stop their cries and within a few days many fell sick and died. The stray cats disappeared while owners with pets reported them either missing or had to throw them out of their homes; the poor felines became hysterical and would hiss and claw at anything. By the fifth night it was the rats, squirrels, and other small mammals that had begun to empty from all the nooks and crannies of the town while they all fled southwards as the falling snow continued to increase. That was when people truly began to get scared.

Rossby Centre had reported back after Anders had submitted his findings. They told him that every single country had been losing contact with their satellites in earth orbit and there no longer was any chance that they could predict the weather using satellite maps. They would have to rely on field reports from now on until the foreseeable future. Meanwhile, the local police had been swamped with reports that a group of local hunters had disappeared while looking for game near the base of Kebnekiase, the tallest mountain in the country. A small team of four police officers went off in search for them and failed to return as well. Mass panic had begun to spread and just two days earlier the Swedish government in Stockholm ordered the evacuation of the entire town. It took less than a day before Kiruna was deserted, save for himself and a few constables still staying at the police station. Anders appealed to his superiors at the Swedish Meteorological and Hydrological Institute to let him head south as well, but his last orders were to sit tight because a climate team was heading out to meet him.

It was just before nightfall that two police Volvos, equipped with snow tires, had been seen heading into the outskirts of town. Anders finally sighed with quiet satisfaction in the feeling that he could be relieved and would be on his way back to his native Stockholm to be with his girlfriend, whom he had lost touch with ever since the nearby mobile cell site had ceased to function just a few days before. Even the powerful police radios in the station had encountered a lot of static interference and were only transmitting information to and fro half the time.

As Anders and two police constables stood outside the front entrance of the police station to greet them, the cars drove over and soon stopped beside the sidewalk and a small group of additional police reinforcements from the south got out of the vehicles, along with a dark-skinned man wearing a deep blue parka.

The man walked over to Anders and held out his hand. "I am Dr. Ranju Nandwani, from the UN, are you Anders?"

Anders shook his hand. "Yes, Anders Olsson. I am the representative for SMHI over here. Would you like to come in the station?"

"Yes, that would be nice, thanks," Ranju said as he followed Anders inside.

The police station was largely deserted. Most of the staff as well as a few detainees had already been evacuated. It was also the only inhabited building in the entire town as everyone else had left a few days before. With the additional six police constables and Dr. Nandwani, there were now eleven of them in total. Everyone was grateful that the heaters were still functioning as they took off their cold weather jackets and stretched out their stiff bodies after the long drive up north.

Anders sat in front of a steaming mug of coffee in the conference room, along with Ranju and Sergeant Dure Johnsen, the commander of the station. "I was told to wait for you, Dr. Nandwani. What can I do for you?" Anders said.

Ranju took short sips from his own mug. "I'm a special inspector with the UN's World Meteorological Organization. I've come to find out the cause of the cold front that's sweeping southwards towards mainland Europe. We believe the source may be emanating not far from here."

Anders frowned. "I'm sorry, I thought SMHI was sending a replacement for me so I could be relieved of my duties so I could go south."

"We can all go back soon, but first I need to find the possible source of these strange weather patterns. Once we've located and identified the source, we all can report back to Stockholm," Ranju said.

Dure Johnsen's voice was devoid of emotion. "The situation out here is getting worse by the day. I would think that it's time we all evacuate by tomorrow."

"But it's imperative that we find out what's causing the cold front," Ranju said, almost pleading. "Tens of millions of people in both Scandinavia and mainland Europe could be in danger. We have an extraordinary weather pattern developing in the entire region. The whole of Northern Europe is now being blanketed by snow and it's still August! It's almost like winter and summer have changed places. This is an extraordinary event in history."

"Since I've been here for a week, I have already recorded over two meters of snow falling," Anders said. "I feel it may be more near the mountain ranges."

Ranju looked at his watch. "It's barely four in the afternoon and yet the sun has already set. I thought days were longer in this part of the world."

Anders shrugged. "They're supposed to be, we're not supposed to have any evenings at this time of the year in this region at all. That is why we call it the land of the midnight sun. But now the daylight only lasts from late morning until early afternoon. I don't think the earth has changed its orbit around the sun, but the cold front may be blocking the sunlight."

"What you just said is impossible. Yet it's happening," Ranju said.

"All the more reason to go and get out of here … my men are not happy being here," Dure said.

Ranju looked at him. "Sergeant, unless we find out what the source is, running to the south will be pointless."

"Even if you could find the source, what good will it do?" Anders said. "Mankind cannot magically change the weather."

"Maybe not, but at least we might know the cause and we can at least understand it," Ranju said. "Because right now, the people of the world are in a panic and we have to figure it out or everything is lost."

Dure's face remained impassive. "Do you have a plan?"

"In the last satellite images I saw of this area that we were able to get, there seemed to have been a cold front that developed right above Kebnekaise Mountain. I believe that's east of this city," Ranju said. "Has anyone in the towns north of us reported anything unusual?"

Dure shook his head. "Everything north of Kiruna has been evacuated. The Finns and the Norwegians have done the same on the sides of their countries."

"Wait," Anders said. "We could try to get to the research station in the Tarfala Valley just facing Kebnekaise. I know it was evacuated last week, but Rossby Centre informed me that the weather instruments over there might still be recording."

Dure looked at him with tired eyes. "Four policemen went in that area, including my superior, the chief inspector, to look for some missing bear hunters. They never came back. I'm not about to risk the lives of my remaining men."

Ranju sat up and straightened his back. "Then give me a car. I will go alone."

"I'm going too," Anders said. He said it almost as an afterthought, but he was young and didn't want to be called a coward.

Dure frowned at the both of them. "Even if I wanted to let you both go on your own, I am still responsible for you regardless of what happens. You realize that I am also responsible for my men and whatever happens to them, yes?"

"Then ask for volunteers, Sergeant. The rest can stay here if they wish," Ranju said.

Dure said nothing as he stood up and left the room.

Ranju turned to face Anders. "Do you think he will accept this?"

Anders sighed. "He is part Sami, the original inhabitants of Lapland. His people are dour and practical. But I know him. As much as he is concerned about the danger, he wants to end this crisis too because his own people are suffering … and he knows the only way to possibly do that is to find out what's causing the cold."

They all sat down for an impromptu dinner in the station's canteen just before leaving. The food was typical of the area: cold reindeer sausage, dried reindeer jerky, sautéed reindeer, smoked reindeer, and gravlax. Ranju was a vegetarian and ended up eating some thin crusty bread, boiled potatoes, cloudberries, and some instant noodles he had packed in his bags before heading out to Sweden. Anders didn't eat much because it felt like the last supper for him. The policemen said nothing as they ate heartily. Towards the end of the meal, Dure simply said that they were all going. Nobody protested.

Tarfala Valley was a little over forty miles away. Three Volvo sport utility vehicles made a beeline towards the research station as the evening twilight was obscured by the cold front. The police vehicles had fog lights, but the visibility steadily became worse as they got closer. Dure was driving the middle car along with a constable sitting in the front seat who was armed with a rifle. Ranju and Anders both sat in the back.

Dure cursed as the conditions ahead of him deteriorated to the point where he could barely see the lead Volvo, whose rear was just a few feet in front of him even though all of the headlights were in bright mode. The radios were barely working because of the static, and the speed of the small convoy had slowed to a crawl lest they collide with each other.

Anders turned sideways and faced Ranju. "You came from UN headquarters in New York?"

"Yes," Ranju said as he adjusted the collar on his dark blue parka. "It took me two days just to get to Stockholm, the transportation system in Europe has slowed down to almost nothing. Nobody wants to fly anymore. The same thing is happening in America."

"I heard that portions of France, Spain and Germany are now under military jurisdiction. What is happening?"

Ranju shrugged. "I don't know. It seems people are rioting for some unknown cause. Parts of Europe have also been blocked, either because the government cordoned them off or because of the strange weather patterns. The whole continent is being pounded nonstop by rain and snow. All we know is that it seems to be emanating from this part of Scandinavia."

"Any word on China and the Far East?"

"China has completely closed itself off from the rest of the world, or at least they're trying to. The little news that we're getting is pretty confusing."

"And what about Japan? I have a friend living there."

"Japan is in a state of near anarchy from what I heard. News reports are saying that demons were roaming the streets of their main cities, but I'm not sure believe a word of that."

Anders said nothing more.

After a little over an hour, they could finally see the faint outlines of buildings at the base of the valley. Tarfala Research Station was really nothing more than a cluster of deep-red colored wooden lodges with a couple of shipping containers and a small antenna tower nearby. Anders took out a woolen cap from his coat and put it over his head. Ranju's parka had a built-in fur lined hood, which he pulled over his head before opening the passenger door. All three cars had halted just alongside the station as they all got out. The wind was howling and it was near whiteout conditions as everybody soon had their handheld flashlights turned on. Dure had to shout in order to get his instructions heard as the police constables split into groups of two to search each cabin. Anders and Ranju paired up as they both headed for the main research lodge.

Although he had the keys to the door since they were entrusted to him during the general evacuation a few days before, Anders found the door to be unlocked and so went inside. The interior of the wooden cabin was cold and totally dark except for the illumination from the car headlights that were shining through the windows. Using his flashlight, he noticed that everything was still in place.

"Will there be any power at all?" Ranju said as he closed the front door behind him.

"I think the generator is in the next room, hold on a minute," Anders said as he started walking towards the door at the far end of the room.

Just as he put his hand on the door knob it suddenly flung open, hitting Anders in the face and knocking him down. A shadowy figure came out. As Ranju instinctively aimed his flashlight towards it, he could see that the assailant was in dark winter clothing and had a knife poised over his head.

"Stop!" Ranju screamed as the man looked like he was about to stab Anders.

The man turned and faced him. Ranju could see the ice frost on his shaggy beard but what was really disconcerting were his wild blue eyes, they had the look of a madman. For a short minute, no one moved or said anything. Suddenly, the front door opened and in came Sergeant Dure, who instantly saw what was happening and pulled out a gun from his holster.

"Put down the knife!" Dure shouted at the man as he aimed the SIG Sauer pistol at him.

The man simply let out a wailing cry and dropped the knife as he fell to his knees. Anders instantly grabbed the knife by the handle and threw it further away so the man couldn't reach it as he got up. Dure ran over to them as Ranju kept his flashlight steady to provide illumination. The police sergeant placed the man's hands behind his back and handcuffed him as Anders picked up his flashlight and went back into the generator room, found the circuit breaker and flipped on the power switch. Within minutes, the lights around the camp went up.

Dure sat the man on a chair and began to search him. Other than a packet of dried meat, there was nothing else on him. Ranju turned on the lights within the main cabin as Anders activated the massive floodlights outside using the controls in the generator room.

"Who are you?" Dure said as he sat down in front of the man while holstering his pistol.

The man simply looked away, closed his eyes and whimpered.

Anders walked over to them and let out a gasp as he peered at the man's face. "That man, he's one of the hunters the police are searching for. I think his name is Mihkal, I believe."

"Is this true? You are a hunter?" Dure said to the man.

The man's chin was trembling. Bits of saliva dribbled out from his chapped lips as he answered. "Y-yes, I-I am Mihkal."

Dure put his arm on the man's trembling shoulder. "What happened? Where are the others?"

"T-they're dead!" Mihkal cried.

Dure narrowed his eyes. "How did they die?"

Mihkal was sobbing again. "W-we were nearby when we saw them, everyone ran, but we were too slow, they caught up to us. I saw one of them pick up Lars and started chewing on his head! I ran and ran and I hid here!"

Dure crossed his arms. "Who did it?"

At that moment, a massive roar was heard that reverberated across the entire valley. It sounded like a strange combination of a lion's bellow and a foghorn. For a brief second, everyone looked up in surprise. Then Mihkal started to scream.

Anders, Dure, and Ranju ran out of the front door. The visibility was still very bad as the snowstorm continued to swirl around them, but at least the base lights had illuminated the area so they could see that the other police constables had come out of the other cabins and started walking towards them.

Ramu pointed to the west. "Look!"

Due to the whiteout, they could barely see it. A strange ray of purple and blue-colored light was emanating from the very summit of Kebnekaise and up into what seemed like a hole in the sky. It looked like the fabric of space had been torn open and a vast, dark void could be seen right above the mountain. White wisps of strange, cloud-like air currents could be seen orbiting the shaft of light along with strange, dancing lights that were falling from the hole in the sky, like miniature shooting stars.

"Oh my god," Anders said.

Everyone was looking in the wrong direction so they were all taken by complete surprise as a gigantic, grey-colored pudgy hand, the size of a small car, came in from right above them, picked up a screaming police constable by his head and then disappeared from view. Everybody let out a cry of alarm and scattered as a gigantic fur-clad foot that was as big as a small bus stomped another policeman into the ground, crushing him.

A few of them pulled out their pistols and opened fire as the two monstrous giants wandered into view. They must have been at least forty-feet tall, with sagging folds of skin and hooked noses beneath black beards the size of opera curtains and grey, stone-like flesh. The giants wore rudimentary fur clothing and boots so they at least looked somewhat intelligent, if it were not for their habit of picking up more victims with their massive hands and either crushing them into red pulp, or just popping them in their mouths to chew on.

Anders and Ranju instinctively ran back into the main cabin as the roar of the giants and the screams of the dying men reverberated throughout the doomed base.

"The power! Cut the power to the lights!" Ranju shouted to Anders as he dove underneath the table in the middle of the cabin, while the other man ran for the generator room. Mihkal was struggling to try and free himself, but the handcuffs held him fast and all he could do was to keep on screaming as one of the giants tore the roof off the cabin and sent pieces of it flying into the howling blizzard that was all around them.

7. El Rey

Mexico

They called him El Paco. His full name was Gustavo Felipe Moreno Cabrera, but his mother always called him Paco, which in Spanish meant "free" because he had such a free spirit, even as a little child. He was the youngest of her eight children and her favorite. Even as a child he was a natural leader. Although he had five older brothers, by the time he was fourteen years of age they all respected him and did everything he suggested. That was because they all realized that he was smarter than the rest of them put together. His father hated him though because Paco just wasn't willing to give him all the money that the boy had earned from selling fruit on the streets of Mexico City. Paco gave it to his mother instead so that the family could have something to eat rather than to support his father's incessant drinking and gambling. So he beat the boy until the child could barely stand every chance he got. By the time he was a teen, Paco had had enough and together with his brothers, left home and traveled by foot all the way to Sinaloa, where they cultivated marijuana plants and started selling to local dealers in exchange for cash. Paco did not have much of an education since his father made him quit school when he was only in the fourth grade. Instead, he schooled himself, gathering as many books as he could find to read. By the time he turned nineteen, Paco was now a self-made man and the leader of his own gang. This was after he personally executed a local dealer when the older man insulted him in front of his brothers.

During the 1980's, the Colombians used Mexico as a transit route for their burgeoning cocaine business in the US and Paco's gang became one of their local affiliates. Paco had a very efficient system of transportation: he simply bribed the police and the politicians to make sure the shipments would not be stopped. He also killed any of his men who failed to deliver the cocaine on time. He got so good at it, and was invited to Colombia as the personal guest of Pablo Escobar for a month. As the US authorities tightened their patrols over the Caribbean and Florida in the succeeding decade, the Colombians became even more dependent on Mexico to bring the drugs through to the point where the Mexicans began to establish their own powerful cartels. The Mexicans ultimately became independent as the Colombian government along with the DEA, finally made headway against Escobar and the other Colombian cartels. By the beginning of the new century, Paco was now the de facto leader of his own cartel. He had now amassed a fortune bigger than Escobar had ever made over his lifetime. By this time, he had added "El" to his title and was now known as El Paco. His beloved mother had died peacefully in her sleep with the thought that she had finally raised a good boy and El Paco had an elaborate mausoleum built for her.

But there were always problems. Just as the Mexican cartels' power had risen, so had the attention of the United States. They began pouring in resources to help the Mexican government's efforts to stem the drug trade. The uneasy peace between the cartels had also been shattered as former members started their own families and attempted to take territory away from the old guard. The most brutal of these upstarts were the Zetas, a group of former Mexican special forces soldiers who deserted and became an enforcement arm of the Gulf Cartel, until they decided to strike out on their own. The Zetas engaged in terror attacks, routinely chopped heads off their enemies and massacred scores of civilians along with anyone who came up against them. The Zetas began to take over vast stretches of territory. Being the head of the most powerful cartel in the country naturally made El Paco the number one target for the Zetas, and they tried everything they could in order to kill him. Three of his brothers died in the war against the Zetas, but El Paco was always one step ahead of them, just as he was always one step ahead of the law. Ultimately, El Paco was able to wear out the Zetas as he masterminded an alliance against them with the other cartels, at one point even cooperating with the Mexican government and the DEA in order to locate and have them arrest the leaders of the Zetas group.

After the Zetas were weakened, another problem arose when the government finally turned on him and made him the most wanted man in the country. But El Paco was still one step ahead. He had an army of three hundred heavily-armed bodyguards and informants who warned him every time the police and the military got too close. He had been hunted for over twenty years, and a legend began to grow that he would never be caught as he lived up to the name of El Paco. His stature began to grow even more, when people would tell of him brazenly walking into a popular restaurant unannounced, as he sat down to dinner while his men would confiscate all cell phones, which would then be returned to their owners after he left, and everyone's bills would be fully paid.

El Paco continued to smoke his Cuban cigar. He sat comfortably in his chair while facing the inner courtyard of his ranch-style mansion, just a few miles from Toluca. The fifty-hectare estate was newly built up in the mountains near a protected lake sanctuary. He had decided to come out in the open again, just days after much of the country had suddenly lost touch with the Federal Government in Mexico City, just an hour's drive away. In just a few weeks after the never ending rains started, there were rumors of rioting in Mexico City and within hours, all contact with the city to the outside world had been lost. The Mexican Army mobilized and since most of their brigades were based in the area, they quickly moved in but the regional governments had lost any and every form of communication with them as well. The Congress and governors of each state in the country quickly met to find a solution, but were unable to formulate a consensus. So the standing orders for all remaining military and police forces were to maintain a perimeter just outside of the capital city, no one was allowed to go in until more information was found as to what had happened. The entire country was now nearing a state of anarchy as local governments had been unable to cope with the loss of their national leadership.

As he stared silently out into the courtyard while listening to the incessant falling rain and enjoying the cool evening, El Paco's walkie-talkie that was sitting on the carved wooden table began to squawk. That meant that his guest was arriving. A uniformed maid came by and placed a silver tray with a steaming pot of Colombian coffee on the table nearby. She poured him a cup along with a spoonful of brown sugar, just the way he liked it.

A few minutes later, a bald, clean-shaven man wearing a raincoat and slacks walked into the covered part of the courtyard. He was flanked by four heavily-armed men with assault rifles and body armor. The maid withdrew back to the kitchen as the man stood in front of him and held out his hand, but El Paco just had a blank look on his face as he continued to sit there and smoke his cigar.

Finally, the man withdrew his hand and took off his raincoat before sitting down on the sofa, his empty side holster at his belt. "That's a hell of a way to treat an old friend," the man said in perfect Spanish.

El Paco blew some cigar smoke at him. "You're a friend now, Barton?"

Doug Barton leaned forward. "We've met a few times over the past decade. I'd like to think of you as a friend, El Paco."

"Cops can never be my friends. You know that a cop killed one of my brothers, yes?" El Paco said. "I paid over two million dollars to have him killed, along with every member of his family. It took my men two years to do it because he had many children, and many brothers and sisters."

Barton smiled. "But I'm not really a cop."

"You're DEA," El Paco said. "No difference there."

"We're Federal agents, El Paco. Not police."

"Same thing. Just another cop with a different badge. Where is your partner by the way? I gather this isn't official since he doesn't know about our relationship?"

Barton tried to keep a straight face. His informants were good. "He's back in Tijuana. He doesn't know about this meeting because my superiors weren't quite sure just how he would feel about the offer I'm supposed to give you."

El Paco smiled. "I can't respect a cop who hides information from his own partner. In my line of business, trust is everything. If I feel I cannot trust a man, then I take steps to make sure that my risk will be minimized."

"You mean by killing that man," Barton said.

"Of course. There is no need to delay the inevitable. If a man cannot be trusted, then you must kill him as soon as possible."

"You know what's going to happen if you kill me, right? There are already US troops on full alert, stationed at the border."

"The brigades you have along the border are mostly part-time soldiers in the National Guard, although I admit you do have a few Green Beret alpha-teams and SEALs on standby. But then again, your government is having its own problems with no planes in the air and parts of your beloved country are slowly getting cut off."

Barton shook his head. "We're getting away from the subject here, El Paco. My orders have changed and that's why I've come to see you. We're no longer aiding the Mexican government in arresting you."

El Paco laughed as he sipped his coffee. "Well, considering that your government is no longer in contact with my government since Mexico City has been cut off, then there's not much you can do about me, is there? The governors of the other Mexican states are in a panic and I can now do whatever I want right out in the open."

"Look," Barton said as a matter of fact. "If the situation down here gets any worse, my government will enact its contingency plan. We will start to occupy the Mexican cities along the boundary to establish a buffer zone. We will stop the refugees streaming over the border and that will include dealing with cartel members in a free-fire zone. All we're asking for now is a truce, stop your drug shipments, especially along the Tijuana and Ciudad Juarez routes and we'll leave your people alone. You can have Mexico."

El Paco laughed again. "Barton, you are a fool. Mexico is already mine. Just a few days ago, my men wiped out the entire Cardenas clan. Now the entire Tijuana Cartel is gone and their territory is mine. The Zetas have not shown themselves since the Federal government was cut off. I've won."

"You may think you have this country now," Barton said. "But how long do you think you can hold it? We have very recent intel reports that the remaining troops along the Mexico City outer perimeter have either run away or disappeared. Whatever is in that city will swallow you up as well."

El Paco smiled as he shook his head. "I've dealt with government people before, and I went up against the Army before, and even you and the other DEA agents, even the FBI, and I've always been one step ahead of them all. Whatever foolishness is going on in Mexico City I will deal with once I've consolidated all my territories. My army of assassins grows by the day."

Barton looked away. "You may think you're the king of Mexico, but you're just another drug dealer."

One of El Paco's men cursed as he leveled a Tavor TAR-21 assault rifle at Barton. Even El Paco became slightly annoyed at the boldness of such a man who would dare insult him in his own house, but he waved off his men, who quickly stood back.

"I'm a businessman," El Paco said nonchalantly to Barton. "I sell goods to people in your own country. If you want to blame the misery of your citizens on something, then you can look in the mirror because the answer is staring right back at you."

Barton rubbed his palms together, wiping away the sweat. "Do you know why there're no drug cartels in Chile even though they pioneered the cocaine business? It's because General Pinochet had them all shot and the lucky survivors moved to Colombia and started everything there. If only we had more Pinochets in Colombia and in Mexico we could have won this damned drug war."

El Paco grinned. "You Americans are so stupid. Even if we had dictators here and in Colombia and even if they had us all killed, then someone else in some other country would have been selling drugs to your people. It is the American public who are to blame for your stupid drug war, you consume the most drugs out of any other country in the world, yet your foolish government keeps trying to ban it. You people are the true idiots of this world, you make your own enemies, and you've brought this disaster onto yourselves."

Barton threw his hands up. "Alright, whatever. But be that as it may, my offer to you still stands. Stop the transporting of drugs up north and you have my solemn word that we leave you all alone, otherwise we'll be going in. Do we have a deal?"

El Paco put the cigar back to his mouth and puffed it. "No, I will go on my own. And the best way for me to send this message to your superiors is by giving them your head in a box." With those words he snapped his fingers as his men aimed their rifles at the now visibly shaken Barton.

Barton stood up as the sweat began to drip from his forehead anew while El Paco's men surrounded him. "You can't do this. My government will hunt you down like a dog if you do this."

El Paco was giggling as he leaned back on his leather chair and crossed his legs. "Your government will fall, just like what happened here. Who knows, maybe I can even take over your country when that finally happens."

Just as Barton cursed at him, there was a flash of lightning that briefly blinded everyone. It was followed by the nerve-cracking sound of thunder as the storm increased its ferocity. When one of the bodyguards grabbed Barton by the arm, sounds of gunfire and plenty of screaming could be heard all around them. El Paco's bodyguards instantly surrounded their master. Less than a minute later, the electric power was cut and the whole house was plunged into near darkness with only a few emergency lights that had automatically activated, and the frequent flashes of lightning which gave everyone a brief form of illumination.

El Paco stood up as the sounds of gunfire continued. He strode over to Barton as he drew his gold-plated .357 Magnum revolver from a shoulder holster and pointed it at the DEA agent. "Your men are attacking me, you lying traitor!"

Barton put his hands up as he knelt down. "No, El Paco! I swear to you, there are no DEA agents or police in this whole area. Your own men picked me up and drove me here!"

El Paco cursed aloud. Perhaps it was his arch enemies, the Zetas, who were mounting a surprise attack. "Let's get to the escape tunnel. We'll bring this American fool with us as a hostage just in case," he told his bodyguards as they readied their weapons.

At that moment, two shadowy figures entered the other side of the courtyard from where the kitchen was. Just as everyone turned to face them, Barton could not get a close look at the intruders due to the very dim lighting.

As the two approached, they looked like very thin women with long dark hair that hid their faces and they were wearing pleated skirts and nothing else. El Paco and his men were confused, the strangers didn't seem to be armed and being men, they could never be afraid of women. When the two got to within thirty feet of the group, there was another flash of lightning.

The bodyguards screamed first. Barton simply had his mouth open in shock. El Paco stayed rooted like a statue as the lightning flash revealed their true forms. Although the two looked like women, each one had deathly pallor like that of a corpse. It was not that they were thin, in fact the two were essentially skeletons as it was clear their protruding ribcages had nothing beneath them. Their skeletal arms ended with black clawed hands, while their thin, stick-like legs ended with talons. But the most terrifying aspect was their skull faces, empty sockets where their eyes should have been, with no noses and long, fanged teeth.

Barton finally screamed as the bodyguards opened fire with their rifles set on automatic. But it was of no use as the monstrous, demonic women tore out their organs and ripped their flesh to shreds in less than a few seconds. El Paco knew he couldn't fight them and simply aimed his revolver at Barton's head and fired, killing the DEA agent. His corpse slumped forward onto the bloody brick floor.

Then a curious thing happened, instead of attacking the drug lord, the demonic women simply stopped and stood in front of El Paco as he wailed like a madman. "What are you waiting for, hurry up and kill me like what you did to my men!"

The two demons simply stared back at him with their empty eye sockets.

8. Lament

Iraq

Every part of him was covered in dust. It had seeped into his boots, through his socks and now he could feel the fine grains of sand in between his toes, not to mention his armpits, his beard, and in his ears. He was covered in sand as if he had taken a bath in it. He was hungry, thirsty, and wounded, but he had to keep on running. He was alive and he still had a job to do. He was a warrior and he would keep fighting until they killed him.

Patrick Gyle knew it was high noon judging from the way the sun was positioned directly overhead through the muddled sky. The dust storms that covered the entire region weren't uniformly just blowing buckets of sand around him all of the time, there were long periods of quietness, of a haze-filled atmosphere with dust that seemed to be suspended in space. Like some gloomy fog up in the northern hemispheres, only instead of water droplets, it was made of sand. It gave everything a washed out, surreal look, and it coated everything in hues of light brown and grey. At night, when the winds weren't blowing, he couldn't see anything at all as he would stumble from one step to the next, never knowing what would be in front of him until the last second. His flashlight had already run out of batteries and his hydration pouch was empty. Gyle's right forearm had an improvised bandage from where the creatures tore at him. He barely got out of the way before Matt had sacrificed himself by trying to ram into one of them. But the creature just kicked the armored Humvee and it flew backwards like a toy car. He thought he was dead too, but the creature just seemed to have moved away and didn't even bother with him. He was able to get to the wreckage of the vehicle and cradled Matt's head in his arms, just as his partner coughed blood from his mouth, and then convulsed and finally lay still with his eyes open.

He salvaged what he could from the Humvee. He also tried to get anything from the other wrecked vehicles in what was left of the convoy; then started making his way south on foot. He was hoping to get back to any sort of HQ, so he could warn all remaining US forces about what had happened. He tried to stay hidden in the daytime, resting while half burying himself behind sand dunes, then avoiding any built-up areas as he worked his way southwards at night. It was one of those evenings when he thought he ran into some packs of creatures with glowing eyes that he could see through the dusty haze. He used up most of his ammunition while firing into what he felt was their positions. Gyle was terrified of the clicking noises throughout that night. It was as if the shrill chirps of insects were combined with blood curdling sounds of demon dogs. Those cries haunted him all through the darkness as he kept scanning around with his flashlight, hoping he could shoot those things before they got close. When morning came, he fell asleep almost immediately from pure exhaustion, but when he woke up a few hours later, his M4 carbine and pistol were gone, along with his food supply.

He had been walking for hours now. Although his training dictated it would be better to move at night to avoid the harsh exposure of the sun, Gyle felt that the dusty haze all around him had provided sufficient protection to keep on going. And the second, most important reason was to find a source of water and find it quickly; he had already gone over a day and a half without anything to drink. Even though he had no food either, Gyle knew that finding potable water was the most important thing right now if he wanted to keep on living.

By late afternoon, he had noticed a cluster of stone buildings out on the flat horizon a few miles in front of him. He had been sticking close to the highway and he estimated that he was near the outskirts of Tikrit, just a little over a hundred miles north of Baghdad. He had tried going into a few nearby houses in the past few days, but he found nothing but sand and dust along with a few dried out corpses. He was now hoping that there would at least be a nearby well that wasn't filled in with sand. Hurrying along, Gyle soon made his way to the edge of the compound as he crept up behind a dust-covered car without any wheels and surveyed the place for signs of movement. After waiting for fifteen minutes without seeing anything, he quickly moved towards a cracked wooden door at the back of the two-story structure. The dust-covered door was barely hanging on by its fixture so he pulled it open with a slight creak as its hinges gave way. Peering inside, he still didn't see any movement, and so he stepped into what looked like an abandoned kitchen.

Pulling off the bandana that filtered his mouth and nostrils down to his neck and then unstrapping his goggles, Gyle quickly began to rummage through cupboards and cabinets, hoping to at least find some containers with water or any drinkable liquid. Hidden behind some boxes underneath a dirty sink was a brown rope sack. Gyle untied the top and quickly let out a cry of joy as he pulled out a small can of a locally produced coconut juice drink. The sack also contained some raw potatoes and onions.

Gyle quickly tore the tab off the top of the juice can and started sipping it slowly. It was a bit too sweet for his liking, but he needed the liquid. The onions and potatoes had mold growing on them, but he could probably just eat around that, provided he had more water. After retying the sack and putting it back where he found it, Gyle walked into an adjoining room where he quickly sensed movement near the side of the door.

Rapidly turning and taking a fighting stance, he saw that they were two people huddled in a corner at the side of the corridor from where he had entered. They were wearing abayas, the ubiquitous full-body cloak and black robes worn by women in these parts. One of them was half the size of the other and let out a shriek, huddling behind the taller one. They were veiled so he could only see their glaring brown eyes through the narrow slits of the niqab. As both sides kept their distance and waited for the other to make a move, Gyle made a rapid assessment and seeing that it looked like they were harmless, slackened his shoulders and held out his open palms in a gesture of peace.

Gyle smiled. "As-salamu Alaikum." It was the universal greeting in Arabic. He didn't know much of the language beyond a few basic words and phrases.

"Wa-Alaikum salaam," the taller one said.

Gyle gestured at the two to take their veils off. As both of them did, he noticed that the taller one seemed to be a brown, middle-aged woman while the small one looked to be a girl of about eight or nine years old. Gyle sighed with both surprise and relief. These were the first people he had found alive after several days out in the desert. The little girl smiled back at him as the woman walked forward and shook his hand.

Gyle made a drinking gesture. "Water? Maya?"

"Nem," the woman said as she walked over to a cabinet, opened it, and took out a metal box with a spout on it and gave it to him.

Gyle tipped the liquid into his mouth. The water was tepid, but he needed it badly, drinking until his stomach was full. Wiping his mouth with his left wrist, he smiled again and gave the container back to the woman. "Shukraan," he said, thanking her.

"Ahlan bik," the woman said as she put the container back into the closet and closed it.

Gyle sat down on the dusty carpet. He needed to rest while his body rehydrated. Already the pounding headache at the back of his head had begun to subside as he groaned and leaned back on the wall of the living room. Just as he began to doze off, he quickly snapped back to attention when he felt something touch his bandaged forearm. The woman let out a cry and fell backwards before Gyle mumbled an apology. She got back up and began to examine his arm once more.

"Jurh?" the woman said, indicating that he might have been hurt. Gyle nodded. With that, the woman got up and began rummaging through the closet again, this time producing a cardboard box containing some white linen that she began cutting up, and turning into homemade bandages using a pair of rusty scissors. The little girl sat on the edge of an old sofa and stared at him intently. An hour had passed as the woman carefully unwrapped the t-shirt around his arm and saw the raw, red laceration that had cut into him when he narrowly jumped out of the Humvee, just as a nightmarish creature landed on top of it several nights before. The wound had begun to fester a bit as there was a clear film of liquid on top, but the woman took out a small bottle of what looked to be some local antiseptic. She poured it over his arm which made Gyle gasp in pain. By the time she was finished he had a fresh bandage over his arm for which he thanked her a second time. Indicating that he needed to rest, she helped him onto the sofa and he soon began to doze off as the winds began to pick up outside.

His sleep was deep and his dreams were that of a black and empty void. There was also the recollection of that last battle in which Matt had lost his life. He wasn't sure how long he had slept, but it must have been at least a day. When he started to wake he could hear the woman and the child shouting and screaming. There was light coming from the outside. That was when he realized that he had gotten complacent and he should have checked the area first as his eyes opened. Gyle saw two men standing over him, one was aiming an AK-47 assault rifle at his face while the other one was slapping the woman around with a pistol. The child cried and screamed, trying desperately to hold onto her. The one who had the rifle trained on him wore a faded black shirt and jeans, with empty ammunition pouches strapped to his chest while the other one wore desert fatigues. Both wore black ski masks and were covered in dust, like him.

"Kun hadyaan!" the man in the fatigues said to the woman to be quiet as she collapsed in front of him, crying and holding onto the little girl.

"You American?" the man with the black t-shirt said to Gyle as he pointed the barrel of the AK at his face. His accent sounded like that of an Australian.

"Yes," Gyle said softly.

"Are you alone?"

Gyle nodded.

"You better not be bullshitting me, mate," the man in black said as he glanced around nervously before pointing the rifle back at him again. Gyle figured he could probably get his hands on the guy and disarm him before he could get a shot off, but he was worried about the second guy with the pistol, who might end up shooting the woman and the child before he could take the rifle and kill the two IS fighters with it.

"Look," Gyle said to the man in black. "The war is over for us, so why don't you ask your friend over there to leave the two girls alone."

The man in black's finger tightened on the trigger of his rifle. "You don't give us orders, mate! Where is the rest of your unit?"

Gyle sighed. "I'm the only one left alive, just as I'm sure you and your friend are the last of the Daesh, so let us make peace and go our separate ways as friends."

"I am not your friend, yank," the man said. "You're a prisoner of the Islamic State and you will be judged as an invader and infidel according to Islamic law."

"Look around you," Gyle said. "This war is over, pal. My entire unit is gone. I'm just making my way south until I can find transport to take me home. You and your friend can have this country. You win, okay?"

The man shook his head. "No, mate, you're going to pay for invading the caliphate. You're a soldier and captured soldiers will face a trial."

The other man in the fatigues turned around and stood beside the IS fighter with the black t-shirt and started talking to him in Arabic. Gyle couldn't make out the whole conversation, but it seemed that the other man just wanted some water and they needed to get out of there. The woman cowered behind them as she held onto the child and was trying to calm her down. Looking at them, Gyle figured the guy with the AK-47 had less than a full magazine of ammunition on him, but he couldn't tell if the other guy had more rounds for his pistol. Gyle figured the two IS men were amateurs, they were standing too close to him and he could take them both down, but he would need a distraction of some sort. He needed to be patient, to wait for just the right moment to strike.

"We're no threat to you, please tell your friend that," Gyle said. He needed to get the guy to calm down because his trigger finger was way too itchy right now. "All American forces are leaving this region. You will have your caliphate, the one you've always wanted. That's what you want, right? So why not just let me and the two girls go?"

The man with the black shirt's eyes brightened when Gyle said that US forces were leaving. He said something to his partner in Arabic and the man in the fatigues shouted, "Allahu Akbar!" a few times. The Australian jihadist had turned to his partner when he told him that and Gyle almost had them, but in a split second, the Aussie quickly turned back to face him again. He needed to keep them complacent and try again. The next one should do the trick, Gyle hoped.

"What's your name?" Gyle said to the man with the black shirt. "You sound Australian, mate. I've been down under a few times and I love the country."

"If it's any of your business, you can call me Abu Ozy for short," the man said as he began to relax the grip on his weapon. "But it won't help you to try and make friends with me. You will face an Islamic Sharia court no matter what happens, mate."

"Look, if that's what you want to do with me then so be it. But could you just let the two girls go? They mean nothing to you," Gyle said.

"You think you can bargain with us, mate?" Abu Ozy hissed. "You're not in a position to negotiate."

"Alright then, take me to your leader, your imam," Gyle said.

"What?" Abu Ozy said. "I don't need to take you anywhere, mate. I can shoot you on the spot right here if I wanted to."

"That's not the way it works though," Gyle said. "You have to take me before the Shura, only the council can make a judgment. You did say I have to be tried first, didn't you?"

Abu Ozy got visibly angry. "Shut up! We're in charge here."

"There are no Shuras left, is there?" Gyle said. "How many in your unit are left? You two are the only ones alive, aren't you?"

Abu Ozy brought the rifle up to his shoulder and aimed it at Gyle's head. "I'll shoot you right now, mate, if you don't shut up!"

"Did you see the monsters?" Gyle said. "There are monsters out there, right? They wiped out my unit just as they surely wiped out you guys, didn't they? You ought to be saving your ammo for them."

Abu Ozy's hands began to shake. "No, those are ... demons sent to test us. Allah sent them!"

"If those demons were sent to test you, then you all failed," Gyle said. "Daesh has been destroyed, not by the forces of the West, but by the gods, yes? Perhaps Allah is not the true god after all?"

Abu Ozy was now enraged as his finger began to squeeze the trigger on the rifle. "How dare you speak blasphemies, infidel!"

The wind outside began to howl. The dust storm once again intensified and they all could hear faint clicking noises not too far away. The older woman began screaming as she tried to tug at the other jihadist's legs. Gyle figured she might have encountered those creatures of the night just like him. She was obviously begging to either be let go so she could hide with the child or that they needed to protect her. It was at that moment that Abu Ozy turned his head to look at the frosted glass window behind him.

Now. Gyle sprung from the sofa as one hand pushed away the barrel of the AK, while his other hand reached into the inside of his boot and pulled out a small knife. Abu Ozy instinctively pulled the trigger as the assault rifle went on automatic fire, but the cascade of bullets narrowly missed Gyle as he had successfully turned the barrel to where the other jihadist was positioned, just as he plunged the knife into Abu Ozy's throat, right at the exposed skin just above the bottom of the ski mask. The Australian jihadist began to gurgle out his own blood as Gyle was able to plunge the three-inch knife deep into his throat, severing the carotid artery and puncturing the trachea. As the man fell to the ground and began to convulse, Gyle brought up the bloody knife and dove on top of the second jihadist, who had fallen on the ground after he took a few shots from Abu Ozy's assault rifle. Gyle stabbed the other man repeatedly in the neck and at the back of the head until the jihadist was no longer moving.

Still clutching the knife, Gyle stood up as the adrenaline rush began to subside. It was then that he noticed both the woman and the child were on the ground as well. Kneeling down beside them, he began to see what he could do. As he took off the older woman's niqab he could see that she took a bullet to her forehead and had died instantly. It was then he heard a small coughing noise and he quickly moved to where the child was lying. As he took off her veil he could see that she was spitting out blood. Ripping off her black robe he noticed that she was wearing a dress underneath, it used to be white with some embroidery, but it now had a large red stain in the center of her chest. Quickly using his knife to expose the wound, Gyle could see that the bullet had punctured the middle of her breast bone. Gyle moaned as he turned the child over on her side, but it was clear that the bullet didn't go through, it was in her body somewhere.

"No, no, no!" Gyle screamed in frustration as the little girl heaved one last breath and then her eyes glazed over. He tried CPR a few times, but nothing had come of it.

For a while, he did nothing but sit there among the dead. When he finally did get the motivation to get up, he wiped the blood off his knife with Abu Ozy's black shirt before putting it back in his boot. He checked the magazine of the AK-47, but there weren't any rounds left. Racking the slide of the other man's pistol, he noticed that it was empty too. By this time night had fallen, he could hear the clicking sounds just outside of the building he was in. Gyle opened the closet and wedged himself in by crouching down underneath the lower shelf, right beside the metal can that still had some water in it. With his knife at the ready, he grabbed the edge of the closet door and slowly swung it backwards until it was closed and tried to control his breathing.

It was then he heard the front door open and the clicking noises were getting really close. Even though he had the knife ready to strike at anyone who would open the closet, his hands were trembling. For what seemed like an eternity, he heard the terrible whispering and the chattering all around him as he gritted his teeth and covered his ears with his hands.

When he finally woke up, all was quiet once more. Slowly opening the closet, Gyle held out the knife and looked around. The dead were still where they were. Gyle put the knife back in his boot and took the water canister and walked over to the kitchen so he wouldn't have to see the corpses. After taking a long draught of the tepid water, he poured the rest into his military hydration pouch. He took a few potatoes and bit into them, carefully spitting out the dirty skin and chewing the raw bits thoroughly before swallowing. He ate both onions, making sure he didn't chew on the moldy parts. When he was done, he took the rest and put them in his pockets. Going back to the living room, Gyle took one long look at the woman and the child before taking the empty AK assault rifle and slinging it over his shoulder. Then he went out through the front door and continued on southwards.

9. A Single Step

Arizona

For the fifth time that afternoon, Tara Weiss gave the thumbs up sign at the passing car but as before it just drove on by without even stopping. It was no use. The fifteen-year-old sighed and walked back from the edge of the highway, past the empty parking lot, and back to the front of the deserted strip mall. The pueblo-style storefronts were all locked down. A few even had steel shutters over them. Tara could probably use a rock to try and break in and steal some stuff, but she wasn't like that. She wasn't a thief, so she just sat down behind one of the columns to shield herself away from the afternoon sun, while placing the old blue denim backpack she was carrying in front of her.

When she had finally decided to leave the house for good, her father shouted at her not to bother coming back just as she walked out the door. Tara was tired of getting beaten and slapped around, but she didn't really blame him since he hadn't had a job for two years after mom left him and the rest of the family. She had been sleeping on the street for three days now, but she remembered everything as if it happened just a few minutes ago. The whole scene kept repeating over and over: her putting her best clothes into the beaten-up backpack that her mom had bought her so many years ago, breaking the piggy bank in her room that had been with her since she was five so she had some money, and finally the part where Timmy had stood before her, crying and pleading for her to stay.

That was her one regret, her little brother Timmy. Oh how she hated having to leave him behind. But he was only six. There was no way she could take care of him since she had nothing. A single tear rolled down Tara's right eye as she hugged her knees. She would go and get a job or something and come back for him. Yeah, she would come back in a white limousine and Timmy would get all excited and run into her arms. Then she would say, it's all over now and I'll take care of you from now on. After a few minutes, she just shook her head. It was time to get back to reality. She was just a nobody and she was getting really hungry.

Tara sighed as she undid the top strap of the backpack. Then she opened it to check how much food she had left. After rummaging through her clothes, all she could find was half a chocolate bar. It was part of the pack of twenty that the Pakistani guy running the convenience store had given her. Two days before, she was a few blocks away eating a two for a dollar hotdog sandwich at the guy's store, when suddenly a whole bunch of people swept in and started to take everything. The poor store owner tried to fight them off, but he was beaten up and left bleeding on the ground as everybody just took what they could and left. Tara just stood there as a couple of burly fat guys wearing baseball caps went right past her, then they started throwing everything off the shelves into a grocery cart that they brought along with them. There were all sorts of people in that mob: young and old, men, mothers, teens, and even a few kids. Most of them went after the canned goods, candies, and packaged snacks. Meanwhile, three men armed with guns helped themselves to most of the beer and liquor. By the time they were done, it was as if a whirlwind had smashed through the store, took everything, and left a pile of empty metal shelves behind. Tara had walked over to the store owner and helped him up. The man cried for a bit as he wiped the blood off his face from an embroidered handkerchief before thanking her. As she started walking out past the broken glass and the smashed door, the man called out to her. When she turned around, he gave her a small cardboard box full of chocolate bars that the mob had missed because it was in a hidden alcove behind the counter. Tara said she didn't want it because she was out of money, but the man just said it was okay so she thanked him and left. When she walked by the place again just yesterday, she noticed it had been abandoned, along with the other stores in the area.

It was such a pity her best friend Crissy had moved away. Every time her dad would beat her she would stay the night at Crissy's house. They had been best friends since elementary school and Tara's heart was broken when, during the end of classes for their freshman year in high school, Crissy told her that she was moving away with her family to California. The night before they didn't sleep at all as they just sat together in Crissy's room, surrounded by all those boxes as they talked about all sorts of things, from who was the hottest guy in school to what kind of lipstick Crissy should buy when she got to California, and a whole lot of other stuff. In the end they realized they had to keep talking in order to stop each other from crying. As the morning came, Crissy had to get in the car with her dad, her mom, and her brothers. Tara started running the moment Crissy's dad was honking the car horn and shouted at her to get in the car already. Tara was in tears and just ran all the way back to her room in the mobile home park where she lived and cried her eyes out that summer. Her biggest regret was not even saying goodbye to Crissy when the time had come.

When sophomore year started in high school it was a bad time for her. Crissy was gone and she was alone. Tara did try to make friends with the other girls, but they sneered at her used clothes and lack of makeup and they called her ghetto girl, or white trailer trash. That was also the time when her father started to drink even more and she ended up taking care of Timmy. She made sure he had a bath every night, even though there wasn't any soap, and brushed his teeth, even though there wasn't any toothpaste. Her dad never bought anything other than whisky and beer with his welfare checks. When summer finally started again, school had ended and she would take long walks along the streets of the city just to get away from him. It was on one of those summer nights when she was hanging around in the mall, just walking by the appliance store, when she saw a whole crowd gathered in front of one of the TV displays. It was the news and it was showing all sorts of bad things, like a lot of American troops were missing in the Middle East. Then it shifted to riots in Europe, and then finally it started to show crashed and burning passenger planes all over the country. The day after that was when crowds started to gather in front of grocery stores to buy everything they could afford. That was when Tara found some money on the table while her dad was asleep on the couch. She went over to a small Vietnamese store in a nearby strip mall and bought a few food items that were still available there. When she arrived home, that was when her dad screamed at her and started hitting her really bad. And that was when she decided to go after leaving the groceries lying near the door.

Tara ran her hand along her reddish brown hair. She hadn't taken a bath in awhile but there was nowhere she could go and do that anyway. There was a nearby faucet in an alleyway that she used to get a drink of water. She thought maybe that she could have a bath nearby, but she shook her head as it was freezing at night. Just last evening was when the streetlights didn't turn on and the whole city was plunged into a cold, deserted twilight once darkness fell. It was obvious to her that there wouldn't be any power now and she regretted not having a flashlight. This was a miserable way to live, but she thought the world was going to end anyway. So at least she would be by herself and in control when it would finally happen.

As the sun began to set and the temperature started to drop, Tara got up, stretched, and started walking towards the back alley behind the strip mall. She needed to go get a drink of water before she would huddle up in her jacket and sleep. As she knelt by the faucet and turned the handle, only a trickle of water came out before a sucking nose occurred and then nothing. A creeping sense of desperation and melancholy swept over her. She would need to find some water before she died of thirst. At that moment she heard a small noise behind her and she turned around.

Sitting on its hind legs and facing her was a small Chihuahua. It had brown fur, big bulging eyes and a short brown coat. Tara noticed a blue collar on its neck that indicated that it was a pet and not a stray. The dog just stared back at her.

Tara smirked. "If you're looking for water too, I'm sorry, but this tap is out."

The dog just stared at her for a bit before it started nibbling on its own shoulder.

Tara took out the half-eaten chocolate bar from her sweater pocket. "If you want something to eat, this is all I've got."

The dog stared at her again.

"Okay fine," Tara said as she tore off a bite-sized chunk of chocolate and nougat from the remaining candy bar and offered it to the little dog with her hand.

The dog walked over to her and took the chunk of candy with its mouth and started to chew it.

Tara smiled. "It's good, huh? You must really be hungry to be out here all by yourself."

"Not bad," the dog said as it chewed the last bits of candy. "But I prefer to have my chocolate without sugar in it, like what the old Mayans had."

Tara screamed as she fell backwards and landed on her buttocks. For a few minutes, nobody said anything as the dog just kept staring at her.

She raised a trembling finger at the animal. "Y-you can talk."

The Chihuahua scratched the back of its ear using its hind paw. "And so can you. That makes us even."

Tara blinked several times to make sure she wasn't dreaming. "But I'm a person, you're a dog."

"And we both have a mouth and we both can think," the dog said. "So what?"

"But dogs aren't supposed to talk."

"Says who? Maybe you people just weren't listening to them."

"How did you learn to talk? Did your owner teach you?"

The dog narrowed its eyes. "The only thing my owner taught me was that she was a terrible woman."

"Then how did you learn how to talk then?"

"I think I was born this way I guess."

"Did your mother talk too?"

The dog sniffed the air around him. "I don't have a mother."

"Then who gave birth to you then?"

"Nobody. I've been around since the dawn of creation."

Tara smirked. This animal was a wiseass. "So you're like God, then?"

"Some people have called me that."

Tara grinned. Other than a few homeless people that were just passing through, this dog was the first person she talked to for days. "Just because you can talk doesn't make you a god."

"You might be right about that. Then again, who really knows?"

Tara got up. "You must really think you're smart, don't cha?"

"You're the one who's saying that, not me."

"I must be dreaming," Tara said wistfully. "Or this must really be the end of the world."

"Take your pick."

Tara sighed. "Okay, doggie. What do you want to do now then?"

The dog looked at her hand. "Could I get another bite of that chocolate? I haven't had any for hundreds of years now."

"Sure," Tara said as she tore off another bit of the candy bar and gave it to the dog while popping the rest of it into her mouth. "Like you're supposed to be billions and billions of years old or something?"

"I guess I don't look at time the way you humans do," the dog said.

Tara crumpled the empty wrapper and threw it away. "So now what? We're out of food and it looks like the water's gone too and I'm still hungry. You got any ideas on how we could find some food?"

"There are many paths to take and each trail leads to a different fate," the dog said.

Tara rolled her eyes. "What the heck is that supposed to mean? Okay, I'll play this game of yours, doggie. Give me some choices, or at least give me a hint of where these paths are then."

"The first path is the easiest … if you go back to the parking lot that is fronting your shelter, you will meet a man who will give you some food and drink," the dog said.

Tara picked up her backpack and slung it over her shoulder as she turned and started walking out of the alley. "That sounds good to me, let's go."

"But I haven't told you of the other paths yet."

"Who cares, I need some food right now," Tara said as she kept walking. "You can tell me about the other paths later. Come on!"

"The easiest path may not necessarily be to your liking," the dog muttered under its breath as it followed the teen girl.

Sure enough, as Tara walked out of the alleyway and back to the front of the strip mall, she saw a grey van that was parked in the middle of the empty parking lot that faced the highway. Its rear doors were open. A man wearing jeans and a hooded sweatshirt was sitting on the back bumper and eating something out of a can with a fork. He had a deep brown beard and the sunburned freckles on his balding forehead were pretty striking. He looked to be in his later thirties. Tara glanced behind her and saw the dog tagging along before she started moving towards the van.

The man noticed her as she got to within twenty feet. He put the can down in the inside of the van's interior and stood up.

"Hi," Tara said as she stopped a few feet away and raised her hand.

The man smiled. "Hi there."

She put her best smile forward. "My name is Tara and I've been sleeping nearby. I noticed you had some food on you. I was hoping you might have some leftovers that you could spare."

"I'm Larry, nice to meet you," the man said as he looked around. "Are you alone?"

The little Chihuahua came up alongside Tara and she picked it up and cradled it. "Just me and my dog, mister."

"You're here by yourself? What about your folks?"

"My dad is back in the house, but I don't wanna be with him anymore."

Larry nodded. "You ran away, huh? Well, this would be the best time to do it I guess. Very few cops around nowadays."

"I'm surprised nobody came by," Tara said. "But then again, I'm not up to date on the news."

"Everything's gone to hell," Larry said. "No more power, no more food. The ones that could leave have left the cities and try to make a go for living out in the country. They could try to grow their own food out there. The rest are hunkered down in their homes and barricading themselves and hoping that the government will come by with some aid, but I don't think that's gonna happen. Everyone's on their own now. Quite a lot of people have killed themselves too."

Tara looked down. "I hope my dad didn't do anything to my little brother. I hope they're both still alive."

Larry grinned. "Hey, I'm sorry for depressing you like that."

She looked away. "It's okay, thanks for the news updates."

Larry turned and started rummaging through several cardboard boxes at the back of the van. A minute later he took out a metal can and showed it to her. "I've got some canned beef stew here, you okay with that?"

Tara grinned as she took the can. "Thanks, mister!"

Larry took out a metal spoon and rubbed it on a white cloth before handing it to her. "Just call me Larry. Or Uncle Larry if you'd like."

She took off the top of the can since it had a flip-top and started wolfing it down. The meat, gravy and vegetables were cold, but she was so hungry she didn't care. "Thanks, Larry," she said in between swallows.

Larry took out a plastic bottle of mineral water from another box and set it beside her while she ate using the back of the van as an impromptu table. After eating about three quarters of the canned stew, Tara set it down on the concrete pavement, and the little dog stuck its muzzle into it and ate heartily. The runaway teen took several big gulps from the water bottle and then let out a loud burp. Larry laughed.

Tara wiped her mouth with her arm. "Sorry about that."

Larry ate the rest of his canned beans. "No worries, kid. Are you planning to stay here?"

"No, I was hoping to hitchhike to California, but none of the cars that passed by stopped to take me."

"Why California? You got relatives there?"

"My best friend's family moved out there last year. I was hoping to hook up with her," Tara said. "What about you? Where're you going?"

Larry shrugged. "To be honest I wasn't sure. I've been out getting supplies, but then I heard on the radio that a number of dams have burst all along the

Colorado River, so it looks like the West Coast is cut off. Heard of a lot of cities in the East Coast and the South are underwater too, because of all the rains and floods out there."

Tara frowned. "Oh no."

"Hang on," Larry said. "I know a guy that a few weeks ago said he knew this family of preppers up in Wyoming. We could go there."

"Preppers? You mean those people who were preparing for the end of the world and all that?"

Larry took the empty cans and just threw them in the parking lot. "That's them. If there's a type of people who can deal with this whole situation, they can. I heard there's a lot of enclaves out in the countryside that's setting themselves up, but they won't just take anybody. They only take people that can earn their right to stay with them, that means that strangers who try to get in must have the skills or supplies that their community needs so that they could be accepted."

"But I don't have any skills or anything like that."

"Well, let's check 'em out anyway. If you don't like it, we can go somewhere else, Sweetpea. Unless you want to stay here, of course."

Tara sighed. She could stay but then there might not be another person who would be coming by and there wasn't any food around anymore. "Okay, I'll go with you."

Larry grinned and pinched her cheek. "That's the spirit! Go ahead and sit on the front seat, I just gotta do a few things before we get moving."

"Okay," Tara said as she walked to the front of the van, opened the front passenger door and got in. As she looked at the side mirror, she noticed that Larry had taken out a sledgehammer and a bolt cutter from the pile of tools he had at the back of the van. "What are you doing with those?"

"Just sit tight, Sweetpea. I'll be back," Larry said as he hefted the tools over his shoulder and started walking towards the front of the strip mall.

The dog ran over to the side of the passenger door and jumped up onto her lap. "This path may not be to your liking," it said.

Tara bit her lip. "Look, I'd rather take my chances with him for now."

"Okay," the dog said. "This is your choice after all."

"What do you want me to do then?" Tara said as she could hear the sounds of glass breaking and an alarm ringing across the parking lot.

"I cannot decide your path. Only you can do that," the dog said.

"He seems nice to me and I owe him since we ate some of his food, you know," Tara said.

"All men are not what they seem. It may take some time for someone to reveal his true self," the dog said.

"What does that even mean? Could you stop talking in riddles?"

"The pattern is not yet clear. The lines are still being drawn."

"You're just not making any sense anymore."

"To know what you know and what you do not know, that is truly knowing yourself."

"Jeez! You. Are. Not. Making. Any. Sense!"

"Who are you talking to there?" Larry said as he threw the tools in the back of the van along with another box before closing the rear doors.

Tara looked in the rearview mirror and shook her head. "Nobody, just talking to myself."

Larry walked over to the driver's side and opened the door. "Okay, I didn't find much other than a little cash on the registers, I dunno if money is of any use these days, but it doesn't hurt if we have a bit of it."

Tara turned and looked at him. "Did you really have to do that? It's stealing."

Larry just smiled and shook his head as he got in the driver's seat. "Sweetpea, the owners of those stores have pretty much abandoned them or they're probably dead. The world that you know is over. There's new rules now if you wanna live. You still with me?"

Tara looked down at the flooring of the car. She didn't like it but it seemed she didn't have a choice. "Yeah, let's go," she said as she closed the front passenger door.

Larry placed a hand on her lap as he started the van's engine. "That's the spirit!"

10. The Horde

London

He was in a sea of fire. All around him were burning waters. There were people trying to climb up on his little wooden boat while their bodies were aflame, screaming in pain and pleading for help, but he was tasked by the gods to only observe. As he looked down into the black depths, he could see the drowned, but their bodies were burning even though they were underwater. He knew he was either in a dream or a vision of some unfathomable future. It was some strange netherworld, a place where the dead of eons past would go to be reborn once again. But it was also a place of pain and suffering. Was it a vision of Hell or a glimpse into the future of the world? His own self was transparent as he looked at his hands as he held them in front of his face. But they were ghost-like as his limbs looked more like translucent mist than actual flesh; he could see right through them as if they were almost invisible. He could feel himself lighter than air as the winds carried him from the boat and into the mist-laden sky, filled with bolts of white lightning and thick clouds. He was traveling, moving across time and space and into some sort of astral dimension, yet he was somehow grounded on earth. He had a feeling of being buffeted by angry winds as he could see screaming people of all sorts being trapped in the clouds. Tornadoes would sweep in and carry them to and fro from one part of the sky to another, their constant thrashings and screaming were deemed both utterly useless and endless. He could see himself passing over a deep, dark forest of black branched trees, with crawling, squirming things on their bark that seemed like they were part of it all. Looking down at the pale forest, he could see creatures of the woods, walking around; prancing and dancing beneath the shadowy canopies, their shrill cries were like the whisper of insects. On and on he went until he flew over the base of a strange mountain. It was dominated by a pyramidal structure of a giant stone ziggurat, with massive granite steps leading up into the dark heavens. He could feel the winds pulling him upwards until he reached the summit, whereupon he spied on three monstrous beings sitting on thrones made of human bones beside a carved stone table. The first being seemed to be a living skeleton, its bony ribcage visible underneath its cloak of brightly-colored feathers, its corpse-like visage had huge, saucer-shaped eyes and long fangs that belied its malevolent nature. The second creature seemed like a hairless man, but with long antlers growing out of his forehead, his deep black skin seemed to swallow light and his blank face had neither eyes, nor nose nor mouth; nothing but a dark void of entropy as he held a gigantic, wriggling maggot in his right hand. The third being was the most inhuman of all, it seemed more like a wisp of energy that took on a vaguely human form crossed with that of a celestial worm; a screaming, white hot spirit of destruction and desolation. On the stone table were strewn about several small amulets that resembled either men or beasts: a figure of a knight, the statue of a woman holding aloft two snakes, as well as small trinkets that resembled a raven and a little dog, among many others. The three players were presiding over what looked like a game of chance, with the world as the prize. It was then that he heard voices that seemed to call him back to the world of the living and the soon to be dead.

After what seemed to be an eternity, Dr. Paul Dane opened his eyes. As his vision and mind began to focus, he noticed that he was lying on a bed. The room was stark white and had an antiseptic smell. An intravenous needle was stuck in his arm. He felt pain all over his body and especially his head and chest. His left arm was free and he rubbed it gingerly on his forehead as he groaned.

A young man in a grey suit sitting in a chair on the side of the room immediately turned off the laptop he was typing in, folded it, and then ran out through the open door, shouting at the top of his lungs the patient was finally awake. Paul groaned again and closed his eyes as the migraine overwhelmed him. When he opened them again a few minutes after the headache had passed, he noticed the grey-suited man was now standing over him, along with an older man with pale skin, slick black hair and wearing a dark suit while a middle-aged female nurse in her white uniform was checking his arm and feeling his head.

The man in the black suit cleared his throat. "Professor Dane? My name is David Getz, I'm with the State Department. With me is Greg Gover, he's with the embassy. Can you talk?"

The nurse frowned at the other two. "This man has been drifting in and out of consciousness for the past three days, he needs some rest," she said.

Getz looked at her. "I'm sorry, ma'am, but this is a national emergency. I need the patient up on his feet because we need to go right now."

The nurse crossed her arms. "Only the doctor assigned to him can decide whether he can be released or not. Those are the rules."

Gover pulled out a document from his coat pocket and waved it in front of her. "I'm sorry, nurse, but we have a signed executive order from the president of the United States that clearly says that this man needs to be transported back to America, and right away."

The nurse started to walk out of the room. "I'll need to clear it with the administration first."

"Do that," Getz said to the nurse as she walked out before looking at Gover. "Follow her and get the clearance, then alert the extraction team. We need to leave now."

"Okay," Gover said as he too left the room. The corridor outside was very noisy with shouts and the squeaks of hospital wheels all around them. People of all sorts were passing by the outside corridor, their faces gripped by concentration and concern.

Paul's mouth was painful and sticky. "I ... need water."

Getz went over to a nearby table and poured some water from a pitcher into a plastic cup and then handed it to him. "You're in a hospital in

Knightsbridge. The situation is critical; we need to get out of here right now. We debated about just wheeling you out of here in your bed so thank God you woke up."

Paul took short sips. "How long have I been out?"

"Almost four days now. You've had a concussion and some bruised ribs, but you've been barely conscious. You've been having fits and occasional delirium and you needed to be restrained quite a few times from what I heard."

Paul looked at him. "Sir Wilfred? Megan?"

Getz shook his head. "I'm afraid Mr. Pyles is gone, he died of a broken neck from the car crash. Megan Abramson is still listed as missing."

Paul moaned. He wanted to cry but no tears came. "What happened? How did you find me?"

"We found you in the wrecked police car just a few miles from Stonehenge. You were extremely lucky the rescue crews found you just minutes after you crashed. Because as soon as they pulled you out and brought you to London, we lost contact with everyone within a three-mile radius of that area. The Brits sent in army troops from nearby, but they went missing too. After that, the government tried to cordon off a ten-mile perimeter, but it didn't hold. A blanket of fog settled into the entire area the next morning and then things just got worse. UK Third Army Division based in Bulford was reported to be under attack just two days ago by unknown assailants, and then all communications with them fell silent. Just yesterday that blanket of fog reached Heathrow Airport and now we think it's lost as well. Whatever it is, it's coming this way. London is being evacuated, but with the traffic jams, I've had to call the embassy for an airborne extraction because there's no way we can get out of here by car," Getz said.

Paul blinked several times. The situation was all too unreal. "News back home?"

"Not any better. No more commercial flights over US airspace, several dams have burst, including Hoover and a whole bunch of others over the past two days, and that's just about killed power and water over most of the cities back home … not to mention hundreds of thousands now reported dead or missing. Massive storms and floods all over the East Coast and the South, the country is slowly being cut up into little pieces. The president and congress declared a state of emergency, but I doubt that will do anything. With most of our military in the Middle East and Afghanistan, law and order is starting to break down because the cops and what remains of the National Guard are too few to deal with this. Satellite communications are all gone and the internet only works some of the time."

Paul coughed dryly as he was given another cup of water. "Other countries?"

Getz sighed. "Ireland we lost contact with days ago ... the entire island is presumed lost to whatever it is that's attacking. Most of Western Europe is under emergency rule but with the riots and such I doubt they will last long either. The British government has already evacuated to Scotland though it seems trouble is brewing up there too. It doesn't look like anywhere is safe. Scandinavia has been snowed under and Russia isn't talking, but our intel shows they might have lost Siberia to unknown forces. China is under total lockdown, but our intel reports are saying that the government there is also losing control too. Japan is under attack by unknown forces and the rest of Asia isn't doing so well either. We have no idea what's going on in Africa because of other priorities. Major parts of India are said to have been taken over by what we don't know and whatever started in Iraq has spread to Turkey, Jordan, Saudi Arabia, and Iran. The Israelis are contemplating a nationwide evacuation, but where they could go beats the heck out of me because Egypt has also gone dark on us. The UN has tried to call an emergency summit for all its members, but everybody is too preoccupied with their own problems to even think about participating."

"Why am I so important, Mr. Getz?" Paul said softly. "I'm just an anthropology and mythology instructor at a university."

Getz pulled out a smart phone from his coat, queued up a video on it and showed it to him. "What do you think of this? This was a video taken in Bulford when unknown forces attacked and it reached us just before the army units there were cut off."

Paul took a look. The video was grainy, probably from a handheld camera or mobile phone. It showed a group of fully-armed and equipped British soldiers manning a roadside checkpoint. There were sandbag barricades put up near the road and a machinegun team on the ready. As the point of view shifted to what lay beyond the road ahead, it seemed to show only an area covered by dense fog, as if it was some sort of smokescreen that slowly drifted towards them. As the video continued, Paul could suddenly see shapes forming at the edges of the fog and it looked like they were getting closer. Shouts from the soldiers in the video started as they were calling in for reinforcements as well as warning the unknown figures up ahead to turn back lest they come under fire. As another minute passed, the shadowy forms ahead began to take shape. Although they looked human at first, it seemed that they were misshapen. Some had one arm bigger than the other, while others had some sort of shambling gait as they lurched forward. When the enemy faces became clear it was apparent that they were not human. Some in the horde that slowly advanced on them had but a single eye set on their foreheads, others had multiple eyes but with only one or two limbs while a few more were naked with skin as if made of stone. Quite a few others had fanged mouths while a couple had snakelike lower bodies that slithered forward instead of walking to them, and a few others looked like red-skinned, pointy-eared dwarfs with claws instead of hands. It was an army of deformed, monster-like creatures and giants that first moved slowly but as soon as they could be seen clearly, the demons began to advance rapidly onto the startled squad. The video began to lose focus as the soldiers shouted and screamed while firing their weapons until it ended in a snowy haze of white static.

Paul opened his mouth in shock and then after a few minutes, his head collapsed back into the pillow on his bed. He placed his hand over his eyes and let out a low moan. The impossible had just happened. His life and the world would never be the same again. Everything he believed in, everything that he thought was real, was not.

Getz remained impassive, his face a mask of stone. "What were those things?"

Paul opened his eyes and looked at him. "Fomorians. Those things must be Fomorians."

"What's a Fomorian?"

"Demonic monsters from Irish mythology. It is said that before the first peoples of Ireland came to that isle, the Formorians were already there. A great war was fought until the Fomorians were defeated and a new pantheon of gods inhabited the land. It makes sense that if Ireland has been lost, these monsters might make a push here in England," Paul said before pausing. "I know you probably think what I'm saying is insane. But I've had strange dreams while being confined here that seem to coincide with what's happening."

Getz looked at him seriously. "Oh I believe you, Professor. With the way things are going, you seem to be the only one so far who's been able to explain what those things are. Everybody else says it's either aliens or zombies, despite a lack of evidence for either of those two theories. This makes my job to get you home even more important than ever before."

At that moment, Greg Gover ran back into the room. "Nurse is talking to some doctors because it looks like the hospital administration has already left."

"Right," Getz said as he started looking at the IV needle on Paul's forearm. "Go find his clothes, we need to get him up."

As Gover opened a small closet in the room, Getz carefully withdrew the needle from Paul's arm as the latter winced at the pain and he sat up on the bed.

"Just take it easy, sir," Gover said as he placed Paul's trousers and shirt beside him on the bed. "You had a concussion and bruised ribs so we'll help you get outta here."

Paul gingerly put on his trousers as Gover placed a pair of shoes at the foot of the bed. Getz looked out the window and let out a gasp.

"What is it?" Paul said as he carefully began to button up his shirt.

"I can see the fog rolling in across Hyde Park and to the west of us. We haven't got much time," Getz said before looking at Gover. "What's the ETA for our evac?"

"Embassy said twenty-five minutes, that was five minutes ago," Gover said.

Getz glanced at his watch. "Right, let's get him up and moving now. Try to get a wheelchair too, Gover."

Paul gingerly stood up. "I can walk."

As the three of them left the room and headed for the stairs at the end of the hall, they heard screams and gunfire all around the building. Hordes of grotesque monsters began their assault on the makeshift defenses east of Hyde Park and Knightsbridge. Although the British soldiers had ranged firepower, their L85 assault rifles and machineguns could only slow down what looked like a tidal wave of creatures that flung themselves at the barricades. A few Challenger battle tanks opened fire and tore through the beasts, but several giant Fomorians quickly picked up the tanks and threw them like ragdolls across the street as the horde broke through. Two of the remaining Apache gunships used rockets and machineguns to break up the most densely packed formations of monsters, but they too got taken down by thrown boulders from the ground or were attacked by winged Fomorians flying in the air.

Paul had a hard time getting up the stairs as his legs were still weak from lack of exercise. Greg Gover was helping him along while Getz led the way as he drew his Glock pistol from beneath his suit jacket. As Gover helped Paul up the third flight of stairs, he heard a shrill grunting sound coming from downstairs, near the base of the fifth floor stairwell.

It was one of the Fomorians. The misshapen creature had a large, bulbous head, dark grey skin and long sinewy arms that seemed to function as legs while it stood on them in order to move its limbless, bloated torso. Gover screamed when he turned around and saw it as Getz ran back down, trying desperately to bring the pistol to bear.

At the last minute, Gover dove in between Paul and the creature, just as Getz pivoted sideways a few steps above them to see if he could get a clear shot. The Fomorian opened its gaping mouth and out came a whip-like, barbed tongue that shot out like a spring and wrapped itself around Gover's neck, dragging the screaming man right down next to it as the barbs on the tongue began to squeeze its victim's windpipe shut.

Getz fired a half dozen shots at the creature, who barely felt the small holes being poked into its dense, clay-like flesh as its tongue began to drain the still struggling Gover of his blood. Paul screamed as Getz held him back and started to push him up the stairs.

"We gotta do something to help him!" Paul cried as he was now getting dragged upwards.

Getz kept pulling him up. "We have to move, he's gone!"

Paul looked at him as they got up past another flight of stairs. They both could still hear the mulching sounds below. "You're a cold, heartless bastard."

Getz kept his eyes above them as he continued to drag him up by the arm. "The mission was to get you out of here by any means possible. He knew the risks when he volunteered."

When they finally got to the top of the stairs, Getz pushed open the fire door and both men started climbing onto the roof of the hospital. Paul's jaw dropped as he saw the chaotic swirl of battle all around them. Down below were hordes of Fomorians feasting on the dead and dying soldiers as well as on hapless civilians that were caught in the crossfire. He could see a wave of monsters massing near Buckingham Palace a few miles away, just as the few remaining tanks and soldiers were desperately trying to hold them off. Swirls of mist were all around them as a few news helicopters were being chased by horrible flying things on leathery wings.

An AS350 blue-painted Eurocopter flew in from east of Westminster, dodged a few boulders thrown its way, then it headed straight for them. Paul turned to his left as he heard a guttural shriek just as two Fomorians came out of the stairwell that they had just passed through, the two froglike creatures were less than thirty feet away as they began to hobble towards the two men.

Getz pushed him out of the way as he began firing at the creatures. "Edge of the roof. Go! Go! Go!"

Paul's legs were beginning to buckle from the strain, but he forced himself to move slowly towards the southern end of the roof just as the two Fomorians were almost upon them. The helicopter soon made a quick turn and hovered alongside Paul, its landing skids barely touching the edge of the roof. The side door opened and a uniformed man inside grabbed him by the hand. As one of the Fomorians tried to seize Paul's leg with its webbed claws, Getz threw himself at the creature and tackled it as they both fell down the ledge and onto the lower part of the roof.

Paul clambered up and into the small interior of the chopper. In less than a second it rapidly veered away before he could even get the door closed. The uniformed crewman was sitting beside him as he struggled to help Paul put on his seatbelt.

"Hold on!" the pilot shouted as he banked and dove before climbing up again as a winged, man-sized creature with legs that ended with bird-like talons attempted to get close to the helicopter.

Paul grimaced as he hung on to the safety straps for dear life as the sky whirled and twisted all around him.

11. The Birds

Captain Barry "Clyde" Barrow frowned underneath his oxygen mask as he banked his F-22 Raptor in a slow circle over Nellis Air Force Base. His wingman, Lieutenant Martin "McFly" Foles quickly followed his move as his own F-22 followed just behind and to the right of his wing leader. Both Raptors had been flying combat air patrol for over an hour now and they could see the misty outlines of Las Vegas just below them. Although they were built for stealth, each fighter jet carried a pair of external fuel pods in order to give them extra range, their commanders on the ground deeming their radar-evading stealth systems weren't necessary for this mission.

Barrow wasn't happy at all, but he kept his thoughts to himself. It didn't help that Hoover Dam had been breached by unknown causes just two days ago and its destruction reverberated across the entire country. Lake Havasu City and a number of other towns along the river were swept away when ten trillion gallons of water burst through. But the disaster hadn't ended there since the massive floods caused by Hoover ruptured the dams in nearby lakes as well, creating a catastrophic chain reaction across several states as highways and bridges were suddenly ripped apart and whole cities were cut off. Las Vegas was now without drinking water and electrical power and this looked to be just the start. It now looked like the whole state of Nevada might have just been rendered uninhabitable. Barrow was partially relieved that his wife and two daughters were within Nellis when the disaster happened, but it was already decreed that all military dependents would have to be evacuated for safer areas, even though no one could tell where these so-called safe zones would be. Already, there were riots just outside the base as civilians had to be held back by Air Force MPs at the base perimeter, despite the fact that they were just begging for food, water and help from an increasingly powerless government.

But what bothered Barrow the most was a feeling of complete helplessness. Here he was, sitting in the cockpit of the most advanced jet fighter in the world, which had state-of-the-art weapons and dual thrust-vectoring capable engines that could enable the Raptor to super cruise at near Mach 2. Advanced avionics gear with full-spherical infrared coverage acted as a passive radar. It could deploy built-in countermeasures against enemy attacks. The Raptor also had stealth characteristics such as a reduced radar cross-section coupled with a low-heat signature and radar absorbent materials embedded in its fuselage. Still, this very expensive weapon was all but useless against the unknown enemy that was even now busy destroying his beloved country. The most powerful military on earth was so far unable to identify or know who or what it was that was doing all of this. Quite a few others in his squadron had been saying it was aliens from outer space, but it just didn't make any sense to him while the other theories like the religious types who claimed it was Judgment Day scared him half to death. Barrow was a very religious man, he took his family to church on the Sundays when he wasn't deployed and his kids were enrolled in Sunday school; this whole notion about the world coming to an end the moment Jesus finally reveals himself made him nervous ... just a few days ago he was starting to feel guilt over his career as a fighter jock, would The Lord ever forgive him for the violation of God's commandment about not killing anyone?

A beep on his radar display brought him back to reality. "Rapier one-one to Bigwig, I got a contact one fifty miles northeast of my position," he said over the radio.

"Rapier one-one, be advised: Angel is in the area," the Air Force ground controller said. Angel was the codename for Air Force One, the plane in which the president was flying on.

"Roger," Barrow said. "Continuing CAP." He had just remembered that the president would be flying to California today since the weather forecasts were still clear in the Southwest, unlike the East Coast and the Southern states, which were inundated with rainstorms. The FAA had grounded all commercial flights almost a week ago so other than the combat air patrols, Air Force One had the skies all to itself.

One other thing about the mission did bother him though. Even though the authorities never released the cockpit flight recordings from the dozen or so downed airliners to the public, they were in fact able to recover almost all of them from the wreckages. Based on the latest intel that was filtered on down to the military aviators, most of the cockpit recordings seemed routine, almost as if the doomed airliners were blindsided and never knew what hit them. The last one that Barrow heard during the latest briefing did make him a little apprehensive, since the now deceased airline captain had screamed about some sort of flying monster coming at him just before the recording stopped. Several of his squadron mates theorized that the airline captain must have mistakenly identified an unknown enemy aircraft as an airborne creature of some sort, before getting hit by some mysterious weapon that caused his airliner to crash, they surmised. To that end, all available fighter aircraft had been assigned to extended combat air patrols. They were now under full authority to shoot down any unidentified aircraft that was foolish enough to enter US airspace. Barrow's squadron had at least two fighters up in the air at any given time, ready to intercept anything in their range. The rest of the squadron was on standby and fully prepared to scramble at a moment's notice once contact was made. The entire US Air Force was now hunting for whatever it was out here in the skies that took down those planes.

The radio squawked again. "Rapier CAP, be advised we are getting a mayday call from Angel, I repeat, we are getting a mayday call from Angel. They have visual contact with unidentified aircraft."

Barrow's heart leapt as his left arm caressed the throttle. "Bigwig this is Rapier one-one, copy that. I am now heading for intercept course, going balls to the wall at full burners."

With that, both Raptors turned northeast, dropped their external tanks and activated their afterburners. With their dual Pratt & Whitney turbofan engines accelerating to a maximum speed of over one thousand five hundred miles an hour within seconds, both fighters would take less than two minutes to reach the president's plane.

As he looked at his HUD, Barrow began to arm the six AIM-120 AMRAAM missiles located in the Raptor's internal weapons bays. The weapon indicator soon shifted to the color green. "Do you see any other contact on your radar, Marty?" he said to his wingman.

"That's a negative, Clyde. All I see is Angel on my scope," Foles said.

Barrow keyed his radio back to base. "Rapier one-one to Bigwig, I'm not getting any other contacts on my radar."

The Air Force ground controller was on again. "Rapier one-one, this is Bigwig, we are not getting any contacts either from ground based radar, I'm patching you over to Angel Actual so you can talk directly to them."

"Copy that, Bigwig," Barrow said as he rapidly switched frequencies on his radio.

Another voice soon came on to his radio link. "This is Angel Actual, we have an unidentified craft or something just below us, we are climbing at full throttle to try and evade."

"Angel Actual, this is Rapier CAP, we are less than a minute away from you, can you turn and make your heading at … two-seven zero, over," Barrow said as he kept looking at his radar, but he still couldn't see any other aircraft in range as the two fighters began to encounter thick clouds over the area.

"Affirmative, CAP, we are now turning to two-seven zero, over. Am I glad to hear from you guys."

As the two Raptors flew just above the thick grey clouds, they finally got a visual on Air Force One. The president's plane was a blue and white VC-25, the military version of the venerable Boeing-747. They could see that it was making a rapid ascent at full throttle to try to rise above the clouds. Within seconds, the two supersonic Raptors closed the distance and they soon slowed down and maneuvered themselves until they were flying parallel and to the side of Air Force One.

"Angel Actual, where did you see the unidentified aircraft, over?" Barrow said.

"CAP, we were about forty-five thousand feet and cruising when one of our passengers noticed something flying just below us. We quickly made a distress call and climbed above the cloud cover."

"Did any of your crew make a visual identification?"

"Negative, CAP, none of my crew made full ID other than seeing a glimpse of it, but cloud cover obscured full identification."

"Clyde, bogey at five o'clock ... just below us!" Foles said.

Barrow glanced down to the right side of the glass canopy and noticed what looked like a black wing hidden by some clouds below. He quickly put the engines to near full throttle and banked right, his wingman following right behind him. "This is CAP, I have tallyho on a bogey at thirty thousand, turning to engage."

The two Raptors began to use radar sweeps over the clouds, but they still couldn't get a contact as Air Force One veered away and tried to get some distance from them. Barrow cursed. Whatever kind of a plane that was, it must be able to vanish into thin air. The radio was silent other than the heavy breathing of the two fighter pilots.

And then they saw it, or at least a slight glimpse of the creature. It flew up slightly where it poked its head above the clouds before diving back into the mists. It looked like a gigantic black bird, its condor-like wings were close to fifty feet across, its entire body the size of a small building, with a massive, hooked black beak equal in size to the Raptor's nose cone. And it had glowing red eyes.

Barrow pulled at the control stick with his right hand that sent the fighter down towards the massive cloud cover ahead of them as his wingman followed. "Tallyho! I have contact ... it looks like a giant bird. It's almost as big as an aircraft carrier!"

"Jesus, Clyde! Did you see the size of that thing?" Foles said over the radio.

Barrow cursed as his sensors continued to see nothing. "McFly, can you get a tone?"

"Negative, no tone."

"Switching to boresight mode," Barrow said tersely as he toggled his four AIM-120 AMRAAM missiles into free guidance mode, this meant that his missiles could lock onto the first thing it sees after being fired, rather than having to wait for the target lock via radar before it could be released.

Both Raptors descended rapidly, hoping to catch the creature below the haze, but as they flew out just below the clouds, there was nothing but an empty sky down below.

Foles continued to turn his head in order to scan what was at their flanks and behind them. "Where the hell is that thing?"

As both fighters continued flying just below the mists, the once tranquil white cloud cover somehow began to transform itself into a storm front within seconds, as the clouds began to coalesce into a swirling grey haze of high force winds. Electric sparks could be seen as lightning bolts began to flash all around them.

Barrow's grip tightened on his control stick as it began to wobble due to the violent winds now buffeting his aircraft. "What in the hell is going on?"

"Clyde, I think I see something up in the clouds just above us, one o'clock," Foles said as crackling thunder began to deafen their ears. The whole thing was just unbelievable.

Barrow pulled up on his control stick. "Climbing."

As both Raptors gained altitude, they ended up in a swirling, haze-filled fury of rain, thunder, and lightning that was all around them. Barrow's electronic HUD began to go haywire as frequent lightning bolts had touched his aircraft. Although modern day fighters had built in insulators against lightning strikes, frequent exposure would corrode these defenses over time. Barrow felt like his Raptor was hit by over a dozen electrical bolts within just a few seconds as his radar indicator suddenly went blank. Just as he took his left hand off the throttle and started to toggle with the controls of his HUD, the giant bird dove down until it was less than half a mile in front of them.

On impulse, Barrow toggled the weapons switch to activate his aircraft's 20mm Vulcan cannon embedded in its right wing root. Just as he sighted the creature on his helmet, it turned to face them while still maintaining its velocity as a massive electrical bolt surged at them from its open beak. Barrow instinctively made a hard turn to his left as the energy surge only glanced off his aircraft's fuselage. In the split second, he veered away from it, but his wingman wasn't so lucky as Foles's Raptor took on the full force of the mystical lightning bolt. Foles screamed for a split second. The intense energy from the monster engulfed the cockpit and ignited the fuel tanks while detonating the missiles in the second Raptor. The resulting explosion instantly tore the plane apart in midair.

Barrow struggled to keep his plane steady as it entered into an uncontrollable spin. The energy surge had shorted out his fly-by-wire controls and HUD. His Raptor began to tumble out of the sky as the intense G-forces made it hard to breathe and he moved in slow motion. It was as if there were multiple anvils on his chest, shoulders, arms, and legs while the pounding headache got worse and started to blur his outer vision. All he could see now was his gloved left hand that slowly reached down and activated his APGS, the auxiliary power generation system, the one thing that could save him since it had a self-contained battery. The seconds seemed like an eternity as his fingers slowly touched the switch and flipped it on twice. By the second click, he instantly heard the turbines restart themselves as his left hand quickly grabbed the throttle stick; his right flipped the switches back on to get some power before the aircraft hit the ground. All the while, the onboard computer kept giving him the stall warning.

He was less than five thousand feet off the ground as the Raptor's engines got to full throttle and he pulled the control stick up to climb again. Barrow's radar indicator and most of his electronics were malfunctioning due to being burned out by the lightning surge, but he still had his guns. Even though his wingman was probably dead, he still had a duty to protect the president with his life if necessary.

Just as the Raptor finally tore above the storm clouds, he quickly saw that the cause was lost as the monster bird had closed in on the president's plane. Barrow screamed in rage. The creature had somehow accelerated close to Mach 1 as it got right behind Air Force One, even though the president's plane was making a hard right turn and diving to avoid it. Barrow felt like he was living a nightmare as the creature's huge claws started tearing at the veering plane's left wing and finally ripped half the section right off just as its massive beak snapped the tail rudder in two. Air Force One plunged sideways and into the swirling mists below as the monster bird seemed to have noticed the closing Raptor and turned to face it.

"Goddamn you!" Barrow screamed as he fired off several hundred 20mm rounds at the creature as the monster opened its hooked beak and let loose with another lightning blast at him.

As the white energy surged all around him, Captain Barry Barrow screamed in pain and rage as he pulled on the handle of his ejection seat. He didn't hear the explosive bolts in time, blacking out as the searing white heat was engulfed him.

12. The Road

Arizona

When Tara Weiss woke up it was already mid-morning. She noticed that Larry was still at the wheel and it looked like he had driven all night. As they left Phoenix, they had to take a number of detours because most of the main roads were blocked by burning and abandoned cars. They could see rioters clashing with police, a few punks even threw some stones at them, but they narrowly missed the van, as Larry was able to get over a divider and drove away on the other side of the highway. As night fell, there were plenty of clouds as well as flashes of lightning and thunder that gave her the creeps; she felt them so close to the point where she would silently count the seconds between the flashes of lightning and the cracklings of thunder. Tara even got surprised once when she saw a lightning bolt hit a bare tree just ahead of them at the side of the road and rip it in two. The ear-splitting sound of thunder felt like a sonic boom; it even startled Larry and he inadvertently swerved just to dodge it, but what was really strange was not a drop of rain fell even after all that.

The little Chihuahua lay curled up in her lap as it slept. Tara still didn't tell Larry about the talking dog. She felt she might need an ace in the hole just in case things got ugly between them. She kept telling herself that he was kind to her so far and she could probably trust him. Larry kept twisting the radio dial all night as he drove to see if there were further updates, but it was mostly static. Most of the stations had already gone off the air due to a lack of power. He was able to find the occasional Emergency Broadcast System that pretty much just said to stay indoors and not to leave your homes as help was coming. Larry would start to scoff every time he heard that pre-recorded message. Other times they would hear stations that were evidently commandeered as all sorts of people would go on air and complain about how the government was to blame for everything and the lack of any help. As she drifted in and out of sleep, Tara started to nickname those kinds of stations Complaints FM or Ranters AM … it got so bad that she finally asked Larry to just turn the radio off so she could sleep.

But as she finally washed the sleep from her eyes using a wet handkerchief, she realized that Larry was listening to the radio once again. "Who is that?" she said. He appeared to be listening to a calm and compassionate voice that seemed to be delivering a lecture of some sort.

Larry kept his eyes on the road. "Good morning."

"Good morning," she said as she shifted her weight slightly so she wouldn't drop the sleeping dog from her lap. "Who's that that you're listening to?"

"Oh, that's just a message from Pastor Burnley. Seems a lot of radio stations that are still working are now carrying his gospel hour show all of a sudden."

"Who's he?"

"You never heard of Pastor Burnley? He's got a whole TV channel just dedicated to his shows. You watch JBN?"

"JBN? What's that?"

Larry laughed. "The Jesus Broadcasting Network, silly."

Tara shook her head as she took a sip of water from a plastic bottle. "We never had cable in the house."

"Oh, it's not just on cable, you can get it on regular TV too, it's on UHF, I think. I think Burnley even has shows on TBN too."

"I don't watch those things. Boring."

Larry played with the dials again since there was static on the radio once more. "Damn, seems like we're outta range again."

Tara stretched her arms and yawned. "Well that's good. Last thing I wanna hear is some preacher talking all morning. That's just boring."

"I would've thought you were used to being bored since you hung out in that strip mall for days with just your dog as a companion."

"I was more hungry than bored. Anyway, it gave me time to think."

Larry glanced at her briefly. "You want to go back to your parents?"

Tara shook her head. "No. I don't know what I want to do."

"Well, just stick with me for now, Sweetpea," Larry said as he grinned. "We make one helluva team and I've got a plan."

"What's your plan?"

"While you were asleep, I was listening to Pastor Burnley and his words made sense to me. You know, with all that's happening right now I'm beginning to believe in him."

"Oh yeah, what's he saying about what's happening that explains all of this then?"

"He's saying that Jesus is now coming back in a few days and he will judge us all. This is the day of judgment."

"Come on, you really believe that?"

"Why not? Have you got any other explanation for what's going on?"

Tara shook her head. "Uh, nope."

"Okay then, so it looks like Pastor Burnley is right."

"Are you sure?"

"I can't think of any other explanation, can you?"

Tara looked away. "Not really."

"Okay, so we stick with the plan."

Tara looked at him blankly. "What's the plan?"

"Pastor Burnley says for all honest Christians to come join him in Kansas to await the coming of The Lord together. He says he can feed and shelter hundreds of thousands of God's chosen."

"So we're going to Kansas then?"

"That's the plan."

For the next few hours, they took a number of detours around Flagstaff as they could see barricades and burnt cars out in the distance of the city limits.

As they drove along a side road parallel to Route-40, they noticed a group of Mexicans along the road frantically waving at them to stop, but Larry stepped on the gas and accelerated instead as he nearly drove over a frantic old man waving a dirty handkerchief at them. Tara could see their anguished faces as the van passed them by; two wrinkly old women sitting on their suitcases looking dejected by the road along with a gaggle of small brown children who cried and screamed at them. She wished she could have helped them, but Larry had told her the night before that they couldn't take anybody else with them because they just didn't have enough food. As she looked down, she could see the dog was awake and stared back at her. Tara wanted to say something to it, but she didn't want to break cover or make Larry think she was crazy if the dog didn't answer back, so she just looked out of the window again and sighed.

Larry glanced at her. "You know we couldn't take them with us."

Tara bit her lip. "I know. It's just that I feel sad at not being able to help people."

"This is a new world we live in, Sweetpea. I'm not happy about it either, but we have to think of ourselves for the time being if we want to survive."

Tara didn't answer as she just kept looking out of the passenger side window. Half an hour later a loud beep began to sound on the dashboard. Larry took a look at it and cursed.

"What's wrong?" Tara said.

"We're starting to run low on gas," Larry said. "We need to find a gas station soon."

By this time, they had mostly passed by Flagstaff as they took the mountain roads near Humphreys Peak and were now close to the historic Route-66. Another hour passed and Larry was getting agitated as he kept looking at the fuel gauge.

Tara kept peering forward as she noticed something out in the distance of the road. As they got closer, it looked like a gas station alright. "There's a pump station," she said as she pointed ahead to the right.

Larry grinned at first because of their newfound luck, but then he began to frown a bit just as they got closer. "It looks like there's people there, lots of them."

Tara shrugged. "We ain't got no choice. Maybe they're friendly."

As the van slowed they could see that the gas station billboard had been torn down and that there were half a dozen men standing near the fuel pumps. They were all armed with rifles and shotguns. They quickly signaled the van to stop in front of the station. Larry did and then turned off the engine. Two men approached the vehicle, one on either side.

Larry looked at her as he put his hand on the door knob. "Whatever happens, stay in the van, okay?"

Tara just nodded as the two men faced them by the side windows. Tara noticed the older man had a white beard, flannel shirt, and a baseball cap with the confederate flag stitched on it. The old man stood by Larry's side while a younger, bare-chested man in blue jeans and a shaved head walked over to the right side of the van and looked closely at her with a bucktoothed grin. The older man had a scoped hunting rifle slung over his shoulder while the younger one had a semi-auto pistol tucked in his waistband.

Larry grinned at the older man who was near to him. "Howdy, do you have any gas to spare?"

"Where you from?" the old man said.

Larry kept smiling. "From Phoenix, sir. We're just looking for some gas and we'll be off."

The younger man just kept looking at Tara and kept on grinning. Tara smiled back before looking away, keeping eyes peeled forward.

"Where you going to?" the old man said. He had a droning voice that betrayed no emotion.

"We're going to Kansas, sir," Larry said.

The old man's face was like chiseled rock. "What are you gonna do in Kansas, boy?"

Larry giggled for bit to take the tension off. "Well isn't that our business, sir?"

The old man began to squint at him. "I'm gonna ask you again, boy. What're you gonna do in Kansas?"

"Look, sir, we don't want no trouble," Larry said. "We're on our way to Kansas to meet our friends there, they are with Pastor Burnley's congregation, and they asked us to join them there, that's all."

Another man, sitting on a folding chair by the store got up and walked over. He was heavyset and his long white hair was tied up in a ponytail underneath his cowboy hat. He wore a leather vest and jeans and carried a pump-action shotgun. "They just want fuel, Abe," he said to the old man standing beside Larry.

Abe looked at the other man before turning his gaze back to Larry again. "There ain't no government anymore so we're here guarding this station against looters. Are you a looter, boy?"

Larry straightened up in his seat. "No, sir."

Abe glanced in the inside of the van from the driver side window. "What's all that stuff you got in the back of your vehicle there? Did you steal all that crap?"

Larry shook his head in rapid succession. "No sir, that's stuff I bought and other stuff is from my house just before I boarded it up. If you want money for the gas, I got some."

The long haired man walked over and stood beside Abe. "Money is useless now, son. You got anything to barter with? Like food or medicine?"

Larry smiled as his tension was relieved. "Yeah, I got some food, hold on," he said as he got out of the driver's side and walked over to the back of the van and opened it. The two older men followed him as Tara turned her head backwards to observe.

Larry took a few cans of beef stew and handed it to both men.

Abe looked at the can. "How much gas you need?"

"A full tank," Larry said as he gave the other can to the other man.

The other man shook his head. "You've gotta give us more than just two cans for a full tank of gas, son."

Larry put his hands on his waist and looked down on the dusty concrete tarmac. This wasn't going to be easy. "How many cans do I have to give you?"

"Looks like you got a few cases there so we'll take two," Abe said.

Larry shook his head. "I can't give you two cases, we need the food or we'll starve on our way to Kansas. I'll give you a case, okay?"

"If you ain't willing to part with two cases then you only get half a tank, boy," Abe said.

The other man looked at Abe. "Just give 'em the gas, Abe," he said before turning to look at the dejected Larry. "You said you got money, let's see how much you got."

Larry took out a wad of bills from his sweater pocket and handed it to him. "That's all I got left, I swear."

The man with the cowboy hat looked at him closely as he pocketed the money. "I think you're lying when you said you ain't no looter, son. But we're giving you the gas anyway. Abe, take one of the cases."

Another man who wore a Diamondbacks baseball cap came out of the store and started working the pumps. As the fuel gauge began to rise, Larry saw that they were using a portable diesel generator to power the station. He also noticed a fat woman in shorts and two kids looking out at them from the inside of the store.

The bare-chested man who kept looking at Tara finally spoke. "Hey, guys, she don't look like that driver at all."

Abe walked over to Larry as he was beside the van watching it being filled up. "That your daughter, boy?"

Larry answered without looking at him. "Yes, she is."

"You need to look at me when I talk to you, boy."

Larry turned. Even though he was scared, he was starting to lose his temper. "Look, what do you want from us? We already gave you the food and the money! Can't you just leave us alone?"

The bare-chested man pulled out his pistol but didn't aim it as he walked over to them. Tara noticed that he was barefoot.

"You need to be taught some manners," Abe said as he unslung his rifle.

"Abe, knock it off," the man with the cowboy hat said. "We made a deal with them, fair and square. Let them take their gas and they can go."

Tara leaned her head out of the window and looked at Larry. "Daddy, let's go!"

Larry turned around and headed back to the driver's side. He noticed that the tank was full as the guy with the Diamondbacks cap put back the fuel tank lid on his van. As he got back on his seat and closed the door, the bare-chested man tried to make a grab for the little dog as he put his spindly arms through the window.

"No!" Tara shrieked as she held on to the Chihuahua. "This is my dog!"

"You won't be needing it anymore, miss," the bare-chested man said as he kept pulling at the dog, but the Chihuahua immediately bit him so hard that he yelped and instinctively drew his hands back.

"Go!" Tara screamed.

Larry had already started the van and hit the gas as the vehicle drove out of the station tarmac while the bare-chested man kicked at its side while screaming that he had rabies. Larry maneuvered the van and got it back on the road with a screech of the tires.

"Goddamn it," Larry said as he gripped the wheel tightly. "We lost over half the food we got."

Tara looked at the dog. It seemed to be okay as it settled back in her lap. "Be glad that's all we lost."

They kept going on the highway until late afternoon when the sun began to set. The radio was able to catch a short EBS broadcast that said a number of oil refineries in the Southwest would be nationalized.

Tara turned to Larry. "What does 'nationalized' mean?"

Larry let out a big yawn as he kept driving. "It means the government is taking them over."

"Why though?"

Larry snorted. "Look around you, a lot of dams broke and there's no power and very little fuel. The government wants it all so they can control it."

As he said that, the van nearly swerved off the road.

Tara instinctively grabbed the handle above the side window. "Whoa!"

Larry shook his head. "I'm sorry, haven't had much sleep."

She pointed to the left of the highway. "Look there's a house with some trees."

Larry squinted his tired eyes. The girl was right, there was a house up ahead and it seemed to be all by itself right up next to the highway. He didn't see any cars parked around it so he slowed and brought the van over to the front and stopped. As they looked, it seemed that the house had been abandoned. Larry maneuvered the van until it was behind the house in between two pinion pines so that no one would see it while driving along the highway. They got out of the van as Tara carried the dog with her and slung her backpack over her shoulder.

Larry got to the front porch and knocked on the door. No answer. He looked through the front windows and past the slightly transparent lace curtains. There didn't seem to be anyone home so he tried the front doorknob, but it wouldn't budge. Tara just stood there as he walked around the back and tried the backdoor, but it wouldn't budge either, so he went back to the front. The main door had a small glass window above the door knob so he smashed it with a small hammer that he took out from his pocket, then reached in and unlocked it.

As they went inside they noticed that the previous occupants must have left in a hurry. There were a few cardboard boxes sitting on the kitchen table with some dirty clothes. Larry went over to the fridge and opened it. All that was in it was an open carton of baking soda and a plastic squeeze bottle of yellow mustard. He then went to the cupboards and rummaged through them as well as the other cabinets.

"Damn," he said. "They took all the food when they left."

Tara half heard him as she went into one of the bedrooms. It looked kind of like a girl's room since the wallpaper had flowery prints. There was a set of six cloth dolls arranged neatly on top of a high dresser in front of a mirror. She put the dog down and unslung her backpack as she looked at the half-made bed. Sitting in the car for almost a whole day made her back ache. Tara searched through some of the drawers and found some used red lipstick and clothes. It looked like the one who stayed in this room must have been a girl, whether it was a teen or an adult she couldn't be sure since there weren't any pictures around. She sat down beside the bed and stared at the lamp on the nightstand before opening the drawers underneath it. There were a bunch of handwritten letters, a half used bottle of some cheap perfume, a few pennies and a rainbow-colored pen. Tara got back up and moved to the front of the mirror and applied some lipstick. After puckering her lips and seeing her handiwork, she immediately felt guilty for using somebody else's property and promptly put the lipstick back in the drawer. That was when she smelled something cooking.

As Tara went back out into the living room, she saw that Larry had taken out two bowls from the cupboard and placed them on the kitchen table. He was stirring a pot on the gas stove. Two empty cans of clam chowder sat on the counter beside him.

As he ladled some of the soup in her bowl, he noticed her red lips and smiled. "At least the stove is still working. Now we can have a hot meal before bedtime."

Tara yawned as she picked up a spoon. "Thanks."

Larry sat down beside her and started on his bowl. "You found some stuff?"

"Nothing, really."

"Did you go through the master bedroom yet?"

"Nope."

"Okay, I get first dibs on the big bed then, Sweetpea."

"You can have it. I'll be sleeping in the other room."

Larry had a sense of dejection. "Okay."

As night fell, there was still the occasional lightning and the accompanying thunder but still no rain. Tara took a look at the dark clouds outside of the bedroom window before getting up on the bed and curling into the comforter. It smelled faintly of mildew and spritzy hairspray, but she didn't mind. If anything, it reminded her of home. The Chihuahua was curled up on top of the blanket as she closed her eyes and instantly fell into a deep sleep. Just half an hour ago, she was able to use the iron pump out back to bring a pail of cold water into the bathroom for an impromptu sponge bath. She saw a shadow outside of the frosted window while she was undressing, but when she looked out, she didn't see anybody.

Strange dreams of black birds, worms, and lightning storms filled her sleep until she woke up in the middle of the night to a strange squeaking noise coming from nearby. Tara instantly sat up. She noticed that the dog was also alert as it stood beside her on top of the bed facing the door. The sound happened again, it was sort of like a rusty latch being turned. She didn't have a flashlight, but the moon over the desert horizon did give her a bit of an illumination with a twilit view.

The sound came again for the third time though it was somewhat fainter. She sensed it might be coming from the door she locked just before she went to sleep.

"Who's there?" Tara said aloud.

The sound stopped.

"Larry?" Tara said.

The house was still. A faint howl of the wind rattled parts of the hanging roof outside.

This time Tara shouted as hard as she could. "Larry!"

There was a noise just outside her door. "Yeah, what is it?" It was him alright.

Tara cupped her hands. "Did you hear a noise?"

"No. Go back to sleep."

Then the house was silent once more. Tara lay back on the pillow. The noise was gone.

The dog went over to her and put its muzzle near her ear. "Be wary of your ally."

Tara turned to the dog. "What's that supposed to mean?"

The dog gave her a lick on the nose. "I believe he meant to come in."

Tara's eyes opened wide. "Larry? You sure?"

"I'm going back to sleep," the dog said as it curled up near the bottom of the comforter.

Tara thought about it for a minute and sighed before falling asleep again.

13. The Witch

Siberia

Ilya Volkhov smiled at his dinner plate. For the first time ever, they served him three pieces of sausage instead of two to go along with his soup and bread. Ever since the link to Moscow was lost because of the snowed in Trans-Siberian Railway, the head caretaker of the Novosibirsk orphanage had gathered all the children together, then told them there would be a little less food served to them for the time being, so this particular meal had come as a pleasant surprise. He had been in the orphanage ever since he was four, when his mother dropped him off and kissed him on the cheek for one last time and then he never saw her again. Ilya had turned ten years old just under a month ago, before the troubles started. The elderly babushka that was their cook even baked a small cake just for him that Ilya ate a little bit of each day until it turned green and he was forced to throw the rest of it away ... although he did save a tiny piece just for remembrance.

"What are you smiling about?" Andrei said while sitting next to him. They had become fast friends the moment they first met since they were the same age. Ilya had yellow blonde hair and had large, bottle-green eyes. Andrei's hair and eyes were both a deep, dark brown. Ilya had an oval head and a small nose while Andrei's nose was pretty big, so Ilya's nickname for his best friend was Buratino, the Russian version of Pinocchio.

Ilya looked at him. Was he stupid or something? "Look," he said. "We were given three sausages instead of just two. It must be good news."

The dining hall along with the rest of the orphanage used to be a former administration building that was built during the Second World War, while the Soviet armies were in full retreat against the Nazis. After the war, it had served as the headquarters for the local Communist Party until a more modern one was built for them in the 1960's that was located closer to the city center. After that, the three-story building lay abandoned for awhile until it was decreed that it would be a sufficient accommodation for the city's orphans. Several hundred boys and girls of varying ages were moved into it around thirty years ago. Ilya and Andrei were assigned to the third level sleeping hall along with almost forty other boys and they would be living there until either their parents claimed them or they had become adults and would be released.

Andrei cupped his hand to whisper something, so Ilya had to bring his ear closer in order to hear it over the noise of the other children having dinner. "The reason why we're getting an extra piece of sausage is because another one of us has been eaten by the witch, and so his share of food is being rationed off," his best friend said.

Ilya jerked his head back. "You're a liar, Buratino!"

Since all the other kids were in their own conversations, nobody else seemed to butt into their discussion as Andrei's face reddened with rage. "Stop calling me that name."

Ilya laughed as he spooned some potato and cabbage soup into his mouth before sticking a fork into the second piece of sausage. The only thing he didn't like about the soup was the lack of sour cream in it. "Your nose is getting bigger."

"But it's true," Andrei said. "Have you not looked at the empty beds in our dorm? Today I counted who is left and there are only about thirty-six of us from a high of forty-two boys just last month."

"Maybe they were finally reunited with their parents? I think that's a good thing."

Andrei shook his head. "You really are stupid, Ilya. The whole city has been cut off because of the snow so how can their parents even get them?"

"I don't believe that there is a witch in this city," Ilya said as a matter of fact.

"She is not in the city, you fool. She is in the woods, just behind our building."

Ilya rolled his eyes. "How do you know there's a witch out there in the woods?"

"Because I saw her, of course," Andrei said.

"You liar! When?"

"Last night."

"You were asleep right beside me last night, Buratino."

Andrei snarled. He hated being called that. "No, I was awake the whole night! I saw two of the older boys get out of bed and put their clothes on. I watched them through the window as they started walking to the woods. Then I saw her."

"Saw who?"

Andrei ate a piece of sausage as he talked. "This old woman, she had long white hair that was longer than her body—she came out of the woods and I saw them talking. She then led them into the woods and I never saw them come out again!"

"Which of the two was it?"

"Evgeny and Gleb. The two bigger boys who used to pick on us, remember?"

Ilya turned and looked around the dining hall to see if he could find them. When he realized that they weren't around, he put his fork and spoon down. Then he looked back at Andrei again. "I-I don't believe you. This must be a trick you're playing with me."

Andrei smirked. "All these years we've been friends and you never believe a word I say."

Ilya crossed his arms and stuck his tongue out at him. "Because you always try to trick me, that's why!"

"This isn't a trick," Andrei said. "I'm telling the truth. If you want, we go look for them after dinner."

"Fine, we'll do that," Ilya said as he picked up his utensils and started eating again. "But if this is a trick and they are just hiding then I will punch that big nose off of your face, Buratino!"

Both boys waited until the lights went out and everyone had gone to sleep before silently slipping out of their beds and putting on their clothes. After putting on his snow boots, Ilya carefully slid out a cardboard box from underneath his bed and started to rummage through his personal items. Although the night wasn't fully dark as a strange twilight had begun ever since the snow started to fall, the sleeping hall's windows still didn't give him enough illumination so he had to feel his way around his most precious possessions. Ilya's fingers could feel the soft fur of his little toy husky dog along with some string until he felt a small plastic wrapper. As he brought it up to his face and smelled it, he noticed that it was some of the moldy cake he had kept from his birthday. He decided to stick it into his jacket pocket because he wanted to be reminded of that happy day. Ilya also found an old but unused stick of chewing gum that had been forgotten and he took that too. Rummaging through the rest of his stuff, he decided to leave his plastic cars, tanks, and a rubber ball in the box before he finally slid it back underneath the bed. After putting on his jacket and gloves, Ilya took his dark blue knitted-wool beanie cap and put it on the top of his head, then over his ears before slowly making his way to the door.

As he slipped out into the corridor, he found Andrei testing a small flashlight along the darkened passageway.

"Where did you get that from, Andrei?" Ilya whispered to him.

"It was in Roman's shack," Andrei said softly as he pointed out the window towards where the groundskeeper lived. "I snuck in there last week after dinner and found it in his desk drawer."

Ilya shook his head. "But that's stealing."

Andrei shrugged his shoulders as they both started walking towards the stairs. "I'm just borrowing it because we will need it. I'll return it when we get back here."

"You better. Stealing isn't good, Andrei."

Andrei snorted as they silently walked down the stairs. "Are you telling me you never stole anything in your life? Ever?"

"Never, the last words my mother told me before she left me here was, never take anyone else's property and to help anyone that I could."

"That's stupid. You mean you won't steal a piece of bread even when you're starving?"

"No," Ilya said as they got to the front door of the orphanage. "I would rather starve than take something that isn't mine."

Andrei made another snort of disgust as he tried the door knob. Unsurprisingly, it was unlocked as both boys carefully opened the door and got out. In the twilit night, the snowy ground could clearly be seen as they saw the shadowy outlines of the abandoned factories and the dark forests nearby, in contrast to the reflective white snow on the ground. The two boys had looked everywhere inside the orphanage for the two older lads right after dinner, so they hatched a plan to go look near the woods once everyone took to bed.

"Are you sure they weren't inside the building?" Ilya said.

"We already looked, stupid," Andrei said as he started walking towards the edge of the woods.

Ilya rubbed his shoulders. Despite wearing a winter coat and his beanie cap, he could feel the cold slowly seeping into his body. "I don't like this. If we do encounter the witch, we may end up just like the other two."

Andrei turned to face him as he walked backwards and smiled as he pulled out a folding pocket knife from his coat pocket and showed it to him. "If that witch finds us, I'll cut her eyes out."

Ilya's mouth opened wide. "Where did you get that?"

"It's Roman's, I found it along with the flashlight."

"That's two things you've stolen now."

"Shut up already, you holy fool."

Their boots made soft crunchy noises on the loosely packed snow as they made it to the edge of the woods. Ilya could barely see the paths that they used to run and play in just a few weeks ago. Andrei started looking at the ground as he shined the stolen flashlight, looking for clues. Ilya could see the cold vapors of his breath as he exhaled. After a few minutes, Andrei bent down and took something from the ground, then held it up so the other boy could see it too.

It was a small coin. "It's a gold chervonets," Andrei said, referring to the old coins that were used as currency during the times of the Soviet Union as he shined the flashlight on it. "This was Gleb's, I think."

"Gleb owned a coin?"

Andrei grinned as he put it in his pocket. "He showed it to me a few times, said it was real and he was going to be rich when he got out, but Babushka the cook told me it was a fake replica when I asked her about it."

Ilya frowned. "If that was Gleb's, then something must have happened to him. I think we should go back."

"What's the matter? Are you scared now?"

"I'm not scared! But we're just two boys and we will be no match against a witch."

"I have a knife so we will be safe," Andrei said. "When we find out where the witch is hiding the others, then we can tell the authorities and we will be heroes."

"I don't like this. We could get lost in the woods. We could freeze to death even if we don't find the witch."

Andrei shrugged as he turned around, then he turned on the flashlight as he started walking into the forest. "Stop being a girl and follow me."

Ilya hesitated. He was scared and he thought the whole thing was foolhardy. But Andrei was his best friend, and he felt some concern for him in case they both got into deeper trouble. In the end, his loyalty won out over his caution, and he followed Andrei to walk on the faint, snow-covered trail.

An hour had passed as the boys walked deeper into the woods. Andrei's stolen flashlight had begun to dim, so he mostly kept it turned off as there was enough twilight to give the forest a dim, grey look. They could hear a few hoots from an owl and the slight moaning breeze from gusts of cold wind that chilled their bodies. Ilya had suggested that they turn back several times but Andrei was adamant; his discovery of the coin had made him bolder and he was determined to see this through. The forest of Siberian pine trees had cast long, pitch black shadows as they loomed over them like tall, rigid tentacles. It was then that Andrei suddenly crouched down and signaled the other boy to be quiet.

Ilya squatted down as well and slowly made his way until he was right behind him. "What is it?" he whispered.

Andrei held the flashlight ready as he took out the pen knife and unfolded it. "It looks like a small clearing up ahead."

"I don't like this. We are too far away from the orphanage. Let's go back."

"Stop being a coward. Shut up and follow me," Andrei said as he started to creep forward, just beside the tufts of grass that were blanketed by snow.

As both boys got to within sight of the clearing, both opened their mouths wide in surprise. It was a circular expanse of grass that had been pushed under by a great weight. In the middle of it towered a small wooden hut with a single door at its front. What kept the little cabin two stories high were the pair of giant chicken legs that jutted out from underneath its base.

Ilya started trembling as he whispered into Andrei's ear. "We've got to get out of here, that's Baba Yaga's hut."

"The stories can't be true," Andrei said softly. "Baba Yaga is nothing but a tall tale."

Ilya couldn't believe it. His best friend was really dumb. "Are you crazy? Her hut is right over there."

"It's not moving though. Maybe she isn't around."

"What are you planning to do?"

"Let's go inside, it probably has some gold and magic treasure in it. We'll be rich and we won't have to live in the orphanage anymore."

Ilya bit his lip. "You're crazy, we're both going to die and get eaten by her."

"Come on, just follow me."

Ilya shook his head. "No way, I'm staying here."

"Suit yourself," Andrei said as he crept forward until he was near the edge of the glade.

Ilya said nothing as his heart was now pounding furiously while Andrei slowly crept out into the clearing. No sooner had the boy walked two steps, when the giant bird legs became animated and immediately shifted the entire cabin to face him. Both boys shrieked aloud as Andrei turned and started running towards his friend, but almost immediately the chicken legs began to crouch and the entire hut was lowered until it was just a few feet off the ground.

Andrei turned back to Ilya. "See, it wants us to come in."

"Yes, so it can eat us."

Andrei shook his head. "A hut does not eat people. Let's go in for a few minutes and then leave. It looks so small, we both could barely fit in it anyway."

Ilya bit his lip. His friend was right, the hut itself actually looked pretty small, its dimensions seemed hardly bigger than an outhouse. "Okay."

Andrei got close to the door just as Ilya made his way to him. There wasn't a knob but rather a thick wooden latch. Andrei touched it at first and then pulled it back as the door slowly opened outwards. Both boys could see a dimly lit interior. A warm draft of air drifted out to them and the smell of something cooking gnawed at their now grumbling stomachs. Momentarily forgetting their caution over curiosity, both boys went inside.

As soon as Ilya stepped in past the entrance, he stood beside Andrei and his mouth was wide open with amazement. The inside of the hut was much larger than they had anticipated. The main interior was the size of a small hallway, with the thatched roof at least fifteen feet high. An old stone fireplace at the back was roaring with burning and crackling firewood that provided steady warmth to the entire hut and cast an orangey illumination. A large cauldron hung over the fire, suspended by an iron bar and both boys could smell a savory meat stew wafting from it. A cupboard was beside it with stacks of wooden bowls on top as well as various bunches of leaves, roots and herbs that were hung on wooden beams near the ceiling. Ilya noticed that there was another large wooden table over at the other side and it was full of bottles and beakers of strangely colored liquids. Two very large but empty wooden cages with metal locks were suspended over the ceiling. At the end of the room they could see a set of wooden stairs that seemed to indicate that there was another level below.

Andrei turned off the flashlight and put it back into his jacket, but he kept the knife in his other hand. "It's so much bigger on the inside, it just can't be."

"Okay, we saw the inside, now let's go," Ilya said as he turned around and pushed at the door. But for some reason the door refused to open no matter how hard he tried. "I can't get it open!"

Andrei tried to help but no matter what they did, the door remained stuck. Both boys looked at each other with a growing sense of doom. Ilya blinked furiously as his mouth began to tremble.

"Let's keep looking, there must be another way out of here or maybe we could find a key or something," Andrei said.

Ilya was extremely frightened, but he said nothing and merely nodded as they both began to look around. The cupboard contained various wooden plates and utensils as well as assorted spices; it reminded Ilya of Babushka's kitchen back in the orphanage, but this one seemed so primitive. Andrei opened a nearby drawer that seemed to contain nothing more than little wood figurines of assorted animals and people. Both boys noticed that there were wooden barrels along the sides of the room, but they couldn't get them open.

After fifteen minutes of poking around, Ilya turned to his friend. "Did you find a key?"

"No," Andrei said as he pointed to the flight of stairs leading below. "Let's try down there."

"If we go deeper then we're farther away from the door."

"Maybe the key is down there."

Ilya sighed. His friend was so foolish. "Maybe something bad is down there."

"If we don't find a key or a way out we'll be stuck here forever. Is that what you want?"

"No, of course not."

"Okay then, follow me," Andrei said as he slowly made his way to the edge of the stairs. He tried to listen for any kind of noise emanating from below. Not hearing any, he gestured at Ilya to follow him as he started making his way down.

As both boys climbed down the stairs they were now in the cellar of the hut. While this room wasn't as large as the upper hall, there were two oil lanterns that hung alongside the wooden beams that illuminated the small mountains of gold coins and sparkling jewelry along the walls of the room. Ilya gasped while Andrei let out a yell of victory. They had found an old treasure trove.

"I told you we would find money!" Andrei exclaimed as he started scooping handfuls of gold coins into his jacket pockets. "Now we're rich."

But Ilya just stood there, not wishing to take any of it. "It belongs to the owner of this place. It's stealing."

Andrei stuck his tongue out at him as he kept stuffing the coins in his pockets. "You truly are a holy fool. Suit yourself, you will die a poor man."

Ilya just crossed his arms in disgust. "Are you finished now, thief?"

Andrei's jacket was bulging with coins and gemstones as he started to climb up the stairs. "You'll regret not taking any of this."

"I have a clear conscience," Ilya said as he went up the stairs after him.

Andrei kept looking back at Ilya as both boys got up to the main room once again. "You will be a street sweeper while I will have a dacha and a big car and—" but he quickly stopped talking as Ilya pointed to the door with a shocked look. Andrei meekly faced forward.

Standing near the doorway was an old woman. Although dressed in rags, she seemed very tall. Her large hooked nose was plain to see, her reddish eyes were like slits, almost hidden beneath the mass of wrinkles that was her face. Her long white hair was unkempt as it cascaded down her back, all the way to the ground. The old woman's bony arms were long, pale and sinewy.

"Well now, it seems that I have guests in my hut this evening," she said. Her voice was both high-pitched yet ancient, as if the winds of time had channeled itself into a vocal message for all to hear.

Both boys just stood there.

The old woman cackled a bit. "Come, come, children. I'm sure my warm fire and my delicious cooking must have attracted you both here. Have you come of your own free will or were you sent?"

Neither Andrei nor Ilya said anything. Both were still in shock.

The old woman edged closer to them. It seemed as if she floated above the old wooden floorboards. "You must both answer. Have you come of your own free will or were you sent?"

Both boys almost answered at the same time.

"I-I came of my own free will," Ilya said.

"No, we were sent!" Andrei exclaimed.

The old woman tilted her head up as if in thought. "Ah, this is a dilemma. Here we have two boys and each gave a different answer."

"We were sent!" Andrei said again.

The old woman moved closer. "Sent by whom?"

Andrei held the small pocketknife out. "By the police!"

The old woman tilted her head up and laughed. "Why would the police send two little boys to me?"

Andrei stood his ground and waved the knife at her. "We're part of a search party! To look for Gleb and Evgeny! We know you have them!"

The old woman smiled at him. Her long white teeth were crooked. "I am not familiar with those two that you mentioned. And I know you are lying for there are no police anymore, not in these lands, anyway. And you have stolen from my hoard."

"Keep away from me!" Andrei said as he started slashing at her with the knife.

Ilya started to scream and cry as the old woman deftly dodged Andrei's slash, picked him up by the throat and ripped his head off with her bare hands.

14. Demon Wind

Baghdad

Ron Boland frowned at the half-eaten slice of apple pie on his plate. It was obvious that the cooks must have run out of apples in preparing this pastry, so they substituted other root vegetables like beets or radishes or something, and then tried to mask the flavor by just adding more sugar and cinnamon. *Just as well*, he thought as he pushed the plate back further into the table. Buffalo wings night was last night and everybody who wanted to eat them was rationed to no more than five wings each. Five! How can you get full from eating five pieces of chicken wings? The situation was getting worse by the hour and there seemed to be nothing he could do about it.

He was sitting in front of a long, empty white table at the palatial dining room of the US Embassy compound in Baghdad, a walled cluster of buildings larger than Vatican City. After Saddam Hussein's fall, the US government spared no expense in creating the most secure embassy in the entire region and to provide the most comfort for its staff, all at taxpayer's expense, of course. With an independent power plant, its own water and sewage treatment centers enabled the embassy to pretty much function independently, regardless of what would occur outside of the almost twenty-foot-high concrete blast walls that surrounded it. Inside the walls was a totally different world compared to the chaos in the region. The Embassy dining room itself was a Las Vegas style buffet that served different ethnic cuisines from a dozen different countries at all times. There was also a six-lane, Olympic-sized swimming pool, a massive gym, tennis courts, even a regulation-sized soccer field for those inclined to get a little exercise. A multi-story shopping mall near the heavily fortified apartments with bulletproof glass windows pretty much made the whole place seem like a slice of Americana, but one that was smack dab in the Middle East. The rumors were that it cost American taxpayers over a billion dollars just to put the whole thing up, but its true price tag would probably never be known.

It was the one break he had in the past few days since the whole situation went to hell, and so the fake comfort food pissed him off even more. Boland was the CIA section chief of the region and the reports that were coming in was beginning to instill a sense of panic all over the embassy. There was still no sign of what happened to all US forces north of the city as the now gargantuan sandstorm coming in continued to intensify and would soon engulf Baghdad as well. The Iraqi government had already been evacuated southwards to Najaf; at least that was the official version. In fact, most of the government ministers and their families were already in Saudi Arabia and some even fleeing as far as Oman or the United Arab Emirates. The southern regions of Turkey were already lost and they had requested formally to NATO for help, but there would be none forthcoming. Most of Syria was already gone, while Jordan and Israel were entering into some sort of alliance to try to stem the tide of refugees fleeing towards them. Iran was publicly saying they were winning against the unknown enemy, but latest intel reports proved that they were in fact, on the verge of collapse. While Saudi Arabia outwardly stressed for calm, private communications to Washington already indicated that the Saudis were in full panic mode over what was happening and were begging to seek refuge in the US.

But the news back home was just as bad. Yesterday's cables indicated that Air Force One had crashed somewhere over northern Utah. It was attacked by some monstrous bird that could fly at supersonic speeds. The few emergency crews that remained active were still trying to reach the wreckage but due to the floods caused by broken dams, it could be days before anyone could even get into the area. Members of Congress had already been dispersed to secret locations since Washington DC was no longer considered safe. The latest cables reported that the vice-president was already sworn in as the new head of state for the country. The Navy lost an aircraft carrier when it was capsized by a freak mile-high tidal wave in the North Atlantic.

Boland looked around the dining hall as he finished the last of his coffee. Only a few people were eating since most of the embassy staff had already been evacuated. The United States was effectively pulling out not just from Iraq, but from the entire Middle East as well. Just before the president boarded Air Force One, he decreed that all US military forces were needed at home for protection against the still unknown menace, but everyone knew it would take a long time, if ever, to bring the troops overseas back to America. This was the most frustrating aspect of the whole thing. The entire world was now in acute danger, but nobody knew exactly what or who the enemy was. There had been contingency plans made for just about every possible threat known to man except for what was happening right now. Heck, at one point, the US State Department even had had plans distributed to all embassies in case of a possible zombie infestation but nobody, not even in their wildest dreams, had ever thought that this would happen. Boland instinctively shook his head, still trying to get his mind over the whole thing. He was not a religious man, but there was a gnawing realization that the earth was now turning into some sort of strange, mythical Dark Ages. Boland was a believer in science and the natural order to things, but it now seemed that all of mankind's accumulated knowledge and power were useless.

A Marine MP in full battle gear ran into the hall, spotted Boland and moved quickly over to him as he got up. "Sir, you're needed at the Consular Entrance at once. We tried to contact you through your phone, but there was no answer so your office told us you may be here," the soldier said as he barely caught his breath.

Boland got up, then he started to walk briskly with the soldier at his side towards the room exit. "Sorry, my phone was off because I just wanted to have dinner with some peace and quiet."

Both men ran out of the hall and then ducked into several underground corridors as they made their way towards the outer perimeter of the compound. Embassy staffers and military personnel alike were moving back and forth, some carrying bags because they were to be evacuated, while others had hard drives or stacks of classified documents that were needed to be either saved or destroyed. As Boland ran past a few civilians that were on their way to the landing strip within the Green Zone, he could see the fear in their eyes.

It took awhile and both men were somewhat exhausted as they finally trotted out from the underground tunnel, then ducked into a small command post just behind the blast walls near the entrance of the compound. Boland could see massive crowds of Iraqis and other people who somehow made it past the outer fortifications of the Green Zone. These desperate people were now trying to cajole, bribe or complain their way into the embassy itself. The outer iron-barred gate was closed and only a trickle of frantic civilians were being let through one at a time as they were carefully screened by American soldiers with weapons on the ready. He saw one woman that he recognized, a formerly well to do wife of an Iraqi politician, who screamed in desperation as she held up her crying baby above the pushing crowd and begged to be let in.

Boland kept going until he got to the door of the bunker. Two other MPs were there and as soon as they saw him they opened the door and let him through. As he walked into the entrance, he passed by a large communications room with several soldiers hunkered over their radios as they desperately tried to coordinate a defense of the city while trying to evacuate all important personnel. His Marine guide kept walking ahead of him and finally stopped in front of an interrogation room, then opened the door for him. As Boland walked into the smaller room, his mouth was open in mute shock.

Sitting beside the lone table was Patrick Gyle. His beard was scraggly and there was some hair growing at the top of his once bald head. Gyle's right arm was in a makeshift sling and he could see dried blood over the improvised, dusty bandages on it. The rest of his tattered fatigues were caked with dust. Gyle was Boland's operator and he was reported missing almost a week ago when the sandstorm first engulfed the northern regions of Iraq.

There were two other men in the room and Boland knew them as well. General Harry Sunderland was now the CO of all US forces in Baghdad and he was sitting across from Gyle, along with his aide, Major Benjamin Rawls. Both men barely acknowledged him as they continued to stare at Gyle, as if somehow waiting for a confession.

As the door closed behind him, Boland carefully walked over to Gyle and bent down slightly as he looked into the operator's tired eyes. "G, what the hell happened? How did you get here?"

General Sunderland crossed his arms and frowned as he leaned back on his metal folding chair. "We haven't been able to get a word out of him. My men found him near the outer perimeter of the Green Zone just half an hour ago. He was in a car with a dead Iraqi in the front seat."

Gyle said nothing, his eyes just staring straight ahead into space.

"He's wounded. Is there a medic?" Boland said to the two senior officers before turning back to face Gyle. "G, can you speak?"

"Medics are on the way," Major Rawls said. "It could be PTSD."

At that moment, the entire room shook for a few seconds, almost as if it was a small earthquake. The lights dimmed briefly before returning back to normal.

Gyle looked up into the concrete ceiling. "They're here," he whispered.

Boland turned to him. "What? Who's here?"

The door opened and in came an Army captain who was the designated command C2 officer as General Sunderland turned to face him. "Sir, our security forces reported enemy contact at Baghdad airport, then they went off the air," the captain said.

General Sutherland got up and made his way to the door before turning to Boland. "Make sure he tells us everything," he said before walking out of the room.

"G, who are they?" Boland said as he looked at Gyle.

Gyle's blue eyes had a glazed look. "We thought they weren't real but then they just ... appeared. I don't think we've got a chance. We've got to get outta here but there's nowhere to run to."

Major Rawls leaned forward, elbows on the table. "Who are you referring to?"

"T-they were like winged monsters," Gyle said wistfully. "Like those stone statues in the ruins. But they were alive."

Confused, Major Rawls looked at Boland. "What in the hell is he talking about?"

Boland remembered the tour in the museum of antiquities in regards to the culture of the region. He had taken some lectures on it and read some books. Most of all, he remembered playing a pen and paper role-playing game back in his college days. In one gaming session that lasted all night to the following day, he and some others had created make-believe characters who delved into a dungeon filled with monsters that had to be killed in order to get their hands on the fabulous riches that lay within. In one particular room that was described to them by the game's narrator, they encountered a creature with the body of a lion, but had the head of a man with giant wings that enabled it to somehow fly. The narrator of the game explained to them that it was some sort of ancient Sumerian monster called a shedu. Boland recalled that memory years later when he visited Baghdad's archaeological museum and found a stone carving of a creature there that was described exactly the same way.

"You're saying that the enemy are a bunch of mythical beasts?" Boland said. "A shedu?"

Gyle covered his face with his left hand and sighed with exhaustion. "We tried to fight them, but we couldn't. Our weapons were useless. Matt was crushed in the Humvee—they just stomped on it like it was made of cardboard."

Boland looked away. He wasn't sure if he could believe it. "What about the unit you were attached to?"

Gyle just stared down at the floor and shook his head. "All dead."

"How did you get out?" Major Rawls said.

"I just jumped out of the Humvee when it was attacked," Gyle said. "I played dead until I could see the morning light. Their screams, the screams of those boys, I can still hear them every time I close my eyes. All I had was my compass and I made my way south. Every time I felt they were near, I hid in the sand."

"These things, these monsters," Boland said. "Did they come from Mosul?

Did it all start from there?"

"I don't know. They came with the dust storm. Everything that has dust is death," Gyle said softly.

"Who's controlling these creatures?" Major Rawls said. "Is it Daesh?"

Gyle looked at him with pity in his eyes. "Don't you get it yet? Their god doesn't exist. The Muslims, the IS- everyone in this entire country paid for that mistake with their lives."

Major Rawls was getting angry. "I'm your superior officer, son. You don't talk that way to me."

Boland turned to Major Rawls. "He's not yours to order around, Major. He's CIA and unattached to the military."

Major Rawls stood up. "I've had enough of this bullshit." With that, he got to the door, opened it and left.

Boland crouched down, closer to Gyle. "What can we do? How can we defeat them?"

Gyle just shrugged. "You can't fight gods. And you can't fight their angels."

The commotion in the other room got louder. People were shouting and Boland could hear the howling wind outside of the bunker picking up. He quickly got to the door and opened it just as an Army medic was about to knock on it. Boland let her through while observing the communications room. The medic instantly began to look at Gyle's injuries as she placed her medical bag on the table. Boland just stood in the doorway and listened to the comms chatter.

"We've lost contact with Alpha Company at the southern perimeter of the Green Zone, sir," a radio operator who was manning one of the radios said to General Sunderland.

General Sunderland frowned. "What was their last transmission?"

"All their CO said was that the dust storm was picking up all around them with possible enemy contact in the heart of the storm, sir."

General Sunderland pounded his fist on a nearby table. Military internet was down along with GPS and satellite linkups, so all they had left were the FM radios and landlines that were still working. "Goddamn it! Are we in communications with anybody?"

Another radio operator chimed in. "We have riots at the entrance of the embassy compound, sir. People are attempting to rush the barricades. MPs are requesting authorization to use force."

"Granted," General Sunderland said grimly. "Order all units to go weapons free. Go to full lockdown. How many Apaches do still we have airborne?"

"At last count six, sir," a third communications staffer said. "But that was just before the storm hit the Green Zone. Now I can't raise any of them with our commos."

General Sunderland kept looking at the charts. "Do we still have the underground lines to the main embassy building?"

The first radio operator started flipping the switches on his radio. "We still do, sir, though we're getting a lot of static now."

Major Rawls said nothing but looked at his commanding officer and nodded.

General Sunderland sighed. That was it then. "Signal general evacuation. Code grey alpha one."

There was furious activity as all the radio operators began to transmit the evacuation order. This meant that all remaining embassy personnel were to try and make it across the Tigris using the Two Stories Bridge that was located south of the compound. From there, a transport unit was supposed to be waiting for them at the Doha Refinery, allowing them to either bring the convoy south, or head to the Al-Rasheed Airport to the east, right beside Camp Rustamiyah, which was supposedly under Iraqi Army control.

Within minutes of the order, General Sunderland strapped on a holstered pistol to his belt and started for the outer door along with Major Rawls as the C2 staff members began to get up while deactivating their communications systems. As Boland turned around, he could see that the medic had replaced the bandage on Gyle's forearm with a fresh one as she too was packing up.

"You coming with us?" Boland said.

"Do I have a choice?" Gyle said as he got up. *Looks like there wasn't even time for a shower and a change of clothes,* he thought.

Both men got to the outer door of the bunker and briskly walked out. They were both instantly hit with high winds as the dust storm swirling around them picked up in intensity. Gyle's goggles and bandanna were tied to his throat and he quickly put them on. Boland just took out a pair of sunglasses and placed them over his eyes. Both men started running towards the vehicle compound where the transportation was waiting. Boland had to squint as small particles of sand were seeping in between the sunglasses and his eyes. They both could see armed military personnel running all over the place.

A sergeant started waving at them across the street in order to guide them towards the garages. Boland could see a Humvee drive up near the main embassy building just as the ambassador and two aides came out of the building's front doors and started making their way to the vehicle.

Gyle couldn't believe it. "He's still here? I thought he was supposed to have gone already!"

Boland too had to shout because of the howling winds as they kept going while looking at them. "He said he would be part of the last group to evacuate. I guess he thinks he can be a hero."

At that moment, something huge fell out of the sky, and landed right on top of the Humvee just as the ambassador got inside of it. It looked like a giant brown-furred lion and it had bird like wings on its back. Its head resembled that of a horrid looking man with a wild mane of hair and thick beard. The creature's weight and momentum crushed the vehicle as its wheels gave out, its body smashed in like it went through a junkyard car crusher. Both men instinctively crouched down as the sergeant on the other side of the street leveled his M16 and began firing at the creature.

"We gotta move!" Gyle shouted as he started running towards the vehicle compound.

People on the outside were screaming and running in all directions as Boland began to sprint after Gyle. Despite the blowing wind and dust, they could hear gunfire and explosions all around. As the two men were less than forty yards away, they both quickly drew back in surprise as a huge, building sized creature landed on top of the garages and started to singlehandedly crush and kick the vehicles within. The huge M35 two and a half ton trucks were being trampled and tossed aside like toys; the destruction was so unearthly that every time the creature stomped its bird-like foot down, it created a small earthquake that sent both men sprawling onto the dusty concrete. As Boland looked up, he just couldn't believe what he was seeing.

The gigantic creature had avian like legs that ended in talons, while its chest and torso were vaguely humanlike, with a skin color of black obsidian. On its back sprouted four feathered wings in a dragonfly-like fashion, with a pair of forward wings turned upwards and two hind wings that were facing down. But its massive face was that of a hideous demon: rounded, bloodshot eyes the size of satellite dishes; its small, stubby nose formed part of a flat snout and beneath them snarled a car-sized maw with numerous fanged teeth that could chew and swallow men whole by the handful. Its massive arms ended in broad claws that started to smash down at the surrounding blast walls as if they were made of paper.

Boland screamed in stark realization of the truth as he remembered the trip to the archaeological museum. In one alcove stood an idol of a dreaded demigod that the ancient Assyrians and Babylonians both worshipped and feared. As he remembered looking at the idol and at the unearthly monster facing them now, he realized that its features were exactly the same. It represented the unceasing wind of desolation, of endless plagues and death. And here it was, in all its destructive glory. He had thought it was but a myth of an old and largely forgotten peoples; a tall tale to keep the young children in check. But in the end, it was real after all.

It was Pazuzu, the god of demons and the wind.

15. Convergence

Tara Weiss smiled to her herself as she drove the van down along a stretch of the deserted highway. For the first time in days she had felt good. Larry had finally given her permission to drive the car while he lay asleep, stretched out in the back of the van. She did take a driving class when she was still in high school a few months before, but she never took the test to get the license at the local Department of Motor Vehicles office because her dad didn't care and she didn't have a car anyway. They had been on the road for three days now. The van had just passed into the New Mexico state border less than a few hours ago. They probably would have been able to travel faster if they just made a beeline to the Kansas state border, but Larry wanted to specifically avoid the built-up areas and stick to the open road. Since the day began there had been considerably less cars on the back roads that they were taking, but Tara couldn't tell if that was a good sign or a bad one since they haven't been able to talk to anybody else. The radio was turned off since Larry was napping away; Tara was sick and tired of hearing Pastor Burnley's constant sermons about how the world was ending and that the only way to get to salvation was to join his flock in Kansas. That's where they were heading for anyway so she got it already, no need to keep hearing about it over and over again.

Tara glanced at the little Chihuahua that lay curled up in the front seat. The second night they spent was behind a small hill on the side of the highway; she had decided to just sleep on a blanket alongside the vehicle. Even though Larry had offered her the back of the van so they could doze side by side, she had refused. The dog woke her in the middle of the night when it jumped on top of her while Tara lay curled up on the dry grass and started barking. When she woke up, she realized Larry was standing over her and was just staring at the both of them in the dark. When she asked what was going on, he just turned around and went back to sleep in the back of the van. She got a little bit scared then, but her drowsiness won out and she soon fell asleep again. The next morning, Larry allowed her to drive the vehicle for the first time.

As she drove on and kept thinking about last night, the van soon moved into a built-up area of nearby houses and strip malls as Tara was lost in thought. She didn't notice that an old sign that formerly said Albuquerque City Limits had been torn down and replaced with a handwritten sign that simply said "Defiance." She drove into a street that was now in a developed area of abandoned warehouses and sand-colored buildings. That was when the shouting and the ringing of bells could suddenly be heard.

Tara's eyes opened wide as she saw an improvised barricade ahead. As she began to put on the brakes, she saw from the rearview mirror that half a dozen people with hoods and ski masks ran into the street that they had just passed and started throwing caltrops on the road behind them. Tara shrieked as she noticed the iron spikes on the boulevard as the small crowd at the rear of the van started moving forward while brandishing baseball bats and steel rods.

"What the hell is going on?" Larry said as he sat up.

"We're trapped!" Tara cried as she slowed the van almost to a halt just a few meters from the barricades. There were people milling around in front of them and they started shouting at them to get out of the vehicle.

The dog growled and leapt into the back of the van. Larry jumped into the front seat beside her and stomped his boot on top of her foot that was on the gas pedal. "Go, go, go!"

As the van accelerated forward, one of the people behind the barricade lit up and threw a Molotov cocktail, but it missed as it exploded just a few feet away on the side of the pavement. The van quickly careened into a side street as Larry twisted the steering wheel to the left, but they noticed that the avenue was blocked off as well. Tara screamed. Larry noticed that part of the section that seemed to be walled up at the edge of the sidewalk was composed of an upturned sofa and a couple of wooden chairs piled on it. He kept the steering wheel angled right for it. The van rammed through the side of the barricade and sent some broken furniture flying to the street as it continued on. He kept an iron grip on the wheel and pushed the weight of his boot on the accelerator as the van drove past the town and back onto the open road again. Larry's steel-toed boot on the top of her foot was pretty painful, but Tara just bit her lip and tried to fight through the pain as a single tear rolled down her flushed cheek.

Larry finally took his foot off of hers when they realized that there would be no pursuit. There weren't any cars following them as the van slowly pulled to a stop. He turned until his face was inches away from hers and shouted. "Get out of the driver's seat!"

Tara didn't look at him as she opened the driver's side door and limped out. She wore light sneakers and she was sure there would be a bruise on the top of her foot when she got the chance to examine it. She kept staring down at the dusty concrete pavement as he slid into the driver's seat and closed the door. Tara was sure he was going to leave her behind but instead he just sat there and stared out into the front of the van.

After a few minutes, Larry finally turned his head and looked at her. "Get in."

Tara meekly walked over to the passenger side door, opened it, and got inside. Within seconds they were moving again.

For almost an hour, nobody said anything until Larry glanced at her again as he maneuvered the van around a pileup of smashed cars along the highway.

"I told you to keep an eye out. Don't go into any built-up area. I told you that like fifty times," he said as he kept his eyes on the road.

She started to cry a little. "I'm sorry."

"They could have taken us down you know. We could have been killed."

"I'm sorry," she repeated.

He shook his head slowly. "Alright, just be more mindful next time. Okay?"

"Okay."

It took them a little over two hours, but they were able to maneuver around the Albuquerque city limits to the point where they could just skirt the edges of Santa Fe. Every time they would get close to any of the big cities, they noticed there were more piled up cars along the road. Tara grimaced as she noticed that there were burned out bodies in a few of them as they passed them by. By mid-afternoon, they were on a deserted stretch of highway on Interstate-25. Larry spotted an abandoned gas station and there were handwritten signs saying "NO GAS" that were nailed to the front of the store. Larry would have none of it as he tried the pumps, but the electricity was off so he took out a manual hand pump from the back of the van. It took an hour but he was able to get a full tank for it, plus he was also able to fill up the spare plastic jerry can he had in the back. By now, he was in a good mood as they drove out with the sun begging to set. Tara figured they probably had enough fuel to get to Kansas without having to stop for gas again.

Tara said nothing as they drove on for a few more hours until night finally fell. She had expected Larry to tell her to go ahead and drive while he would go to sleep in the back, but he didn't as he just hummed a tune instead while turning on the headlights as the desert moon began to shine its luminescence over the horizon.

Tara looked at him. "Are we gonna stop soon?"

He didn't look back at her but instead just smiled. "Soon."

"When?"

"A few more miles. Then we bed down."

Tara stared out into the twilit night. It was starting to get chilly. "Have you been here before?"

"Yes, there's a place where we can stay, it's just up ahead."

"A place? What is it?"

"You'll see."

Within a few minutes, she saw a cluster of darkened buildings along the side of the road just a few miles ahead of them. It was evidently an abandoned motel. Its elevated vintage sign post wasn't working, but she could plainly see the words Petrie Motel in the outlines of the deactivated neon billboard as they got close. Larry brought the van into the graveled driveway and stopped in front of the manager's office.

"How did you know there wouldn't be anybody here?" Tara said as she unbuckled her seatbelt.

Larry turned off the engine, got out and then stretched his legs on the tarmac. "I didn't. But I figured there was a good chance the owners left."

Tara had gotten out and started looking around. The little dog jumped out from the van and started to take a piss near a concrete column. "You stayed here before?"

Larry grinned at her as he turned on a flashlight with his left hand while taking out a set of keys with his right. "Sweetpea, I used to work here."

"Oh yeah, as what?"

"I used to be the night manager," Larry said as he unlocked the door to the office and went in.

Tara followed. When she got inside, she noticed the brown wooden counter and a sofa for waiting guests. Larry opened up the manager's office, walked in, and then looked out the window at the back to see a large metal box just in the outside of the building. No rust, so it looked to be in good shape, but he wasn't sure if it had any fuel in it. Hoping for the best, Larry located the electrical switch and flipped it on. Within minutes, a loud humming noise began as the generator started and the lights in and around the motel instantly came on. Tara was blinded for a bit, but she quickly readjusted her eyes to the now bright as daylight illumination. Larry began to manually deactivate the exterior lights of the buildings as well as the flashing neon motel sign right beside the highway.

Leaning over the counter and grabbing a few keys from the side wall, Tara grinned and looked at Larry as he stepped out from the manager's office. "Can I use any room I want?" she said.

"You sure can, Sweetpea," Larry said. "Which room would you like this evening?"

Tara looked closely at the set of keys she took. Each one had a number emblazoned on its plastic tab which attached to the keychain. "I think I'll take room twenty-one, sir."

Larry smirked. "Well, you've already got the keys so enjoy your evening, lady. Don't forget to checkout by noon tomorrow."

Tara took the keys, went out and headed to her room. The dog noticed and quickly followed as she unlocked her room door and went in after turning on the lights. It was a stereotypical lodge style interior, with brown wood paneling, two single beds side by side and the door leading to the bathroom at the opposite end. Tara closed and locked the door behind her, then threw her backpack on the other bed before throwing herself on top of the nearest one. It was her first time ever in a motel room. She felt a certain sense of accomplishment that she had at least experienced this in her short life. Her dog just jumped up on top of the other bed and started to get comfortable on it.

After resting for bit, she got up and walked into the bathroom. Tara noticed some small plastic packets of soap and shampoo, as well as some fresh white towels that had been left hanging on the racks. Grinning with excitement, she turned the tap on the sink and was immediately rewarded with gushing wet steam; Larry's generator trick was able to get some hot water too. Within minutes, Tara took the first hot shower she had in a week and then stopped the drain on the tub as she let it rise, then doubled down with a bubble bath that wrinkled her fingertips and toes as she relaxed in the warm, sudsy water. She felt like she could just stay in the nice, clean bathtub all night.

As she wrapped a towel over her wet hair, Tara noticed that the dog walked into the bathroom and stared at her.

"Whatchu looking at?" she said playfully.

The dog lay down and began to rub its back on the bathroom mat.

"You want a bath too?" she said.

"No," the dog said. "Just came to warn you."

Tara's brow furrowed. "Warn me? About what?"

"Something's going to happen."

Tara quickly stood up from the tub, grabbed another towel and began drying herself. "What's gonna happen?"

"The future is cloudy, but I can sense possible danger."

"Now you're scaring me," Tara said as she wrapped the long white towel around her body and opened the bathroom door.

Just as she walked back into the room, Tara gasped. Larry was standing in the middle of the place, staring at her intently, the door to the outside slightly open. Taken aback, she instantly retreated into the bathroom again. "Larry, what are you doing in here?" she demanded.

Larry had a blank look in his eyes as he twisted his head sideways as if to check if anyone was looking at them. "I let myself in since I've got the master keys to this place. Who were you talking to back there?"

"Nobody," Tara said as she poked her head out of the door. "I was just talking to myself okay? Can you please leave?"

"Not just yet," he said. "I wanted to talk. About us."

Tara sighed. This was getting irritating. "Can't it wait till dinner? I just got out of the bath and I'm half naked. Come on, Larry, this isn't funny anymore."

"Come out here, I wanna talk to you."

"Larry, I told you…"

"Come out of there! Right now!"

His angry shout had startled her. When he was mad, he sounded like her father. Tara meekly stepped out of the bathroom and sat at the bottom edge of the nearest bed and looked down on the floor, knees firmly locked together. Tears welled in her eyes, but she fought to contain her own hurt feelings and to keep them from falling down.

Larry stood over her. "Look, we've been together for a few days now and we've gotten to know each other. I think I'm now starting to like you. As in really like you."

She didn't say anything.

"I've done a lot for you," Larry said. "I've driven you around and I've saved your life. Many times over. So I think it's only fair that I get a little bit of love back."

She looked up at him in confusion. "I-I don't get what you mean…."

Larry placed his right hand on her bare shoulder. She shuddered as his calloused hand touched her moist skin. "Just a little love is all I need, Sweetpea."

"No!" Tara said as she shifted her shoulders so his hand fell off as she moved away from him and stood up. "I-I'm not ready for this, I'm only fifteen."

This time Larry's left hand grasped her arm and held it somewhat tightly. "The world's changed, Sweetpea. Laws don't matter anymore. Now it's all about survival. I'm not a bad man, I just want a little thing in return. Consider it payment for my services."

"No!" Tara shouted as she tried to twist away again. "Leave me alone!"

His backhanded slap caught her square in the jaw as she fell sideways, her head bouncing off the side of the mattress until she was down on her back, lying on the carpeted floor. Larry started to pull down his pants. As he knelt on top of her, his large hands pinned her arms to the ground while there was a slight air current near where the main door was.

Tara screamed. "No, please don't do this!"

"Shut the hell up," Larry said softly as his left hand started to pull away the towel that was wrapped around her body. She tried to twist away from his arm, but he was too strong for her. Tara grimaced and shrieked as Larry used his own forehead to keep her head down on the floor.

Just as he started running his tongue along her throat, Larry's head jerked back all of a sudden, as a hand that was gloved in black leather appeared to be grasping the back of his throat. Larry started to choke as he got up, but was instantly thrown backwards and he smashed into a side table before lying in a heap on the floor. Tara opened her eyes, turned and saw a tall man with a grey crew cut. He was dressed in slacks and wore a hunting vest over a yellow-striped polo shirt as he stood over them. The man had a pistol belt with a holstered Glock 21 and several spare magazines dangled along its sides. The little dog had run out of the bathroom and was staring at all of them.

"Will you look at that," the man said, laughing a little. "That's the little dog I was looking for."

Tara didn't say anything as she sat up on the floor and faced them. Larry started to get up but stopped and quickly stayed back down. The man had pivoted to face him and had placed his hand on the holstered Glock pistol, ready to draw and fire.

"Stay down," the man said to him as he moved closer to where the dog was, picked it up and examined its collar. "Yup, this is the little dog, alright. This must be some sort of miracle. I not only find the pet I'm looking for, but I run into an old acquaintance as well."

Larry rubbed the back of his bruised head. "Who are you?"

The man put down the dog and stood over Larry. "You don't remember do you? I'm one of the guys in the task force that helped put you away for a few years, if I recall."

Larry pointed up at him. "I do remember now, Officer Haggard."

"Detective Joshua Haggard," Josh said. "Funny you just showed up this evening. I thought you were still in prison, Larry."

Tara gasped.

Josh looked at her and chuckled. "Oh, he didn't tell you, did he? I bet you don't even know his last name, or else he just gave you a false one, right?"

Tara nodded meekly.

"It's okay, girl. Go ahead and sit on the bed. I want you to see this," Josh said as Tara got up from the floor, sat at the base of the bed and wrapped herself with the quilted blanket.

"Look, Detective, I didn't know you were here," Larry protested.

"Shut up, Larry," Josh said. "Even if you did know, would that had stopped you from raping this girl?"

Larry bit his lip.

Josh looked back at Tara. "Let me give you both a proper introduction, this here, lying on the ground is Larry Hanley, two-time burglar, convicted rapist, occasional drug dealer, and three time scumbag loser." Then he turned to Larry again. "So when did you get out of prison, Larry? Did they let you go or are you a fugitive? Don't lie to me now."

"They let me out just over a week ago," Larry said softly. "Just before the world went to hell."

Josh nodded contemptuously. "Gone to hell is right. So where did you get the van?"

"I found it."

"Where?"

"In a parking lot by one of the malls in Mesa, the keys were still inside," Larry said.

"And like the petty thief that you are, you just took it," Josh said as he pointed to Tara. "What about her?"

"She was hitching a ride, that's all," Larry said.

Josh looked at her. "Is that true?"

Tara nodded meekly. "Y-yes."

Josh turned his attention back to Larry again. "What about the dog? Where'd you find it?"

"That's her dog," Larry said.

"Is that true?" Josh said to her. "Where did you find it?"

The dog ran over to Tara and sat by her feet. "I just found it on the street, sir," she said.

Josh smiled as he shook his head in amazement. "And here I was, going to Kansas now that my wife is gone so I hold up in one of the rooms here for the night, and then all of a sudden the lights come on! I thought this must be a sign from our Lord, and I think now that it's a true miracle indeed, yessiree. After my wife's best friend shot her to death, she ranted about some demonic dog they were trying to kill and how it was all an accident. She gave a description of course, and the type of collar he wore as well as its breed and fur color. I thought she was nuts but seeing this little dog right here, right now, just spells out fate in my books, don't you both agree?"

Tara and Larry said nothing.

Josh wagged a finger at the dog. "Ah, Bibsy, there's a claim you caused the death of my wife, but I find that hard to believe, at all. But with all that's happening now, I dunno what to believe, but I guess I'll just have to place my trust in the Lord."

"You can have the dog and you can have her, for crissakes," Larry said. "Just let me go, I'll take the van and be outta here and you'll never see me again, Detective Haggard, I swear to the almighty."

Josh smiled as he picked up a wooden table leg that Larry had broken off as he fell down. "Why in the hell would I let you go, Larry? You just burglarized this motel here and you attempted a rape on a minor. You'll be going back to prison for a long, long time, now."

"Okay, look, just take the van then, it's all yours. There's food in there and tools and such. Just let me go, please," Larry said.

"I don't let criminals go, it's not in my nature," Josh said to him.

Larry saw the table leg in his right hand. He was sweating all over now. "Please, the whole world has changed! You can let me go, there aren't any laws anymore! How can I be committing a crime if there's no order?"

"Why, you're wrong, Larry," Josh said as he hefted the table leg. "I'm the law and order now."

Larry held up an open palm to him, both as a gesture of peace and submission. "Okay, okay! You're the law now, you're everything! If you want to put me back in jail, then fine! Just don't hurt me, please!"

Josh chuckled as he shook his head. "I'm afraid I can't put you in jail either. You see, I don't think there are a whole lotta law enforcement personnel still doing their jobs anymore. So that means even if I do haul your ass to the nearest jail, nobody will be able to prosecute you, much less book you in."

Larry started to cry as Tara's mouth began to open wide in dread.

"But you know, you're right, Larry," Josh said. "There are no more laws because nobody follows them anymore. So you know what that means?"

Larry looked up at him, tears and mucous streaming down his grizzled chin. "You'll let me go?"

Josh looked at him intently. "No, but since Internal Affairs is pretty much gone, it means that I don't have to hold back when I apprehend criminal scum like you anymore."

Larry shrieked as Josh smashed him in the forehead with the table leg. His head jerked backwards as a big, bloody gash appeared. A puddle of blood began to form on the carpet as Josh hit him again and again until his entire face and head was just a bloody pulp and he finally stopped breathing.

Tara screamed once, then she covered her eyes though she could still hear the sticky sound of flesh and bone being pounded.

16. Resolve

Brooklyn

The building elevators were not working because there wasn't any power throughout the whole city. Joe Pascorelli took the stairs all the way up to the eighth floor as he used his flashlight to guide him along. In the nearly twenty-five years he was on the force, his dark brown hair now had streaks of grey in it as it complemented his salt and pepper moustache. His paunch was beginning to tighten the NYPD lieutenant's uniform around his waistline, and it slowed him down as he finally got to the top of the stairway, but that was the least of his worries right now. Opening the fire door that led out into a twilit corridor illuminated by a faint light coming from the open window at the far end, Joe rested his legs for a bit before walking up to the eighth door on the right and knocked a few times.

A short, brown-skinned lady with silver hair tied neatly in a ponytail answered the door. "Yes?"

Joe took his officer's cap off. "Mrs. Mendoza, my name is Lieutenant Joseph Pascorelli of the New York Police Department. Ma'am, I would like to—"

The old woman cut him off with a wave of her hand as she smiled. "Hello, Joe, please do come in," she said as she stood back to let him inside.

"Thank you," Joe said as he walked into the small, three-bedroom apartment. He could see lighted candles all around. It gave everything a soft, yellow illumination as he switched off his flashlight and strapped it back on his belt. "It's great that you still remember me, Mrs. Mendoza."

The old woman closed the door behind them. "Please, call me Josefina. Can I get you some coffee or some water? Forgive me, but that's all we have right now."

"No, thank you, ma'am, I mean, Josefina." Joe grinned. "I already drank and ate before I got here. How's your food supply going?"

Josefina smiled and shrugged. She had a simple purple dress underneath her knitted sweater. "We can survive until the next handout. It would be nice if I could get more medicine for her, though. Please sit down," she said, pointing to the nearby sofa.

"Thanks," Joe said as he sat down on the sofa, placed his cap beside him and rubbed his right leg. He had injured it in the line of duty many years ago and it gave him cramps when he put too much weight on it. His wife Maria had asked him if he wanted to have an operation to fix it, but Joe always hated scalpels and needles, and so held it off until the pain gradually subsided into a dull ache when the weather would get too cold.

Josefina sat down in an easy chair beside him and placed her wrinkly hands on her lap. "How is everything out there?"

Joe sighed as he looked out the window. The rain was incessant and continued to fall day and night for weeks now. "Not good, we've lost about half the force already through either injuries, sickness, or just plain desertion," he said before looking towards the small corridor to where the bedrooms were located. "Is she still willing to see me?"

Josefina smiled faintly, the wrinkles under her beady eyes gave her face even more lines. "She didn't answer when I told her you would be coming, but she won't ignore you. I think she's just getting ready."

"I didn't really want to put her under this awkward situation and God knows she needs the rest after what she went through, but we really need more men ... or should I say more women, back in uniform right now."

Josefina nodded. "She knows her duty, Lieutenant. She's still a cop."

At that moment, a door leading into a bedroom opened and Valerie walked out. She had a jogging suit on along with a sweater. She walked towards them with slippers on her feet. Valerie's right arm was bandaged but the doctors had told her that no ligaments were severed, thank goodness, so all she needed was to rest it until the skin grew over the wound. Her face however, was another matter entirely: the knife slash made a vicious cut from in between her eyebrows, down her cheek, to just above the right side of her chin. There was a long white bandage that ran along her facial wound and was held in place by medical tape; that bothered her because the protruding binding gave her double vision every time she tried to center her field of view. With over twenty stitches still holding the cut in place, she knew she would never be beautiful when the dressings would finally be removed.

Joe stood up and held out his hand. "Val, it's so nice to see you again, how are you?"

Valerie shook his hand but said nothing as she sat down on a wooden chair on the opposite side of her mother.

Josefina made a slight smile and stood up. "I'll make us some coffee," she said as she started to walk to the kitchen.

For a few minutes, Joe just sat there as he looked out of the window again. The only other sounds in the room came from the howling wind and the pounding of the rain outside. But the noises inside soon took over, as the clanking of ceramic cups and the boiling of the kettle meant that Josefina had started brewing coffee.

"Val, is everything alright?" Joe said to her.

Valerie finally turned and looked at him. "I've been resting for the past few days so other than looking like Frankenstein, it's been fun."

Joe smiled and looked down on the floor. "It's great you still have that sense of humor, Val."

"Did you come just for a casual visit, Lieutenant?"

"Actually, not just that. I came to see if one of my detectives is fit for duty again. The bottom line is that there aren't many of us left. If you don't want to come back, I understand, two other officers already told me so this morning. Things are getting really bad and there's not much we can do to stop it."

Valerie shrugged. "I don't have much of a face left and this bandage is giving me double vision. Are you sure you want me back on the force at this time?"

"I need anyone I can get right now. We're putting together a task force to try and retake lower Manhattan, volunteers only. Have you been updated on the news?"

"Just the radio because we still have some batteries," Valerie said. "But it's sporadic and we only get the news once in awhile. Most of the time it's just white noise."

Joe sighed. "We've had to withdraw all the way north from Hell's Kitchen, down to Tribeca, and over to the Lower East Side. That whole area is now designated as a no-go and it's getting bigger. Anybody who can is leaving the whole city, but from what I've been hearing, I don't think anywhere in the country is safe. We've set up checkpoints along Brooklyn Bridge and all of the other bridges, but I don't think it'll hold. If whatever's causing this decides to move towards Staten Island or Brooklyn, I don't think we could stop them, not with the few officers we have left."

"Still no idea what's causing it?"

"We think it's some sort of cult. But I don't know how they grew to this size in such a short time. We've been getting reports of monsters in Central Park, but I just don't believe it, it's too fantastic already."

"Monsters?" Valerie said. "What kind of monsters?"

Joe shook his head. He had a hard time believing in what he was saying. "Some of the news reporters showed us video feeds of people in the park getting attacked by things. They looked like naked white women, only they are so thin, they're like walking skeletons, but they had the strength to rip people in half."

Josefina placed a tray with a ceramic pot and cups on the short wooden table between them and started pouring some hot, steaming coffee. "They are the tzitzimitl."

Joe's eyes widened. "The what?"

Valerie rolled her eyes. "Mama, please. We don't have time for a mythology lecture."

Josefina shook her head. "Mi hija, you keep trying to deny what is there, what you saw."

"Mama, what you're saying cannot be true," Valerie said. "Those old stories were myths and legends, they cannot be real."

"Wait," Joe said. "Those things you just said, what exactly are they?"

Valerie looked at him disapprovingly. "Lieutenant, come on, surely you don't want to listen to this nonsense?"

Joe held up his hand. "I'm sorry, Val, we don't have any idea what we're dealing with and I've seen things that I cannot accept as real, but now I don't know what to believe."

Valerie frowned and crossed her arms, but didn't say anything as her mother sat down on the easy chair and looked at the police lieutenant approvingly.

"I am going to tell you some stories that were passed down from my family since I was a child," Josefina said. "The tzitzimitl were goddesses from the stars and the Aztecs believed that when they would attack the sun, it would cause an eclipse. They lived in darkness and were fated to return when the gods could no longer keep the world alive. The Aztecs believed that they had to enact rituals to keep these demons at bay by lighting fires and praying to keep the sun over the earth. The tzitzimitl only dwell in darkness, so if you are in daylight then they cannot harm you."

"Okay," Joe said. He was intrigued. "How do we kill these things?"

Josefina shook her head. "The tzitzimitl are gods and you cannot kill them."

Valerie frowned. "So you're saying that we might as well surrender now and get eaten alive, Mama?"

"Mi hija, you should listen to your elders rather than disrespect them," Josefina said. "The tzitzimitl can be both good and evil. They may inflict disease on one person, yet heal another. You must find the cause as to why they are here."

"A trigger," Joe said. "How do we do that?"

Josefina took out a necklace she was wearing underneath her sweater. "This is an old Aztec charm given to me by my grandmother. She said that this will save me if I ever encounter an Aztec demon. Valerie has one too, that is why she survived her ordeal."

Valerie got up. "Mama! How dare you talk about what happened to me like it was some sort of crazy religious story. I was attacked by a bunch of crazy cult members and my partner is dead! How dare you!"

Joe also stood up as he placed a hand on Valerie's left forearm. "Val, I'm so sorry about Myron, but what your mother is saying is the only thing that makes sense right now. We need to know more."

As she sat down, Valerie began to cry. She remembered only brief glimpses of what had happened a few nights ago. The horror still lived in her mind. Of Myron lying on top of her as they tore him to pieces, Her partner's screams mixed in with gunfire all around them, as the Emergency Services Unit team got there just as she almost drowned in sea of blood. She could still remember the pungent, metallic taste and the smell of it all. She recalled the night at the hospital when they had to wheel her out of there when it too was attacked. And most of all, she remembered the first time since the attack when she looked at herself in the mirror, with the long red slit with black stitches that ran along the length of her face. At the time, she wanted to kill herself but couldn't because there wasn't a gun lying around. And finally when her mother asked her to live with her, so she could take care of her daughter. Valerie had had a few visitors, including the vice-mayor, who wanted to give her a medal. Even when she felt she didn't really do anything except survive a situation where her partner, half a dozen ESU team members, and two paramedics had died. How could she have survived when so many did not?

Josefina stood up, walked over to her daughter and placed her hands gently on her shoulders. Valerie buried her face in her mother's dress as the tears continued to flow. Joe looked away. He knew this stage of grief and he thought about leaving and coming back some other day, but a slight gesture from Valerie's mother indicated that he should stay, that made him slump back into the sofa.

After a few minutes that seemed like an eternity, Valerie had at last calmed down as she wiped away the tears with her mother's handkerchief. Josefina went back to the kitchen and brought out a plate of baked, sweetened breads with a sugar glaze on top of them. Even in lean times Mama Josefina always prided herself on being able to provide food for the family.

Joe smiled as he shook his hand in a polite refusal when Josefina offered him some of the sweet bread, but then he took a piece anyway after she gave him the evil eye. "Muchas gracias," he said. "So what do you call these kinds of breads anyway?"

"De nada. They are called pan dulce," Josefina said as she sat down on the easy chair once more. "Very popular in Mexico."

"Freshly baked?" Joe said.

"Si, I baked them this morning."

Joe took another bite out of the bread. Thank goodness everybody was calm again. "How did you manage that? I thought all the gas mains in the city were out."

Valerie blew her nose. "When the troubles started, Mama immediately bought two propane gas tanks and had me set them up for her. I think she has enough gas in the stove for a few months, at least."

Joe smiled as he looked at her mother. "Smart, real smart. Did you have an inkling as to what was gonna happen?"

Josefina looked down on the floor. "I had been having dreams for the past few months. Very bad dreams."

"She would call me in the middle of the night," Valerie said. "She was absolutely terrified. I tried to calm her, saying they were just dreams of things that could never happen, but she insisted they were real."

"These dreams of yours, Mrs. Mendoza, did they include the monsters we're seeing on video?" Joe said, leaning forward.

"Yes, I dreamt of the tzitzimitl, and of other gods too," Josefina said. "They have come back from the past and plan on revenge."

Joe furrowed his brow. "Revenge? What do you mean? What are they getting back at us for?"

"Many reasons," Josefina said. "We no longer worship the old gods and they feel disrespected. We have killed many animals and have pillaged the earth—we have grown too numerous and wicked."

Joe sat back and sighed. He had been raised Catholic but forgotten all about it ever since he became a cop. Now it all came back. "Like the book of Genesis and the flood? Because man had grown too evil, too lazy, is that it?"

Valerie looked at him. "Of all the people who would believe this, I thought you'd be the last person who would, Lieutenant."

"For the first few days I didn't believe it," Joe said. "But now with everything that's going on I'm beginning to change my mind. The city council has held meetings with CDC, doctors, psychologists, even brought in military advisors, but nobody can come up with anything that makes any sense. But here I am in your mother's apartment and what she's saying is the only thing that fits the narrative."

"Somebody famous once said 'when you've eliminated the impossible, all that's left must be the truth,' or something like that," Valerie said. "Do you think you could convince the city council and the mayor with this?"

"Well, considering that we're about to lose the city and everything we've tried isn't working, I think I can make a case, but I'll need to talk with Commissioner Donovan about it first," Joe said.

"Donovan?" Valerie said. "You think he's gonna believe all this?"

"He's tough as nails and very practical," Joe said. "He actually made the suggestion for this task force. If I can get some results, then maybe the rest will listen to us."

"There is something else," Josefina said. "From what my daughter told me she found in Baruch House, you will have to deal with a very powerful god."

"What? The pile of skinless corpses?" Joe said. "It must be some sick serial killer cult that's doing this. We shot a lot of them, but we had to get outta there because we couldn't hold the building. It seems there're more and more of them around."

"You are dealing with Xipe Totec," Josefina said. "The Flayed One."

"Xipe what?" Joe said.

"Xipe Totec is the Aztec god of fertility," Valerie said. "Mama used to teach me the old Aztec stories when I was growing up. This god requires human sacrifices and when the priests sacrificed those sacrificial lambs, they flayed them and took their skins to wear them."

Joe shook his head. "That's just sick. What kind of sicko mind would dream of wearing another man's skin?"

"The flaying of the skin represents the symbol of fertility in old Mayan culture," Josefina said. "It is like the casting off of old vegetation in order for new crops to grow. This was extremely important to the ancient people of Mexico. Without abundant crops, they would face starvation. When Xipe Totec needed to be reborn, the skin he wore would dry and crack until it peeled away to reveal his true self, his golden skin."

"They must have had one hell of a way to look at things back then," Joe said. "That kind of reasoning now would land you in prison nowadays, if not shot dead first."

"The ancient Mexica lived in different times and they had different values," Josefina said. "One cannot judge what they did then with the very different set of values we have now."

"So you're saying those skeleton demons are under this Xipe Totec god?" Joe said. "How could we fight against them? What can we do?"

"The gods of the Azteca had their destructive side," Josefina said. "But they could also be beneficial to mankind. Xipe Totec was the god who blessed the crops and would sometimes cure the sick, or he could cause floods and pestilence to others."

"So they can be good or evil then," Joe said. "How can we get them to reveal their good side?"

Josefina wagged a finger at him. "You must find the reason why the gods have returned. You must find a way to please the gods so that they will leave us all in peace once more."

"Where do we start?" Joe said.

"We may need to look at old reports right at the beginning when this whole thing began, any sort of investigations or complaints made by people who we thought were crazy, but who might somehow corroborate what we know now," Valerie said.

Joe looked at her. "Does this mean that you're on the task force now, Detective?"

Valerie nodded. "I owe it to Myron to see this through. He didn't deserve to die like that. And I have to do my part to help fix this city before it's too late."

Joe smiled. "That's great news. We have a new HQ set up over at the

Empire Fulton Ferry dock. We're calling in the National Guard too. You can report in tomorrow morning."

"Tomorrow my ass," Valerie said. "I'm gonna report in tonight. We've got lots of things to cover."

Josefina looked at her daughter. "Remember to keep wearing that talisman, mi hija. It will protect you. These gods cannot be beaten by force, but they can be tricked. I have taught you everything I know, and you must use that knowledge now to help humanity in its darkest hour of need."

17. The Chosen People

Kansas

Steve Van Dyke parked his bright red Chevrolet SUV in front of the ministry building and got out. A fair-haired man in jeans and a checkered shirt walked down the steps and asked for his identification. Steve could see the man had an assault vest over his chest. It contained at least half a dozen spare magazines for the modified AR-15 semi-automatic rifle he had slung over his shoulder. Steve was pretty familiar with the weapon and it was obvious the other guy needed some more training on using it. Steve noticed he had the safety off. The civilian version of the US military's M16 would probably go off and injure an innocent bystander, but since the barrel wasn't pointing at him, and he had yet to speak to the pastor, then he felt it was better to let bygones be bygones, for now anyway.

The man gave him back his driver's license. "Okay, the pastor has been waiting to meet you. It may take awhile though because he's currently taping a broadcast. I'm Art, by the way, head of building security."

"Nice to meet you," Steve said as he looked up at the sky and adjusted the black Stetson on his head. "Can we go inside? I think it's gonna rain again."

"Oh, sorry," Art said as he turned around and began to walk up the steps. "Follow me, I'll take you through the administration block and over to the studios."

After walking up the white steps, they went through a glass double door and entered the lobby. Steve noticed about a dozen armed guards with an assorted range of semi-automatic rifles. But without uniforms, they looked more like a ragtag posse than the supposedly well-trained defense force the pastor had promised him. Each one had a white armband that signified they were part of the Rock of God Church security. Although there was a metal detector situated near the entrance, Art just waived the both of them through by winking at one of the other guards, who was lounging around the folding tables and waved back while sipping on a mug of coffee. *Very sloppy*, Steve thought. They didn't even search him, or pat him down, otherwise they might have found the Glock 26 that he was carrying in a concealable holster near the base of his spine.

As they walked past the main corridor leading to the auditorium, they immediately turned right and began moving into an enclosed glass walkway that served as a connection to the annex building. Steve noticed that there was a hive of activity along the offices located nearby. He could see from the glass windows a dozen huge eighteen-wheeler trucks at the back parking lot. The transports were being unloaded by volunteer staffers, while more armed sentries stood by as they rode on an escalator going up to the second level of the building.

Art slowed his pace so he ended up walking right beside him. "I heard you came up from Dallas. How are things going in Texas?"

Steve just shrugged, he was almost six and a half feet tall and had broad, muscled shoulders from his time as a linebacker in high school. "Some people back there were saying that the fate of the country would be decided along the Texas border with Mexico. So they were trying to get anybody with a gun and a car to go down to the border to try and defend it."

Art glanced at him with obvious concern, but he kept walking. "Is it true about they say?"

"What do they say?"

"Pastor Burnley and the others are saying that Mexico is now the land of Satan. Is it true that nobody knows what's going on down there anymore?"

Steve's demeanor didn't change. "All I know is there's a massive fog and rainstorms covering anything south of the border and no radio communications. Anybody who went down south hasn't come back."

"Did you make your way through Oklahoma? What's the situation over there?"

"I went through Amarillo. All I heard is things might be bad in Oklahoma too."

"That sucks," Art said. "My wife's family is from Oklahoma City. I hope The Lord is doing all he can to protect the good Christians there."

"I thought all the church members had brought their families over here," Steve said as they walked into a large square building, then passed through another set of double doors before heading down a narrow white corridor.

"Her family ain't members of this church, but of another," Art said as they stopped in front of a black metal door that read SILENCE PLEASE above it. "This is where I leave you, just go in through that door and the pastor will meet you after his taping session."

Steve shook his hand once more, then opened the door and walked through. The studio had a high ceiling and he could see catwalks above, along with assorted lighting and huge black curtains that served as background drapery. There were long, thick cables all over the floor as he stepped gingerly around them, while making his way around the front side of the hall. A little bit to his right, he could see the set that was made to look like a cozy living room with sliding doors at the back. It had a green screen as a background further out. Sitting on two ornate chairs that faced three strategically placed studio cameras on wheeled tripods were the hosts of the show. Pastor Erik Burnley and Janet Clancey were alternately addressing each other or talking directly to the cameras.

"And I must pass the message once again to our loyal viewers and listeners of this broadcast. There is no need to fear. God is with you. God feels your pain and he feels your worries. All is not lost, your soul can still be saved. How? By simply embracing the Lord and believing in him with all your heart. Forgiveness is still possible- so don't despair, my friends. Jesus will be coming very, very soon, so now is the time to repent and embrace the will of The Lord," Pastor Erik said into the camera facing him. The pastor was approaching his mid-fifties, but he still looked lean and sun-tanned. Erik was a prominent figure since he was as tall as Steve. He would shave his scalp every morning so he was sometimes nicknamed the bald preacher. He had inherited the ministry from his late father, Pastor Michael Burnley, a former Texas oil millionaire who had found God and moved to Kansas to set up a ministry back in the 1960's. Burnley's little congregation ultimately grew into one of the world's largest megachurches.

Steve looked around. In addition to the video crew, he noticed there was a control room across from where he was; it was accessible by the stairs to the catwalks. He could see the director along with several technicians from behind the glass partition. Standing at the rear of the control room was a portly man dressed in a suit and wearing a white cowboy hat, along with a silver-haired woman in a white dress. Steve instantly recognized him as the Kansas state governor along with his wife. *So it's clear whose side he's on*, Steve thought.

"As far as your closing thoughts for this evening, Pastor, when do you think our Lord Jesus will be coming?" Janet Clancey said to the camera. Steve didn't know her personally, but he had read about her. A former Hollywood actress, Janet was the star of a top-rated situational comedy on national TV, but she gave it all up when she had a religious conversion and soon became the co-host of Pastor Burnley's prime-time religious talk show on his personal network.

"A very good question, Janet," Pastor Erik said to her before turning his gaze to the camera once more. "I cannot tell our audience the exact date of our Lord's return, but I can guarantee it will be any day now. You've all seen it with your own eyes and experienced the horrors of what is happening to the world. This, my friends, is the apocalypse. These are the final days of the Earth, and if you want eternal life, if you want eternal salvation, then the time is now for you to give yourself to The Lord. But you won't be alone, for every good Christian is with you. If you are lost and you need shelter, then come join us here in Kansas. We have room for you to join the Rock of God Church. As I've been telling this to our church members for years, I predicted this would happen."

"That's right," Janet said to him. "Two years ago, you predicted that the apocalypse would come soon, and you urged all of us to prepare for the second coming of The Lord. We even have proof that you said it, and we will be repeating that episode after this broadcast for those of you that still have some doubts about Pastor Erik's message to the world."

"Thank you, Janet," Erik said as he smiled at her. "But I can't take all the credit for this because after all, I am but a messenger for our Lord Jesus Christ, and it is only through Him that we will be saved."

Janet nodded. Steve could see that there were multiple cameras on her as well. "And how prepared is the Rock of God Church for the apocalypse, Pastor?" she said.

Pastor Erik chuckled. "Another good question, Janet. Ever since I gave that speech about the second coming of The Lord all those years ago, our church donations have skyrocketed. We have used these gifts from our loyal members to build the Rock of God Church into an institution that is now functioning as a preparation point for our Lord Jesus's return. We have our stadium right here in McPherson County, right by our headquarters that can house up to two hundred thousand of the faithful. The stadium has an all-weather dome and tents are not a requirement, but some of our more resourceful church members have set up their own. The parking lot around the stadium consists of multiple acres, and we have room for all sorts of cars. And if you want to bring your own RV or camper, then we have facilities to support those too. And don't worry about electricity or food, because we have set up several distribution centers on church property to feed our loyal members. And one of our most gracious members, Governor Lloyd Mallory himself, who happens to be in the studio right now," Pastor Erik said as he waved to the control room before turning to face the camera once more. "Governor Mallory has graciously donated the state's petroleum reserves to our humble facilities, so that we will have ample power for anyone who wishes to join us here."

"So should anyone want to join our church here in Kansas, they really don't need to bring anything with them then?" Janet said to him.

"The only requirement is that they give themselves to God, and to believe with all their hearts in our Lord Jesus Christ, and we will accept them, just as

The Father accepted his prodigal son back to his fold," Pastor Erik said, smiling. "But of course, if anybody brings along transportation, food, tents, blankets, as well as guns and ammo, we will gladly accept those donations because we may need them to help those less fortunate."

"We have a question from some of our viewers about the enemy that we're facing," Janet said as she read off the teleprompter beside one of the cameras facing her. "They're also asking if we ought to listen to the Federal Government and their emergency broadcasts that claim everything is under control, and people should stay where they are."

Almost immediately, Pastor Erik's visage became a serious one as one of the studio cameras made a close-up of his face. "Let there be no mistake that Satan's forces have grown in tremendous power. The Devil is here now: he is in Mexico, in Iraq, in Europe, in China, in New York City, and all those other places where man thought he could live away from God, and from the teachings of our Lord Jesus Christ. This is why I'm asking for anyone who wants to join us to bring their weapons here because we will have need to defend ourselves while we await our Lord. The Federals will not help us because they have thrown away their allegiance to God. They have instead thrown in their lot with the communists, the gays, and the liberals, and they have led many of us astray. They will all be cleansed in fire when The Lord returns. The only one we can depend on is ourselves now, which is why I am asking all good and decent Christians to join us here in Kansas, join us in the final battle because there is no doubt that we will win and ascend back to Heaven with our Lord Jesus. It's a matter of belief, those others in those places I've mentioned have been destroyed because they refused to believe. Proof in what I've said is now all around you, so how can anyone still doubt what I've been saying all along? If you care about your soul, and your family, then you must join us here, it is the only way you can attain salvation. Come to Kansas and join with us now before it is too late."

As the taping ended, Steve watched as the governor walked out of the control room and headed over to Pastor Erik and both men shook hands and gave each other a warm hug. A crewmember nearly bumped into him, as the technician was moving one of the cameras to the rear of the studio as other crewmen began to dismantle the set. Pastor Erik quickly recognized him and walked over, along with the governor.

"Steve, how nice of you to make it," Pastor Erik smiled warmly as he shook Steve's hand. "Might I introduce you to Governor Mallory, of our great state of Kansas."

"Governor Mallory," Steve acknowledged the shorter man as he shook his hand. "It's an honor to meet you."

"Pleasure's mine, son," Governor Mallory said.

"Steve here was a lieutenant in Dallas SWAT," Pastor Erik said. "Let's all go to my office, shall we?"

The walk led them back into the main building through the glass concourse. Governor Mallory's wife had stayed behind so she could chat with Janet Clancey. The three men went ahead and took an elevator to the top floor. Pastor Erik placed his thumb on the biometric scanner on the elevator's control pad, which then gave an affirmative as it brought them up to the penthouse suite.

"Did you just come from Texas, Steve?" Governor Mallory said to him.

"Yes," Steve said as the loud ping indicated that they reached the top floor. "Took me two days to get around the blocked roads and the flooded areas, otherwise I would have been here sooner."

Pastor Erik walked out into the room first. "Lloyd, have you been in contact with Governor Bishop of Texas?"

Governor Mallory stepped out into the carpeted office. His cowboy boots were also white leather. "As you well know, I just came from that big governor's conference in Colorado Springs a few days back, and I've also talked with him on the phone just before the main lines went down. He has his way of doing things and I have mine. That damned fool wants each and every one to volunteer and head to the Texas border to fight the devils and demons in Mexico. Of course, I disagreed with all of that."

As Steve walked into the office, the elevator closed behind him. He saw that the glass walls around the penthouse was unusually thick, that was when he realized that it was bulletproof, the kind of layered glass they used in building embassies overseas in high risk countries. The furniture was mostly tan leather, with numerous couches, oak coffee tables, and padded chairs. Pastor Erik walked around his massive, solid oak office desk and sat down on a high leather chair. Governor Mallory sat on a guest chair opposite him and began to pour himself some whisky that he took from a silver tray sitting on the side of the desk. Steve walked over to them and sat down on the other, identical chair.

Pastor Erik leaned forward and placed his elbows on his desk while clasping his palms together in a triangular gesture. "I've brought Steve over because I would like him to go over our compound security," he said as he looked at the former SWAT operator. "Did you have any other officers in your team that would like to join us here in Kansas, Steve?"

Steve just shook his head. "The only ones left in my squad who didn't go off and join up with prepper groups have gone south towards the border to help defend it. I'm sorry."

"Ah, that's too bad," Pastor Erik said. "We could use more experienced personnel here. What do you think of Art, my head of security?"

Steve smiled. "He's an amateur. I've noticed many things wrong with the perimeter the moment the guards at the gate let me through. Seems most of your security team are either kids or middle-aged family men with guns."

"Well then, I'm putting you in charge of security as of right now," Pastor Erik said. "Do what you need to do in order to keep us secure here."

"Okay, I can implement new security measures ASAP," Steve said. "Do your men have any riot gear?"

Pastor Erik arched an eyebrow. "Riot gear? What in heaven's name for?"

"On my way here, I've noticed that law and order was already breaking down. People were setting up barricades in Wichita, and that's only about twenty-five miles from here. In a few weeks, water and food will become scarce and people may head towards this compound. I've noticed that most of the church's surrounding area is only protected by chain-link fences. It won't be enough," Steve said.

Governor Mallory took out a cigar from his coat pocket, then bit off its rear portion and spat it out onto the ashtray before taking out his solid gold lighter. "I might be able to help with that, son. I've talked to General O'Neill and he'll be giving us access to the armory over at Great Bend. Once he gives me the go-ahead this evening, you can have your men and their trucks over there and take what you need."

Pastor Erik clapped his hands. "Wonderful news, Lloyd! What about the Kansas Guard units themselves, will they be willing to join our growing congregation here?"

"I'm afraid I can't officially do it, Erik," Governor Mallory said as he began puffing on his cigar. "I would get lynched by the rest of the state, and maybe the damned Feds at Homeland Security would try to come here and force me not to, so I would say the best way is to recruit men from the National Guard units individually. O'Neill told me he won't have a problem with that as long as it's all done under the table. Heck, he could barely call up half of the men at this point since everybody's deserting anyway. It will take some time, but you ought to be having some ex-guardsmen with tanks and choppers here soon enough- the loyal ones to the church anyway. My office is coordinating with them so just be patient and give me a few days on it."

Pastor Erik was clearly in a good mood. "Wonderful, wonderful! I can't believe this is all going according to plan. I had a vision about the coming apocalypse years ago, you know, and I took steps to prepare for this eventuality. I steadily bought up most of the land in this county, fenced it off so now we have farmland with which to grow crops, just in case The Lord's return is delayed. My men took control of the local oil refinery just two days ago, so that means we have plenty of power for our private electrical grid and fuel for our vehicles."

Governor Mallory chuckled. "Don't forget that damned water treatment plant you secretly built."

Steve was surprised. "Water treatment plant?"

Pastor Erik winked at him. "That's right, Steve, while you were away from the congregation and settled in Dallas, I had a water facility built at the west of the main compound. I also secretly acquired the rights to the refined petroleum storage facility in Conway, since it's less than a mile away. If our Lord Jesus Christ decides to come back in six months, or even a year from now, then we will still be here, waiting for him. Now, why didn't you bring your wife with you?"

Steve looked down. "I'm sorry about that, Pastor. I tried to make my marriage work with Tammy, but no matter how hard I tried, she just blocked me off."

"Don't be so hard on yourself," Pastor Erik said. "When you wrote to me and said you were going to keep working as a cop in Dallas, did you keep tabs on them? Perhaps we may be able to get them and bring them here so that they can join you."

"Thanks for the offer, Pastor, but it's a lost cause," Steve said. "She took the children with her to Oregon and joined one of those New Age Satanic religions they practice over there. They're all damned in my eyes now and I consider them lost to me permanently."

"Ah, well too bad for them then, their souls will be burning in Hell very soon I expect," Pastor Erik said. "We have plenty of room for you here, Steve, so I'll fix you up with a suite in the adjoining apartment complex we've recently built here in the compound. Unless of course, you'd like to join up with Governor Mallory here and his family over at the bunker."

"Bunker?" Steve said.

"That's right, son," Governor Mallory laughed again. "While Erik here loves living in his penthouse suites, me and my wife prefer the safety of the underground bunker located two levels underneath this same building. It was built to withstand a nuke attack, if I recall."

Pastor Erik beamed with pride. "Yes, it was. Several layers of reinforced concrete, with additional seams of sand and gravel between them. This was the time when the church board had voted to make a bomb shelter since they thought, and wrongly I must add, that it would be Muslim terrorists that would threaten us here in the future. But as it stands now, I proved them wrong."

"How many more people are you expecting to come and join the church here, Pastor?" Steve said.

"Well, let's see," Pastor Erik said. "We've had about seventy thousand active members before this apocalypse started, and as of yesterday's count that number has more than doubled to about one hundred fifty thousand by now, and I expect more to be coming."

Governor Mallory kept puffing on his cigar. "Do you think we're going to have the facilities available if say, a million people started coming over?"

"Area-wise we have the land since the church property is several hundred square miles," Pastor Erik said. "Long term food supply may be a problem for that many people, but I believe The Lord will be coming any day now, so I don't think it will be a long-term problem."

"Any word from the other churches?" Steve said.

Pastor Erik leaned back on his chair and crossed his arms. "Well, Joel Ostermann over at Blackwood church in Houston, and his seventy thousand followers wanted to join up with us here, but I still remembered that silly remark he made about me in one of his sermons on TBN so I told him no."

"Which sermon was that?" Governor Mallory said.

"He was saying that I was some sort of false prophet of doom because I kept talking about the coming apocalypse in one of my sermons on JBN a few years back. He didn't say my name on air of course, but I'm sure he was referring to me," Pastor Erik said.

Governor Mallory giggled a little. "Come on, Erik, can't you find it in your heart to forgive the man? I mean, it's not every day that your prophecies are proven right and his proven wrong."

Pastor Erik shook his head. "His flock is too big, they could end up being a threat to us. Besides, I'm so sick and tired of him and the others who preached about the prosperity gospel and all that. If there is a false prophet, it's him and the others. I don't want them tainting the followers of our church because we're the one true church of The Lord. Not even the Vatican can say no to that. I never preached about material gain as God's reward, every time I ever asked for a donation was to help build this compound for the coming return of our Lord. Those other churches won't make it either. Pretty soon, I'm sure we will be the one and only vanguard for The Lord's return."

Governor Mallory threw his arms up in a mock gesture of surrender. "Okay, all I was suggesting was that we could use his money to get more stuff for our church is all."

"Money's now a secondary need," Pastor Erik said. "What we need are guns and foodstuff, lots of 'em."

"We should have all the weapons we need once we can access the armory," Steve said.

Governor Mallory smiled. "Well, son, I can even get you artillery, nothing like a howitzer cannon to wake your friends up in the morning."

Steve adjusted his Stetson. "Well, we won't need that right away, just maybe the riot gear, as well as a few APCs and helicopters ought to do for now."

Governor Mallory winked at him. "You'll have it by tonight, son. I guarantee it."

"We've got about close to fifty thousand church members with guns," Pastor Erik said with obvious pride. "That pretty much means we're a small army. With armored vehicles and helicopters, even the Feds will think twice about whether they want to mess with us or not."

Governor Mallory tilted his cowboy hat upwards so a portion of his balding forehead showed. "Erik, my office has updated me that you will soon have at least a regiment of National Guard troops at your disposal, so don't worry, everything is going well."

"So far so good then," Pastor Erik said. "Everything is falling into place. All we have to do now is to wait for our Lord's return, and he will deliver us from this broken world we call earth. Eternal life in Heaven must be so sweet and I could just taste it right now. My father said just as he was on his deathbed that he saw a glimpse of paradise, it was like a blissful garden with a flowing breeze and eternal sunshine, where one could hear chirping birds and the soft chime of the wind. And then he died. I can't wait to see him again once this is all over and done with."

Governor Mallory chuckled. "Amen."

18. State of the Union

When the small convoy of unmarked SUVs finally pulled in front of an inauspicious country club, Dr. Paul Dane had hoped that this would be the final stop for awhile. He had been whisked away onto an aircraft carrier after narrowly escaping from the battle of London just two days ago. Paul was quickly put in the rear seat of an F\A-18 Super Hornet, flown over the Atlantic, and back into US territory in record time. The Navy pilot of the aircraft had flown using afterburners at supersonic speed and refused to travel in a straight line, always using evasive maneuvering that put both a tremendous strain on Paul's chest, as well as nearly making him throw up in his oxygen mask. The one respite he had during the whole flight was when the pilot finally flew straight and steady during the air to air refueling with a Boeing KC-46 Pegasus tanker over the mid-Atlantic. When they finally landed at the Naval Station in Norfolk, Paul promptly vomited out the half cup of coffee they gave him when he got onto the carrier, just a few hours before.

"This way, sir," a six-foot four-inch black Marine sergeant in full combat gear who was sitting beside him in the vehicle said as the cars stopped. The Marine got out of the passenger door of the SUV and motioned at Paul to follow him.

The rains had continued incessantly and it looked like the country club was closed from the outside. They had passed through the heavily-guarded front gate and into the long, inner road, then onwards to the roofed driveway leading to the front of the main building. As Paul got out, he had been briefed that most of the southern states were completely inundated by flooding. New Orleans was in the process of evacuation, as well as some other coastal cities below sea level, but the levees all across the country had already been broken and a great many people were presumed dead.

Military people at the naval station had given Paul a pair of Navy Working Uniforms with which to wear, but he declined, preferring to keep wearing his old blue sport coat and heavily used walking shoes. He did however buy a new white dress shirt, socks, and a pair of khaki trousers at the Navy Exchange. The other pair of pants was torn and moist with sweat and he had to throw them away. As Paul stood beside the SUV, he stretched his back out for a bit and then followed the sergeant into the main lobby.

It was a hive of activity. Paul was shocked as he could see heavily-armed military personnel equipped with M4 carbines and M240 machineguns all over the place. There were also members of Congress milling around the crowded foyer. Whatever was going on, it was involving the entire US government. Paul clutched at the stack of notes he had been carrying, ever since they gave him some time to look at the latest intelligence reports coming from all over the world. He had spent hours in debriefing rooms, talking to military and civilian survivors of disasters that had happened both in Europe and in the continental US. At first he thought he was in some strange nightmare, but after seeing the dreaded Fomorians up close in London, Paul knew that this was a new reality that had to be accepted. The alternative would be nothing short of madness.

An Air Force captain walked up to him. She was tall and pale, with her short, auburn hair carefully held down underneath her cap and offered her hand. He noticed that she had a pistol strapped to her hip holster. "Professor Dane? I'm Captain Laura Niven. I'll be your AFISRA military liaison from now on."

Paul adjusted his newly-issued glasses as he shook her hand. He had lost his original pair at Stonehenge and was lucky enough to get to an optometrist at the naval station in time. "I'm sorry, Captain, AFISRA? I'm not familiar with that word."

"It's short for Air Force Intelligence, Surveillance and Reconnaissance Agency," Captain Niven said. "You have been assigned to the Department of Defense, and my duty is to work closely with you on gathering intel while you help with drafting contingency plans against the enemy."

Paul shook his head and made a nervous laugh. "I'm sorry, but I'm a civilian, how could I be in the DOD now?"

Captain Niven looked him straight in the eye. It wasn't a joke to her. "By Executive Order. Martial Law has been declared and your country needs you. You'll need to prepare for a briefing so I need you to come with me, right now."

Paul nodded and began to follow her. There was an open door that led to a large service corridor, and he walked in after she showed her ID to a group of men in suits carrying Heckler & Koch MP5 submachineguns who were standing by the entrance. After looking at Paul's newly issued ID, they gave him a thorough body search with metal detectors and then allowed him to pass through. Going through a largely deserted kitchen, Paul was stunned to notice that part of the wall had been opened, which revealed a hidden blast door made of solid steel at least six inches thick. As he continued to walk behind her, he realized that this so-called country club was just a front for what now was obviously a hidden bunker for the US government.

Paul quickened his pace until he was just behind her. "Excuse me, I'm supposed to give a briefing? As to what exactly and when?"

Captain Niven kept up her brisk walk and didn't even turn to look at him. "You are to brief the JCS, UCC, and the president on the nature of the enemy and their capabilities, as well as any contingencies on how to deal with them." She looked at her watch. "That briefing should start as soon as we get into the room in a few minutes' time."

"What? I'm supposed to brief the president now? I don't even know where to start!" Paul protested. "I don't even know what the JCS or UCC is."

"Joint Chiefs of Staff, as well as the Unified Combatant Commands, specifically USNORTHCOM or US Northern Command," Captain Niven said. "NORTHCOM's mission is to protect the homeland from the threats we are facing now with all US military and civilian forces at its disposal."

"Look, I've been flown over the Atlantic and I've barely had any sleep. I've been reading reports and interviewing survivors for the past few days, and I still don't know what this is all about," Paul said as they turned into another corridor. "I'm a mythology professor, for crissakes." He didn't tell her that he really didn't want to sleep either, because of the recurring nightmares and visions that haunted him every time he closed his eyes.

Captain Niven finally turned to face him as she stopped in front of a white-painted double door. "At this point, you know more than we do. You had two supernatural encounters in the UK, and you're the only one qualified to make this briefing, and to answer questions from both the government and the military."

Paul sighed. "Okay, but even what I know may not be enough."

She turned, then knocked twice and the door was opened outwards by two men in suits. As they were ushered in, Paul noticed that the center of the large room was dominated by a long table of dark oak wood. All around it sat the most powerful people in the world as they faced a large video monitor that nearly covered the opposite wall. The former vice president had just been recently sworn in; he was now the de-facto leader of a battered country that was once the most powerful nation on earth. Sitting to his right was the Secretary of Defense. The Speaker of the House was but two chairs away. Paul realized that the men in suits were undoubtedly from the Secret Service to protect the new President of the United States, one of them pointed to two empty chairs along the side of the wall. Captain Niven and Paul quickly sat down on them as most of the people sitting on the table continued to look at the incoming video feeds which detailed the latest reports.

As he quickly went over the stack of papers he carried for a last minute review, Paul glanced over at the president. It had been only a few days when Air Force One and his predecessor went down with all hands lost. Less than a quarter of the American people had actually seen his televised oath of office since there were very few television and radio stations left that were still operational. Paul could see that the past few days had literally aged him, he looked tired and emaciated, his silvery hair hung limply on the top of his head. All of the military people sitting in the table were wearing battle fatigues, not a single one was in dress uniform, and every one of them had a pistol strapped to his hip. The nation was clearly at war. With whom, Paul wasn't so sure.

"Everybody here?" the president said after glancing in Paul's direction. "Let's get this thing underway."

"Very well, Mr. President," Admiral Charles Zimmerman, the commanding officer of NORTHCOM said. "We'll start with Major Cochran from INSCOM. He will update us on the current sitrep."

An Army officer who had been sitting beside Paul instantly stood up and walked to the front of the video monitor, as he too carried a stack of reports.

Paul whispered into Captain Niven's ear. "What's INSCOM mean?"

"US Army Intelligence and Security Command," she said to him in a very low voice.

Major Cochran cleared his throat as he stood in front of them. "Mr. President, our situation is currently precarious. I'll start with our borders: Canada is essentially snowed under by the strange weather phenomena that has engulfed Northern Europe. It's like an ice age up in the north just a few hundred miles away from us."

The president lightly tapped the table and turned to his left. "John, how are we with accommodating the Canadian government?"

John Smalley, the president's Chief of Staff, coughed before answering. "At present, Prime Minister Archer, his family and his staff, are currently staying at the Greenbrier. We are in the process of renovating it since it was turned into a museum. That was after we abandoned it when the press found out that it had a government bunker back in the Sixties, but it will take months for obvious reasons. They aren't complaining at this point."

"Just as well," the president said. "Most of his country is in a snowstorm and the ones who could get down here know it isn't any better. What about the rest of Congress?"

"Most of Congress, their families, and staff are at the underground bunker in Raven Rock Mountain Complex," the Speaker of the House said. "There's a few senators and congressmen who don't want to leave Washington DC, so to hell with 'em. I'll be heading over to Mount Weather as soon as we've finished here and coordinate with you once you get to NORAD. With three separate locations, continuity of government will be maintained."

"We're not even sure if we can maintain landline communications that far away," John Smalley said before turning to look at Major Cochran. "What is the sitrep in regards to our communications?"

"I'm afraid it's not good, sir," Major Cochran said. "We have no contact with our orbital satellites, and the floods and adverse weather have severely damaged our telecommunications infrastructure. Even our FM radios aren't reliable due to unknown interference. The only way we can get communications through some of our agencies and bases is through direct courier."

The president shook his head in frustration. "Goddamn it, what is the situation with our nuclear silos?"

"We only have a few hundred nuclear warheads in fixed silos when this whole war began, sir," Major Cochran said. "With the exception of the base in Kings Bay, Georgia, we are still in contact with the others, sir. The silos in Bangor, Malmstrom, and Minot are inoperable due to the snowstorm, sir."

"What's the situation in Georgia?" the president said.

"Mostly it's the weather, sir," Major Cochran said. "We can't get any constant lines of communication so we sent some military units down there. We're still waiting for updates. NORTHCOM has given orders to evacuate most of the military bases in the affected areas of the South, but the going is slow."

"Goddamn it," the president said as he turned to look at Admiral Zimmerman. "Make that your first priority. We've got to make sure all our nukes are under control."

"I've already given out the orders to maintain communications with all SAC bases at all cost, Mr. President," Admiral Zimmerman said. "Just give me a few days."

The president just nodded. There wasn't much point in getting angry since he knew that everybody was trying their best. "What about Mexico and our southern border with them?"

"General Montelo was sent in with US Army South to establish a buffer zone in northern Mexico. We lost contact with them two days ago and the massive rainstorms in that area now seem to be right up near our borders as of today," Admiral Zimmerman said.

"Jesus Christ," the Secretary of Defense said. "So we've lost an entire army corps now?"

"What are the estimated casualties for our entire military so far?" the president said.

Major Cochran took a quick look at his notes before answering. "We can't get a definitive number at this point, sir. But if we are to assume that our overseas forces that have been cut off as ineffective or labeled as MIA, then I would say about close to around five hundred thousand total, and that includes casualties within the continental United States, sir."

Admiral Zimmerman looked away. The other generals and admirals of the Joint Chiefs began to murmur. The losses to the US military was catastrophic and a historic first.

The president raised his hand and signaled everyone to quiet down. "Okay, we can talk about this among ourselves later. Anything else we have on the border, Major?"

Major Cochran bit his lip before responding. "Governor Bishop of Texas is at the border and he's personally commanding our units down there, in direct contravention of our Federal chain of command. He has also managed to convince the governors of New Mexico, Arizona and California to start marshalling their own National Guard units and commit them to their own respective southern borders with Mexico. There's been talk of those states openly seceding from the union."

The murmurings among the senior officers began again while the president just shook his head in total disbelief.

"Who's in command of the Texas National Guard down there?" the Defense Secretary said.

"Major General Len Williams," Admiral Zimmerman said. "He's been telling his men not to obey the governor's orders until he gets approval from NORTHCOM and the Executive Branch of the Federal Government. His men have low morale and there's plenty of confused messages coming in from both sides."

"Tell him to take orders only from us and to disregard any directives from the governor, is that clear?" the president said. "Same goes for all Guard units and reserve forces we have in those states. Under no circumstances are any of the commanders of those units to obey orders from any of the governors until NORTHCOM's say so. I want to place all military units in the country under federal service as of now."

"Yes, Mr. President," Admiral Zimmerman said tersely.

"What about the coastline?" the Secretary of Defense said.

"Most of our naval assets in the continental United States are in their respective ports, with the exception of the Theodore Roosevelt carrier group that's in the southern edge of the Celtic Sea. They are overseeing the evacuation of our forces from Europe, but they will withdraw tomorrow due to sightings of ghost ships that have been approaching them. The Nimitz battlegroup is withdrawing from the Sea of Japan because of sightings of sea creatures in the area and is heading back to the Pacific coast. Most of our submarines have returned to base, but we have lost contact with about eleven of them while they were at sea, nine attack subs and two Ohio-class ballistic missile boats. As you well know, we have not deployed any new naval task forces due to the fact that we lost two aircraft carriers for as of yet unexplained reasons," Major Cochran said.

"What are the rumors about what happened to the Reagan and Bush carrier groups?" the president said.

"It's all unconfirmed, but a mile-high tidal wave formed in the mid-Atlantic right where the George HW Bush task force was and pretty much capsized most of the ships in that fleet," Admiral Zimmerman said. "We still don't know what happened to the USS Ronald Reagan though some of the survivors of that carrier group are claiming they were attacked by a gigantic sea serpent in the Pacific near the Korean coast. I just can't believe those reports."

The Secretary of Defense pounded his fist on the table. "Those were our two newest carriers too!"

"There have been numerous unconfirmed sightings of gigantic sea creatures and other strange phenomena on all major oceans," Major Cochran said. "Not to mention sightings of antique ships manned by creatures that the British encountered in London just before all communications with them was lost. The UK government in exile is currently at their embassy in Washington DC, though they are only a skeleton crew since their prime minister and most of his cabinet ware holed up somewhere in Falsane. That was when we last heard from them two days ago."

"What's the status of the evacuation of all US forces overseas?" the president said. It was a recognized fact now that the whole world knew that the United States was withdrawing all of its military forces back to North America.

"Very slow," Admiral Zimmerman said. "We've been concentrating on getting the troops back first and the heavy equipment in later. We can't airlift them out in large numbers due to the fact that we keep losing a huge amount of aircraft every single day. Those monster birds that brought down Air Force One have extended their range out to the coasts, and every single military aircraft now has orders to avoid and evade those things at all cost. Our air transports are vulnerable as hell. All we can do is get our troops on ships, but like the previous report said, our boats are getting sunk as well, so we're withdrawing them too. If you want to commit more carrier groups out to sea, I would advise against it at this time until we know what exactly it is that we're dealing with."

"So you're saying our troops overseas are trapped until further notice?" the president said.

"I'm afraid so, Mr. President," Admiral Zimmerman said.

"Goddammit," the president said. "What's the situation in the Middle East?"

"No change, sir," Major Cochran said. "Most of Iraq is pretty much lost. The Saudis are begging for aid. We have reports that the Iranian government is facing both an internal revolt from its own people as well as the unknown, external threat coming from Iraq. Turkey has lost most of its southern border. They are urgently requesting assistance from all NATO members but it looks like we will lose them too. Israel has approached us about the possibility to help evacuate their citizens, but we do not have any available assets to even consider that. Our troops in Afghanistan and Pakistan have been cut off, and we have not heard from our commanders there in days. Something is happening in Egypt as well that may be similar to the situation in Iraq, but since worldwide communications are down, we are only getting in second-hand information, most of it unconfirmed rumors. Needless to say, we've lost contact with most of our embassies overseas. The ones that we are in contact with have been ordered to evacuate immediately."

A four-star Marine general of the Joint Chiefs raised his hand. "Going back to NORTHCOM for a minute here, are there situations in any of the other states that require urgent attention?"

"New York City is becoming an acute problem, sir," Major Cochran said. "The mayor and the governor have begun the evacuation of Manhattan Island. They're saying that some sort of killer cult has taken over that part of the city, but so far it's unconfirmed. Most of our northern states bordering Canada have been hit by massive snowstorms and blizzards, cutting off most the people and our bases there. The Canadian refugees trying to head south have compounded the problem. The other states in the Midwest are in some form of anarchy as quite a lot of people are demanding food and water supplies. Most of the country's electrical grid has been destroyed, and a number of anti-government militia groups have sprung up all over the place. With Hoover Dam gone, there was a chain reaction and almost every town that was along the Colorado River has been flooded over. California and the West Coast are largely cut off west of the Rocky Mountains. Provo River has also been flooded due to massive rainstorms sweeping that part of Utah. Las Vegas has no power or water and we are getting reports of large scale rioting and starvation over there. Also, we are receiving reports of large scale desertion from police and emergency services from all states. Military desertions are at an all-time high as well. The calling up of all military reserves has been met by numerous delays because of this as well as the near complete destruction of our national transportation and telecommunications infrastructure."

A number of sighs and groans emanated from the people sitting by the table. Everyone realized it, but nobody wanted to admit it. The United States was slowly being torn apart.

Major Cochran continued. "Due to communications being down, and the withdrawal of our naval assets, EUCOM and AFRICOM have been cut off from our chain of command because they are based in Germany. Most of our troops over there have not reported in. The few survivors that we evacuated and debriefed have told us of some sort of ghosts and monsters running rampant in the major cities as well as heavy fog that is obscuring long range visibility. We are trying to consolidate the remaining Combatant Commands into NORTHCOM here in Virginia, but it will take time."

"How secure are we here in Virginia right now?" the president said as everyone quieted down again.

"US Army North is still in the process of reorganizing and reforming. It will take another few weeks, Mr. President," Major Cochran said. "There are numerous problems of getting the National Guard and Army Reserve units to full strength. Also, we have had numerous reports of supposed ghosts and demons in the Virginia area as well as in other parts of the continental United States. We've lost contact with a number of military bases and units stationed in just about every state. Unit commanders reported encountering some sort of devil, or giant, or spirit and then we never hear from them or their unit again. We've had similar reports from state police departments saying the exact same thing. We've obtained video and sound footage from a number of these encounters and we are still evaluating as to whether the evidence we have is real or not."

"Good lord," a four-star US Army general said. "Where the hell are our front lines?"

"At this stage, sir, we have no idea if there are any safe areas within the country, or for the rest of the world. We are still assessing the situation," Major Cochran said. "It is best to assume that we are vulnerable from all sides and we recommend setting up a three hundred sixty-degree defensive perimeter for every installation and location that we still have under our control."

"We've lost our overseas allies, we're under siege by an unknown enemy or enemies, and we don't have a clue as to what's going on," the Secretary of Defense said. "Gentlemen, unless we do something, then we are about to lose America."

Now the murmurings around the table were getting louder. An Air Force general began to openly pray while another Army general started shouting and cursing to no one in particular. Major Cochran looked down on the carpeted floor, then walked back to the chair by the side of the wall and glumly sat down. John Smalley got up, walked over until he was behind the president and began to whisper something in his ear. Paul was still going over his notes when he felt a tap on his arm from Captain Niven, who indicated that he needed to get ready. The president pounded on the table with his fists and the commotion rapidly subsided as John Smalley walked back to his chair and sat down.

"Alright, enough of that!" the president said. "This isn't getting us anywhere. I've been given word that we have an additional briefing from someone who might have first-hand knowledge of what exactly is going on. John, can you introduce this man to us?"

"Thank you, Mr. President," John Smalley said as he looked at Paul. "Professor Dane, could you please go up, front and center, and brief us as to what you've experienced?"

Paul bit his lip, got up and walked up to the front of the video monitor. "Mr. President, gentlemen, and ladies," he said while briefly glancing at Captain Niven, who maintained her rock-like composure. "My name is Paul Dane, I'm a professor of anthropology at Harvard."

"A mythology professor, what in the hell?" the Air Force general who was previously praying said.

"Pipe down and let him talk, goddamnit!" Admiral Zimmerman hissed.

Paul cleared his throat. "Most of you, if not all of you, will probably find what I am about to say hard to believe, but from everything that has happened, it seems that the unthinkable has come true. I just came back from London a few days ago where I witnessed an attack on a modern day city by an army of mythical creatures. I've interviewed over two dozen survivors, both civilian and military, from attacks that have occurred here in the United

States, and I have seen countless video footage of some very different creatures in the area, but they were also thought to be mythical in nature."

"So what are these things?" the president said.

"They are mythological gods and creatures of ancient civilizations that once inhabited the earth," Paul said. "It seems that the myths that have been handed down to us were not imaginary at all, these ancient legends were in fact, real and the gods and demons depicted in these stories are actually in existence."

The entire room was silent. One could hear a pin drop if not for the low static noise emanating from the video monitor and the slight hum of the ventilation system.

"Wait, are you talking about the old Norse gods like Thor, and Odin, and the Greek gods like Zeus?" Admiral Zimmerman said.

"Although we have no confirmation that any of the deities from the Norse or Greek pantheons have been sighted yet, a number of gods from other parts of the world have revealed themselves," Paul said. "I saw with my own eyes the Fomorians, which are demonic creatures from Celtic mythology, devastate London. I barely got out of there with my life and a number of people died getting me back here."

"So what kind of gods are we dealing with in Mexico then?" the president said.

"It seems highly likely that we are encountering gods and demons from Aztec myths and they are coming up north," Paul said. "The Aztecs worship some very malevolent gods, from Huitzilopochtli, Tezcatlipoca and Tlaloc, these gods we would consider highly evil and destructive in our modern day views of morality due to the fact that they demanded human sacrifices in order to be satiated."

An Army general began chuckling in disbelief. "Wait, are you expecting us to perform human sacrifice in order to prevent them from invading the United States?"

"No," Paul said brusquely. "What I am saying is that we have to find a way to send them back to whatever other dimension or afterlife that they came from. There must be a reason why they appeared just now, we need to find what that reason is."

"What about the monster birds that took down Air Force One, are those things Aztec as well?" the president said.

"They are from Native American mythology and are called thunderbirds. We had thought that these creatures were dreamt up by Native Americans as an explanation as to where the sound of thunder came from," Paul said.

"Okay then, how do we kill it?" the Secretary of Defense said. "We've sent in our Raptor, Viper, and Eagle squadrons against those things and we've lost all of our aircraft and most of our pilots. Heck, our drone fleet is pretty much useless. What about nukes?"

"I don't think you can kill them," Paul said. "Mythical creatures cannot be fought by ordinary weapons."

"So you're saying is then we're as good as dead?" Admiral Zimmerman said. "We've no chance against any of these gods and creatures?"

"No, I'm not saying that," Paul said. "We need to develop a plan to find their weaknesses and deal with these things."

"If these gods are real, then where the hell is our god, the Lord Jesus Christ?" the Air Force general said. "Shouldn't he be coming back to save us from these devils?"

"Either he hasn't appeared yet or perhaps it was the Abrahamic god that was the imaginary one," Paul said.

John Smalley sighed. "So you're saying we've been worshipping the wrong god all this time?"

Paul tried his best to keep composure. "There is that possibility, yes."

The president looked at him closely. "Professor Dane, do you have any suggestions as to what we do now?"

Paul let out a deep breath. "First of all, we need to find out and identify which of the gods and supernatural creatures we know of has appeared and are walking the earth. Since there are hundreds, maybe even thousands, of ancient gods and creatures that we know about, then we need to establish a database of what they are and where they are. Then, we will need to know just what is the extent of what their capabilities are, and what their intentions will be for us. Also, we will need a team of scholars and researchers who can find out whether these gods have the exact same power and behavior as they do in these ancient stories."

The president looked at John Smalley. "John, I want you to give Professor Dane every resource and asset that he needs to get this team up and running as quickly as possible. Also add him and his liaison as part of the National Security Staff, effective immediately." Then he turned his attention back to Paul. "Make sure you prioritize these Aztec and American Indian gods first on your list, Professor. Now, assuming you're able to get this done then what is the next step?"

"For every evil god that was depicted, there were also benevolent gods and creatures that helped mankind as well," Paul said. "We need to find these so-called 'good gods' and perhaps make them our allies to help us fight off their evil counterparts. There were also a number of mortal men and women who were able to outwit and sometimes defeat the evil gods and monsters and they were called heroes. Since these mythical gods and monsters apparently exist, then perhaps these so-called heroes might be around as well?"

19. Devil's Advocate

Beersheba

It was just after lunch when his distant Uncle Ariel called him up and said that he would be dropping by for a visit, so David Zim was able to make a quick trip to the nearby store and bought a box of baklavas. When he got back to the house, he washed the dirty dishes in the sink and placed them in the cupboard before preparing the freshly ground coffee. David's wife Tzipi had wanted to meet their old uncle, but she had to be back at the university for an emergency staff meeting. So by the time he got there, she just kissed her husband goodbye, and left Ariel a note instead. As he looked at his watch, David knew that the drive from Jerusalem to his place would take about an hour and a half under normal circumstances, but he knew there wasn't much traffic these days. He still had some time to relax so he sat down on the sofa. The afternoon sun cast yellow shafts of light past the open windows, and into the cream-colored living room.

Almost immediately, he heard a car pull up in the street below. David quickly got up and walked over to the front door and opened it. Peering outside, he saw a white Toyota sedan parked along the side of the street. As he walked down the steps, he saw his Uncle Ariel being helped out by a younger man who was obviously his driver. Short and stocky, with a balding scalp and a silvery beard, dressed in a white short-sleeved shirt and grey slacks, Ariel Weizman was already pushing seventy. But he still had an appetite for good food and pastries, hence the reason why David had made a last minute purchase for some snacks to go with the coffee, since he normally didn't eat any sweets.

"Uncle Ariel, shalom," David said as he ran up to the old man and shook his hand.

"Shalom, David," Ariel said as he closed the car door behind him. "Is your lovely wife here?"

David smiled and gave him the note. "I'm sorry, Uncle Ariel, she had just left because they needed her back at the university."

"Ah, just as well," Ariel said as he put the note in his shirt pocket. "It's you I wanted to talk to anyway. You're not too busy are you?"

"Not right now," David said as he put his hands into the front pockets of his royal blue slacks. "In fact, I've been waiting for the call up these last two days, but I've heard nothing. All my other colleagues have already been deployed, but I'm still here."

Ariel winked at him. "That's partly my doing. I need you to go with me."

"Oh, do we have time for coffee?" David said to him and looked at the younger man too. "I've got a freshly brewed pitcher in the house along with some baklava."

Ariel chuckled. "Ah, you still know my weakness. Okay, let's go upstairs," he said before turning to face the younger man. "Ory, you stay here. You can have your refreshments when we leave in awhile."

"No problem, sir," the younger man said as he leaned on the hood of the car while taking out a pack of cigarettes.

David helped him upstairs so Ariel didn't need to use his walking cane. As the old man sat down on the sofa, David brought out a tray with the promised baklava, then started pouring two cups of steaming black java that had a hint of cardamom. By the time David had sat down, his uncle had already eaten two pieces of pastry and was munching on a third.

David smiled as he began to sip his coffee. "Too much of that will give you diabetes, Uncle."

Ariel took a break from the baklava and started on the coffee as well. "At my age, diabetes is the least of my worries. Are you still keeping in shape?"

"You know we do, Uncle. My unit requires that even when I'm not on assignment. There's an apartment block nearby that's ten stories. I run up and down the stairwell every day," he said. David was part of the Mossad, Israel's feared national intelligence agency. After serving in the military, he was recruited as he was taking advanced classes in Ben-Gurion University. It was at the college where he also met his future wife Tzipi. Although they had been trying hard to have children for the past four years, luck was against them so far.

"That is good. With the way things are going we will need everyone in shape."

David placed his cup down onto the coffee table. "Is it really that bad? What happened in the Knesset today?"

Ariel sighed and leaned back on the couch. He had been a government minister for as long as David knew him. "Oh, you know, the usual infighting and arguing. With all the kvetching we have, it's a surprise we ever get anything done there these days. The truth is, we won't have anyone to depend on but ourselves. Israel will always have to fight her own battles, I've told them that over and over again."

"So the Americans won't help us then?"

"The Americans have their own problems. They have lost most of their overseas troops and they have taken a beating in their homeland as well," Ariel said. "In fact, they are asking us for help— they have requested that if we come across any American soldier or civilian that we help them to get back to the US, as if we even could. The prime minister has tasked the government to see if we could make an emergency evacuation by sea if our northern border is threatened."

"I don't think we have enough naval assets for a seaborne evacuation of all Israeli citizens," David said. "Even if we did, where would we be going to?"

Ariel shook his head. "That's what I told them, but they wouldn't listen. We could be looking at a second exodus, David. We may have to initiate a second Jewish Diaspora as our people will live among gentiles once more. An even worse case scenario is we end up as captives of a resurgent Babylon. I would have never thought this was possible just a few days ago. Now, it feels that the tide of history has once again turned against us. We fought so hard to have a land that is finally ours and now it seems it was all for nothing."

"Yes, it is bad. The Palestinians are in full revolt. The call up for reserves is almost complete yet I'm still here, waiting for orders. All my other colleagues are either in Jordan or in the West Bank. I want to do something, Uncle."

Ariel took another piece of baklava from the box. He knew it was bad for him, but he always had a habit of eating more in times of stress. "I was born three years before Yom Ha'atzmaut, our day of independence. That was when the entire Arab world rose up against us. But I was too young to remember the details, other than hiding along with the other children in a special room somewhere in the kibbutz where I was born in when they would attack. During the time of the Six Day War, I was a young man who fought with the paratroopers when we finally recaptured Jerusalem. All that is now a distant memory now when compared to this enormous threat we are facing. Tell me, David, have you heard of the term devil's advocate?"

"I have heard of the phrase. I know it means adopting a contrarian position."

"Have you heard of it within intelligence circles at all?"

David thought about it for a minute, then he shook his head. "No, why?"

Ariel sipped on more coffee in order to moisten his lips. "Let me tell you a story. After the Six Day War, we thought we were unbeatable. Israel knocked out the Arab nations we fought against so quickly, we thought that there was very little threat to us in the future, and we were permanently secure. Then Yom Kippur happened six years later. The Egyptians had caught us by surprise so by the time we started mobilizing, it was too late. As you well know, we normally fight by attacking the enemy first, destroying their offensive firepower before they could be brought to bear against our tiny nation. During the Yom Kippur War, we were unable to do it and we took a lot of casualties. We came very close to defeat in that war, David. Two of my brothers died and I still miss them terribly to this day. We were able to overcome the enemy but at great cost. After that war, there was a full reassessment of our intelligence agencies and it was found that we relied too much on majority consensus and groupthink. Therefore, we needed to reorganize AMAN, the IDF's military intelligence agency, in order to prevent overreliance on one-sided intelligence gathering and analysis. We therefore created a devil's advocate division within AMAN. They were a special unit and they were specifically tasked with to provide a counterpoint, a contrary position in order to have a different opinion so that every and any possibility would be considered, not just those belonging to the majority. Do you understand that?"

David's eyes had widened. "I do indeed, Uncle. So this means that even remote possibilities to our intelligence reports would be considered and not just thrown away into a rubbish pile then?"

"Exactly," Ariel said. "When reports started to come in with regards to what was happening in Iraq and in other places, our devil's advocate team in AMAN proposed a radical intelligence report on the type of enemy we will be facing soon."

"From just reading reports in the Institute, I can hardly believe what they have been saying," David said. "Many people in my office just cannot believe it either. The old gods have returned? Can you believe that, Uncle?"

"I can tell you that AMAN now believes it. They didn't at first, of course, but the constant flow of information has apparently proved the devil's advocate team right and we are now implementing their proposals," Ariel said as he leaned on his cane and started to get up. "We need to go now. I've got something to show you."

As the car drove out of Beersheba and headed southeast towards the small city of Dimona, David sat in the backseat beside Ariel and started reading the latest reports, just as Ory kept his eyes on the mostly deserted highway. Israel was a small country and most of its citizens were called up by the military and deployed to the borders, so there were very few cars left still driving around. It took them less than fifteen minutes to arrive in front of a walled compound manned by armed IDF soldiers. After showing their identifications, they were let through past a reinforced metal gate with a machinegun emplacement. The car then drove into a covered driveway in front of what looked like an old factory building.

Ory stopped the car and helped his uncle out. David kept holding the stack of reports in his hand as he got out of the other side of the vehicle. "What is this place, Uncle Ariel?" he said.

Ariel walked up to the front of the building as he led with his cane as Ory stayed by the car. "You'll see, come on and follow me," the old man said.

Although he let his uncle lead the way, the old man was so slow that David was able to walk slowly beside him. "These reports are saying that the Babylonian gods now rule over Iraq and are heading southwards. If the US military couldn't stop them, what chance do we have?"

"You'll see," Ariel said as they started walking along a bare corridor. "Have you heard of the name Khaled Hadawi?"

"Of course," David said. "Who hasn't? Hadawi has been all over the news for years and even more so now. He is the famous Palestinian sculptor, known worldwide for his art even though most Muslims frown on it. But the latest news is that the Palestinians say he was kidnapped by us and of course we are denying those reports."

Ariel kept a straight face while he walked slowly. "The reports are true. We did take him," he said.

David arched his eyebrows in confusion. "What? Why would we want to kidnap an artist for? Hadawi isn't a radical."

Ariel stopped in front of a metallic double door. There was a strong, earthy smell coming from it. "We didn't exactly kidnap him. We asked him if he could help us. Since Muslims frown on idolatry, we had to tell him the real reason for it and so in the end he agreed … sort of," he said before pointing at the door. "Go ahead, open it."

David pushed at the double doors and they gave way. As he looked out into the main hall he gasped. For a few minutes he just stood there, not sure if what he was seeing was real. Finally, he walked through the open doorway and started to look closer at what they were creating.

All around him were gigantic clay statues. Almost twenty feet tall, they looked vaguely humanoid in shape, with large heads attached directly onto broad shoulders. They had long, ape-like arms extending almost to the floor and short legs ending in stubby feet. They looked like huge gorillas made out of reddish clay. Around a dozen sculptors seemed to be working on the more detailed aspects of the clay statues while a number of workers with plastic buckets were either applying more clay on the unfinished parts, or were keeping the statues moist by spray hosing them with water. David noticed that there were giant humidifiers attached to the ceiling and there were elevated walkways above the main floor, with fully-armed IDF soldiers wandering about.

Ariel walked up beside him. "Well, what do you think about the plan that our devil's advocate team proposed?"

David turned to look at him with wild, surprised eyes. "You- you're creating golems."

Ariel smiled faintly. "I knew you would recognize them. After all, you did attend a graduate course in anthropology over at Harvard all those years ago. If I recall, your instructor was the great Professor Paul Dane."

"I heard he was last seen in Stonehenge before England was overrun. He is probably dead by now."

Ariel smirked. "Oh no. Not dead. He made it out of London and is now back in America, I believe. Now you can see why we have redeployed your colleagues in Mossad for other missions but we kept you waiting until now- you are the one who is qualified for special tasks such as these. Tell me, from your studies, what do you know about golems?"

David turned back to look at the statues once more. "They are creatures made from clay and magically given life. Tradition states that they are the mythical protectors of the Jewish people. According to the Talmud, Adam, the first man, was created from clay and was nothing more than a robot until God breathed a soul into him. Golems are unable to speak and can only be commanded by their master."

"Very good, David," Ariel said. "When I talked to your katsa in the Mossad, your case officer said you were the one who could deal with this since you're one of the few in the Institute that has intimate knowledge of anthropology. This is in addition to your skills as a field agent. No one outside of the prime minister and select members of the Knesset, the IDF special division and the Mossad know about this project. With the public focused on events at our borders and the Palestinians, then we have a chance to keep this project under wraps until we are ready to deploy our own supernatural soldiers to fight the mystical forces that threaten Israel."

David turned back to look at his uncle again. "But how can you even get this to work? Assuming that our enemies are truly paranormal in nature, how can you animate these golems? Without some sort of divine guarantee or some help from God, then these statues will be nothing more than lumps of red clay."

"We have someone knowledgeable to guide us," Ariel said. "From what he showed us, we believed we are on the right track."

"But who?" David said as he once again turned back to look at the golems and began to walk closer to them. As he started to walk among the workmen, he noticed that one sculptor in particular was putting up the finishing touches on one of the completed golems near the back of the hall. As he moved closer, the sculptor turned around and gazed at him with tired and pitiful eyes.

David took one long look at him and gasped. It was Khaled Hadawi. The Palestinian artist had a metal chain clamped around his ankle and the other end of it was bolted down to the floor. The old man was unkempt, dressed in muddy overalls and looked exhausted. It looked like he could barely stand as his trembling hands clutched at his clay modeling tools. David reached out to him and the old man fell into his arms.

Ariel sighed in disappointment and began to limp slowly towards them. "David, let him go. He has work to do."

"Please, help me," Khaled begged as he could barely hold onto David's shoulders.

"Uncle," David said as he supported Khaled in his arms while looking at Ariel. "This is wrong! He is being held here and it's clear he is being worked to death, he must be freed and he must get some rest."

A booming voice was heard above, where the walkway was. "You there! Get away from him! Guards, separate those two!"

Two IDF soldiers quickly came over and took Khaled away. David tried to stop them but a third soldier got in between them and drew his pistol. Ariel pushed himself to walk a bit faster until he got to David and led him away as the soldiers unchained Khaled, then they carried him into a side door and out of sight. The other workmen continued on as if nothing had happened.

Ariel kept a hold of David's arm. "What are you doing? Do not interfere."

David was trembling with rage. "We cannot be doing this. This is illegal!"

The voice above them shouted once more. "Silence! You are nothing more than a guest here. If you do not behave, you will be thrown out!"

David looked up and for the third time today, his eyes widened with surprise. Standing above them on the upper walkway was a man he didn't think he would ever see in public again. Rabbi Elijah Ba'al was a truly controversial figure, he was once a very influential member of the Chief Rabbinate of Israel, the supreme authority for Judaism in the country, until he was forced out because of his radical views about the Talmud. Rabbi Ba'al had been accused of heresy and was officially censured via herem, he was excluded from the Jewish rabbinic community by way of being shunned and ignored. For twenty years it was rumored that he had begun to gather his own followers, but no one in mainstream Judaism paid him any attention and he had drifted away from the public eye. Now he was here and obviously in charge.

The two men watched him slowly walk down the metal stairs and onto the ground floor as he turned and started moving towards them. The rabbi was wearing a white robe and underneath that he wore a black coat and trousers, his jet black yarmulke was on the top of his head. Tall and stocky, with a large, puffin nose, fiery red beard with streaks of silver, oval spectacles and a perpetual grim visage, Rabbi Ba'al looked like he just stepped out of an ancient temple, his tzitzit dangling out of his front trouser pocket. David could see that he had huge hands, like that of a bricklayer.

Rabbi Ba'al walked right up to them and pointed a stubby finger. "Ariel, who is this man, and why is he disrupting my project? Can you both not see that the country is about to be invaded and what I am doing is the only thing that can save us? How dare you come in here and do this!"

David was beet red with rage. "You are keeping a man here against his will. You illegally kidnapped him! Don't you know he is one of the reasons why the Palestinians in the West Bank are rioting right now?"

"The only time I could care about an Arab is when they are useful to me," Rabbi Ba'al said. "In this case, he is useful to Israel too. He is a very good sculptor. Without him, we would be so far behind this whole project would have been delayed for weeks. We don't have that kind of time."

David sneered. "You're nothing but a heretic and a fraud. I do not believe you can even animate these clay statues. The Knesset may believe your lies, but I don't."

Ariel tightened his grip on the younger man's arm. "David, please. The rabbi has a plan. We we're given a demonstration of it. I know you are upset but you need to control your temper. This is not the time to go on a morality crusade. Israel's existence is in the balance. We will deal with the ethical consequences in the future."

David looked at his uncle. "What demonstration? Can't you see that this man is nothing but a fraud? He is deceiving you all!"

Rabbi Ba'al glared at him. "Fool! Despite all that's happening in the world you still refuse to believe. Very well, follow me." With that, the rabbi quickly turned around and started to walk towards a large door at the opposite side of the hall from where they came in. The two men followed behind him.

As they got in front of the door, Rabbi Ba'al took out a set of keys from underneath his robe and unlocked the entrance. As he swung the door open, he bade the two men to go inside. David took his uncle's arm and led him in. The interior was a smaller room that looked like a laboratory with the exception of a large fire pit at its center. At the center of the smoldering crater of ash, there was apparently a transparent glass jar that was about two feet high and something was stirring inside of it. As David got closer he began to notice that there was some sort of creature inside and it was moving as it acknowledged his presence. For the fourth time that day, David's eyes widened with shock and surprise. Inside the glass jar was a being that looked like a miniature man, it had a head, a pair of arms and legs and it had a face. But the creature had the features of a misshapen dwarf, one eye was bigger than the other, stunted legs, a curved spine and it had a hole where the nose should have been. Completely pale and hairless, it was no more than a foot tall and snarled at him with sharp, crooked teeth.

David recoiled in horror. "T-that's a homunculus! You created a homunculus!"

The rabbi had closed the door behind them and had walked over with Ariel standing beside him. "This was the demonstration I made with select members of the Knesset and AMAN. I was disgraced by the Rabbinical councils years ago, but I have proven that my readings of the Kabbalah and my teachings are the truth. I shall be the one to save Israel and the Jewish people."

David shook his head. A part of him still couldn't accept it. "How? How were you able to create such a thing?"

"Ten years ago, I had found a clue as to where to find the original copy of the Sefer Yetzirah," Rabbi Ba'al said. "My followers searched for a long time to pinpoint its location until we finally stumbled upon it by mere chance. It was in the possession of an old Arab antiquarian in Egypt and he did not want to part with it, saying that it was part of his family's legacy to safeguard its contents. So myself and two of my most trusted assistants broke into his house one night to try and get it. He caught us in the act and I had to kill him."

David grimaced. "So you admit to murder then? And the other name for the Sefer Yetzirah is the Book of Creation, a very common book on Jewish mysticism that can be found in many libraries. You killed someone just to steal a stupid book that's already widely published."

Rabbi Ba'al bellowed in anger. "Wrong! My copy of the Book of Creation is the original one. It contains many chapters on magic that was removed by succeeding generations of foolish scholars in an attempt to suppress its true power! But that wisdom is not lost anymore for I now have the knowledge to create golems to protect the Holy Land from the pagan gods who seek to destroy it and its people."

"How were you able to animate the homunculus?" David said.

Rabbi Ba'al walked over to the edge of the fire pit. The homunculus became agitated and was trying to get out of the glass container, but it couldn't. "I used bits of dead flesh and molded it before infusing it with the soul of a criminal. The government allowed me the use of Palestinian prisoners as experimental subjects, so I was able to get plenty of practice."

David turned to look at his uncle. "This is madness, surely you can see that? This man will bring ruin to Israel."

Ariel stared back at him. "The Defense Committee along with the prime minister has approved his project. The forces against our country are so powerful that we now realize that the IDF has no chance against it. We either go with Rabbi Ba'al's plan or we face a second genocide of the Jewish people. This must be done."

David turned away. "I-I cannot in good conscience be a part of this. This is black magic. It's evil and goes against the teachings of God and Judaism."

"Again you are wrong," Rabbi Ba'al said to him. "What I am doing was suppressed by our ancestors, but I am bringing the full power of our faith to safeguard us. We are God's chosen people and he gave us the means to defend ourselves through this."

Ariel walked over to the younger man and placed a hand on his shoulder. "David, we need you. Your country needs you. The prime minister and I agreed that you are the one qualified operative that can lead a mission for the sake of the survival of our country. If you're not going to do it for yourself, then at least think of Tzipi, do you want her to die when the pagan gods invade Israel?"

David looked down on the floor. It was all too much. But he loved his wife as well and he couldn't bear the thought of failing to protect her. "What do you want me to do?"

"I need you to find a man for me," Rabbi Ba'al said. "I had doubts he ever existed, but with the events that have been happening, there is a fair chance now that he does because the Book of Creation told me so."

"AMAN and Mossad have been working round the clock to pinpoint his location," Ariel said. "He may either be in the Sinai or the Saudi Arabian desert. If he is in the former, then it should be very easy to find him. If he is in the latter, we will provide you with a full team of operatives to support you, David."

David looked up and sighed. "Who is this man?"

"Legend calls him the eternal man, the man who never dies," Rabbi Ba'al said. "He has the knowledge of creation because he was there when the old gods were still young. My studies of the book reveal he is a needed component in the creation of the golems. Without him, we will not have a chance. You must find him and bring him to Israel at all costs."

Ariel said nothing as he glanced at his distant nephew. He was hoping that the younger man would make the right decision.

"I will do it. But not for you. I am going on this mission only because my wife and my country are in mortal danger. Otherwise, I would make sure you go to prison for murder," David said as he stared at the rabbi. "I have read stories of the golem and you seem to have overlooked one very important thing."

Rabbi Ba'al sneered at him. "And what pray tell, would that be?"

David couldn't even hate him anymore. All he saw now was a misguided, delusional man. "Every golem story ends the same way: the creature always turns against its master."

20. The Magus

Upper Manhattan

Just as Elliot Ledwidge began to stir the cream of mushroom soup in the little red pot on the stove with a rubber spatula, the lights in the kitchen began to flicker and dim for a few seconds before returning back to normal. For a moment, Elliot did nothing as his momentary fright froze him in place, until he realized that the soup was starting to burn, so he quickly turned off the gas and breathed a sigh of relief.

After carefully placing the steaming pot on the marble countertop, Elliot quickly dashed over to the electrical panel beside the barricaded front door. He took a look at the readings of the standby generator that was located on the roof. As he looked the fuel indicators, he made a few quick calculations. He estimated that the generator was now running on the second and final liquid propane tank that had been installed a few years back. The gas cylinder had been recently serviced only a few months ago. That meant that there was about seventy-two hours of electrical power left, maybe more if he kept up the rationing like he did when this whole incident started. Putting the bad thoughts back from the present, Elliot returned to the kitchen and poured the mushroom soup into a ceramic bowl, then placed it on a tray. Opening a cupboard, he took out an airtight plastic container and removed the top from it, then took out some soda crackers from their wrappings and placed them on a little plate beside the bowl of soup. Elliot took out a chilled plastic bottle from the refrigerator and poured some filtered water into a fist-sized glass and placed it on the tray as well. After putting the water back in the refrigerator, he opened the taps on the sink. Still no running water and it had been like that for three days now. It looked like the dirty dishes would have to wait a little bit more. Based on what he heard on the battery-powered radio, he was surprised the tap had run out just recently. Both Elliot and his master had been trapped in this penthouse for over a week already. When would the promised emergency services teams finally come by and rescue them? Oh well, either way he would be with his master until the end.

Elliot was intensely loyal to him. That was why the master had chosen him over all the other aspiring candidates. Unlike the others, Elliot wasn't married, and that probably played a factor in the master's decision to make him and only him as his personal manservant. He wasn't married because Elliot just didn't like women. In fact, he really didn't like men either. What he really liked were little girls because they were so angelic, so pure. And his liking of them had put him in prison where he served out his sentence in silent anonymity for more than eleven years. A year after his release, Elliot had been drifting in and out of menial jobs with no future and no friends. That was until he met the master. He had tried to join the Freemason Guild in New York City, but was rejected because of his criminal background. So he drifted on and away, going from one town to the next, living day to day with no purpose, until an old friend from one of the mystical groups he used to frequent introduced him to the master. Since the master was currently looking for a new manservant to replace his elderly valet who had recently passed away, Elliot begged and cajoled his way to an interview. The master would require someone who would be devoted to his needs for twenty-four hours, seven days a week. There would be no holidays and no rewards, only a silent acknowledgement for the honor of having served him. Of course, if he was chosen, then Elliot would be given perks: free room and board, free food, and a nice salary that was deposited into a trust fund and would only be available to him if he was too weak or infirm to serve any longer. Since he had nowhere to go, and with no ties to anyone because his mother had passed away when he was still in prison, Elliot was chosen and he wholeheartedly accepted. Now, twenty years later, he was still around, dutifully serving the master.

As he placed a hand-knit cloth napkin on the tray, Elliot shuddered as he heard a sudden blast of thunder outside. Days before, he had boarded up the windows of the apartment after seeing ghostly figures in the park below. *Better to close oneself off than to have to face reality such as that*, he thought. He was not much of a spiritual man, the reason he was drawn towards the occult had more to do with the rituals, the fascinating symbols, and the people he met more than anything else. But the events that had happened in the past two weeks disturbed him. The master, however, seemed supremely confident that everything was happening according to plan, what that plan was Elliot had no idea, but he had faith in his superior. Just days before the rains started, the master had ordered Elliot to make sure that the backup power generator was sufficiently fueled and serviced by a technician. He also told Elliot to purchase enough food and bottled water for the both of them to last for a month. The delivery guy who came upstairs to bring in the goods wondered if they were preppers or something. *But if that person was still alive today he would no doubt be envying the master's meticulous plans for survival*, he thought.

Elliot walked slowly towards the inner chambers as he carried along the tray. How he had wished to be able to go out and buy some fresh vegetables. All they had left in the penthouse was either canned or frozen peas, carrots, and fruit cocktail, but he dared not venture out of their sanctum. Only a few nights ago, he had heard screaming coming from the front door which led to the outside corridor and the loud banging on it, which he ignored until it went silent once more. The master's directives had ordered him to move the wooden six-foot tall dresser from his room and be pushed up as a barricade against the front door. He did just that, so he figured that no one would bother them while they go about their business now. In order to preserve fuel for the generator, he dragged the mattress from his bedroom out into the corridor and slept there; the only places he had kept the lights on were in the kitchen, the corridor, and of course, the master's chambers.

Just as he was about to knock on the inner door, he had suddenly remembered that he needed to be quiet and so he tried the door knob. It opened with a slight squeak so he pushed the door forward a little, just so that he could see a bit of the inside of the anteroom in case the master was there.

He wasn't. The anteroom was a sort of smaller waiting room that had another door at the opposite side which led to the master's main chamber. There was an oval table in the middle, with a couple of matching chairs. All around the walls were bookshelves lined with ancient, arcane tomes. Carefully placing the tray onto the black wood table, he noticed that the day's previous plate of food that he left behind hadn't been touched. He had thought that he might go and open the inner door and take a peek to see if the master was well, but he had thought better of it and decided not to. His strict orders were never to disturb him if the inner door was ever closed. The only time Elliot had done so was eight years ago, when he had heard a loud thud as he was cleaning the anteroom and he had thought that the master had fallen and needed help. When he burst in, he ended up interrupting one of the master's rituals involving the sacrifice of a small dog and he had to apologize profusely. For the next several days after that, the master had stopped speaking to him and Elliot cried himself to sleep for the next few months, thinking that he would soon be dismissed from his duties and shamed forever. But in the end, the master forgave him but had warned him never to do it again. There was utter silence in the room now and Elliot had thought the master was asleep, so he carefully placed the previous day's plate of food back onto the tray and silently walked out, carefully closing the door behind him.

The main chamber was a high-ceilinged bedroom that had been converted into both a private study and an occult workshop. Like the anteroom, most of the walls were lined with bookshelves, overflowing with all sorts of rare and forgotten manuscripts as well as a few ancient scrolls. The windows of the room once held an excellent view of Central Park down below but due to recent events, it had been haphazardly boarded up with panels of plywood. Beside the window was a narrow wooden pallet with a thin mattress on it which served as a bed. The whole place smelled of dusty old paper combined with the pungent sweat of old men and incense.

He sat cross legged and was facing a small alcove, to the right of the door. The niche along the wall once held a small statue of Pan, the Greek god of the wild, but it had been removed and placed in storage years ago. Now the alcove was empty, save for a three-foot-wide pentagram engraved with gold and lead on its floor. An incense burner was suspended by a chain link embedded in the ceiling hung just above the recess as the smoke wafted down, which gave the five-pointed star engraving on the floor a hazy outline. The master had been meditating for days on end now, only getting up to eat a small meal and having a drink of water at the adjoining room before returning to his ritual once more.

Although Elliot called him the master, to everyone else he was Seth Solomon. He had been born to a wealthy family of bankers during the time of the Great Depression, and he was now the last of his line. As an only son, he was given everything he wanted. His father had spent the dwindling family fortunes to make sure his heir received the proper education befitting a man of his class. But it all changed when his father was diagnosed with cancer and he had summoned his son to his deathbed. As Solomon looked on in sadness and horror, his father's bony hand clutched at his arm and told him how scared he was of dying. His father was once a giant of a man and now, lying in the bed was a shrunken, skeletal derelict that had begun to breathe his last. Solomon then heard a loud clap in the room when his father finally died despite the fact that it was only the two of them there. That experience opened his senses to the supernatural. It was then that he made a promise to himself, that he would do everything he could to stave off death.

Since he had been the only child, Solomon and his team of lawyers maneuvered and manipulated the law to make sure that his mother was kept out of what was left of his father's fortune. His mother was soon shipped off to a cheap nursing home, where she died penniless and forgotten a few years later. Using the proceeds of his inheritance, Solomon embarked on a worldwide scholarly research for all things esoteric and arcane, to find the secrets of mastering death. Solomon had tried them all. As a teenager, he had met Crowley, who had once been called the Great Beast, as the old English occultist was already dying from the complications of his heroin addiction. Solomon had been able to receive basic instructions on Thelema just before the old prophet finally succumbed to the ravages of time. Later on, he even dabbled in LaVeyan Satanism for a few years, until he realized that it was nothing more than a sham designed to get its practitioners laid more than anything else. Solomon had also a few spent months with Castaneda, learning all he could about the Tensegrity movement, before ultimately dismissing it as made up nonsense. His most promising experience however, was with a group of shadowy occultists of the Temple while he was in Germany. Through them he was able to piece together clues which had led him to the find of an immensely powerful artifact. Soon, he was able to discern the location of the seal of King Solomon, a purported magical ring that was worn by his namesake.

As he continued to stare into the misty emptiness of the alcove, Solomon subconsciously rubbed the brass ring on his right hand and remembered the people that he had to kill in order to get it. He was an old man now, and he knew there wasn't much time left. But the being had already come once before, just a few weeks ago, and had warned him of the coming tide of destruction that humanity was to face. It was a very short conversation, but it had proven to him that there was indeed another world out there, a place where the spirits and demons that had been thought as nothing more than superstitious nonsense, were all indeed real. All of his sacrifices, all of his efforts, all had been vindicated in the end, and the thought of it gave him renewed energy. Now he needed to take the next step and commune with the being once more, in order to finally unlock the secrets of life and death. He was so close now, a lifetime of exertion was now focused on this one goal, and not even the monsters waiting outside of the door would stop him.

It had been hours since he had gotten up to take a drink of water. Solomon had already lost feeling in both of his legs, but he kept at it, silently chanting the incantations over and over to evoke the being that had revealed itself to him but a few days ago. He had not slept for several days now, but his will kept his eyes open like slits as he continued to stare into the misty alcove. His lips moved silently while he rocked back and forth in order to put some circulation in his deadened legs and feet. His black robes had already been soiled when he could no longer hold his bladder, but he needed to keep up with the ritual as he kept telling himself to chant just one more time, just one more incantation, and the being will come again, it had to come.

For an unknown length of time, Solomon continued his silent invocation until the pain of keeping his eyes open finally made him blink several times, until he ultimately kept them closed and he soon began to drift into a restful slumber.

"Solomon."

Almost immediately, he opened his eyes. It was the voice. The voice of the being. He remembered the tone and the accent. It was like listening to a million chattering insects all at once. A small, mist-like figure began to form in the alcove.

"Solomon."

Solomon licked his dry lips. His voice was a croak. "Yes. I am here. I have been chanting for weeks now and I am weak. Very weak."

"I had other tasks that needed to be done before conversing with you again."

Solomon felt his body revitalized with renewed energy. "I have questions. I need answers, and I need them right now."

The misty figure in the alcove began to coalesce. "Of questions that you have, of answers I cannot promise."

Solomon shifted his hands so that the ring was prominently seen. "I must know! Can you give me renewed life? I am an old man, near death, and I must have more life!"

The being now had the features of an ordinary man as he stood over Solomon. He looked very average in his dark suit, like a Wall Street banker on his way to work. "Of these things, all have a price."

"Name the price then," Solomon said. "You want my soul or something?"

The being laughed. "We already have that."

"What then?"

"More souls, more essences."

"I have given you five souls over my lifetime," Solomon said. "Isn't that enough for five lives?"

"The five requires one more, I like even numerologies."

Solomon thought about it for a second. "Very well, I shall give you a sixth life."

"Then with the sixth life paid, you shall be lent six more years," the spirit said.

"Fine," Solomon said. "Now I will also need protection, I need to get out of here."

"You ask an additional bargain."

"Yes, of course!" Solomon hissed. "What is the point of giving me six more years if the creatures out there will end up destroying me anyway? I need you to protect me from those things."

"An additional bargain requires an additional payment."

"What more do you want, another soul?"

"The ones outside require a service of a different kind, for they are of a different pantheon."

Solomon arched his silver eyebrows. "Those creatures outside, they are not with you?"

"There are many factions in this war. If you want my protection, then I must bargain with them not to harm you."

Solomon pursed his lips. "From what I heard on the radio, the creatures out there are of the Aztec pantheon then? Are they minions of Xipe Totec, the Flayed God?"

The spirit simply smiled. "Tricksters take many forms."

"What does that mean?"

"I shall say no more," the man said. "Lest I anger him, and the Hidden One makes war upon me."

Solomon narrowed his eyes. There was more to this than he was being led to believe. "Very well then, what is the price for the other bargain?"

"There is … a relic that you must retrieve and bring to the sacred place."

"What kind of relic?"

"The god inside the tree."

"What?"

The being began to fidget. "Go to the ancient collection and retrieve the god inside the tree. Bring it to the sacrifice, and commit it to the altar. Once that is done, the Hidden One will grant you safe passage out of the city."

Solomon took mental notes of what the being said. "Very well, I shall do this. Once the task is done and I give you the sixth life, I would like to make another bargain, this time for power. I want to rule a part of this world as a king."

The figure began to fade into the hazy mist. "One bargain is agreed upon by me and another agreed upon the Hidden One. Fulfill these bargains firstly and then we shall see...."

Solomon held out a restraining hand. "Wait, I still have more questions!"

"Remember ... both bargains." With that, the being faded into nothingness as the alcove stood empty once more.

Solomon slumped onto the floor. He was exhausted, weak, and hungry, but his mind was racing. He needed to solve the riddles spoken by the demon and he needed to do it now. There was no time for rest. After spending a few minutes catching his breath, Solomon willed himself to stand up and barely succeeded, his knees were wobbling and nearly buckled as he leaned on the side of the wall for support. Limping into the bathroom, he threw off his soiled robes and began to wash himself using the pail of tepid water that had been left there by his manservant since the water mains had stopped working days ago.

A few minutes later, there was a shout that came from the anteroom. "Elliot, get in here!"

Elliot had actually been listening by the door when he heard the master begin to shout, but he wondered who he was talking to since Solomon was obviously all alone in his inner chambers. Quickly getting up from his chair by the door, Elliot immediately straightened his tie to make sure he was presentable, and then he gently turned the lock and peered in.

The master was dressed in a black suit. Although it was clear he was emaciated, Solomon sat down and began to swallow mouthfuls of the cold soup that was sitting on the table. He was hungry and needed fuel. "Move the dresser out of the way from the front door, we're going out," he said.

"Yes, master," Elliot said as he turned around and walked up to the dresser and started to pull it backwards.

"Get me some more food first, I'm famished," Solomon shouted from the anteroom. "And clean my bathroom before we go out, it's filthy!"

21. The Thousand Steps

New Mexico

They had made it as far as the small, deserted town of Wagon Mound using Interstate-25. That was when Josh Haggard saw the highway underpass had collapsed on itself. The nearby stream had turned into a raging river of mud, which meant that they would have to find an alternate route to get to Kansas. The former Arizona police detective silently cursed as he turned the van eastwards towards the Las Mesas de Conjelon, a small mountain overlooking the town. They headed towards the Kiowa National Grassland, a huge expanse of prairie once protected by the US Government. Josh hated this van since it belonged to Larry Hanley, the ex-convict he killed the night before. But then again, he didn't really have much choice since his own car had broken down, and he was holding up in the very motel that Larry and this runaway girl had decided to stay at for the night. It was only when the lights came on that Josh had realized that someone else was in the motel. Whoever it was knew how to start up the emergency generator, so he sneaked around and bided his time to find out. By God's grace he was able to intervene in time to prevent a crime in progress. Larry had wanted to rape this girl he found, but Josh had put a stop to it, then he dispensed his own brand of justice to make sure the perpetrator would never stray from the law again.

Tara Weiss sat at her customary place on the front passenger seat with the little Chihuahua curled up in her lap. She barely slept that night after seeing

Josh beat Larry to death. When she asked the former cop if she could just please leave, he said go right ahead, but the dog was his to keep. Since she had grown to love the little animal and she knew its secret, Tara felt a sense of obligation to protect it. So she went ahead and climbed aboard the van after Josh woke her up. He told her she could go with him to Kansas to join up with the Rock of God Church, or just stay behind. The dog seemed to shake its head slightly when she told Josh she might as well tag along. She wasn't sure whether it was approving her choice or warning her to get away before it was too late. As Tara looked out of the side window of the van and stared at the blunt peak of the mountain they passed by, she realized it was her only choice.

They had spent all afternoon trying to maneuver along the Canadian river, it had once been a small desert stream running across the road through the grassland, but now they saw that it had flooded the small road in front of them. Josh couldn't tell how deep it was, but if he pushed on, the van would have to go through about forty yards of flooded road before it could get to the dry part of the highway on the other side. The only other alternative was to go off road, north through the prairie, but without any road to guide them, or make another long detour southwards to Santa Rosa and hope that the swollen river ended there. But to go southwards would mean a detour of at least fifty miles, and Josh doubted the van would have any fuel left for it so he bit his lip, turned the steering wheel left and proceeded to go off road through the prairie grasslands.

After a couple of hours, night had fallen. Tara was bouncing up and down on the front seat as the van continued to barrel through the plains. The evening sky was clear and she saw the full moon shining brightly overhead. Josh was going parallel along the river's edge, hoping he could find a shallow section of the waterway so he could turn the van eastwards and drive through, but so far all he could see was the flooded banks along its side. As her hand grabbed onto the handlebar on top of the side window to keep herself steady, Tara noticed an orange glint to the west, turning that way she noticed that it looked like somebody had made a small bonfire a few hundred yards away from them.

"Look, there's some people over there," Tara said as she thrust out her left arm and pointed.

"Huh?" Josh said as he turned and looked to his left as he kept his foot on the accelerator.

At that moment the van's right front wheel hit a small depression that was hidden in the tall grass of the prairie. The sudden bump and Josh's overcompensation of the steering wheel instantly tipped the van over on its side, as its forward momentum made it slide down into the edges of the muddy riverbank. Josh let out a curse while Tara screamed as everything in the cabin tilted ninety degrees to the right. By the time it was over, the driver's side door had opened where the vehicle roof was supposed to be and Josh climbed out. Tara called for help, but he ignored her as he jumped down into the ground and took a look around.

Tara unbuckled her seatbelt and saw the dog running around the side of the van that was now the bottom. She scooped it up with one arm and then climbed out through the driver's side. "You could have helped me, you know," she said to Josh as she got down beside him.

His one-handed backslap to her face sent her reeling into the ground. The dog started barking at him but soon quieted down when Josh half turned and placed his hand on the holstered pistol on the side of his belt.

Tara let out a few tears as she wiped the blood from her lower lip with her right wrist, but she stayed down. "What'd you do that for?"

"That's for distracting me while I was driving. See what you made me do? Now the van's tipped over."

Tara tried to blink the tears away. "I-I'm sorry, I didn't mean to."

"Just shut up and let me think," Josh said as he walked away.

Tara sat up and looked down at the twilit grass. The little Chihuahua ran over and curled itself on her lap while licking her hand.

Josh could see the moisture in his breath as he sighed loudly with his mouth. Great, now they were stranded in the middle of nowhere. Even with the little bimbo's help, he doubted he could right the vehicle with just the two of them. As he stared out into the night, he noticed the bonfire a few hundred yards away. *There must be people over there, but what kind?* he thought. Would they be able to help or were they bandits who would try to steal their supplies? Either way he needed to find out.

After a few minutes, Tara noticed Josh walking back towards her. Expecting another slap, she tensed her shoulders and avoided eye contact, but the former police detective just walked right past her and got to the rear door of the van. As he opened it, she noticed he took out his Remington 870 pump-action shotgun, the one with the flashlight attached, and then closed the van up again.

As Josh walked up alongside of her, he also did a brass check on his Glock pistol to make sure there was a round in the chamber. "Come on," he said as he passed her by.

Tara got up, picked up the dog and cradled it in her arms and followed. She walked silently behind him as they both made a beeline for the bonfire. When they got closer they both saw that it was a group of American Indians huddled by the fire. They looked like an extended family with about a half-dozen male adults, three old women, and a child that looked to be about eight. The men were mostly old, their silvery hair glittered in the moonlight. What looked like a grandmother was stirring a small pot by the fire. They had dark wool blankets wrapped around themselves as they sat and stared at the flames. When Josh came into view they hardly noticed him.

"Howdy," Josh said as he stood a few feet away from the bonfire and faced them. "What are you people doing over here?"

None of them made eye contact. Tara walked up until she was a few feet beside Josh. She could see their wrinkled brown faces were given an orange hue by the reflection of the firelight. Either they ignored him or they didn't speak any English, but she couldn't believe the latter since this was America.

"Hey," Josh said, his voice rising. "I'm talking to you folks. No habla English?"

"Maybe we ought to just leave them alone, Detective?" Tara said.

Josh glared at her. "Shut up, I'll do the talking around here."

Tara looked away from him. She didn't want any more trouble.

Josh turned and looked at them again. "Now, I'm gonna say this once more. What are you people doing over here? This is Federal land."

The youngest man in the group, he looked to be about thirty, Josh reckoned, spoke up but didn't make eye contact as he kept poking the crackling bonfire with a stick. "Mister, why don't you just go and leave us alone."

"First of all, I'm a cop and you all look like illegal squatters here," Josh said as he cradled the shotgun so it pointed sideways, out into the night, even though his finger was close to the trigger. Within a split-second he could get into a firing position if any of them gave him any trouble. "Second of all, I'm gonna need your help as my van got overturned down by the river a few hundred yards away. Now, what tribe are you folks?"

"Navajo," an old man said as he adjusted his blanket and kept close to the fire.

Josh nodded sarcastically. "Navajo. That's great. Okay then, here's my deal, I will overlook your squatting and vagrancy in this here park, as long as you boys help me out and get my van upturned. Deal?"

Nobody answered. From the corner of her eye, Tara noticed the small child huddled behind one of the women and they looked at each other as the little boy smiled at her. Tara wasn't sure if it was the bonfire or the moonlight, but it looked like the boy's eyes were glowing in the dark when they made eye contact. Even though she was confused by what that meant, she instinctively smiled back.

Josh's patience had run out. He quickly spread his legs so he was properly balanced as he began to point the shotgun in their direction, but not to anyone in particular. "Okay, now I'm ordering you all to get up. You're all going with me and you'll do your share to right my car. Is that clear?"

Nobody moved. Tara held her breath because she knew what he was capable of.

Josh's left hand racked the slide pump as he chambered a 12-gauge shell into the Remington shotgun, then he pointed it towards the men. "Get up, all of you. And put your hands in the air. Now!"

At that moment Josh sensed something to his left, at the far end of his field of vision. It was a blur of movement in the darkness that had seemed to be far off when he first sensed it. But now, just a split-second later, it felt so close that he could touch it. As he turned to his left, a large, white-furred wolf leapt up at him as its jaws clamped down on his throat. Josh screamed as he let go of the shotgun to try and grab at the beast before it could get to his neck, but it was too late as the wolf's jaws ripped his jugular open and his blood began to spurt on the grass where he fell, as the beast continued its relentless attack. Tara's mouth was wide open as she noticed the Navajo men and their glowing eyes as they finally looked at her. She had stayed rooted to the spot as she saw how their forms began to shimmer as if it weren't their bodies at all. Within a blink of an eye, there were now a pack of wolves, grey and white furred and as large as one of the big show dogs she once saw when visiting the state fair with her brother last year. They had all somehow transformed into animals as the entire pack soon pounced on what was left of Josh. It was then that all the stress and the shock of what had happened finally took its toll on her. She closed her eyes and fainted while hearing the growls and sensed the smell of blood in the night air.

When she finally awoke it was late morning. As Tara sat up, she noticed that the dog was sitting nearby as it scratched the back of its ear with it hind leg. The bonfire was now a smoking pile of ash and the Navajo were gone. After getting up, Tara walked over to where Josh was attacked. All she saw was some bloodstains on the faded grass and his shotgun lying nearby. The dog made its way over to her as she sat down and partially unzipped her dirty jacket.

"I thought they were going to kill me next," Tara half-whispered. The last two nights she had seen someone die before her eyes. When it had happened the first time in the motel, she was hysterical and had to cry herself to sleep, but now she just felt numb.

The dog sat down in front of her. "There was no reason to kill someone that wasn't a threat to them," it said.

"It seemed that they all changed into wolves just like that. I saw the kid's eyes … they were like glowing in the dark, like the eyes of a cat at night."

"The eyes are the hallmarks of the yee naaldlooshii. The practitioners of the Way always begin to exhibit tell-tale signs of their power," the dog said.

Tara turned towards the Chihuahua. "The yee what?"

"They are known as skin-walkers," the dog said. "They are witches that have attained the power to change their shape. When the man intruded upon them and threatened them, they assumed the form of wolves to defend themselves."

"So they're like werewolves then?"

"Similarities perhaps, but the skin-walkers are more like sorcerers that use magic to change their forms because of their mastery over the dark arts."

Tara furrowed her brow. "How do you know all of this?"

The dog had a very strange accent. It had trouble speaking consonants like "V" and "M" because of its snout. "I have been around."

"Okay, I give up," Tara said. "You've been speaking in riddles to me ever since I met you, and it seems you can foretell the future—you keep telling me about these paths. I'm pretty sure you look like a dog, but I think you really aren't one. Just who or what exactly are you?"

"The ancient peoples in these lands worshipped many gods before the various empires from across the sea conquered them."

"I read about this in school," Tara said. "They worshipped animals or something like that?"

"The peoples of this land believed that animals were as intelligent as humans and anything that moves is alive. They believe that spirits and beings reside in all things, and the land and everything in it must be given respect. Animals are regarded as both gods and spirit guides for the people. Even when the beasts were hunted, the people always gave their respect to the animal after it was killed and eaten," the dog said

Tara smirked. "So that's it then? You're my spirit guide?"

"The choices you have are yours," the dog said. "No one forces you on the paths that you have taken. You must choose the path that will take you to your goal."

Tara sighed. "Look, I don't know what I want to do. A few weeks ago I just wanted to get away from my dad because he kept hitting me. Then I ended up with Larry, and then that ex-cop. Now they're both dead and I'm stuck out here. I'll probably die too."

"You are at a crossroads," the dog said. "There are many paths around you and you must choose … for only then does your destiny reveal itself."

A few tears slid down her ruddy cheeks. "I'm just a kid. And I miss my little brother."

"Is that the path you wish to take?"

Tara pushed her knees up and placed her chin on them as she wrapped her arms around her shins. "I just want the world to go back the way it was so I can get a job, and then take Timmy to live with me."

The dog stared back at her with its bulging brown eyes. "If you want to make the world a peaceful place, then it shall be a long path you must undertake, one filled with many dangers. There were many ancient tales of heroes who rid the world of monsters, so perhaps you shall be the focus of a new legend."

She wiped the tears on her cheek with her wrist. "I need to do something. I gotta help Timmy. Will you guide me to that path?"

"If that is the path you wish to take, then so be it," the dog said. "It's been ages since I last aided mortals, perhaps it is time to do so once again."

Tara narrowed her eyes and looked at the dog closely. "I remember now. There was a kid's book I read in class about a spirit guide. I think it was a dog or a coyote or something like that and it led the hero on a journey as an advisor or something. That story was about you, wasn't it?"

"I was known by another name and I chose another form back then."

"What did they call you back then?"

"Some tribes called me Coyote. Others called me the trickster."

Tara stood up and grinned. "I knew it! You're the Trickster God."

"I have been called that," the dog said.

She winked at the dog. "Trickster God sounds too long, I'll just call you Bibsy."

The dog growled. "That was the name given by my last master and it was a terrible one."

Tara laughed as she zipped up her jacket and started walking towards the riverbank. "Okay, as long as you guide me the right way I'll call you Trickster, if you give me trouble I'll call you Bibsy."

The dog ran alongside of her. "That was not funny."

Tara giggled as she made it to the van. The vehicle was still there as it lay on its side along the riverbank. She opened the rear door and looked for some food and found two unopened cans of soup. Tara reached in and grabbed her backpack and then placed the two cans inside of it before slinging it over her shoulder.

She turned to look at the dog. "We've got one, maybe two days' worth of food before we start starving. Where's this next path supposed to take me?"

"In order to journey into the Spirit World, your senses must be further attuned," the dog said. "I know of an old man that you can talk to and he lives a few days walk from here. You will need his instructions and teachings."

Tara frowned. "Spirit World? Is that like the land of the dead or something? I don't think I'll like going there. Do I have to die first?"

"If you want peace to return to this world and to be reunited with your little brother then this is the journey you must take."

Tara thought about it for a minute before giving out a smile as she shrugged. "Ah heck, I got nothing better to do anyway. Might as well try to be a heroine and save the world then. Lead the way, o' Trickster God."

22. The Otherworld

The boy could no longer remember what time or even what day it was. For some strange reason, he felt neither hunger nor thirst, and he wasn't tired either. Of course, when he would close his eyes, he would sleep and dream, but even then, he just didn't feel the need to rest and would only do it when she entered the room so he would not have to look at her.

Ilya Volkhov was trapped, suspended in a wooden cage that hung over the hut's ceiling … for how long now he didn't know. He saw the old woman kill and eat his best friend Andrei. She simply tore him into little bits and pieces with her bare hands, then threw the parts into a black cauldron by the fire. She then licked the blood off the wooden floor with an enormously long black tongue. Ilya closed his eyes in shame when he remembered because he just stood there and watched. But as he thought about it further, there was really nothing he could have done. He was just a child and she was a monstrous, evil witch who just couldn't be defeated.

His mouth trembling in fear and rage, Ilya made a silent vow to himself that if he could somehow escape and survive, he would avenge the death of his best friend, the one he called Buratino. He had thought long and hard on how to escape and as time had passed, he felt his courage growing as he nurtured it with fond memories of his friend and of his desire for vengeance. While the old woman would move around the room and do her various chores, he would pretend to be asleep so as not to catch her attention, observing with half-closed eyes to see if there was a time and an opportunity with which to escape.

As he heard her singing an old Slavic tune while she rummaged through her treasure trove in the room below, he realized this would be the best time to initiate his plan. From his past observations, she would usually go back upstairs and then go over to him and open the door to the cage so she could feel how thick his arms were. Ilya had read an old storybook in the library of the orphanage where he grew up in. The book told a fairy tale about a little boy and a girl who were held captive by a fearsome witch. In that story, the witch had always felt up the boy's arm in order to see just how fat he was, so she could eventually kill him and eat him, but the children finally tricked the witch and killed her instead. Ilya hoped that this witch wouldn't have known about that fairy tale, but he had a slightly different plan as he rummaged through his jacket. That was when he finally took out the piece of chewing gum he had saved just before they went out into the forest.

Hearing her coming up the wooden stairs, he immediately unwrapped the piece of gum before popping it into his mouth, and then started chewing. As the old woman made it up the stairs and looked around, she noticed that the boy in the cage was awake and looking at her.

"Ah, so you have finally awoken from your long sleep," she said as she moved towards him. "I was hoping to talk to you now that you are rested."

"I do not want to talk to you, witch," Ilya said. "You killed my best friend."

The old woman moved closer, her long, beaklike nose almost touched the bars of the cage. It was like she was floating on air. "Your friend was telling lies and he was stealing from me. I merely exacted justice for his greed and deceptions. The balance must be maintained."

Ilya mustered up some courage as his anger overtook his fear. "You didn't have to kill him!"

The old woman grinned. He could see her long yellow teeth as she began to unlock the cage. "In my abode, I decide what is fair or not. Now, let me see how you have grown."

She instantly grabbed Ilya's left arm and pushed back his jacket sleeve so she could see his pale forearm. The old woman ran her hand along it, feeling the soft flesh and the bones underneath.

As she kept her attention on his arm, the old woman didn't notice Ilya take the gum out of his mouth with his other hand, and stick it in the hole on the side of the cage where the latch was supposed to rest after it was to be locked.

Letting go of his arm, she pushed him back deeper into the cage. "You are still very thin. You do not eat the food I offer you. How do you expect to grow up?" the old woman said as she closed the cage door and turned the lock with her key, which she then took out and placed within the folds of her tattered black robes.

"Because I'm not a cannibal," Ilya said brusquely.

The old woman tilted her head back and laughed. "I cook all sorts of things in my pot, boy. Today I have chicken and vegetables simmering away in it. Are you sure you won't like to have some of that?"

Ilya shook his head and closed his eyes. "No."

The woman laughed once more before taking a wooden bowl from her cupboard and ladled some food on it, then began to eat. After the meal, the woman then sat down on an ancient wooden chair by the roaring fire and sang more ancient songs until she finally dozed off.

Now would be the time, Ilya thought, as he got on his knees and tried to push on the cage door, hoping that the gum had dislodged the latch for the lock to open. But as he pushed there was nothing. The cage door didn't budge. As the heat of frustration began to wash over him, he tried again. Still nothing.

Ilya's chin began to tremble and his eyes started to tear up. No! He just couldn't give up like this. He didn't want to be killed and eaten by this witch—he had to do something. Finally, he couldn't take it anymore as he lay down on his back and used his legs to press against the cage door with all of his might.

With a shrill creak, the door began to give way. Ilya quickly looked over at the old woman to see if she noticed the sound. She was still sitting in her chair, snoring.

Bracing himself, Ilya pushed at the cage door once more. This time the lock only made a slight shriek as the latch recoiled and the cage door swung open with a wooden squeak. Ilya once again looked to see if she woke up, but the old woman still hadn't moved from her chair.

The cage lay suspended at about ten feet over the room, so Ilya carefully lowered himself using his legs first, until he was dangling with his arms just above the long table that occupied most of the hall. As he finally let go and landed on the table with a soft thud, his right boot knocked a wooden cup that was on the counter and it began to roll sideways towards the edge.

Ilya quickly crouched down and made a grab for the cup just as it fell over the rim of the table. The cup almost slipped through his fingers, but he was able to hold onto it, just a few feet from the floor. Silently sighing with relief, he placed it back on the table, as he carefully made his way towards the door just as he heard a snort behind him.

Slowly turning his head with a sense of dread, Ilya looked back. The old woman was still snoring away and bits of food had come out of her nostrils. Shaking his head and facing the door, Ilya tried the latch on it. Unlike the cage, this one had a simple wooden bar that slid over the lock and the boy had no trouble sliding it back and opening the door, before finally stepping out through the opening and into freedom.

As he ran through the forest, Ilya was quite sure he was nowhere near the orphanage. As he saw the gargantuan gnarled trees all around him, he soon began to realize he might not even be in Russia at all. The weather out here was no longer winter, it seemed to be either spring or fall since there was no snow. The towering trees were like hundreds of feet tall and their trunks were as thick as skyscrapers, their leaves the size of dinner plates. Ilya wasn't sure where he was going, but he just kept running, hoping to make some distance before the old witch could realize that he had escaped and would no doubt come looking for him.

A strange, multi-colored bird flew past him. Ilya kept on running as his breath began to slow and only then did he note that there was something up ahead. He had thought about perhaps climbing the trees, but the nearest branch was at least forty feet above him, and there wasn't any way he could get a handhold on the smooth bark of these strange plants. He had thought it was night when he first got out through the door of the witch's hut, but now he realized that it was neither the evening nor daylight either. The whole forest seemed to have a strange, unearthly glow, like some sort of celestial luminescence that lighted his way and kept things visible.

It was then that he realized that he had ran into a small clearing. As he stood by and caught his breath, he noticed a figure had entered into the clearing on the other side. As he prepared to run, he soon realized that the figure was a man. His curiosity getting the better of him, Ilya moved closer to get a better look. The man was sitting on a silvery boulder and was polishing a very long spear. He was dressed in black medieval armor, the kind of protection that knights had and he had a black fur cloak wrapped over his shoulders. Before the boy got close, the man noticed him and quickly stood up as he turned to face him.

Ilya's eyes were wide open as he raised his hands to his chest, palms forward. "Hello, sir."

The man had a great brown beard that almost touched his chest. He looked to be at least seven feet tall. "Hello to you, young traveler. What are you doing in this part of the forest?"

Ilya tried to catch his breath. "I-I'm lost. I just escaped from a witch that killed and ate my best friend."

The man tilted his head and snorted in disgust. "So, Baba Yaga is on the loose again is she? That old hag never learns."

"P-please, sir," Ilya said. "I need your help. I just want to go home, back to the orphanage."

The man looked at him quizzically. "Orphanage? I'm afraid you will not find a place like that anywhere here, boy. What is your name anyway?"

"Ilya Volkhov, from Novosibirsk," the boy said.

The man bowed. "Greetings to you, Ilya Volkhov. I myself go by many names, but the most commonly known one for me is Radegast. I am here to hunt some game, but as you can see, I have been out for a long time and I have nothing to show for my efforts. The guests at my banquet will be very cross indeed. In fact, I myself am very hungry since I've not had any food nor have had any drink since I left the hunting lodge."

Ilya then remembered something that he still had in his pocket. He knew that proper manners when greeting a stranger meant the sharing of food and drink, but all he had was a moldy piece of cake from his last birthday party. Hoping that the stranger wouldn't eat it and instead just consider it as a token of hospitality, Ilya took out the old pastry from his jacket and held it out to the man. "All I have for food is this piece of moldy cake, it might give you a stomach ache if you eat it though," the boy said as he offered it.

Radegast laughed as he took the boy's gift and he popped it into his mouth. "Mmm, that is a very sweet cake and it satiates my hunger considerably. I am now in your debt."

For the first time in a long time, Ilya smiled. At least he brought some happiness to someone for once. "You're welcome, sir. Could you tell me how to get out of this forest so I can keep running before that witch finds me?"

Radegast bowed to him. "I'll do much more than that, boy. Your kindness has incurred a debt in which I cannot repay except through helping you. How would you like to join me in my lodge for a banquet? Do not worry about Baba Yaga, you are under my protection now."

Ilya grinned. "I would be very grateful if you would, Mr. Radegast."

The god laughed once more. "Just Radegast is fine, Ilya. Let me lead the way then!"

As he sat down on a wooden bench in a corner of the banquet hall, Ilya wondered if this was all a dream. Just moments before, he had been walking in a forest of gigantic trees that reached out to the sky, and then all of a sudden a path had appeared before them. Minutes after that, they came upon the edge of the woods that faced a twilit veldt with a hilltop at its smoke-filled horizon. No sooner that they had walked towards that hill that its base soon appeared right in front of them, and a path which led them up to a great wooden hall. Now here he was, a little boy surrounded by glowing men and women wearing strange and ancient garments, as a great bonfire roared at the central pit of the room. Radegast had seated himself on a carved wooden throne near the roaring fire and told the boy he could sit anywhere he wished.

Looking around, he had noticed that the people around him had a strange cyanic glow about them, it was as if they weren't fully materialized and looked to be ethereal spirits of some sort. They all seemed to be quite happy as they drank liquid light from metal cups while singing and dancing without any apparent fatigue.

A glowing woman dressed in a tunic and carrying a wooden pitcher came over to him. "Greetings child, and welcome to Radegast's hall. Would you like something to eat? Perhaps a manna pie, or some roasted ambrosia?"

"No, thank you," Ilya said to her. "I'm not quite sure, but it seems I just don't get hungry here."

The woman grinned. "Very well, if you need anything, don't hesitate to give me a sign." With those words she walked away to attend to the other guests.

As he leaned with his elbows on the banquet table to try and overhear the others, Ilya soon heard another woman's voice just behind his left shoulder. "That's because your body is still living, while you're in the land of the dead."

Ilya opened his eyes wide and turned around. Standing behind him was a tall woman. She had blue hair that seemed to float in the air, even as she moved quickly and leapt over the table above him, and then landed in a sitting position opposite him as she leered at his surprised face. Ilya could see that she was garbed in a combination silvery tunic and dark blue corset that hugged her shapely figure. Other than her hair which seemed to be constantly shifting as if it was suspended underwater, her eyes had a fiery glow like rubies in the night. Unlike the other guests, she didn't glow.

The woman's right hand extended a narrow finger that rubbed the boy's chin. "My, what a handsome child you are. So what brings you to the land of the spirits?"

Ilya could barely bring the words out of his mouth. "W-who are you?"

The woman instantly stood up from the table and smiled at him as she made a quick acrobatic twirl before quickly sitting down again. "They call me Ozwiena. I am a goddess by the way, just in case you didn't know."

"A-a goddess?" Ilya said. "What kind of goddess?"

"A goddess of sound," she said, smiling. "When you hear the cries of a bird in the morning sun, or the whispers of deceit in a conspirator's chambers, or the sound of a tree branch falling in the forest, everything passes through my ears and I sometimes carry these messages to other gods, and perhaps even men ... but only to those that I admire, of course."

Ilya swallowed. He had to think fast. He needed to show good manners, but he had nothing more to give. Then he came up with an idea. "I-I am pleased to meet you. I am honored to have the attention of a mighty goddess. Although I do not have anything with which to offer as a gift, if I may, could I give you a kiss on the cheek and perhaps you would consider it as a gesture of respect?"

Ozwiena tilted her head back and laughed. "You are an astonishing boy! Not only are you handsome, but you are indeed very clever. You may kiss my cheek," she said as she turned her head sideways in anticipation.

Ilya leaned over and just as his lips were about to touch the unearthly woman's cheek, she instantly turned, faced him and then gave a long kiss on his mouth instead. Ilya was surprised, but he kept his composure as they locked lips for nearly a minute before mutually withdrawing.

Once more Ozwiena giggled with delight and she clapped her hands. "That was most excellent! It's been a long time since I've kissed a mortal. You have made this night quite memorable, and now I am in your debt."

Ilya's cheeks were beet-red from embarrassment, but so far nobody else had seemed to notice. It was the first time that he had ever kissed anyone, and he did it to a goddess, no less. "Could I ask you something?"

"Most definitely," Ozweina said as she locked her fingers together and stared at him intently. "Ask me as many questions as you like, I know all that goes on in this world and in the other lands, as well."

"You said I'm in the Spirit Lands. Does this mean I am dead?"

"Not you, no," she said as she pointed to the others. "Do you see that they glow with astral fire? They are spirits of the ancestors of your world. They have passed on eons ago and yet some of them go to this hall to pay their respects to the gods, and enjoy a bit of merriment before they go onto their journeys."

"Where do they all go after this place?"

"Each spirit goes on a separate voyage. Every path one takes in life brings one to a different path in the afterlife."

"Okay then, if I'm not dead then how did I get here?"

"You were kept prisoner by Baba Yaga for quite a long time as I recall," Ozwiena said. "Her abode travels between the many worlds, and it was in this particular world you escaped to when you got out of her hut."

Ilya nodded. "Then how do I get back home?"

She winked at him. "Is that what you really want? To go back to the orphanage?"

Ilya looked down at the table. "I just wish my mother would come back for me. I just want to be there when she does."

Ozwiena shook her head. "She can't. Not right now. She's trapped."

Ilya's mouth hung open in shock. "She's what? Where is she trapped? I must go find her!"

Ozwiena shrugged. "She is with many others, trapped in Chernobog's lair."

Ilya's fists slammed on the table. "Tell me where this Chernobog is. Tell me!"

The goddess smirked. "You are a clever little boy, but you will be no match against the Black God, for he is a powerful being who cannot be hurt by mortals. He has returned and is currently ruling over your lands as we speak."

"You mean the snow storms over Russia and the world are being caused by this god?"

She nodded. "Parts of it are caused by him, but there are other gods that have now returned and they have their own goals. The Fomorians now have those isles in the north and the giants are in command of the frozen wastes, while Ahriman, Erra, and Pazuzu rule the Levant as the Hidden God plots in the New Land, for he has an alliance with—"

"Ozwiena!" Radegast bellowed from across the hall. "Stop bewitching the child and come here! Veles wants you!"

"I must go," Ozwiena said as she stood up. "Perhaps we shall speak again." And like a passing bolt of lightning, she was gone.

Ilya was speechless as his little fists were shaking on the table. His mother was a prisoner and his best friend was dead. How could he possibly defeat a powerful god and his minions? His mouth trembled as tears began to flow down his cheeks.

A soothing voice towered above him. As he looked up he saw that it was the ghostly servant girl. "Why don't you drink some of this to wash your sorrow away? This is a hall of happiness and mirth. One shouldn't waste tears in such a joyous place," she said as she placed a wooden bowl on the table in front of him, pouring a phosphorescent golden liquid into it.

"Thank you," the boy said as the girl smiled at him once more, then walked away to refill the other's cups. Ilya looked into the bowl. The strange liquid bubbled and swirled as if it was cold lava. He stared into it deeply as he could see some sort of figures in its liquid reflections. The first thing he saw was a girl, slightly older than he was, as she was walking along a desert and a little dog followed her, while giant black birds hovered in the air. The next vision was of a soldier with a great thick beard who raced across the desert in a military vehicle with a wounded friend sitting beside him. The third vision was that of a much older man who wore glasses and a coat as he faced what looked like a giant glowing maggot that seemed to be hundreds of feet tall. Ilya shook his head as the visions rapidly began to fade away and he soon realized that he was staring back into the glowing liquid that was in his bowl once more.

Ilya waved at the servant girl and she came over to him, smiling. "What is this liquid? I thought I saw visions while I stared at it," he said.

The servant seemed surprised. "You must have some sort of special gift. You are the first guest that has ever seen visions within that bowl. The drink is nothing more than fermented moonlight, sweetened by nectar from the great tree of life."

Ilya picked up the bowl and drank the liquid in one big gulp. The mystical juices felt like a sort of energy washing over his entire body, and imbued him with a newfound strength and power. "Tell me," he said to the servant girl. "Are their paths in this land to return to my world?"

She smiled. "In the Spirit World, one can travel across time and space. All you have to do is will yourself to a destination, and the path shall reveal itself before you."

Ilya nodded. So that was how Radegast was able to guide him to his banquet hall so quickly. All he had to do was to wish hard enough and he would be able to travel across the various planes of existence to find his mother and defeat that evil god. What he needed now was a plan. And some friends to help him.

23. Alamo

Rio Grande

Major General Len Williams shook his head in both frustration and disbelief at the reports coming in that evening at the National Guard command center in Sullivan City. He had ordered all National Guard and Army Reserve units on standby, but half of them were no longer answering his communications. What made it even worse was that there had been second-hand reports that were received through other channels. They claimed that military and volunteer units had begun firing on the Mexican refugees that were streaming through the border in cities all along the Rio Grande, despite his express orders not to engage or resist their crossings into US territory. General Williams was a veteran of both Iraq and Afghanistan, and he could feel the bitter tang of disappointment as wholesale units were beginning to disobey orders. *The military is close to collapse*, he thought. General Williams frowned as he stood over his communications officers, who were monitoring the situation in the command post.

The tent's outer flap opened and in came Colonel Grant Merriman, the executive officer. The rain had intensified in the last few days, and his combat uniform was soaking wet. "General, I've got word that there's been intense fighting in Brownsville. A few units of the Texas State Guard began to open fire on the refugees from Mexico, and one of our National Guard units attempted to intervene. No word on casualties yet, but they are reported to be high on both sides."

"Goddamn it," General Williams muttered under his breath. He had been designated as the commander of the Texas National Guard just over a year ago. There were some controversies because of his outspoken views on politics and of his friendship with certain controversial figures in the black community. Being African American himself, he had recently attempted to temper his outspokenness to the point where it hardly mattered anymore. But now there were many within NORTHCOM who had begun to suggest that he be replaced, especially as the military was now under intense pressure by outside forces, and due to the immense casualties they had taken in this crisis. "Are we still in contact with our units in Brownsville?"

Colonel Merriman took off his wet cap and shook his bald head. "I'm afraid not, General. We're even starting to have trouble communicating with our units in McAllen and they're right next to us."

"Jesus," General Williams said. His command post was here in Sullivan City, less than a mile from the Mexican border. If they were losing communications with their units in McAllen City, then that meant that their entire position along the border was now untenable. With less than twenty thousand soldiers manning a front that stretched from the Gulf of Mexico to the El Paso border, which covered a length of over a thousand miles, his command had no chance to possibly contain the millions of refugees from Mexico that were desperately seeking sanctuary in American territory, much less repel an attack from demonic forces. The enemy had already destroyed an entire US Army task force that had been deployed into Northern Mexico. Everyone now felt that this was a suicide mission, but they went through the motions anyway. They felt that the government would come up with a solution, and their eventual sacrifice should be used to buy time until a way was found to somehow turn the tide.

Colonel Merriman walked over to the map board on the far side of the command tent and started to look at the colored pins on it. "My suggestion is that we redeploy all our forward units from the Del Rio southern flank all the way to Brownsville, and reform them in front of San Antonio."

General Williams stood beside him. "That would mean losing the entire southern tip of Texas. I don't think NORTHCOM would ever approve of it.

244

We'd lose most of the units we have left because we're all native Texans, and we'd all rather die to the last man like in the Alamo than give up a single inch of ground, no matter who the enemy is."

One of the communications operators who was monitoring the radios raised his hand. "General, we got a call from one of our OPs in Hidalgo. They report explosions and heavy gunfire to the south coming from Reynosa, the Mexican City."

Both men walked over and stood behind the radioman who reported it.

General Williams looked at the colonel. "Well?"

"Reynosa has got the remaining units of what was left of the Mexican Army," Colonel Merriman said tersely. "If they are engaging, then that means those Aztec demons will soon be hitting the border."

General Williams frowned as he made his choice. "Okay then. Listen up, everyone," he said as the other communications operators in the command post looked up at him. "I want you to order all units to pull back to the San Antonio defense line. Code is bravo two-zero-zero. Have all units authenticate and acknowledge."

As the communications operators began to issue orders on their radios, the tent flap to the outside once again opened, and a large group of a dozen uniformed men cloaked in dark green military ponchos came inside.

Colonel Merriman immediately ran over and confronted them as he placed his hand on the pistol that was holstered on his hip. "Hey, this is a restricted area, identify yourselves!"

Several of the men pulled out M4 assault rifles from beneath their dripping wet ponchos and leveled them at the executive officer, who took a half step back in shock. General Williams calmly walked over and stood beside the colonel. The other comm operators who had noticed the intruders looked up in apparent surprise, as a couple of them stood up and took off their headsets.

One of the intruders took off the hood of his poncho to reveal his face. Grey-haired but still youthful looking, Governor Jack Bishop of Texas stared back at the National Guard commanders with a grim look on his face. "General, you know who I am, right?"

General Williams frowned as he stood his ground. "Of course I do,

Governor. Now what in blue blazes are you doing here and why are your men pointing guns at my command staff?"

"As of this moment, you and all your men are under the command of the State of Texas," Bishop said as he turned to look at the radio operators. "Order all National Guard units and reserves to maintain their positions and do not retreat a single inch. We have volunteers as well as extra units from the Texas State Guard that are on their way and will be reinforcing them. The state of Texas will remain free as long as I'm governor."

General Williams grimaced. The Texas State Guard was a paramilitary defense force, and supplemented both the military and civilian authorities in times of emergencies. Although their personnel were trained and equipped like military units, the Texas State Guard was not part of the US Armed Forces command structure. They instead acted as a legally recognized and well-armed militia in times of peace and was controlled exclusively by the state governor and the Texas General Assembly.

Colonel Merriman maintained his confrontational posture, although he didn't make a move to draw his pistol. "The Texas National Guard has been federalized. You know this, Governor. You need to pull your men out of there right now."

Bishop drew a chrome-barreled Colt 1911 from underneath his poncho and aimed it at the colonel as he thumbed the safety off. "As of now, the State of Texas has officially declared independence. Therefore, all National Guard units, including all military reserves, are under my command. You are to order all your units to maintain positions and fire on anything that crosses the border, is that clear?"

General Williams turned his head and shouted at his communications staff. "Disregard that order! We are under the command of NORTHCOM and as the designated CO here, I am ordering the governor and his men to get outta here, right now!"

"Where the hell are our MPs? I'm calling base security," Colonel Merriman said as he took out his walkie-talkie, but he instantly froze when the governor aimed his pistol right at his face.

"If you push the talk button on that thing, I'm gonna blow your head off,"

Bishop said nonchalantly. "Texas State Guard troops have surrounded your command post and they have orders to fire if you attempt to resist, so calling the MPs to save you won't do a damned thing except get y'all killed."

General Williams put a restraining hand on the colonel's elbow but kept his eyes on Bishop. "You are making a big mistake, Governor. This is treason. You'll all be arrested for this."

Bishop shifted his aim to the general. "I am doing this for Texas. I will not lose this state to the Mexicans, or those demons that they unleashed. Texas will be defended and will resist. Your goddamned commander-in-chief is nothing but a useless idiot, so from now on the people of Texas will take matters into their own hands when it comes to defending this great state. You are either with us or against us, so make your choice right now."

For what seemed like an eternity, nobody else said anything, or moved a muscle as the radios continued their chatter and the heavy rain outside continued to pour down.

Suddenly, one of the radio operators who was still wearing a headset instantly looked at her display. "Say again OP thirty-one, say again," she said.

General Williams turned his head in her direction. "What is it?"

"Observation Post thirty-one is in Cuevitas, General," the radio operator said. "That's less than half a mile south of us … they reported enemy contact and then fell silent."

"Keep trying to reach them," General Williams said to her. "As to the rest of you, order the pull back."

"Belay that order!" Bishop screamed as he aimed the pistol at the general. "Tell all units to stand and hold, right now!"

"I will not do so," General Williams said calmly.

"Have it your way then," Bishop said as he began to pull on the trigger.

"Out of the way, General!" Colonel Merriman said as he jumped in front of General Williams while drawing his own pistol.

Bishop fired as three of the comm operators stood up and drew their holstered pistols. The .45 caliber bullet from the governor's gun hit Colonel Merriman in the center of his chest and he fell on top of General Williams. The governor's Texas Guardsmen turned and opened fire on the radio operators who were trying to bring their own guns to bear on them.

As his ears were ringing from the deafening gunfire all around him, General Williams saw that the colonel's eyes were wide open and glazed over … he was dead. Pushing back the corpse of his executive officer, the general tried to reach up to his desk and grab the headset to his radio that was tuned to NORTHCOM command in Virginia. Just as he crouched up and pushed the talk button, a bullet struck the back of his lower spine and he fell down onto the floor. Drawing on his remaining willpower, he tried reaching up for the headset one more time. A another bullet went through his upper back, bounced around a bit in his ribcage and exited from his left shoulder and he finally slumped over the dead body of his second in command.

Governor Jack Bishop got up from the floor as the smoke rapidly began to clear. He could smell blood and cordite in the air as his ringing ears heard a few distant groans and death rattles. Looking around, he noticed two radio operators were still standing with their hands in the air as his men aimed their assault rifles at them. The rest were on the ground, either dead or soon to be dead as they were bleeding out.

"Goddamn it," Bishop muttered as he checked the communications systems in the tent. A few radios and a number of video display monitors had bullet holes in them but most looked to still be operational. "Get these people outta here and find me some replacement personnel to man this station," he said to his men.

As the two prisoners were led outside, he pushed away the corpse of a dead guardsman from the table after realizing that the radio was still functional. While cycling through several frequencies, he started hearing a commotion outside.

One of his men ran back into the tent, his M4 rifle was dripping wet with rainwater as gunfire began erupting outside. "Governor, they're attacking us!"

Bishop looked up from the table. "Who's attacking? The National Guard?"

The man looked scared and hysterical. "No, sir. It's those monsters, they're all over the perimeter!"

"What?" Bishop said as he grabbed the pistol he had left on the table and ran outside.

The rains were getting stronger as the night sky became opaque with haze and gusts of howling winds. All around him he could see flashes of lightning as well as weapons fire. The command tent had been situated on a school parking lot and there was a chain link fence around it. Several dozen of his Texas State Guardsmen had parked their half dozen Humvees with machinegun turrets in a semi-circle around the command post.

Bishop opened the car door and then jumped into the front seat of one of the vehicles. The Humvee driver was trying to frantically switch frequencies on the vehicle's two-way radio gear.

"Where in the hell is Colonel Sands?" Bishop said as he slammed the front seat door shut to keep out the pouring rain.

"I'm not sure, sir," the driver said nervously. Bishop remembered his name was Blaine, a young kid who joined up just weeks ago. "He got a radio distress call from our lead unit at the outskirts of the city facing Cuevitas, so he took most of the convoy and sped off just under ten minutes ago. Now I can't reach him."

Bishop grabbed the radio receiver from him as he began to fiddle with the radio controls. "For God's sake, let me do this."

As Blaine looked out at the front windshield he instantly let out a cry of surprise. "Oh lord, look at that!" he said, pointing at the perimeter fence, less than fifty yards away from them.

Bishop looked up and instantly recoiled back into his seat, his shaking hand nearly letting go of the radio receiver. Just beyond the fence was a horde of pale-skinned skeletal creatures with jet black damp hair that hung limply down their shoulders, partly covering their flaccid breasts, just above their emasculated ribcages. Their long arms ended in black talons and they wore skirts that had shrunken human skulls hanging on strings around them. Their eye sockets were empty and sunken, as if someone had ripped out their eyeballs and left nothing but a hollow black void of nothingness with which to stare down their victims just before they would kill them.

The other Texas State Guardsmen had seen them as well. The gunners who were stationed on the vehicle turrets immediately turned their swivel-mounted M2 Browning heavy machine guns and opened fire. As the massive

.50 caliber rounds began streaming into their direction, the demons immediately leapt up into the sky, and within seconds had landed on top of several Humvees as they began tearing and ripping into the hapless men sitting on the open turrets. The men on the ground began to run and fire in all directions, some of them even started to run away.

"Let's go! Let's go!" Bishop screamed. Blaine immediately shifted gears and floored the vehicle's accelerator since the engine was already idle. The Humvee accelerated forward as it drove past the carnage and out into the rainy street. The city was mostly deserted due to the standing evacuation orders, so the Humvee skidded along the wet pavement as Blaine fought for control while trying to compensate for the adverse weather conditions as he accelerated.

Visibility was less than twenty feet as the Humvee drove through the sheets of rain that kept pouring relentlessly from the storm clouds above. As the initial adrenaline and fright had started to wear off, reason and logic had both begun to reestablish themselves, Blaine began to slow down as he sensed the danger was left behind.

"Goddamn that was close," Bishop said as he slumped back into the front seat.

Blaine kept his eyes on the road as he made a turn along a deserted intersection. "What the hell were those things, sir?"

Bishop closed his eyes as he remembered reading the reports from the Department of Defense. "Some sort of Aztec demons. Apparently, those stupid wetbacks in Mexico must have done something to awaken those monsters, and now they're making their way up north to us."

"Demons?" Blaine said nervously. "How in the hell do we fight that?"

"I don't know," Bishop said as he felt a drop of rain on his cheek. As he wiped it away with his hand he looked at Blaine. "Is there a leak in this vehicle? I'm starting to get wet."

"No sir," Blaine said. "Private Calhoun was on the turret gun so maybe you ought to ask him."

"Huh?" Bishop's eyes widened as he realized the Humvee actually had a gunner stationed on its turret. He quickly turned around, then let out a gasp a split second later.

As he looked up at the turret in the back area of the Humvee, Bishop saw that Calhoun had already been torn in half, only his lower torso and legs were left standing under the open turret. The governor could see bits of entrails and blood all over the back seat. It was then that he noticed that one of those demons was actually sitting on top of the vehicle and then used its claws to climb in through the open turret to sit right behind them. Its leering mouth filled with jagged sharp teeth was now inches away from Bishop's terrified face.

Both men screamed as the demon began to tear at them with its claws. Blaine's throat was sliced through and his dying hands let go of the steering wheel. The Humvee swerved sideways and then fishtailed into the side of an abandoned building.

24. The Flood

Arabian Desert

They had been driving across the desert for almost two days now. The grey dust of Iraq had now given way to the vermillion sands of Arabia. Patrick Gyle kept his hands on the steering wheel of the Toyota Land Cruiser while Ron Boland rested in the back seat. Both of them had barely escaped the attack in the Green Zone. They had jumped into the Tigris River and made their way south after stealing a sedan from a terrified Iraqi man who was prostrate on the ground, begging the ancient gods of Babylon to spare him and his family. They didn't come out of it unscathed though, as Boland's left leg was horribly mangled when a winged demon landed on it before flying off again. Gyle had fashioned a makeshift splint for him. He wanted to leave Boland at a local hospital when they made it south to Najaf ahead of the sandstorm, but Boland refused. He made the painful decision to go with Gyle, because he told Boland of the dream he had about an ancient man sitting in cave who had been calling out to him. They weren't sure about the significance of Gyle's visions, but it was enough motivation for them to try and head southwards, across Saudi Arabia, with the hopes of finding that man. Boland theorized that with everything that had happened, he needed to find more intel before he could report back to Washington. The last thing he wanted to do was to return in disgrace.

The car's windshield was caked with dust as Gyle took another swig of the water bottle that lay beside him in the front seat. The Land Cruiser was brand new and still smelled faintly of factory synthetic leather mixed in with their sweat. They had made it into a car dealership in Najaf City. The sympathetic owner had given them the car keys and his blessing. He told them to take the vehicle and do with it as they pleased. Boland had later told him that the man who owned the dealership was in fact a courier for the Israeli Mossad. He could be counted on as an ally when Gyle had wondered why the man gave up the car so easily. After quickly loading it with water, rations, and jerrycans full of diesel that Gyle had placed at the back, they immediately sped off towards the south until they crossed the invisible border as his visions led the way.

Gyle checked the Land Cruiser's dashboard computer. The GPS display was indicating that they were less than twenty miles north of Ha'il, a small city in northwestern Saudi Arabia. He had marveled at their luck since the GPS maps had already been preloaded by the resourceful Iraqi car dealer, so all he had to do was to manually adjust their current position by triangulation. He was pretty much being guided by his feelings now, as if the old man in his dreams had been calling to him. He drove in the direction where he felt was the right way and he had been doing this for days now, only stopping for a few hours in the night to rest and refuel the vehicle's gas tank.

Boland began to cough dryly as he opened his eyes. Gyle glanced back in the rearview mirror to see if he was still okay. As their eyes met, Boland silently made a thumbs-up sign with his hand, and then promptly closed his eyes again while slumping back into the seat. *The man must be in a lot of pain because of his busted leg*, Gyle thought. *And yet he insisted on going with me. That takes a lot of guts.*

Although he was mostly driving off-road, there were times when he went along the highway. But even then, both the roads and the areas they passed through were mostly deserted, except for the occasional car, or a gaggle of Bedouins on their camels heading southward. Gyle would cycle through the radio for any recent news. From what they heard it was obvious that Iraq had fallen to the supernatural gods and demons of the blowing sands. Even though the Saudis proclaimed that they would defend their borders, Gyle did not see a single Saudi military unit the moment they crossed through. English language news reports on the radio had intercepted top-secret government cables that revealed the Saudi government and their military units had retreated south towards Mecca, the holiest place in Islam. That would be the city where the Muslim faith would make its final stand, as the Saudi government implored all those loyal to the teachings of the Prophet Mohammed that they would form a ring of steel around their holiest shrines, and defend it with their lives. Gyle scoffed at the ridiculousness of it all. He knew they were worshipping the false god because the real ones were in fact just up north and coming this way.

As he turned the car into the highway near As-Sufun, Gyle glanced at a ring of mountains to his right. His hands began to tremble as a warm feeling began to cascade over his body. This was it, the old man was nearby. Taking his foot off the accelerator, the car slowed down as Gyle began to bring the vehicle towards the base of the small mountain range. There were dry riverbeds called wadis that cut along the mountains. Gyle began to drive the Land Cruiser through them, the vehicle kicking up small clouds of dust as its wheels turned slowly on the loose sand. He had seen a glimpse of the city of Ha'il a few miles away on the horizon, but he noticed there was no movement or vehicles near the outskirts, so he guessed that the whole place must have already been evacuated. He drove on for another hour, as he twisted and turned along the wadis until the hairs on the back of his neck were so electrified they seemed to run a current through his spine.

Turning off the car ignition, Gyle turned around to look at his CIA case officer. Boland lay stretched out in the backseat, the makeshift splint on his right leg was straightened out to keep his injured limb steady. "Ron, I think we're here," he said to him.

Boland opened his eyes again and pushed at the seat cushion in order to sit up. "Where are we?"

"About a few klicks west of Ha'il. That city looks deserted by the way."

Boland took out his own plastic bottle of water from the rear compartment, and took a sip to moisten his dry throat. "Are you sure this is the place?"

"I can feel the tingling all over my body," Gyle said. "I know what I'm saying sounds far-fetched, but the man with the answers is somewhere here, I can feel it."

"After everything I saw in the Green Zone," Boland said softly. "I can pretty much believe anything now."

Gyle had a Beretta M9 pistol on his hip that he took off a dead soldier that was lying in the Green Zone a few days back. He did a brass check by slightly thumbing back the slide to make sure there was a round in the chamber. "You want to come with me?"

"With this blasted leg I'd be only slowing you down," Boland said as he popped a few aspirin tablets into his mouth before sipping more water. "I'll guard the vehicle."

Gyle thumbed the safety of the gun and gave it to him butt-first. "Keep this, then."

Boland shook his head. "That's for you, just in case that old man's hostile."

"He won't attack me, I can feel it," Gyle said as he offered him the gun again.

This time Boland took it and placed it on his lap. "Okay, if you get into trouble, don't make me come limping after you, G."

Gyle nodded as he opened the front door and slid out of the driver's seat. As he stretched his back, he began to survey the area. The mountains didn't look particularly tall, the highest elevations looked to be around a hundred feet, though he had a feeling that he wouldn't have to climb since his last dream was of a cave, which meant that he needed to look at ground level.

The late afternoon sun was being blocked by the mountains so it gave the wadi an overcast look. Gyle began to walk along the dried riverbeds that had naturally carved their way along the base of the mountains over the centuries. For an hour, he did nothing but follow the smooth paths of sand as he walked deeper into the base of the mountain range. As he made another turn by just walking along the dried riverbed, he noticed a large desert bush at the end of a trail that led to the base of a rock spire just ahead of him. A strange feeling came over him as he realized that he was close.

Gyle walked over and stood in front of the dried shrub, he realized that there was a soft breeze coming from behind it. As he walked around it, he saw that it actually hid an entrance to a cave. Taking the flashlight from his belt, he turned it on and crouched down as he ventured inside.

Whether it was formed naturally or hewn by hand he couldn't tell. He crouched and made his way in further. A slight upward draft of cooling air continued to drift by him. Gyle could smell myrrh and cedar coming from somewhere. The descent along the cave tunnel was narrow and he nearly fell as his boots slid down the smooth limestone floor, until he slowed down and began to gingerly choose his footing. Gyle reckoned he had gone down about a hundred feet below the mouth of the cave when the tunnel finally ended, and he stood before a massive underground chamber.

Fist-sized rays of light illuminated the cavern, so he turned his flashlight off and clipped it back on his belt. As he looked up, he figured there must have been thousands of these tiny holes up on the cave ceiling that led out into the sky, it gave the effect of standing over a night sky full of stars. Looking around, Gyle saw that a small, underground stream of flowing water crisscrossed the cavern floor and wild plants grew all around him. The far side of the cave had a cliff side loft with a makeshift wooden pallet that was apparently used as a cot. Peering further out, Gyle could see that near the bed was a wooden chest, as well as a metal cooking pot near a smoldering fire pit. A handmade wooden table with various tools lay nearby. As he kept looking around, he soon heard the sound of footsteps.

Gyle reacted quickly by crouching down as he slid into the side of the cave tunnel, away from the beams of light shining down, and into the shadows. As the sounds of movement got closer, he noticed an old man appearing from where the loft was. The man started to make his way down using a narrow trail along on the side of the limestone wall. He could see that the old man was clothed in nothing but a tattered robe and wore sandals, his long white beard and wild mane of hair made him look like a stereotypical hermit of the sort that one usually sees in old movies. As the old man made it to the base of the cavern, he raised a bony hand in a gesture of peace towards Gyle.

Since he had been obviously discovered there was no point in hiding any further, so Gyle stood up and faced the old man as he walked into the center of the cavern. The old man didn't seem to be hostile, so Gyle raised his hand with an open palm at him in return.

The old man smiled and gestured at him to come closer. "Welcome, my friend. I am of no threat to you. Would you like some tea?"

Gyle took a step before stopping abruptly. Even though events of the past week had shaken his beliefs in practically everything, there was still a part of him that couldn't believe it at all so he compensated by returning back to his old, cautious ways. "I saw you in my dreams. And you speak English. Who are you?"

The old man nodded. "Ah, that is the way with dreams. I saw you in my dreams as well along with some others, like the woman with the scar, and the two children, wandering all by themselves in the netherworld. Dreams are important because it is the god's way of talking to you, especially when they have no voice. As far as my speaking to you in your language, I have had plenty of time to learn most manner of tongues that all men speak."

Gyle came closer. "So let's talk about dreams then. I dreamt of this very cave and it led me from Baghdad and across the desert. I've seen many people die on my way here and I am no closer in knowing what the hell is going on than I was when I first saw those demons in the dust."

"I was not calling you with my dreams," the old man said as he bent down, then he started to take some leaves from a flowery plant growing at the edge of the underground stream. "But perhaps the gods are using us as part of their plans. But then again, who really knows the will of the gods except maybe the gods themselves."

"For the last two days, every time I closed my eyes, you kept appearing before me and you'd tell me the same thing."

The old man stopped and looked up at him. "And what were these things of which I would tell you?"

"You kept saying that the world was in danger and that I was needed," Gyle said. "But for what, I don't know. The dream just ends without any further explanation."

The old man looked up at the ceiling as if thinking to himself before sitting down on a smooth rock near the stream. "That is strange. My dream is of you wandering the desert. Then I dream of the others, and they are also making their way across different parts of the world."

Gyle shook his head. "I don't know of the others. My name is Patrick, and you still haven't told me your name."

The old man smiled as he shrugged. "I've been called many names. I remembered the time they called me Ziusudra, then later on they called me Atrahasis. Then after that Utnapishtim, but I guess my most popular name is Noah. Ah well, they are just names, names that are ultimately lost through time. As far as the others, I have a feeling that you will meet them in your journeys."

Gyle sat down near the other side of the stream. He was weary and just wanted to rest, but the way the old man described things meant that his ride still had a long way to go. "I thought this was the final leg of my journey. So you are that Noah then? Of the great flood?"

The old man grinned. His crooked teeth were stained yellow. "That story has been told many, many times, with each time a little different than the last. First it was said that there were many gods, and one of the gods took pity on me and my wife, and told me to build a great ark. Then the story changed again into just one god that told me to build a ship to contain all the land animals of the world, to keep them alive until the waters receded. And so on."

Gyle looked at him closely. "Well, what really is it then? Was it a number of gods or just one god telling you all this?"

The old man just shrugged and put up his bony arms in a gesture of resignation. "It was such a long time ago, I don't remember anymore. Then again what does it matter if it was one god or many?"

Gyle leaned over so the old man could see he was serious. "It matters because the whole world is under attack by either many gods or all under the guise of one god, that's why. I need to know what can be done to stop them. If there's a way to kill them."

The old man waved a crooked finger at him. "Ah, you are a warrior and warriors always try to find a way to kill things. Remember, you are no longer fighting other men, but gods and their allies now. You may know of ten thousand ways to kill a man, but killing a god? That is another matter entirely."

Gyle sighed. "Okay, I guess I might as well call you Noah. So tell me, Noah, how do I fight these gods if they cannot be killed?"

The old man thrust out his lower lip. "I don't like the name Noah. Too common nowadays."

"Okay so what do you want me to call you then?"

The old man looked up again as if deep in thought. "Let me see … the oldest name I can remember is Ziusudra, which means 'found long life' but… ah, that is too much of a braggart's name. Let me see … okay, how about the second name that I remember having which is Atrahasis, meaning 'extremely wise' … so, yes … I think that name is better."

"If it means genius, then isn't that as cocky as naming yourself Ziusudra?"

The old man laughed. "You're right, but I would rather be known as someone smart than as some immortal. Living forever is not something to be proud of."

"You have a strange sense of pride."

"Being called an immortal sometimes gets to me, you know," Atrahasis said. "All those years, staying alive, while the people around you die. Or of that great hero coming to visit me and asking for a way to live forever, and I had to tell him that it was a doomed journey. But he insisted, so I told him where to find a magical flower to keep him young forever, yet he lost it after only one night because he was careless, and it was that lesson that finally made him give up his vain quest."

"You mentioned that you had a wife," Gyle said. "Is she an immortal too?"

"Yes, she was," Atrahasis said ruefully. "She left me a long time ago to be off with other men. I do not know where she is now. I have heard of some stories that she went mad when all of her other husbands died of old age or of sickness, while she never did. It was so long ago I even forgot her name. I am sure she is still out there somewhere, and I hope she has found some happiness at last, if only for a short time."

Gyle looked down at the stream. He noticed there were luminous cave fish swimming in it. "I also have a wife, and children. And I'd move Heaven and Earth just to be with them again. I hope they're alright."

"Do you wish for the world to return as it once was? You realize that is no longer possible."

Gyle stared at him. "So what's your solution then? Do nothing? My country is being ravaged by other gods, creatures of pure evil, and even now my family might be dead. I've got to do something. There must be a way to defeat them."

Atrahasis contemplated his words before speaking again. "The gods are immortals and they have great power over us, that is why we call them gods and we are but men. On the other hand, these gods are very much like us, for they have the same feelings as men for they too fall in love. They hate, and they too feel sadness. There are other means with which to defeat them than battle."

"I'm a soldier," Gyle said. "It's what I do. I don't know how to do anything else. Will you help me? Please?"

The old man reached into his torn and dirty robes, then took out a withered petal as he held it aloft for Gyle to see. "When I told you the story of this great hero who went in search of immortality, I told him to find this flower at the bottom of the deepest sea. That he did, and he showed it to me and allowed me to take a piece of that plant before we parted ways forever. All I have is this little petal. It will not endow you with immortality, but it may grant you some strength and power over men. But beware, for this power has a curse … it will transform you and your lifespan will be shortened because one cannot be like the gods when one has the body of a man."

Gyle thought about it for a moment as he recalled the good times he spent with Marie, with the twins. He remembered his time in the military and his friends. All that was gone now. It was now nothing but gods and death all around him. And all he knew was how to kill. "I'm willing to make that sacrifice," he said with finality as he moved closer.

"Very well," Atrahasis said and gave him the petal.

Gyle examined the withered leaf. It still seemed soft to the touch and it glowed with a strange amber luminescence, as if it was still alive. He placed it into his mouth and chewed for a bit before swallowing it. The taste was strange, like chewing on a strange herb that tasted unlike anything he had ever eaten. As it traveled down his throat and into his stomach, it began to feel like molten lead had been poured down his gullet. That was when a sudden wave of nausea overtook him. Gyle began to retch violently before he vomited a stream of yellowish bile on the cave floor.

"And so it begins," Atrahasis said as he stood up and looked down at him.

Gyle's body was wracked by sharp, searing pangs of pain. His eyes began to tear blood from the pure, unadulterated agony that was now overwhelming him. He could feel his skin as if it was on fire, just as the pores began to pop and blister. Gyle was now lying on the floor as he struggled violently with himself, his kicks and spasms were like those of a dying animal. He felt as if his heart was going to explode and he could not catch his breath. He began to wonder if the old man lied to him, and what he ate was nothing more than virulent poison. Then the pain was simply too much and everything faded to black.

When he opened his eyes once more, he noticed at least six men were standing over him. They all wore tunics, flowing cloaks, and head cloths that hid their faces so all he could see was their eyes. At first glance, he thought they were Bedouins because that was what they would normally wear, but he soon realized they were in fact imposters because of the way they carried themselves, and of the weapons that they had brought with them.

As he tried to get up, one of them immediately made a flatfooted kick to his shoulders that sent him once more on the ground. Gyle noticed that Atrahasis was sitting on the far edge of the cave and they were placing handcuffs on him. One of the other men who had been staring at the old man being bound turned around and made his way towards him.

Gyle's voice came out guttural, almost as if it was an animal who tried to speak for the first time. "What are you doing to him?"

The man looked at him. "You are Patrick Gyle of the CIA, are you not?"

"Yes," Gyle said as he realized who they were from their heavy accents. "And you are our allies, you're Israelis."

The man didn't answer him.

"What are you doing to him? Why are you taking him?"

The man flicked his eyes as if caught in a lie. "We have our orders, just like you. I'm afraid you need to come with us as well. We want to talk to you and with what happened in Iraq."

Gyle started to get up again, it seemed that his aches and pains were gone, and he somehow felt lighter, perhaps even stronger. "You're not taking him anywhere and I'm not going with you."

One of the other men, the same one who hit him before, tried to knock him back down again with the butt of his AK-47 assault rifle. But Gyle was too quick for him as he immediately sidestepped away from the blow and his kick sent the man flying back halfway across the cave. The other men quickly brought their rifles to bear on him as Gyle put his hands up in the air.

The man he was talking to was livid as he gave orders in Hebrew for the others to tend to the one who got kicked, then he aimed a pistol at Gyle. "Why did you do that?"

"He attacked me first," Gyle said. "Why am I being held by you people? The US and Israel are supposed to be allies."

Another man who was aiming a rifle at Gyle's back gasped. "David, look at him! Look at his arms!"

Gyle turned his head sideways and looked at his own outstretched arms. He saw that his exposed forearms had began to slough off their skin as loose folds of them hung limply over his arms, exposing some sort of thick, lizard-like skin underneath that was hard to the touch. "Oh my god," he said.

The man with the pistol began to shake his head. "What are you? What happened to you?"

Gyle placed his palms near his face. It looked like the outer skin was also peeling off as it exposed a new type of outer covering that was akin to pale leather and plastic. It was semi-hard to the touch, and Gyle had almost no feelings of sensitivity over his body anymore. "What have I done?" he said softly.

That was when he saw the first group of Israelis take Atrahasis, and started pushing him into the cave tunnel that led up to the surface. As he began to move again, Gyle could feel the skin on his legs peeling away, as he ran faster than he had ever run in his life. He made his way to where they were bringing the old man, but then he soon heard gunfire as it reverberated within the cave. That was when he felt the bullets hit his upper legs, and he fell face down on the limestone floor. As he tried to get up, another bullet hit him in the back and embedded itself in his collarbone. Then the waves of pain began again and once more he lost consciousness.

David Zim took off his Bedouin headwear and sighed with relief. Two of his men ran forward and checked on the American. For a brief moment, he thought the man would somehow get away and maybe even kill him and his men just to free that old man. It was obvious that Patrick Gyle had somehow been altered into something fast and lethal, and his men had to react as if their lives were in danger. The state of Israel could no longer depend on her allies, she was on her own now and her people would need to do whatever it took to ensure their own survival. *If the Americans were put in this same position, then they would think and do the same.*

One of the men who was examining the American turned to look at him. "David, this man is still alive somehow. It looks like most of his wounds are superficial."

"Then we take him with us as well," David said. "How is Eitan doing?"

Another operative was checking the stunned man who Gyle had knocked back to the wall. "He has a few broken ribs and maybe a concussion I think, but he will make it."

Another man on the far side of the cave, near the tunnel, was carrying a TAR-21 Tavor battle rifle that had just been fired and he slung it over his shoulder. "Boland isn't going to be too happy about this, that's his man we shot right there."

"I don't care what that American fool thinks," David said to him before turning to look at another man. "Rafael, what time does our extraction arrive at the airstrip?"

Rafael had a portable radio on his back and was speaking into the receiver. "About two hours from now."

"Let's get going then," David said. "Do we have special restraints on that plane?"

Rafael nodded. "Yes, that crazy rabbi told us during the briefing that we may be encountering beings that may have great strength, so we brought along some heavy-duty animal restraints that we got from the zoo in Tel-Aviv."

David nodded. "Make sure they're both heavily restrained and if you have any drugs that can keep them sedated then apply it on them too. I do not want either of them conscious on the flight back home. Same goes for Boland."

25. Convoy

Kansas

The convoy of vehicles had been on the road along US Route 400 for nearly an hour. They had left McConnell Air Force Base just after dark, so as not to arouse any suspicions with the rioters at the base perimeter. The plan was to turn north at the highway's terminus near the Missouri border, then head east towards Warrensburg until they would reach their final destination at Whiteman Air Force Base. Leading the convoy were two M1127 Stryker wheeled armored fighting vehicles. The Strykers had Browning M2 heavy machineguns mounted on their top turrets, and they were followed closely by three Humvees equipped with M249 light machineguns. A single M977 HEMTT heavy transport truck and another Stryker brought up the rear.

Gary Larue frowned as he looked at his watch for the umpteenth time. He sat in the back seat of the first Humvee that was moving in formation behind the second Stryker. Unlike the ad hoc mix of Air Force and Army reservists he was travelling with, Gary was in fact a civilian. He was a senior administrator for the government's National Nuclear Security Administration. The agency was tasked with maintaining and safeguarding the nuclear weapons stockpile for the entire country. He was heading the mission to transfer a large store of nuclear warheads safely to the base in Missouri. Sitting right beside him was Captain Chuck Teller, the commanding officer of the convoy. Gary had an instant dislike of him when they had met just a few hours before. Captain Teller was consistently ignoring his suggestions to bring the convoy out as soon as possible and instead had wanted to leave at night; that meant a delay of several hours. The top brass over at Whiteman AFB would be twiddling their thumbs and wondering how much longer it would take to transport a significant portion of the country's nuclear warheads from a neighboring state, just 250 miles away.

After stealing a glance at the Air Force captain who seemed to be asleep, Gary looked out the window on his side of the Humvee. Electrical power had been out for days now all over the state. The highway was pretty much deserted except for an occasional car that was rapidly told to veer off by the turret gunners in the convoy. The streetlamps that had once guided commuters at night had been inoperative and this gave Gary an eerie feeling, since the only illumination along the road was now from their vehicle headlights. He could see an occasional bonfire out in the distance, but the rest of the journey would be traveled along a highway of night along a twilit horizon, as the full moon made a faint illumination above them.

The mission was pretty much straightforward. Due to the rioting at McConnell, it was deemed necessary that the forty W87 thermonuclear warheads that were secretly being stored in the base would have to be moved over to the more secure facilities at Whiteman. The HEMTT truck traveling two cars behind carried the devices in secure containers. Gary had supervised the handling of these converted MX Peacekeeper ICBM warheads from their underground storage bunkers and into the truck's rear containers. The security briefing earlier today had stressed that the only possible threats could have come from unconfirmed ghost sightings along the highway or perhaps from some survivalist groups. But since the convoy was equipped with wheeled vehicles then their orders were not to stop for anything the moment they were on the road. Captain Teller even bragged to his men that if any of those preppers would be stupid enough to try to hijack his convoy, they would be dealt with severely using all the massive firepower he had available. Gary had wished that they had some air support like Apache gunships or Blackhawk helicopters, but unfortunately there were no aircraft of any kind to spare.

As the convoy began nearing the eastern terminus of the highway, Gary noticed that Captain Teller had at last managed to wake up. The man beside him straightened up in the backseat and looked at his own watch. Now it was Gary's turn to relax somewhat as he now slumped back and tried to close his eyes to get some rest. They would be moving into the state of Missouri very shortly as the convoy began to turn north. The fleet of vehicles soon passed a thick copse of trees along the highway.

Almost instantly, floodlights opened up all around them. The lead Stryker stopped just yards away from a school bus that had parked itself across the northern turn of the highway, thereby blocking the entire road in front of them. The HEMTT truck was barely able to apply its breaks in time, as it almost rear ended the fourth Humvee in front of it. All of the gunners in the convoy were instantly alert, but they couldn't aim their machinegun turrets. The men were temporarily blinded by the powerful lights that were once hidden behind the tree line along both sides of the road.

Gary instantly sat right back up as he looked out into the trees. He could see vehicle mounted searchlights on trucks had positioned themselves behind the trees. An unknown force was surrounding the convoy and he could see silhouettes of men with rifles in prepared positions. "What in the hell is going on?" he said as his eyes could only squint while being in the center of so much bright light.

"Attention," a voice that was amplified by a megaphone said. "Attention, Air Force and Army convoy. We are the Soldiers of the Lord Jesus Christ and we have you surrounded. We urge you to step out of your vehicles peacefully or we will use deadly force against you."

"What the fuck?" The Humvee driver, a young man of nineteen and a part-time reservist said. "Are they kidding me?"

The voice from the trees came on again. "Attention convoy, you have ten seconds to comply or we will start shooting."

Captain Teller drew his M9 Beretta pistol from his hip holster and activated his walkie-talkie with his other hand. "Everybody, out of the vehicles, this is an order."

The Humvee driver turned his head and looked at the captain with an incredulous look in his eyes. "Sir, are you sure about this?"

"Just do it, son," Captain Teller said softly as the driver opened his door and walked out.

It was then that Gary realized the awful truth. "You set us up, you son of a bitch," he said to Captain Teller.

The Stryker at the rear of the convoy suddenly began to back up, then started to maneuver to turn around. A wire-guided TOW missile came flying in from the tree line and hit the vehicle on its side which stopped it in its tracks. A deafening bang followed and smoke started to emanate from the Stryker. A loud scream began, then a hatch was opened as a soldier who was clearly burned all over his body climbed out of the stricken Stryker, before falling down to the ground beside the vehicle as flames began to erupt all around it.

"Dammit," Captain Teller mumbled before engaging his walkie-talkie again. "I say again, this is Captain Chuck Teller, I am ordering all units to abandon your vehicles and surrender. Now!"

The two Strykers in the lead were commanded by the executive officer and their engines immediately started up, their machinegun turrets started firing into the tree line along their flanks, hitting and knocking out a couple of the floodlights. The first Stryker broadsided the empty school bus as it attempted to push it off the highway. Just as the abandoned bus began to give way, an M1 Abrams battle tank suddenly appeared less than a hundred yards in front of the Stryker, just as the latter had pushed the bus from the middle of the highway. Seconds later, the tank fired its 120mm cannon as the sabot round easily penetrated the thin front armor of the lead Stryker. The wheeled vehicle instantly exploded in a shower of sparks as roaring flames began to pour out of it. Little popping noises began as the ordnance inside of the stricken Stryker had started to detonate.

The second Stryker had seen what had happened, and the vehicle instantly stopped firing as the men inside began to open their hatches and clambered out, their hands in the air. Gary cursed as the squads in the Humvees also got out of their vehicles and put their weapons down before surrendering. As he looked around in despair, Gary noticed that Captain Teller had his gun pointed directly at him.

"This is treason, goddamn it," Gary hissed. "You set us all up and a number of your own men are dead!"

"I had to make a choice," Captain Teller said. "Either see my country be dismembered, and go down following orders from a commander in chief I have no trust and respect in, or give my soul to the one true Lord Jesus Christ. The choice was an easy one to make. Now get out of the vehicle, Mr. Larue. I won't say it again."

Gary opened the car door on his side and slid out. He noticed a large group of men coming out of the tree line and started to make their way towards the convoy. They were wearing combat fatigues with body armor and were well-armed. Gary turned around and looked at the captain once more. "Don't think any of you will be getting away with this, you traitors. When I get back and tell NORTHCOM and the president about everything that happened here, then your puny little rebellion will be put down, just like the Confederates were taken down all those years ago."

"You won't be going anywhere," Captain Teller said as he fired two shots into Gary's chest. The NNSA administrator fell to the ground and his last thoughts were that his chest hurt so bad, he just couldn't breathe.

Steve Van Dyke walked over to Captain Teller as the latter was standing over the body of Gary Larue. The ammunition explosions from the two Strykers that were destroyed had begun to die down. The captured men of the convoy were being rounded up before being led into the tree line, where another convoy composed of very different vehicles had parked many hours earlier. Steve looked at the body on the ground and shook his head.

Captain Teller holstered his pistol after thumbing its manual safety. "He wasn't going to surrender, so I had to finish him. If given the chance, he would escape and try to report back to his superiors in Washington or wherever the hell they are holing up in now."

"That's too bad," Steve said. Unlike the others who were wearing standard issue military camouflage, he was dressed in his blue and black SWAT gear as he cradled his M4 carbine. "And a pity about those two Strykers, we could have used them too."

Captain Teller nodded. "Yeah, but I knew my XO would be trouble, that's why I requested armored support and made him stay in the lead Stryker. He was Army and pretty loyal to that one crew and they to him, because they served in Afghanistan. This way they all died together."

Steve looked at the heavy transport truck behind them. "So how many warheads do we have in our possession now?"

"There're at least forty of those thermonuclear warheads in the back of that truck," Captain Teller said. "Our original mission was to transport them over to Whiteman, but the Rock of God Church can have them now. I assume you got specialists that can work those things."

"Well, we have people that claim they can work them," Steve said. "As to whether they really can, remains to be seen. Pastor Erik has started to interview a number of military deserters and I'm sure we can find a nuke technician or two that can work these things sooner or later, since there's just been so many that have gone over to our side, like yourself. All we need now is to get a couple of those nukes ready to go, and after that there'll be no way the US government would be able to touch us once we got it, unless they want a thermonuclear exchange to happen."

"I hope all the lives we've sacrificed today was worth it then," Captain Teller said as he held out his hand.

Steve shook it. "I'm sure it is. I'd like to thank you. The Soldiers of the Lord will need experienced military officers like you, and I'm sure you'll be given a commission once you meet up with Pastor Erik. We needed these nukes in order to survive. Now we're truly legit and those commies in the US government will have no choice but to leave us alone from now on. Now we are safe so we can concentrate against fighting the true enemy."

Captain Teller looked at him quizzically. "What true enemy are you referring to?"

Steve looked out into the night as the floodlights were being deactivated. All the remaining illumination left were the burning Strykers. The fires turned everything into black silhouettes against a flickering orange background.

"Why, the armies of Satan of course. As we talk, right here right now, they're busy marching all across the world and they'll be here very soon … so we need to be ready for the final battle."

26. A Different Reality

It had already been a few days, and Tara Weiss was feeling both tired and hungry. She had been sitting silently near the mouth of a shallow cave on top of a small hill, overlooking the desert scrublands below. Sitting opposite her was a wrinkled old Indian that the dog said was either a Yaqui, a Navajo, or something else. It had been a few days and she could barely remember what was said anymore. Tara was drifting in and out of consciousness. The only sustenance the old shaman would allow her to partake of were a few sips of water every few hours. Her stomach had ceased growling, and instead all she felt there was just a gnawing emptiness.

When Tara and the dog first climbed their way up on the solid rock plateau, he was already sitting there as if waiting for them. The trickster dog had told her that the old Indian was in fact a shaman, when Tara asked what that was, the trickster explained that a shaman was a type of man who could speak with spirits. When Tara then asked if he was some sort of magician the dog said yes, because this particular shaman was also a brujo, or sorcerer. As soon as the brujo saw her, he gestured for her to sit down in front of him as the dog ran off somewhere. Tara had sat down and became bored a few hours later. She finally asked the old man if she could stand up and stretch her legs, but the brujo emphatically said no. Hours after that, when she complained that her back was starting to hurt and that she could barely feel her legs, the

272

brujo told her she needed to find the right spot on the slab of stone she was sitting on and the pain and discomfort would go away. For the next hour, Tara had shifted and moved slightly to the left and then to the right without any success until she realized there was a small cleft on the far edge of the boulder. It seemed to have been sat upon by numerous people over the decades. An indentation had formed on the rock which resembled the seat of a chair. As she finally sat down on the cleft, the pain in her lower back subsided and a strange warmth cascaded over her body. That night, she could see the giant thunderbirds drifting over the storm clouds in the far horizon as the mauve and pewter skies slowly turned to a grey dusk.

Just as she closed her eyes for a bit and then opened them once more, she found the old man had built a small bonfire in front of her. As her eyes became mesmerized by the leaping yellow tongues of flame, the brujo sat down on the opposite side of the fire and faced her. Tara could see that his eyes were glowing in the dark, just like the skin walkers that she had encountered just a few nights before.

The old man looked at her closely and then started talking. His voice felt both timeless and hollow. "What is your name?"

"Tara, sir," she said. Her throat was dry so when her voice came out it was like a croak of a small frog.

"Out here I am called El Brujo," the old man said. "And I am honored to meet with you for you have been chosen."

Tara blinked. "Ch-chosen? I-I don't get what you mean."

El Brujo looked out into the night. "Many stories have been told of the Fifth World and of the gods and spirits that inhabit it. The First World was called Nihodilhil, it was a world of darkness and that was where the Divine Spirit began its journey towards the Fifth World, the world of the present. The Trickster was there too and he was called Coyote by my people, but I understand he took on many forms, and many names among the other peoples of the world. Now it is the time of the ending of the Fifth World, when all the gods of old have come back and the Sixth World must now be brought forth, but only after the gods have either been satiated or tricked into doing so."

Tara shook her head. The old man was speaking in riddles. "I-I'm sorry. Did you mean that this world is about to end and that a new world will soon be taking its place?"

The old man nodded. "When the old gods made their presence felt, the barrier between our world and the land of the spirits have been weakened. This means that all sorts of beings can travel between the worlds, just as it was in the past ages. These breaches must be healed once again if we are to usher in the new age."

"How do you intend to do that?"

"One that is pure of heart must travel between the worlds and find a way," El Brujo said. "That will be your path. It will be a long journey, and you will have many trials until you are able to become a being of power. But do not despair, for you shall have the help of allies in your journey. In fact, you have already one that will take you to the first gate."

"Y-you mean Bibsy? The dog? The one they call the trickster?"

"Yes, Coyote will be one of your friends for he has taken a liking to you, but beware his excesses for he can turn his tricks on you as well."

"So you're telling me not to trust him?"

"The trickster god has many guises, many forms, many shapes, and with so many appearances, he also has many personalities, some will be good and others malevolent, such is the way with tricksters. Some of his forms will be very helpful to you, yet others may have the opposite effect. You must be able to determine his capabilities and make a wise decision in order to use his gifts properly."

Tara nodded. "I see. So how do I make these judgments? How will I know if I made the right call?"

"You will learn in due course as you journey onwards through the portals of time," El Brujo said. "But in order to learn the ways of true magic, you must overcome the four challenges that you will encounter tonight."

Tara's eyes widened as she looked around nervously. "Four challenges? What are they? How do I fight them? Are you going to give me a weapon or something?"

El Brujo shook his head in disappointment. "You must overcome these challenges not with battle, but with your mind and spirit."

Tara started to calm down. "I'm sorry, I-I thought I had to fight or something like that."

El Brujo gestured with his hands. "The first of your four challenges has arrived. It is called fear."

"Fear?" Tara said as she suddenly felt an evil presence all around her. As she once again looked around, she could see a thousand yellowish eyes staring back at her through the darkness. Tara shrieked and felt the urge to get up and flee towards the shallow cave, but a part of her urged herself to calm down once more, as she fought her own instincts that were telling her to run away. That was when she remembered watching a movie on TV about anger management and one of the techniques that was taught was to control your breathing, and she began to take deep breaths as she slowly began to regain her composure. Within a few minutes, her heart rate had returned to normal and the adrenaline that was building up in her body began to subside. Her fear had metamorphosed into a sense of tranquility as she calmly stared back at the thousand eyes of the night. Almost immediately the yellowish mass of eyes blinked away and vanished into the darkness.

For the first time in two days El Brujo smiled at her. "Good, you have overcome the first challenge. To deal with fear you must face it calmly and without emotion, for when dealing with it when using other feelings such as anger or sadness, then that would only lead to more suffering. Now you must stare into the fire and face your second challenge, for now that you have conquered fear then you are ready for your next trial."

Tara did as she was told and stared at the flames. For a moment, all she could see was the flickering firelight, but as she concentrated she began to see other visions, other meanings that she had previously been unaware of. That was when it all began to make sense to her. Tara had realized that the journey that had brought her to this mountaintop had been through her own choices all along, as if she subconsciously willed it to happen. It was she who had decided to travel with Larry out of Arizona. It was her choice to run away from home, and it was her choice that made her encounter the skin walkers a few days back. Tara finally understood that the paths in life were not predestined, but were deliberately chosen paths for the individual, that in turn led to other paths down their separate journeys. A million myriad paths lay before her, and a million more new ones would open up as soon as she ventured down one of them.

El Brujo sensed the change within her. "Ah, so you have at last overcome the second challenge. That of vision," he said. "Your mind is now aware of the many paths that lie before you, and where these paths will take you, but you now understood that every path is a choice, and every choice you make creates new choices. Only by taking a step back and understanding your fate and that of the world as a whole can you now truly understand what it means to master the art of vision."

"It's all starting to make sense now," Tara said. "I can't believe I've acted so stupidly so many times because I failed to see the consequences of my actions, or how it would affect others! I-I think I might have caused the death of two people."

"No," El Brujo said. "You must also be aware that other individuals choose their own paths in life. They died making their own choices, and met their fate because of those choices. Think about it, would they have altered their choices had you not been traveling with them?"

Tara stared back into the flames once more. "No, I guess not."

"Good, then you have learned that not everything can be changed, but the awareness that fate can be altered will become another choice," El Brujo said. "Now, face your third challenge."

Tara closed her eyes and within seconds began to see visions in her mind. She could see that she was walking along a strange, glowing forest and her companion was a tow-headed boy. The second vision that came to her showed her standing over her dad and he was begging for his life as she pointed a gun at him. The end of the second vision came with her pulling the trigger, but Tara was instantly taken aback, as she willed herself in that vision to take her finger off the trigger and to not kill her father, even though her younger brother Timmy was cheering her on in the background. The third vision came when she and the blond boy from her first vision encountered a very ugly man with antlers on his head, who stood in front of a glowing portal to another world. As she opened her palm and looked at it, there was a large maggot that was the size of her fist, wriggling and squirming on it. Sensing that the worm was evil, she closed her fist and crushed the life out of the maggot as it spewed out green and grey juices, its blubbery skin split open in several places, and it died. But then a part of her realized that she once again went too far, and she replayed the vision once more, this time instead of crushing the large maggot to death, she instead placed it on the stem of a small plant, where it spun a pupae. Within seconds, out came a golden butterfly that flew off into the stars. A sense of tranquility washed over her as the visions faded out and Tara opened her eyes once more.

El Brujo once again noticed the change in her. "Very good, you have overcome the third challenge, which is called control. There are many people who have power over others and these people tend to use their power much too often, and without restraint and that leads to destruction and despair. A true being of knowledge does not seek power in order to destroy or to dominate others. They use restraint as a means to guide these lesser ones into becoming greater beings. The knowledge in using one's power properly, and in small amounts without destroying to achieve small things, is far more important than using one's power for conquest and dominance. This has been the fault of many gods since they have used their own powers for malevolence instead of learning to control their inner urges before using such things."

"So to have power without restraint or control is more dangerous than not having any," Tara said.

"Yes," El Brujo said as he pointed upwards. "You have learned quickly. The trickster chose you well. Now, onto your fourth and final challenge."

Tara looked up into the night sky. A question began to form in her mind. Did she really want to be a hero to save the world? Or was it just to gain respect of others such as her friends in school, the ones who laughed and made fun of her? Did she really plan on forcefully taking Timmy away from her own dad? Was her whole goal just to take advantage of her gifts or to help others find their own way? That was when she began to realize that her motivations were shallow and self-serving, and so she began to weep at her own false sense of pride. The night wind blew some of her tears away as she wiped the rest off using her wrist. It was then that Tara realized that she needed to make this journey not out of pride, but out of a sense of obligation with which to help.

El Brujo smiled. There were large gaps in his old and rotting teeth. "At last you have conquered the four challenges, the last of which is pride. For pride makes one do things for their own benefit rather than for others. A true hero conquers his own pride in order to help others. Now you are ready to begin your journey, for only after you have overcome yourself can you truly be called a being of power."

It was at that instant that the little Chihuahua appeared beside Tara. The dog was carrying something in its mouth and gently placed it in Tara's hand. As she looked at the little thing in her palm, she saw it resembled some sort of withered leathery button, glowing with a faint green bioluminescence.

Tara looked at it confusingly. "What is it?"

"It is called peyote," El Brujo said.

"Peyote which I took from a spirit world," the dog said. "I had just come from there."

Tara looked at them both. "What am I supposed to do with it?"

"Eat it, obviously," the dog said as it sat on its hind legs and stared at her. "Chew it until the juices flow and then spit it out."

"Okay then," Tara said as she placed it in her mouth and began to chew. The taste was extremely bitter and akin to eating dirt. Tara felt like vomiting, but she was able to control her urges and kept chewing to get it over with. Soon her mouth felt extremely dry as if all the remaining saliva in it just evaporated, and her mucous membrane was unable to produce any more. Less than a minute later, all feeling and taste in her mouth and even her chin was gone. She started seeing red and green spots in front of her eyes that blocked most of her field of vision. As she held her hands in front of her face, she could see that they had become transparent. It was as if her palms had become like mist. Tara could see the veins on her wrists. She could see the blood travelling along her body as if it were a luminous dye on an x-ray machine. The flames in the bonfire had changed color from yellow to cyan blue, and the warmth of the fire now felt like a cold blizzard.

All that she could hear was the whispering voice of El Brujo. "Your journey to the spirit world begins," he said.

"Follow me," the dog said as it got up and started walking towards the cave.

Tara could barely feel her legs as she got up. It was like she was walking on air. As she looked around she could see the stars whirling around in the night sky. A gigantic thunderbird flew overhead and hovered just beneath her, its flapping wings sounded like claps of thunder as it regarded her with eager curiosity.

As she got to the entrance of the cave, she saw that the inner cavern was glowing. It looked like a passage to another dimension as it showed a forest clearing bathed in a cyan twilight, just like the vision that she had earlier. The dog had already stepped across the portal, so she went ahead and followed it in.

27. Preparations

Brooklyn

"Alright, listen up," Lieutenant Joe Pascorelli said to the assembled police officers and ESU operators in the impromptu meeting room. The ESU was analogous to the SWAT teams that the other police departments used. "I'm giving tactical field command of this task force to Detective Val Mendoza. She's got the experience and the knowledge as to what we're facing. I know there's some of you with a more senior rank than her, but she is one of the few survivors of the recent attacks, and she has a special insight on what we could do to stay alive and fight this thing. So without further delay, the floor is yours, Detective," Joe said as he gestured for her to step forward.

Valerie Mendoza moved ahead from where she had been standing near the side of the room, and faced the team of cops in front of her. She had heard of the snide remarks about her face the moment she came back on duty, but beyond that there was a grudging respect for her since she had somehow survived, while many of the others did not. As she looked around the room at the grim and serious faces, she remembered Myron telling her way back when that she had the makings of a future police chief. She had laughed it off when he said that because she thought he was just making a joke. How she missed his guidance, but she knew she had to keep her composure and not to show signs of weakness or indecision. In these times, a lack of confidence would be fatal for all of them.

"Let's get this out of the way first. I've heard all the nicknames you people gave me since I got over here," Valerie said to them. "From Scargirl, to Scarface and all that, so if anyone mentions it in passing, it's no big deal because I'm used to it, okay?"

There were a few faint smiles, but everyone kept the serious look. *So much for making a lousy joke at a time like this*, she thought. A few days ago, she had taken the bandage off of her face to see the long pink scar marring her face. She had gotten some surprised looks, but mostly, the cops in the command post seemed to view it as a badge of honor, a battle scar for a wounded, but still able warrior.

She continued. "As you all know by now, we have had to evacuate Manhattan. We still have some police and National Guard units holding Washington Heights up in the northern part, but most of the island is now off-limits to police and emergency rescue teams. We have barricaded the bridges and subways leading into the island and so far we have been able to check the enemy's advance, but things are changing rapidly even as we speak. That's actually the good news. The bad news is we're also starting to lose control of parts of Brooklyn, Queens, and New Jersey to unknown forces so we're actually being hit from all sides. Now you may all wonder as to the reason why we're are planning to go back into Manhattan Island when it looks like we're being surrounded, but based on the intelligence we have gathered, we believe that there is something in the island, right at the center of the city, that is the cause of all this. And if we can get to that source and neutralize it, then we could put an end to the troubles."

A police sergeant in full riot gear raised his hand. "Detective, what exactly are we fighting against?"

"I'll tell you what I went up against," Valerie said. "We think it's some sort of cult worshipping an Aztec god called Xipe Totec. He is known as the Flayed One, and he is a fertility god. The ancient Aztecs believed that in order for crops to grow and for the land to have a good harvest, then ritual human sacrifice must be made in order to appease this god. The sacrificial victims have their skin sliced off of them and the flayed skin is then worn by the priests until they are dried and are peeled off. It symbolizes the shedding off of dried corn husks to reveal the act of renewal and the changing seasons."

Almost immediately the crowd of police officers began arguing with each other, some of them expressing outright disbelief, while others began to claim that it was the end of the world and they were all dead.

Joe shouted at them to be quiet. "Alright, pipe down and let her finish!"

"There have been other reports about some sort of ghost or monster attacking people on the streets and in Central Park. The government has received some video footage, but they have not commented on it yet," Valerie said. "We think that these are Aztec demons and monsters that are allied with Xipe Totec. We've read the reports that claims gunfire is ineffective against these things, so we have requested that the National Guard supply us with flamethrowers, but that request has yet to be approved. As of right now, since we don't seem to have any effective ways of dealing with those things, then it's best we avoid any encounters with them."

Another cop raised his hand. "What if one of those demons attempts to storm the barricades on one of the bridges, or in the subways? Do we just run?"

"We don't have any further information on how to deal with those things yet," Valerie said. "At this point, just do what you can, and try to survive."

An ESU trooper wearing full battle gear crossed his arms. "Oh great, so if we see one of those things coming at us, then it's just put our hands up and kiss our own asses goodbye?"

The room erupted into verbal chaos. Joe had to pound on the wall a number of times to bring everything back to order once more.

"We've received reports that some of the first incidents happened near the Museum of Natural History on the Upper West Side," Valerie said as she pointed to a map that was taped to the wall behind her. "So we're planning to send the task force to that area to see if there is any sort of connection. We've also tracked down and interviewed a few staff members of the museum to see if there was anything strange had occurred a few days before these incidents started happening, and they can confirm of a remote possibility for a cause to all of this."

Another ESU trooper raised his hand. "We're in Brooklyn. How do we get there?"

"Washington Heights is heavily contested right now, so we're going by convoy and cross into Manhattan using the Queensboro Bridge across the East River, then make a beeline to the museum," Valerie said. "The National Guard will be lending us a couple of armored personnel carriers, so we ought to be okay. Our main goal will be to enter the museum and deploy the forensics teams to search for anything that could pinpoint the cause of this. ESU teams will be deployed to protect forensics while they go about their job."

"What makes you so sure that the answer to our problems lies in the museum?" an NYPD detective in plainclothes said.

"We've had one of the museum staff members here yesterday, he's an archaeologist and he insists that strange things began to happen when they brought in part of a petrified tree trunk from North Carolina, or something like that," Valerie said. "It's the only one lead that we think that has a connection to what's happening right now. Any other questions?"

No one said anything. A few looked at each other, but everyone realized that the hard and grim task of investigating any lead in order to stem the flow of chaos needed to be done. They all were volunteers and each knew what the risks were.

"Okay, dismissed," Valerie said. "We'll reconvene in a few hours once the APCs have arrived."

As the meeting broke up, Joe went over to her and put a reassuring hand on her shoulder. "You did good, kid. Was this your first ever briefing?"

Valerie smiled faintly as she turned around. "Myron did let me do a morning briefing about six months ago, but I think that was more for fun than anything else. Now I feel I might be seeing the last of some of these guys when I saw their faces in the room."

"Don't worry about it," Joe said. "We're all professionals and we know what the stakes are. If we don't do this and put a stop to whatever's going on right now, then nobody else will. Let's go get some coffee."

As they walked out of the tent, they quickly heard a rumbling noise from where the staging area was and both started running towards it. Police and National Guardsmen quickly readied their weapons. Everyone was expecting an attack on the Brooklyn Bridge for days now and this could be it, they thought. Valerie and Joe both drew their pistols as they got to the edge of the compound. There was a hastily-erected chain linked fence around a series of tents and mobile office trailers that was essentially the makeshift police headquarters for the area, so a breach meant that they were all vulnerable.

The moment they got to the gate, they stopped in surprise as they saw what it was. A small convoy of a half dozen Stryker M1126 Infantry Carrier Vehicles came into the staging area, along with a number of Humvees. Heavily-armed soldiers in body armor and night vision goggles soon exited the vehicles as the cops and National Guardsmen stared back in amazement.

"Jesus," Joe said, "It's the government."

The rear door of one of the Strykers opened, and out came a grey-haired man with a beard and eyeglasses. Unlike the soldiers in combat fatigues that flanked him, he was wearing an old sport coat and trousers while accompanied by Delta and SEAL operators with thick beards wearing baseball caps. Valerie noticed a female soldier walking alongside of him as he spoke with one of the cops on guard duty who soon pointed towards her. Valerie holstered her pistol as the older man approached him.

"Hi, I'm Paul Dane," the man said as he smiled and held out his hand. "Are you Detective Valerie Mendoza?"

Valerie shook his hand. "Looks like you found me. This is my superior, Lieutenant Joseph Pascorelli."

Paul shook Joe's hand as well. "Detective, I need to talk to you as quickly as possible."

"Hold on a minute," Joe said. "If I recall, you're supposed to be a world famous author or something like that, what's with all these Fed types guarding you?"

"Professor Dane is part of the US Government's new task force on dealing with this crisis," the female soldier standing beside Paul said. "He's with the Department of Defense and we will be assuming command over this entire area as of now."

"Under whose authority?" Joe demanded. "And who are you?"

"I'm Captain Laura Niven," the woman said as she took out a piece of paper and handed it to him. "We're acting under the authority of the President of the United States via executive order."

"Look, there's no need for hostility here," Paul said sheepishly. "We're here to work with you to try to deal with this emergency. Is there someplace private we could talk?"

Despite the tension Valerie smiled. "Yeah, we can go to one of the office trailers. Come on, follow me."

The room was cramped, but it did give them shelter from the constant rain. Paul had also requested the presence of the researcher from the American Museum of Natural History who tipped them off, so they waited a half hour as the man was picked up by a military escort since he was just living nearby. Dr. Edwin Worlich, a noted archaeologist, sat on the opposite end of the table, his balding forehead was somewhat matched by his khaki-colored suit. Paul had met him before and knew him to be a very learned and honest man as he sat to the right with Captain Niven beside him. Valerie and Joe were facing them as they both wondered what was going on.

"It's good to see you again, Edwin," Paul said as he shook Dr. Worlich's hand.

Dr. Worlich rubbed the bald spot on his head and then adjusted his thick eyeglasses. "Likewise, Paul. From what I've seen, it looks like you're the head of a new Federal agency or something like that."

Paul grinned. "More like an ad-hoc task force. In fact, I'd like you to join us."

"Since the museum is now off-limits and higher education has been shut down for the time being, I guess I might as well accept then, otherwise I have a feeling you'd draft me anyway," Dr. Worlich said as he leaned back on the metal folding chair and smiled faintly.

Captain Niven turned to look at Valerie and Joe. It was obvious that she found the pleasantries to be pointless and just wanted to get down to business. "How credible is this lead of yours?"

"We've gone through thousands of tips that the entire police department had gotten in the early days of this whole crisis, and the tip Dr. Worlich gave us was the most credible based on what's happening so far," Valerie said.

Joe leaned forward. "So could you go back to the beginning and tell us what happened, Dr. Worlich."

"As you all know, I'm one of the curators of the museum's Division of Anthropology," Dr. Worlich said. "About two weeks ago, we had uncovered the remains of a petrified tree on Hatteras Island, off the coast of North Carolina. We were able to transport it to the basement level of the museum, and began the painstaking process of examining it. The reason why we felt this particular tree was special enough to warrant closer study is because there were strange symbols that were carved on the trunk … me and my assistants believe that it may have been written in Powhatan."

Paul's brow furrowed in slight confusion. "Powhatan? But the Algonquin tribes of that area never had a written language, it was all verbal. Are you sure?"

"Not completely sure, but I suspected that it was, and I was preparing a paper on it," Dr. Worlich said. "The symbols that were inscribed on the trunk had an extraordinary resemblance to cuneiform script and Mayan hieroglyphs. I gotta tell you, Paul, it was an extraordinary find and I was able to convince the board to get a transportation budget on it when one of my grad students uncovered it on Hatteras. After we got it to the museum, strange incidents began to happen. That's when the rains started and one of my assistants disappeared while working on the trunk a few nights later. We called the police and they searched the entire museum, but not a trace of him was found. A few days later came the evacuation order, so the senior staff closed the building and we all left during the initial phase. The cops called me back for an interview just yesterday about this and I told them all I know."

Paul's eyes narrowed. "Hatteras Island, do you think it might have something to do with the Lost Colony, Edwin?"

"Could be," Dr. Worlich said. "Either way, it looks like we're going to have to wait until this whole mess is over with before we can start researching it again. I'm just glad we were able to lock it up in the vaults for safekeeping."

"Hold on a minute," Captain Niven said. "You're losing me here. Can you explain the significance of this island? And what is this Lost Colony you're talking about?"

"The old name for Hatteras is Croatoan Island," Paul said. "There were theories that the lost colony of Roanoke may have settled there after their disappearance on Roanoke Island."

"Roanoke?" Joe said. "I'm not too familiar with it. Can you explain further?"

"The Lost Colony was a sixteenth-century British settlement that was based in Roanoke Island," Dr. Worlich said. "Sir Walter Raleigh founded it and it was England's first attempt to establish a permanent colony in the New World. A little over one hundred colonists lived there, surrounded by small tribes of Croatoan Indians. In fact, the first English child born on American soil was named Virginia Dare, and she was a part of that colony. The Roanoke Colony were the ones that introduced tobacco and potatoes to Europe. Now the ship that brought them there left to return to England for supplies, but when they came back three years later the colony was gone."

Valerie rubbed her chin as she was taking it all in. "Gone? What do you mean gone?"

"I mean every living person in that colony was missing when the relief force got there," Dr. Worlich said. "The settlement was deserted. Not a living soul was behind the wooden walls they had set up for defense just three years earlier. There were no signs of battle; it was as if all the inhabitants of the colony just dropped whatever it was that they were doing and disappeared into the wild."

"No clues? Nothing at all as to what might have happened to them?" Valerie said.

"One very cryptic clue," Paul said. "The only thing that they found of any significance was a single word carved on a fencepost in the village stockade. It merely said: Croatoan."

Valerie seemed confused. "That's it? Just that one word and nothing else?"

"That's it," Dr. Worlich said as he clasped his fingers together on the table. "The ultimate fate of the colony has never been solved. Granted, both England and Spain were at war and so it took years for a relief ship with supplies to get back to Roanoke, because England needed every ship it had in order to fight the Spanish. So it often took years to support the colonies out in the North American continent. Even the Spanish themselves were looking for that colony, but they never found it."

"The one-word clue that was left there might pertain to Croatoan Island, but there never was any proof that the colonists settled in that place," Paul said. "The colonists were instructed to carve a Maltese cross on a tree trunk as a sign that if they were forced to leave Roanoke, then there would be a message to the relief parties, but no such carving was ever found."

"There has been some archaeological evidence uncovered about fifty miles away from the original site of the Roanoke colony, but it's pretty sparse because of shoreline erosion," Dr. Worlich said. "The true fate of the Lost Colony is one of the great unsolved mysteries of history."

Captain Niven crossed her arms and frowned. "So what you both are saying is that what's happening right now might be some sort of curse? Because you brought the archaeological remains of that so-called lost colony into the museum in New York?"

Valerie looked at her. It was obvious she was skeptical. "Granted, it's pretty thin in regards to motive, but we don't seem to have any other leads to go on. This one lead coincides with everything, well almost everything anyway."

"What do you mean?" Paul said to her.

Valerie leaned forward so they all could see the scar on her face. "I've survived an attack by a large group of cultists just days ago near the East Village. They had flayed the skins of their victims and were using obsidian knives as weapons. My partner was killed. I believe the only thing that saved me was that I wore an old Aztec charm on my neck that was visible after I fell. My mother is full-blooded Aztec and she told me that the god Xipe Totec is walking around Manhattan right now."

Paul looked up in confusion for a minute. "Xipe Totec? The Flayed God? Are you sure?"

"It has to be," Valerie said. "I'm sure you government types have also seen the video footage of those creatures attacking people in Central Park, right? From their appearance alone it was obvious those were tzitzimitl, Aztec demons that looked like skeletal women."

"I've seen the footage and I'm not disagreeing with you," Paul said. "It's just that from the database we've set up, it seems that these so-called Pagan gods and their demons are formally tied to a geographic location as to where they originated. I myself survived an attack by Celtic demons called Fomorians in England, but my point is why would an Aztec god that's tied to Central America be doing here in the Tri-state area?"

"Well, since you did mention the Fomorians, and they were based in Ireland yet they somehow made it to London, right?" Dr. Worlich said. "Perhaps the Aztec gods may be making a push up north to us?"

Paul nodded. "That's certainly a possibility, but I would have thought that they would go through the southern states first. If what Detective Mendoza is saying is true about Xipe Totec, then how was he able to bypass the south?"

Dr. Worlich shrugged. "They're gods, obviously. I guess their power is pretty absolute at this stage."

"Which brings us to the next question," Joe said. "Suppose we do find a connection with that relic you have in the museum. What then? How do we kill a god?"

"My mother said that you can't kill a god," Valerie said. "The most we can do is to trick him in order to foil his plans."

"She's right," Paul said. "We may need a plan once we get into the museum. How to deal with Xipe Totec and how to deal with those demons."

"Guns don't seem to affect them," Joe said as a matter of factly. "We've requested some flamethrowers. Perhaps if we burn them down, it might do the trick, but so far our request has not been approved."

"You'll get them by late this evening," Captain Niven said. "We have a contingent of special forces troops here with us. They're veterans of Iraq and Afghanistan, and we're in the process of equipping them with special weapons that might be able to help so they will join you in the push to the museum."

"Which brings me to another question," Joe said. "I must request that Detective Mendoza be given tactical command of this operation. She knows the area and has experience."

"Just because she survived one attack doesn't mean she's experienced in dealing with these creatures," Captain Niven said brusquely.

Paul put his arm up to calm things down. "Hold on a minute, we're all in this together. Detective Mendoza, will you consent for allowing our soldiers to go with your team? You will have overall tactical command, but you must be willing to give them leeway if things get dicey out there."

Captain Niven looked at him in surprise. "Now wait a minute, this is now a Department of Defense operation and we have qualified military personnel who will be put in command and General Benteen is—"

Paul cut her off with a wave of his hand. "The president gave me the authority to chair this task force. If the NYPD feels that they have enough expertise for this mission, then they can retain command of their own units."

Valerie placed her hands on the table as a sign of concession. "I'm not a soldier and I have no experience in warfare. All I would like to do is to get my forensics team into the museum and have a look at this tree trunk. Whatever the government wants to do is their business as long as they don't interfere with what my men are doing. They are free to give out orders to their own soldiers, and I will definitely cede command to them if we're attacked, deal?"

"Deal," Paul said with finality as he ignored Captain Niven's angry glare. "Since this could be a very significant lead, I'm going along too."

Captain Niven's eyes were now wide as saucers. "What? You're the head of this task force. The area is too dangerous and I will not allow you to take that risk, Professor."

Paul shrugged. "Somebody has to go down to that museum basement and get a thorough examination of that tree. If there's any clue we can get in regards to solving this crisis, then it's imperative that we have all hands on deck."

"I cannot permit this, if anything happened to you we would have no idea on how to continue to deal with this crisis," Captain Niven said.

"Someone with some knowledge of anthropology has to be down there to deal with whatever it is that's written on that tree. If we can make an assessment on the scene, it would be of great help in solving this mystery," Paul said.

Dr. Worlich cleared his throat. "With all due respect, Paul, she's right. You're too valuable to be sent into the lion's den. Since I'm currently not doing anything, I volunteer to go in with the troops."

"This could be a suicide mission, Edwin," Paul said to him.

Dr. Worlich shrugged and smiled. "I'm divorced, the kids have their own families now, and as far as I know, they're safe. Anyway, I am part of the museum staff and I know my way around there. Unless I do my part, this whole thing could get worse."

Paul turned to look at his military liaison. "You need to give him the best protection necessary, it all hinges on whether Edwin can decipher the meaning of the writing on that tree bark."

"I'll do you one better, Professor Dane," Captain Niven said. "I'll be going with him and you can monitor us both from the command HQ."

"That's it then," Joe said. "All we can do now is wait for those weapons you ordered and we're good to go."

"And don't forget to pray to whatever gods we have on our side," Valerie said.

28. The Transformed Man

Ron Boland stared at the orthopedic cast on his left leg, the plaster had solidified and it was obvious that he couldn't bend the knee. That meant that any kind of running was out of the question. Then again it wouldn't have made any difference, since his right wrist was handcuffed to the metal frame of the wheeled bed that he was lying in. He was in some sort of infirmary. The room had white painted walls and a single steel door was located on the far side. All he remembered was lying in the back of the Land Cruiser out in the middle of the Arabian Desert. The moment he had closed his eyes someone had hit him with a stun gun. The rest of his short term memory was a blur. He vaguely remembered being put on the back of a cargo plane and the next thing he knew they were treating his leg.

He had been awake for several hours now, and was busy counting the tiny holes in the ceiling panels when the door opened and an old, portly man wearing a yarmulke and hobbling along on a cane walked inside and closed it behind him.

Boland looked at the older man. "What the hell took you so long, Ariel? And why am I handcuffed to this goddamned bed?"

Ariel Weizman found a metal stool and dragged it over near the bed before sitting down on it. "Shalom. The team was just taking precautions, Ron. In your line of work, I'm sure you understand these kinds of operating procedures."

"Fine," Boland said. "So now explain the restraints on me."

Ariel shrugged. "Again, we have precautions. In this day and age, we cannot afford to make a single mistake."

Boland kept his composure even though his anger was rising. "So is this how you treat your allies, Ariel? If I was to report this to my government, it would create a diplomatic incident, you know that."

Ariel threw his hands up. "I know this looks bad and I'm sorry. But I'm only following orders. The word on up is that anyone that we take in that has anything to do with Subject Noah is to be treated as a potential threat."

"My leg is in a cast because it was busted up," Boland growled. "Do I look like a threat to you?"

"Normally, we wouldn't have put you in restraints and instead would have allowed you to stay in a secure room with proper supervision, but right now we are short-staffed and we've got no one to spare," Ariel said. "We're at a critical stage right now because the dust storm has reached the Jordanian border."

"Ariel, I cooperated with your side fully. I gave my area coordinates in the desert to your people. And yet they hit me with a stun gun and sedated me," Boland said. "We had an agreement that if I allowed your men to interview this Subject Noah, you would then find me and my operative a way back to the United States. Am I missing something here?"

Ariel looked away. "A new situation has arisen. This Subject Noah has more intelligence value than we previously surmised and something happened to your operative that compels us to keep him here for the time being. So long as you do not make any trouble for us, I can arrange for a way to get you back to America."

Boland's eyes narrowed. "What happened to Patrick?"

"We're not sure. He was in the cave along with Subject Noah and they were talking—apparently the target was somehow able to … transform him into something else."

"What? What do you mean transform him? Is Patrick still alive?"

"Your operative is undoubtedly alive. In fact, he survived several gunshot wounds to his torso and apparently has made a full recovery. He is currently in another part of this installation and we are doing some tests on him."

"You're full of it."

Ariel sighed at the American's lack of tact. "No, Ron, I am not. His skin has apparently molted and the new skin he has is almost bulletproof. He has also gained tremendous strength and speed. It was a miracle that our people were able to neutralize him, but then again, I think it was because he was still undergoing the process of transformation. Reading the reports, it was like him turning from a tadpole and into a frog."

Boland shook his head. Everything that had happened in the past few days was simply unbelievable, but in the end it was true. He felt that nothing could surprise him anymore. "Why did your men try to disable him? Was he hostile or something?"

"Let's just say that he was uncooperative when we tried to apprehend Subject Noah," Ariel said. "He tried to interfere, so we used force to take him down. We sedated him and he's still unconscious as of now."

"Whatever happened to him is irrelevant. He's still an American citizen and you have no right to keep him here."

"Once we run the tests on him and analyze what happened as to how he became like he is now, then he will be free to go," Ariel said. "Provided that he refrains from any future hostility, of course."

"What about Noah? Where is he?"

"Subject Noah is uncooperative as to how he was able to somehow transform your operative," Ariel said. "But we have found other uses for him so we're keeping him here in Israel for the time being."

Boland scoffed. "This wasn't the deal I made with you people."

"Would you have preferred to walk out of that desert on your own, with those demons right behind you? Be thankful that we saved your life, Ron."

Boland grimaced. He could hardly maintain his composure. "Whatever. Now get me out of these handcuffs."

Ariel leaned on his cane. "Do I have your word that you won't try anything stupid?"

Boland looked him in the eye. "Yes."

Ariel got up slowly from the stool. "Very well, I shall call for an escort and then they will take off those handcuffs. You will then be placed on a private jet and flown back to the United States. If you keep quiet about this incident, then your man will be returned to you in a few days once our tests are done. Even if you do make a stink about this, it won't harm the special relationship we have with your country, you know that. We've been doing everything we've ever wanted to anyway and your own government has never threatened to cut off our aid or sever our ties so your complaint will be useless, but I think you already know that."

Boland said nothing.

Ariel turned around and headed for the door. Boland slipped out of the handcuffs since he had already unlocked them even before Ariel had come in. His captors did not remove his wristwatch, nor did they notice a handcuff key that was taped to the bottom of it so Boland was just biding his time until he heard the full story. Boland leapt forward and tackled Ariel from behind. The old man grunted as he fell face forward. Boland got his arm around the old man's neck as the CIA administrator began to search him with his other hand.

As Boland forced him up, Ariel shrieked in pain. Boland found a keycard in the old man's pocket, along with his wallet and car keys, but nothing else. *Pity he didn't carry a weapon with him,* Boland thought.

"Please … my neck, I-I can't breathe," Ariel said hoarsely as he struggled against the taller man's arm around his neck.

"You goddamned bastards," Boland said as he held the keycard up in front of him with his other hand. "Always in it for yourselves again, eh? Now tell me, does this keycard give you access to the entire facility?"

"Y-yes!"

"Okay," Boland said, "Now where are you holding my operative?"

"One l-level below us, please, it hurts!"

"How many guards in this level?"

Ariel was gasping. "Argh."

Boland partially relaxed his grip. "How many guards?"

"O-only four on duty in the security room in the level below us. M-most of the guards are located at the upper floor where they're making the go-golems…."

Boland's eyes widened. "Golems?"

"Y-yes, they are our country's secret weapon against those Babylonian devils."

"You delusional idiots. Okay, how many guards up in the ground level before I can get to the transportation area?"

"A reinforced platoon of fully-armed IDF soldiers," Ariel said, breathing heavily. "You're never going to make it out of here alive, Ron. You have to surrender now."

"We'll see about that. Come on."

As Patrick Gyle regained consciousness, he was instantly aware that he couldn't move his arms or legs. When he tilted his head, he soon noticed that his four limbs were bolted down with two-inch industrial steel clamps, as he laid spread eagle on a metal slab that served as an examining table. Across the room, he noticed glass partitions that divided it into sections as people wearing white lab smocks and surgical masks were apparently observing him while staring at their computer consoles. As Gyle looked down at his own body, it was clear they had stripped him of his clothing as if he was a corpse lying in a morgue. But what really surprised him was looking at his skin, for it seemed like he was in a brand new body. It felt like he was wearing some sort of pale, leathery armor with strange bumps and ridges and it had grown to at least an inch in thickness. He tried to lift his arms, but the clamps held him tight no matter how hard he tried.

The Israeli doctors and scientists who were studying him expressed both shock and awe at his condition. When they tried to draw blood for a sample, all of their syringe needles had failed to penetrate Gyle's thick outer skin, in fact every single needle had broken upon impact. Thicker, industrial syringes were quickly ordered, but they were still awaiting delivery due to the crunch in the country's supply chain because of the complete call up of all military reserves. When the subject's original skin had fully sloughed off, they kept the remains in an autopsy lab for examination, but it had rapidly decomposed, and within minutes had turned to fine ash. One of the scientists remarked that the subject was now a eunuch since his genitals had molted away and there were no visible reproductive organs apparent when they made a second examination of him. When they attempted to check for injuries after the extraction team had reported that the subject had taken several rounds to his body, they could no longer find any entry wounds, as the thickening new skin had apparently closed over them. When the subject briefly opened his eyes while they were examining him for injuries, they were shocked to notice his new eyes were crimson in color and had no pupils. Since they needed to wait for more specialized test instruments, all they could do now was to just observe the subject as he fought against his restraints.

There were about six of them, half were medical doctors and the rest were veterinarians. As they kept talking about how incredible the subject was, the fire alarm had sounded and they just stood around in confusion. They had never been trained in an event of a fire in the facility and therefore didn't know what to do. A few minutes passed, and the outer door leading to the corridor opened and in came Ariel while Boland was limping right behind him. The CIA administrator held one of the old man's arms behind Ariel's back in a painful grip. Just minutes before, the two men found a supply room and Boland put on a lab smock so he could disguise himself as they both limped past the unmanned security corridor, then into the lower level just as he tripped the fire alarm so as to distract the guards.

"Sir, what's going on?" one of the doctors said as she held a coffee cup in her hand.

"Shut up. All of you stand over there!" Boland shouted as he had produced a scalpel and placed it at Ariel's throat with his other hand.

"Boland, what are you doing?" Ariel gasped as the other man pushed him forward towards the consoles. "You can't free that man, he's dangerous!"

"He's my operative and he's an American," Boland shouted as he made his way to the consoles while keeping Ariel in front of him. "You can't keep him prisoner like this."

Some of the scientists began to overcome their initial surprise. Two of them held their hands forward in a gesture of peace while another man, who had a silvery beard and wore thick glasses, reached for a landline phone.

"None of you move!" Boland said as he pressed the scalpel against Ariel's jugular. A single drop of blood was visible on the old man's throat. "If you reach for that phone, I'll kill him!"

The others stopped moving and stood still as Ariel shrieked from the pain on his arm and at the scratch on his neck. Boland glanced over at Gyle past the glass partitions. He just couldn't believe what he was seeing. His operative looked like an unholy offspring of a crocodile and a human being. He could see the hairless, pale armored skin, and the unearthly face that made eye contact with him and stared back with blood red eyes. Quickly overcoming his initial shock, Boland glanced back at the lab scientists before he began scanning the consoles to see if there were any controls that he could use to loosen the restraints.

As he noticed Boland was now too distracted, the man with the beard moved quickly and closed the distance to the two men as he made a grab for the scalpel that was on Ariel's throat. Boland sensed it, but he was too late as the doctor used both hands to pull his wrist back and away from the old man's throat. Realizing he only had a few seconds before the others gathered up their courage and overwhelmed him, Boland used his other arm to push Ariel forward and into the doctor as he pulled back his other arm and let go of the scalpel. Both Ariel and the doctor fell forward as Boland turned around and started to push every single key on the consoles, hoping one of them would free Gyle. The others quickly ran over to him and started grabbing his arms.

Gyle had noticed the commotion as the group had swarmed on top of Boland and began to wrestle him to the ground. Another door across the other side had opened, and four armed security guards had burst in with pistols drawn. That was when he realized that one of the restraining bolts in the clamp on his right arm had loosened somehow. Whether it was because of Boland's frantic and random button pushing on the controls, or it was because of his constant resistance against the restraints he just wasn't sure, but now there was a chance to be free as he pulled at the now loosened clamp with all his strength. A few seconds later, he heard the sound of grinding metal as the restraint finally gave way and he was able to slip it off his right arm. Gyle could now hear panicked shouts across the room as someone realized he was partially free. He quickly grabbed onto the other arm restraint and he pulled at it with both arms until it too gave way. That was when he saw three of the guards had ran out from the partitioned area and stood right next to him as they aimed their Jericho 941 pistols at his body.

"Stop what you are doing!" one of the guards shouted in heavily-accented English. "If you do not stop, we will shoot!"

Gyle ignored the warning as he used both hands to free his left leg by ripping out the steel clamp that held it. Just as he got the first leg free, one of the guards started to fire at him, a split second later all three guards had opened fire. But all Gyle could feel was some slight pressure on his skin as the 9mm rounds seemed to bounce harmlessly off of him.

One of the guards had emptied his magazine and was frantically reloading as Gyle finally got all of the restraints off of him, then he leapt up into the ceiling. The three guards stopped shooting and just looked up in astonishment. They saw Gyle had dug his claws into the ceiling panels and was just hanging on right above them like some giant, pale lizard. Gyle had been amazed at his newfound strength and lightning fast speed, but his mind was clouded with rage at what they had done to him as he leapt down and smashed on top of one of the guards. The impact had crushed the poor man's skull and ribcage and he lay in a convulsing bloody heap. Gyle grabbed a second guard who just stood there screaming in terror and threw him at the glass partition with just one arm. The hapless guard went through the glass walls like a brick made of flesh and bone as a few of the lab testers screamed and made a run for the exits.

The third guard had dropped his gun, fell on his knees and begged for mercy while crying for his mother. Gyle just walked past him and through the broken partition as he stared down at Boland and Ariel, who were both lying on the floor as they gawked back at his fearsome image.

Boland sat up and their eyes met. "I'm sorry, Patrick. Sorry for betraying you to these Israelis. They made a bargain to take us safely out of the Middle East, but they screwed us."

Ariel rapidly shook his head. "No, no! Your superior Boland begged us to get him out of there, he was the one who betrayed you … it was he who gave your locations to us!"

Boland glanced back at the old man with pure hatred in his eyes. "You lying bastard."

Ariel frantically shook his head as he couldn't take his eyes off of Patrick. "No, no, it's true, Boland wanted a lot of money to bring you and the eternal man to us—"

But Ariel's words were cut off in mid-sentence as Gyle had grabbed him by the throat and pulled him up to his eye level. The old man's legs were now dangling off the ground as he gasped for air. Ariel tried to loosen Gyle's grip, but it was like trying to stop an industrial vise with just his hands.

Gyle's voice had turned guttural, it sounded like a growl of a monstrous dog. "Atrahasis, where is he?"

Ariel kept gasping, he couldn't catch his breath. "The l-level down below … aargh … last corridor to … th-the right…."

Gyle let go and the old man crumpled to the ground. He looked at Boland for a brief minute and said nothing. Boland looked down at the messy floor and didn't say anything either. Then Gyle turned and walked out of the exit and into the corridor.

Although the guards had disabled the elevators, Gyle nevertheless opened the lift doors and just leapt down to the lower level of the installation. He could see that this level wasn't quite completed yet. The builders had evidently left one wing exposed to solid rock as they had not yet finished digging out the earth at this depth. Following Ariel's directions, Gyle walked down the concrete-lined corridor to his right. A few people had seen him and they immediately got out of the way while a few just fell to the ground and screamed in terror. He ignored them and kept on going until he got to the door in the final corridor and opened it.

Gyle saw that it was a smaller room than where they had kept him. In the middle was a hospital bed surrounded by medical machinery. As he walked over, Gyle could see intravenous tubes all around the floor as he stopped at the foot of the bed. Lying on the hospital bed was Atrahasis, his gaunt figure dressed only in a hospital gown, his flowing white hair and beard had been shaved off; his arms were held down by restraints on the side of the bed frame. Intravenous needles had been stuck into his forearm and his blood flowed freely from it and into several machines that had tubes running from the floor and lay embedded into the nearby wall. Gyle quickly tore off the needles from his arm and ripped out the restraints as the old man stirred to life.

Atrahasis's voice was a faint whisper. "Thank you, my friend."

Gyle easily picked up the old man using his now massive arms. "There'll be many soldiers in the upper areas. I'll shield you as much as I can if they decide to fire at us. I can't guarantee full protection if we do it that way unless I hide you first—I could go around and kill everyone before bringing you out."

"There is no need for more killing," Atrahasis said. "Did you recall that there are rock tunnels in this place?"

"Yes, I passed by one such corridor just awhile ago on my way here."

"Then let us go there for I can guide you to a portal that will bring us to Irkalla, the underworld. They will not be able to follow."

"Very well," Gyle said as he carried the old man out of the room.

Rabbi Elijah Ba'al stood by and stared at the carnage in the examining room. Medical orderlies had finally carried the body of the dead guard out on a stretcher. There was broken glass and machinery all around. Ariel Weizman limped over to him as he kept rubbing his sore throat with one hand and led with his cane in the other.

"So they got away then?" Rabbi Ba'al said.

Ariel's voice was hoarse and it was painful to speak. "Unfortunately, yes. We do not know how they got out since they never made it to the upper levels. My men swept the area multiple times and there isn't a single sign of them."

"They are unique creatures," Rabbi Ba'al said. "I was not surprised we were unable to keep them for long."

Ariel shook his head slowly. "That's it then, we failed. The Holy Land of Israel will be lost. Our people will be scattered again."

"Perhaps not," Rabbi Ba'al said. "We have extracted enough blood and life force from the eternal man to animate at least forty golems, according to my estimation. We might as well proceed to stage three of the project."

Ariel looked down on the floor. More blood would be spilled now, but what mattered was the country's survival. Everything else was secondary. "So you want to deliver the Palestinian prisoners to the staging area now?"

Rabbi Ba'al nodded. "Yes, there is no time to waste."

29. The Larva

The moment she stepped through the portal, Tara Weiss kept her mind focused. She realized that the little Chihuahua had somehow transformed itself into a large coyote as it stood there waiting as the portal closed behind her. She was now standing in some strange desert that resembled the scrublands of the place where she had just come from, but the sand was bluish in color and it glowed faintly. Looking up at the sky, she noticed that there were no stars shining in the darkness at all, but she could see other planets in the distance and they seemed so close that she could make out their surface details. Their incandescent bodies illuminated the twilit world all around her. It felt like the entire sky was crowded with other worlds that she could fly off to, if only she had wings.

As she finally turned her attention to the coyote, Tara smiled at it as she zipped up her jacket. "You were a little dog in my world, but you look like a big coyote in this one, Bibsy."

The coyote looked at her grimly. "I hate that name."

Tara laughed. "But that's the name your owner gave you, right?"

"She sure did."

Tara shrugged. "Okay then, what would you like me to call you?"

"Coyote the Trickster would be fine."

Tara gave it the thumbs up. "Alrighty then, Mr. Coyote Trickster. What do we do now?"

Coyote looked around. "You said you wanted to save the world, right?"

Tara shrugged. "I did. But how do I do that?"

"Well, we are in the Spirit World so anything is possible."

Tara stared up into the heavenly sky. "So this Spirit World that we're in, is it like, you know ... Heaven?"

"Sort of."

"What do you mean 'sort of'?"

"Many ancient peoples had different stories that interpreted the other worlds. The Yaqui for instance, believed that there were five separate worlds: the desert world, the mystical world, the flower world, the dream world, and the night world. Others believed in an afterlife which wasn't any different than the world that they came from, while still others believed that one world held eternal suffering and the more deserving ones go to a place of eternal bliss. All these worlds have many meanings and it is only limited by your own power."

"Wait," Tara said. "Are you saying that this world changes depending on how you feel about it or how you sense it?"

"That's one way of putting it."

"So everyone's beliefs in the afterlife are all here? In this world that we're in right now?"

"More or less."

Tara thought about it for a minute. "So this place, it can be Heaven or Hell and I can go to either one and it all depends on like, my imagination or something?"

"To a certain degree, yes."

"Wow," Tara said. "So this means I can travel back and forth, all I have to do is will myself to do it, right?"

"You're starting to get the picture," Coyote said. "You must know where you are going in order to create the path ahead of you."

"Okay, I think I'm getting it now," Tara said. "So if I concentrate on a place to go to, then the path will open itself up before me? What if I don't think about anything and just keep walking ahead?"

"As to your first question the answer is yes. As to the second one, anything can happen because you may end up in someone else's path."

Tara nodded. "Okay, I get it. So the first thing I need to concentrate on is to how help America because the whole country is going down the tubes."

"Ah, well there are many causes to that," Coyote said.

"Well, I need your guidance then," Tara said. "Where's the biggest problem that the country is having right now?"

Coyote rolled its eyes. "Hmm, where do I start? Firstly, the thunderbirds are angry so they are destroying anything up in the skies."

"That's bad, what else?"

"Then you've got the Lords of the Night coming up from the south. They are very, very nasty gods, so I think it's best you get some additional allies first before trying to defeat them."

"Good point, I'll have to take a rain check on them. Next."

"Then you have the Hidden One who will soon be reborn in the great city to the east."

Tara furrowed her brow. "Wait a minute, he sounds familiar. I had a vision about meeting a boy younger than me, and I had this giant gross worm in my hand, so when you said the Hidden One, I totally remembered that dream."

"Ah, that is indeed him. If he is allowed to grow into the dark god, then he will do great destruction to the country you are from."

"Okay then, we need to stop him first," Tara said. "How do I go about doing that though?"

"The key was in your dream, think harder," Coyote said.

Tara closed her eyes and concentrated. "Okay, before I had the worm in my hand, I met that boy and he was in a giant forest … okay, I think I'll have to find him first. So all I need to do now is to get to the forest."

"Ah, now we are getting somewhere," Coyote said.

Tara opened her eyes. On the far horizon she could see a forest that seemed to glow neon green out in the distance. She knew that she would find the boy there so she started walking towards it. The coyote grinned and began to follow her.

Manhattan

When the rioting began, the staff of the American Museum of Natural History immediately closed their doors to the public and began to lock down the entire place in order to safeguard its contents. They weren't sure how long until order would be restored, so they had kept the emergency generators on standby in case there was limited power within the city; because they made sure the alarm systems were still active. Over a week went by and the museum itself seemed miraculously untouched, despite all the recent damage to the other buildings nearby when the monsters began to attack civilians in Central Park. While there was burning and looting all over the rest of the city, the museum itself stood strangely silent as a tomb. But it all came to an abrupt end that evening, when a convoy of armored vehicles with machinegun turrets sped their way through from across the East River and into the Upper West Side.

Once the lead Stryker in the convoy had turned toward the museum's parking garage, it instantly smashed through the iron-barred gate, rumbled in and down into the underground garage. The Stryker stopped at the closed glass entrance doors to the museum, while the other vehicles followed and began to park themselves in the once empty carport. Almost immediately, the rear doors of the Strykers opened and fully-armed soldiers and ESU troopers in battle gear streamed out and began to secure the area.

Valerie Mendoza opened the front passenger door of the Humvee that she was travelling in and got out, just as she drew her Glock pistol. Dr. Edwin Worlich along with Captain Laura Niven came out from the backseat of the vehicle and crouched down beside her. Valerie could almost immediately tell the difference between the cops and the soldiers. The ESU team members were all in dark blue uniforms underneath their black body armor, while the special forces operators were wearing TACAM and NWU digital woodland camouflage patterns on their combat fatigues. She noticed that quite a few of the soldiers wore beards, probably a habit they had carried over from their service in Afghanistan and Iraq, while the ESU troopers were all clean shaven. Valerie also saw that the black ops soldiers seemed more confident and relaxed, while the ESU troopers seemed tense and ready to explode at a moment's notice. One police trooper made a hand signal to her to signify that they were going in. Valerie recognized him as Lieutenant Frank Carbone, the tactical commander of the ESU contingent. She nodded back to him in acknowledgement.

Using bolt cutters, the teams were able to breach the museum doors and soon split up. Several squads headed for the Theodore Roosevelt Memorial Hall in order to secure the front entrance, while others began to head down to the basement area. Valerie stood up and beckoned Dr. Worlich to follow her as Captain Niven brought up the rear. When Valerie entered the museum, she took a look back and noticed one squad of soldiers unloading a forklift that they had towed on a wheeled platform behind one of the Humvees, while another squad struggled to bring in a large plastic crate from the rear compartment of a Stryker. Rapidly turning her head back and concentrating on the task at hand, she thought no more of it as the three of them began to follow right behind a squad of ESU troopers while they headed towards the basement stairwell.

Brooklyn

The command tent was a hive of activity. Dr. Paul Dane stood alongside Lieutenant Joe Pascorelli and Police Commissioner Donovan. The three of them stood behind the military radio operators and General Russell Benteen, the NORTHCOM commanding officer. Two fully-armed soldiers from the DOD were standing guard near the entrance flap.

"Task Force Omega has entered the museum, no enemy contact," a C2 officer who was supervising the radio team said.

"Make sure they have one team covering the Grand Gallery exit as well," General Benteen said to the communications officer who quickly acknowledged.

Commissioner Donovan turned and looked at Joe. He was a big man with a shaved head and he wore all the citations above the police badge on his uniform. "You sure this is gonna work, Joe? The department is at the breaking point."

"It's our best lead," Joe said. "And our only lead. The fact that DOD is here means they feel the same way. I have a good feeling about this."

As he looked at the others in the tent, Joe noticed that Dr. Paul Dane was deep in thought. Something was clearly troubling him.

Paul quickly looked back at Joe. "Did Edwin give you pictures of the writings on that petrified tree bark?"

"Yes, they're right in that brown folder," Joe pointed at a nearby desk. "Is something wrong?"

Paul walked over to the folding table at the side of the tent and began to sort through the pictures. When he found two photographs that contained the close-ups of the suspected Powhatan writings, he began to examine them closely.

Joe walked over and stood beside him. "Professor Dane, what is it?"

Paul kept on looking. He had sensed something familiar about the ancient script. There was a dream he had only days ago and in it he was in some strange netherworld where he stood before a gigantic tree and its bark was similar to the trunk in the photographs. "I'm not sure," he said. "Something just doesn't make any sense. I'm beginning to doubt that Xipe Totec is behind this."

Joe frowned. "What makes you say that? What about the flayed skins on the victims and those demons in the park? Aren't they consistent with that Aztec god?"

"I know," Paul said. "But there's something we're missing. I'm sure of it."

The Otherworld

They both finally made it into the giant forest. Tara was amazed at the size of the trees, they looked like foliage from earth, but they were hundreds of feet tall as their branches blotted out the dark sky. Their green leaves and the grass underneath glowed faintly and so she could see quite clearly without any need for additional light. There were no trails so they just moved on the flat, grassy ground around the massive trunks. Coyote had led the way since Tara had asked to see if the Trickster could use his nose to find the boy's scent. Sure enough, after a few minutes, Coyote led her to the edge of a small glade where they spotted a tow-headed boy wearing a winter jacket crouched down while he picked at the grass.

Tara had a feeling that time was running out so she decided on the direct route. She just walked out into the center of the glade and raised her hand at him. "Hello."

The boy looked up and immediately stood as soon as he saw her. He looked a few years younger than she was. "Who are you?"

Tara walked up to him with an outstretched hand. "Hi, I'm Tara. Nice to meet you, but I am in a bit of a hurry since I already saw you in my dreams, so I figured I would just come up to you for a quick intro."

The boy looked at her suspiciously, but then he remembered his own dreams as well so he shook her hand. "I am Ilya, from Russia."

Tara smiled. "Nice to meet you, Ilya from Russia. You speak pretty good English. I didn't know they taught that language over there."

Ilya Volkhov frowned. "You hear English? I do not speak English."

Tara's eyes widened as Coyote ran up and sat on its hind legs beside her. "Wow, this world is something else."

"In the Spirit World, all languages are one … even those of the animals," Coyote said.

Ilya pointed at Coyote. "Is that your talking dog?"

Tara laughed. "Not exactly, he's actually a Trickster God called Coyote so he's not a dog."

"A coyote is a type of dog," Ilya said.

Tara rolled her eyes. "Whatever. Okay, now that we've been introduced I was wondering what you're doing here?"

Ilya looked at her closely. He was still somewhat suspicious. "I should ask you that."

"Well, I asked you first," Tara said fitfully. "So you have to answer first."

"Very well," Ilya said. "I am looking for raskovnik."

Tara looked confused. "Rasa-what? What's that?"

"It is a magical plant," Ilya said. "I need it to find my mother."

Tara scratched the back of her head. "Okay, what does it do?"

"When the babushka in the orphanage where I lived told me stories, she told me about the raskovnik. The plant is like a key that can unlock anything, and it can uncover hidden things if one eats it," Ilya said as he started looking down at the ground again.

Tara looked around. "Okay, what makes you think it's here?"

"A goddess told me to find a quiet spot in the forest and I think I have been here for many hours searching, but so far I can't find it," Ilya said as he crouched down and began to closely examine the grass around him.

Coyote began scratching his ear with its hind leg. "That's because only special animals can find that plant."

Ilya looked up in astonishment. "What?"

"You need to find a tortoise because they know what it looks like on sight," Coyote said. "Or an animal god, like me."

Ilya ran up to the Trickster God. "Then you must find it for me, please!"

Tara crossed her arms. "Ilya, we'll help you find it, but you must help us as well. There's a god that is about to destroy a big city in my country and I need your help to stop him."

Ilya looked at her intently. He wasn't expecting to meet this girl and her strange dog. He had planned to be the one hero who would save the world and make his mother so proud of him that she would take him back and they would live happily together again. But then he remembered his friend Andrei and how lonely he was. He quickly recalled that the goddess had told him that he would need friends and allies, for he would not be able to do it alone. And he liked to help others as well so this was his best chance to do both.

The boy smirked. "Very well, I shall help you," he said to Tara before turning back to face Coyote. "Now, help me find the raskovnik."

Coyote moved its right front paw by an inch and underneath it was a small cluster of glowing yellowish clovers. "It's right here."

Ilya threw his hands up in triumph. "Yes! Thank you," he said to them as he quickly ran over and scooped up the plants and put it in the side pocket of his coat. He had a sense that he was being played, but his joy at being able to get the plant that he needed chased all his suspicions away.

"Okay," Tara said. "Now that you got what you need, can you help us?"

Ilya walked up to her and smiled. "A bargain is a bargain. So what do you need for me to do?"

Tara rubbed her chin. "Well, I had this dream about an evil god called the Hidden One and he lives in some sort of very old, very huge oak tree. We need to stop him somehow."

Ilya winked at her before turning around and walking off. "A great big tree? Why didn't you say so? I passed by a very big oak tree in another clearing not too long ago, follow me!"

Tara's eyes widened as she ran to keep up with the boy. "Wait up!"

Manhattan

"Looks like it's all clear," Valerie said as the team of ESU troopers had walked down into the lower basement level with her. The basement of the museum was subdivided into multiple partitions. There was a massive industrial elevator at the end of the great hall for loading large crates of antiquities and other artifacts from the parking garage. The crates would then be examined carefully by the museum staff before it would be put on display upstairs for the public. They were able to get the emergency generator working, but only a fraction of the lights was active, so quite a lot of areas in the entire building were still in shadow. The ESU teams fanned out as they tried to cover as much ground as possible while making sure the area was secure. One team went over to the elevators, while four other troopers began to go through the smaller storerooms along the adjoining corridors one by one.

Dr. Worlich started walking down a dimly lit corridor as he headed for the American Indian storage rooms. "Everything's intact, so far so good," he said while taking out a security key from his pocket as he stood in front of a pair of double doors. "It should be just about here."

Walking a slight distance behind him, Captain Niven kept her M4 assault rifle at the ready while Valerie headed up the rear. Dr. Worlich twisted the key and unlocked the door, then quickly walked in.

It was a large hall, almost as big as the one they came into and also dimly lit, as only a few ceiling lights were active. There were a number of large wooden crates along the side of the room that were as large as shipping containers.

"That's it," Dr. Worlich said as he got to the front of a tall crate and unlocked the padlock before pushing back the wooden panel. The petrified trunk was of a deep brown color and as thick as a small car. The trunk stood upright at close to ten feet high as it sat on a wheeled platform. Dr. Worlich grabbed the handle on the side of the platform, then began wheeling it out until it was just beneath one of the active lights in the hall so he could get it properly illuminated.

As Dr. Worlich set up a tripod in front of the trunk and placed a camera on it, Captain Niven tried to use her walkie-talkie. As she pressed the receiver she got a lot of static. "Must be the interference because we're underground," she said to no one in particular.

Valerie saw that everything looked okay so she started walking back towards the main stairs. "I'm going to check up on the other teams, I'll be back."

Dr. Worlich didn't even notice Valerie's departure as he concentrated heavily on setting up the remote video camera before turning it on. Then he went to a nearby table that had wheels on it and rolled it out until it was right next to the trunk. He then took out a penlight from one of the tools on the table and moved over to the trunk. Dr. Worlich began to minutely examine the writings on it while placing the headset over his ears and activating the video microphone. Captain Niven wandered off into one of the corridors, as she checked up on the security teams in the level.

Brooklyn

"We have video feed, coming in now," one of the military radio operators said as one of the formerly blank monitor screens in front of them went live. They could see the close-up of the tree trunk as Dr. Worlich began a cursory examination of it.

Paul stood with the others as he held up the pictures that were taken before with the live video feed of the tree trunk to compare them.

"It's clearly not fossilized," Dr. Worlich spoke through the video feed. "Because permineralization would take millions of years for it to happen, but the fact that this tree bark is rock hard even though it's supposed to be only a few hundred years old, so this is a baffling phenomena."

Paul noticed that General Benteen had his own walkie-talkie and he sensed that the general had some sort of private communications with his soldiers that were in the museum. He quietly observed as the general kept talking into his radio receiver. It was something about "failsafe" and "code zeta," but he couldn't articulate the rest.

Dr. Worlich kept talking through the live feed. "As you can also see, the writings that we suspect are Powhatan were thought to have been carved into the trunk, but now that I am examining it closely, it seems to have been branded onto the tree bark by as of yet unknown means. If you look at this particular symbol here," Dr. Worlich said as he used a remote control on the camera to go to a close-up of a strange glyph on the trunk. "It seems to resemble an eye with a hand over it ... what that means, I do not know at this time."

As he heard those words, Paul held up the pictures he was carrying once more. That was when he realized that they had all been wrong. Wrong about everything. Paul gasped as he realized the awful truth. They had all been deceived by the Hidden God.

Joe heard Paul's cry and looked at him. "Professor Dane?"

"Oh my god," Paul said. "It's not Xipe Totec! We've got to warn the team down there! The enemy is Okeus! The Hidden One! It's Okeus!"

Everybody turned and looked at him, confusion and terror in their eyes.

General Benteen looked at Paul incredulously. "What in the hell are you talking about?"

Then the video feed went dead.

Manhattan

Valerie had made it up to the first floor of the museum when she noticed something peculiar. While she had noticed that most of the other soldiers had set up defensive positions to guard the entrances and exits, she saw that one particular group had brought up a forklift from the parking garage. The lift was carrying some sort of man-sized plastic container which they then transported over to one of the side galleries, close to the center of the building. Her suspicions aroused, Valerie instantly hid in the shadows as she crouched down and began to silently follow them.

As they moved the plastic crate into a massive hall that housed the mammal exhibit, she noticed that the man leading the squad was Lieutenant Blake Rockatansky, he had introduced himself earlier to her that night and he was the designated field commander of the special forces contingent, that meant that he was in full contact with his military superiors in the DOD. While the ESU police troopers mostly carried assault rifles and shotguns, the special ops soldiers were carrying an eclectic mix of weapons, among the six of them she noticed two were equipped with those new civilian X15 flamethrowers that were hastily ordered, while another two were carrying some sort of multiple grenade launchers. Clearly these people had no concern for collateral damage as napalm and high explosives would cause severe destruction to the museum if they were ever used.

Sensing that they still hadn't noticed her, Valerie made a quick dash from behind as she ran over to the side of a free-standing glass display that enclosed an upright, snarling polar bear before peering out and trying to get a closer look as to what was inside of the box. As she squinted her eyes, she noticed that the crate actually contained some sort of white cylinder as she crept up to get a better view. That was when she felt a heavy push on her back and she fell face down on the floor. The force of the blow made her drop her Glock pistol and it clattered away. As she tried to get up, she felt severe pressure on her back to keep her down and smelled a combination of sweat and tobacco just above her.

Standing over her with his boot on her back was a soldier. He pressed down the barrel of his M4 on her neck. She noticed he had night vision goggles over his eyes. So that's how he saw her. "That's as far as you go, lady," he said softly.

Valerie cursed and looked up as she saw Blake walking towards her. The other soldiers didn't even glance her way as they used a dolly to elevate the cylinder out of the crate, then set it down near a glass display of two buffalos standing in a snowy backdrop. That was when she saw the yellow and black trefoil symbol stamped along its side. "What in the hell?" she shouted. "That's a nuclear bomb for chrissakes! What are you people doing?"

Blake stood over her as he adjusted the flamethrower pack on his back. "This is a damned pity, Detective. Even with that scar on your face, I still liked you. Now why did you have to go around sneaking up on us like that?"

Valerie was clearly upset. "What the hell is this? This mission is supposed to be a forensics investigation. Why in the hell did you guys bring a nuke in here? I would have never have authorized this! No way Professor Dane would approve of this! I want to hear what he has to say right now!"

Blake crouched down so she could see his stone-faced visage at nearly eye level. "Stop shouting, Detective. I'm under orders to insert the device here at all costs. Now if your SWAT guys make trouble like what you're doing right now, then I'm afraid we're gonna have to engage them and that would mean a lot of dead cops. I don't want to have to do that, but I will if I have to? Now if you behave, we'll let you up, or do you prefer to be restrained and sedated?"

Valerie nodded. "Fine, I'll behave."

Blake stood up and backed away as the soldier behind her withdrew his foot from her back. As Valerie got up, she noticed the soldier with the night vision goggles had taken her Glock pistol, removed the magazine, and emptied its chamber before disassembling it and throwing the parts on the floor.

"Now let me be clear," Blake said calmly. "My mission orders come directly from General Benteen. If this museum is breached, then he is authorized to order me to activate the weapon. You and your men have ten minutes to get to safe distance before it detonates."

"I get it," Valerie hissed. "So you people didn't even tell Professor Dane about this did you? This whole thing was a government operation from the very beginning and what are we supposed to be? Cannon fodder?"

"I'm just a soldier, ma'am, all this how, where, and why is above my pay grade. I just follow orders," Blake said as he pulled out a walkie-talkie from his utility vest and pressed on the receiver. "Echo Six to Omega Actual, the device is in play, over."

Brooklyn

As everyone was confused to what Paul had just said, General Benteen was listening to his walkie-talkie. "Roger that, Echo Six, you will detonate the device on my command. If we lose comms at any time after this, you have full authority to detonate the device at your discretion, over."

The voice on his walkie-talkie came back loud and clear. "Roger, wilco."

"What is going on?" Paul said. "Did you place some sort of bomb in the museum? I wasn't told of this!"

"Calm down, Professor," General Benteen said. "I got my orders direct from DOD. If the museum is overrun, a nuclear device is to be detonated so that the enemy doesn't get any access to the relic."

Joe was shocked. "Wait a minute, you got a nuke in there? What about our men?"

General Benteen looked at him. "Don't worry, there will be ten minutes before detonation, plenty of time to get clear, unless there's a rapid breach by the enemy."

Joe was livid. "This is insane!"

Commissioner Donovan walked right up to the general's face. "My men have families and there are still people holed up in that city. I can't let you do this."

General Benteen backed up and quickly drew his pistol. The soldiers near the entrance took the safeties off of their weapons and aimed it at the police. "This is not a debate," the general said as he once more keyed the walkie-talkie on his other hand. "Echo Six, we've lost contact with the basement, send in another team to check it out, over."

"Roger, wilco," Blake said over the communications link.

"General, do not do this," Paul said. "Nuclear weapons are useless against Okeus, he's a god. All you will end up doing is killing a lot of innocent people. Please reconsider this."

"I have my orders, Professor."

Paul took a deep breath. "General, the government just doesn't have the full picture. We are here in operations, right at ground zero. And I'm telling you that nuking the museum won't change a damn thing. We tried to fight the thunderbirds and the demons but none of our weapons work against them. We need to find another way to defeat them. Conventional weapons aren't the answer."

General Benteen sighed. "Who is this Okeus anyway?"

"He was worshipped by the Powhatan tribes. He is supposed to be the evil counterpart to their chief deity Ahone. The colonists called him the devil. He had been hiding behind the identity of the Aztec god Xipe Totec, but now we know that he's the one behind all that's happening in New York City. Detonating that nuke won't affect him," Paul said pleadingly.

The general thought about it for a minute. "Alright," he said. "I'm going to order my men to keep the device on standby until I know more of what's going on. But if your colleague in the museum can't work out a solution, then I'll have my men start a countdown."

Paul sighed with relief. "Thank you, General. Just give us some time. Please."

General Benteen keyed in his walkie-talkie again but now all he got back was static. "Goddamn it," he said as he turned to his radio operators. "See if you can get me the museum team right now."

For the next few minutes the entire C2 team tried frantically to get into contact with somebody, anybody, but now all they were receiving was white noise.

Manhattan

Blake placed the walkie-talkie back in his belt as he gave Valerie a smug look. "Looks like you heard it from the CO himself, if we lose comms with HQ then we detonate at our discretion," he said as he turned to the other soldiers. "Duke, take a team and head downstairs to the basement area to make sure everything's okay."

One of the spec ops soldiers who was carrying a flamethrower instantly turned and ran off into the back exit of the hall. Valerie saw that there were only six of them now and if she was going to make a play, then she would need some help.

Less than a minute later, they all heard a commotion coming from the front entrance as the sound of running and gunfire reverberated from the hall's main entryway. All the other soldiers except for Blake immediately began to position themselves behind cover. Seconds later, the ESU field commander, Lieutenant Carbone, ran into the hall along with five of his men.

"Val, I've been looking all over for you!" Carbone said. "We got contact in the Roosevelt Memorial Hall, some of those cultists are trying to force their way through the…" His voice trailed off as he realized that Valerie had her hands up in the air. Then he noticed the white cylinder lying horizontally near the far display.

"Carbone! They got a nuclear bomb primed here, we gotta stop them!" Valerie screamed as she dived for cover behind one of the displays.

At that moment, four of the soldiers opened fire from prepared positions. Blake drew his pistol while Carbone turned and ran for cover. Two of the ESU SWAT troopers were shot in the face and went down instantly, while another took two pistol shots in the chest and fell backwards onto the floor. Carbone took a bullet in the leg before managing to get behind a free standing display while glass shattered all around him.

Blake got behind cover as well, just as Carbone fired back at him with his Glock pistol but missed. As a wounded ESU trooper tried to get up, two more rifle shots simultaneously hit his temple just below the ballistic helmet he was wearing and he died instantly. As more ESU troopers made their way into the entrance of the hall, Carbone signaled at them to take cover as another one of them went down from a precise headshot before they scattered. One of the soldiers fired two 40mm grenades from his Milkor MGL grenade launcher. The high-explosive warheads impacted near the hallway entrance, completely destroying one of the large open doors and part of the wall. Some of the wounded cops that were hit began to scream in agony.

A few minutes before the firefight upstairs, Dr. Worlich had just finished talking on the microphone in his headset when he heard a loud noise behind him. As he turned around, he noticed that the video camera had fallen into the concrete floor along with the tripod. "How in the hell?"

And then he noticed them. Two men emerged from the shadows and walked up until they stood a few feet from him. The taller man had a slightly balding forehead with black hair and wore glasses as he helped to support the shorter man, who was old and wrinkly, with a sharp nose and long white hair tied down in a pony tail. Both wore black suits that seemed to blend in with the darkness around them.

Dr. Worlich just stood there in complete surprise, the pen light still held in one hand. "Who are you?"

The old man stood before him as he gestured to the other one to move back and was dutifully obeyed. "I'm Seth Solomon, and I've been waiting for you."

"Hold it right there," Captain Niven said as she came out from behind one of the crates while she aimed her assault rifle at the two men. The taller man shrieked and put his hands up. "I don't know who the two of you are, but you're not supposed to be in here," she said. "Get your hands up, old man."

Solomon smiled as he glanced at her. "The only one who won't be here is you, young lady."

Dr. Worlich saw something that came out of the shadows behind Captain Niven. What it was he really couldn't be sure. It seemed to resemble a man but it was transparent, almost like an invisible spirit. The being instantly grabbed her from behind, then threw the young woman across the room with such force that she went right through one of the wooden crates with a loud crash. Dr. Worlich was now too terrified to scream as the shadowy form advanced on him. He could feel a vise-like grip on his neck as he dropped the penlight and grabbed at his throat but all he could feel was his own windpipe being crushed. After a few minutes he slumped down on the floor and lay still.

Solomon subconsciously rubbed at the brass ring on his right hand. "So, now you have two more souls, that makes it a total of seven that I have given you."

The being turned around. "No, these souls were not sacrifices- they were unwilling. The Hidden One still awaits the sixth."

Elliot Ledwidge, who happened to be the taller man, just silently gaped in both surprise and terror. He couldn't believe what he just saw. His master was indeed a magician who had just summoned a ghost to do his bidding, and who just killed two people right before his very eyes. Even though he couldn't hear what the ghost was saying, it was clear that all the things he heard about what magic were true after all.

Solomon turned to look at his gawking manservant and sighed. "Elliot! Get over here and help me get close to that tree trunk!"

"Y-yes, Master," Elliot said as he quickly moved over to Solomon, took the old man by his arms and walked him until they were both right beside the petrified tree.

Solomon now pressed his hands against the hardened trunk. They both had been here since mid-morning and had waited until darkness fell, but the basement was locked and so the spirit had told him to wait because other mortals would be coming. Sure enough there was a loud convoy that came in the middle of the night. The wandering cops who searched the place were never able to find them because the spirit being killed anyone that got close. When the time finally came to reveal themselves, Solomon was silently instructed on what to do. As he ran his withered hands along the trunk, he noticed it began to move. It was like putting one's hands on a man's chest, he thought as he could see the once rigid bark rhythmically vibrate until a small tear was now visible near its center.

Elliot gasped in shock as the rip along the bark became bigger and finally the inner part of the trunk had opened to reveal something inside of it. Solomon placed both his hands into the inside of the trunk and grabbed onto something sticky and wriggling. When he pulled out, there was a large white maggot the size of his fist squirming in his hands

He turned to face his manservant. "Kneel."

Elliot was too scared to protest, so he got on his knees as the old man hobbled above him until Solomon's sticky hands were holding the grub was just above his face. Beads of sweat had begun to pour down his manservant's forehead. He was so nervous he couldn't breathe.

"Now Elliot," Solomon said. "You shall do one final task for me, you are to accept the worm into your heart. Your forgoing will bring out the Hidden God and he shall be free to reign in this world once more."

Elliot began to shake. "B-but Master, I…"

Solomon glared at him. "No more protests. You swore your undying loyalty to me did you not? Now prove it!"

Elliot began to cry. "Y-yes."

"Then open your mouth to receive the Hidden One," Solomon said as he held the squirming grub worm over his lips.

Elliot whimpered as he closed his eyes and opened his jaws. Solomon stuffed the maggot into his manservant's mouth, then he covered Elliot's lips with his hands so he couldn't spit out the grub. Elliot started to choke as the maggot worked its way down his throat, his muffled screams came from the pit of his soul. Solomon hobbled backwards as Elliot fell to the floor and began to convulse in pain and terror.

The being hovered right next to Solomon, its shadowy form becoming more opaque. "Well done, Solomon. The sixth soul has now been consumed. The bargain has been met."

Elliot's body became bloated as his stomach began to expand. Within seconds, he looked like a dead cow lying on its side as something within him stretched the skin like a balloon. His arms and legs disappeared as the bulbous pale flesh expanded until it was a blob that was now the size of a small car.

At that moment, a group of four soldiers burst through the door. For half a second, they all just gaped at the monstrous transformation as the expanding fleshy blob had grown into the size of a bus that was now crowding the center of the hall. Reacting quickly, one of the special forces operators moved forward as he activated the nozzle of his X15 flamethrower and sprayed flaming napalm over the creature. Another man readied his multi-grenade launcher.

The giant bulbous thing writhed in agony as it was sheathed in flames, Solomon turned to the being that hovered beside him. "I have done my part of the bargain so you must grant me safe passage now!"

"Follow me, there is someone waiting for you," the spirit beckoned as Solomon hobbled after him and they both disappeared back into the shadows.

As the second man began firing high explosive 40mm grenades into the creature, the other two men kept firing at it with their M4 assault rifles. The first soldier kept up with the flame thrower. The X15 had a sixty-second total burn time and the operator wanted to make sure he would use all the fuel in it. The explosions rocked the building, but the creature discarded its outer shell as it lashed out and rolled its gigantic, worm-like body on top of the screaming soldiers, crushing them like matchsticks as it began to grow even larger until it began to burst through the ceiling.

The Otherworld

They had found the clearing in the center of the great forest just a few minutes before. The three of them hid behind one of the large trunks and watched. A huge oak tree dominated the center of the clearing; its bark was gnarled and ancient as it was bathed in a glowering orange fire.

"Look," Ilya said as he pointed towards the base of the oak tree.

Tara could see two ghostly forms standing on opposite sides of the oak. They both looked like American Indian men and were almost identical though one had very handsome features, while the other's visage was twisted and distorted into something malevolent. Both figures had antlers growing from the sides of their heads. "Who are they?"

"There you can see Okeus and his counterpart Ahone," Coyote said. "They are the two primary gods of the ancient people who dwelled in the eastern coast. One of them is about to be born into your world."

"We need to stop them," Tara said. "Let's get down there."

Manhattan

The firefight upstairs had turned into a stalemate. The ESU troopers had the numbers and they controlled the entryway into the great hall, but the soldiers had the firepower and were dug in as each of them shifted from one prepared position and into another, all the while maintaining a steady rate of fire at anyone who tried to get in. Valerie was lying prone on the ground, but she was on the far side and the spec ops soldiers were too busy concentrating their fire towards the entryway to notice her. Carbone took out a handkerchief and made a makeshift tourniquet on his leg as he tried to get a bearing on the situation.

Valerie began crawling towards the edge of the display that she was hiding behind. "Carbone! Are you okay?"

"Stay there, Val," Carbone said as he sat up behind his cover. "Blake! Why in the hell did you shoot my men?"

"Tell your men to back away from this hall, Carbone," Blake said as he crouched low behind a shattered case. "I have my orders!"

At that moment, the entire hall shuddered as if hit by an earthquake. Everyone instantly froze in complete surprise as a loud rumbling sound began underneath them. Then the ground began to move as cracks appeared in the center of the hallway floor. The remaining undamaged displays began to topple over as the surrounding walls and ceiling started to collapse. A split second later, there was a rupture in the floor as the head of a giant worm pushed its way out. Carbone screamed in terror before the monstrous creature turned to him and bit his head off along with the upper part of his torso.

Even the experienced spec ops soldiers began to scream and panic along with everybody else as they all started running in every direction. As Blake got up and looked around in sheer terror, he saw one of his men, the soldier with the night vision goggles, slip and fall off the edge of the ruptured floor, and then was crushed by the giant grub worm as his body fell down into the basement. Blake knew that the position was untenable as he sprinted towards the device. The modified B83 nuclear bomb had an instant detonation fuse in addition to the timer, so all he had to do was to take the key that he wore in a necklace around his neck, and twist it into the key lock on the side of the cylinder.

As more of the floor collapsed, Blake tore off his backpack that had the flamethrower and threw it to the side before jumping over a tottering display. He made one last sprint as he got to where the bomb was sitting. Thankfully, they had placed it in front of one the main bulkheads in the building so the floor around it had yet to collapse. He could already see the concrete support beams cracking as the gigantic maggot grew even bigger. As he opened a flap along the side of the cylinder, Blake holstered his pistol and used both hands to pull out the keychain from underneath his ballistic armored vest. As his hand clutched the key, he inserted it into the lock and was just about to twist it when Valerie tackled him from behind and they both fell over to the side, near the edge of the gaping hole in the floor.

Blake instantly rolled and then got up as Valerie dove at him once more. She tried to put him in a headlock, but the spec ops soldier elbowed her in the chin and she fell back onto the floor, stunned. As she fought through the pain and tried to sit up, she saw Blake move towards the cylinder just as the remaining floor shifted again. Blake almost fell over the side as more of the floor collapsed right beside him. He struggled to regain his balance, the key he had in his hand fell away and flew down into the basement level. As he roared in frustration, Valerie crouched and leapt up into the side exit and into another hallway, just as both Blake and the bomb were crushed when the giant worm rolled its body sideways as it burst through the roof of the museum. Valerie started to run towards the Grand Gallery exit as the walls began collapsing all around her.

Brooklyn

Most of them had walked out of the command tent and stared across the river. They too had felt the earthquake and they could see the giant worm's monstrous reflection up in the night sky, as if it was some sort of ghostly image that had projected itself onto the rain clouds above. An intense, roaring noise like that of a shrieking bird, reverberated across the entire city as the great god Okeus had started to come into being.

"Oh my god," Paul said as the rain had intensified.

Joe shook his head in disbelief. "What is that thing?"

The Otherworld

The great oak tree looked even bigger now that they were alongside of it. The two spirit manifestations of Okeus and Ahone seemed to be just standing there as if suspended in midair. Ilya noticed a silvery thread of energy that was emanating from Ahone's avatar and it connected like a current to the tree. Okeus's aura was blood red as the evil god's energy tendrils were also connected to the oak's trunk from the other side.

"Look, there's something here," Tara said as she stared at the trunk of the tree.

Ilya walked over and stood beside her. Lying on the outside of the trunk was a very large white maggot trying to eat its way into the bark.

Tara immediately remembered her dream. "This is the symbol of Okeus! We need to kill it. I need to find a rock so I can crush it."

"Gods cannot be killed," Coyote said as it sat down on its hind legs to observe what the two of them would do.

Tara looked at the trickster in frustration. "Then how do we defeat it then?"

Ilya thought about it for a minute before looking at Coyote. "Wait, you said that they were two gods, right? Or are they just different sides of one god?"

"The ancient peoples believed that the many gods could have good and bad aspects to them," Coyote said. "Even the most malevolent god could also become a protector to their people."

Tara frowned. "I don't get it."

"That's it then!" Ilya exclaimed. "If we cannot destroy the evil god then we combine him with the good one. It will be a stalemate, like in chess. That worm is a larva—it can grow into something good or into something evil … if we show its true form, maybe it can grow as one god who can be both."

"And the balance will be restored," Coyote added.

"Okay," Tara said. "How do we do that?"

Ilya grinned as he took out some bits of the magical raskovnik plant from his jacket. "If the worm likes to eat, then feed it this. It is said to uncover the truth in whoever eats it and unlocks all doors."

"That's a plan then," Tara said as she grabbed the maggot and set it down on the ground. "Eew, that was gross. I can't believe I had to touch it."

Ilya placed the bits of raskovnik in front of the grub worm. "Now let's see what happens next."

Almost immediately, the maggot chewed on the magical herbs. Seconds later, it began to glow as it grew bigger. Sensing danger, both Ilya and Tara began to back away, but the grub worm had suddenly turned into a bluish wisp of energy that divided itself into two halves. The ghostly figures of Ahone and Okeus each started to move. Both gods took an equal share of the energy pool as both their forms began to merge into one. Within minutes, there were no longer two avatars but a single god that stood before them. As both Ilya and Tara stared in wonderment, the god placed a hand on each of their foreheads before finally turning around and walked into the great oak tree's trunk as they too merged as one. When Coyote walked over to the two astonished kids, they now saw that the oak tree had somehow gotten bigger and was now glowing with a multicolored, mystical aura around it.

Tara and Ilya looked at each other and grinned. There was a feeling of peace and accomplishment between them as they sensed that they had just averted a major catastrophe in their own world.

"Gimme five!" Tara said as she and Ilya clapped their hands together in triumph.

Ilya recoiled as soon as he touched her palm. "Your hands are sticky and disgusting!"

Brooklyn

As everyone stood watching with a sense of growing hopelessness, the gigantic reflection of the maggot suddenly began to shudder and collapse in on itself. A few seconds later, there was a loud scream like that of a dying animal heard across the city with such force that nearby windows shattered and doors flew open. The simulacrum of the larva had disappeared as its energy wave seemingly began to dissipate into the night sky.

Paul looked up as the rains suddenly stopped and the clouds began to miraculously clear over the brightening horizon. Some of the police offers gave a loud whoop while others began to scream and holler with delight.

General Benteen had been looking out from the entrance of the command tent. Then he finally walked over and stood beside Joe, Paul, and Commissioner Donovan. "Just what the hell happened?"

Commissioner Donovan didn't even look at him. "A miracle, that's what."

"We need to get EMS crews over to the museum," Joe said as he turned and headed back towards the command tent.

Commissioner Donovan looked at Paul. "Did that giant worm somehow die or something?"

"I don't know," Paul said. "Perhaps that larva was a sign of change since worms like that grow into something else once that stage of their existence is over. I'd like to think that it transformed into something beautiful, like a butterfly."

"Let's hope it didn't change into something even worse," Commissioner Donovan said.

30. The End of the Beginning

Manhattan

By the time the emergency teams arrived at the museum, it was already mid morning. As Valerie Mendoza stood beside the rubble that had once been a historic landmark, she realized that she had just somehow escaped the wrath of a very angry god. She looked up, and was immediately surprised to see that the rain clouds had miraculously parted as the morning sun shined over her. Valerie closed her eyes in quiet satisfaction as she could feel the heat on her face for the first time in weeks.

The convoy of emergency rescue teams came over fifteen minutes later. There were about a dozen other cops that had survived the giant grub worm's attack and the ensuing destruction of the museum. And about half of them were hurt. A number of emergency crews took the ones who couldn't walk onto stretchers and into the back of the half-dozen ambulances in the convoy. Valerie refused medical attention, but she did take the offer of a blanket as she wrapped it around her shoulders.

A Humvee parked itself beside her. Dr. Paul Dane came out from the passenger side door along with Lieutenant Joe Pascorelli. She hugged them both and told them what had happened. Just as she had gotten out of the museum, the giant maggot had somehow begun to shudder and collapsed in on itself as an energy surge was all around it. Within seconds, there was nothing left … almost as if it never existed.

"That was a near thing," Paul said wistfully. "Manhattan would have blown up if it wasn't for you."

"I think it was something or somebody else that saved me," Valerie said. "I'd like to meet whoever it was that did it."

Joe gave her a playful punch in the arm. "Maybe it was Myron. He's your guardian angel now."

"Maybe," Valerie said.

"So I guess it's all over then," Joe said.

"Nope," Paul said to him. "We've still got big problems all around the world. This isn't over yet."

"I can't help but think that maybe God was the one who saved us," Joe said. "If that's really what happened then maybe there is justice in the world."

"Either that," Valerie said. "Or it was just us."

Siberia

"God, I can't believe how cold it is where you live," Tara Weiss said as she walked along with Ilya Volkhov and the little dog along the snow-covered trail in the moonlit night. The jacket and sweater she wore just wasn't enough to block the cold, and she felt they needed to get to shelter soon. As they had passed through a portal and were now in the forests of Siberia, Coyote changed back into a little Chihuahua once more.

Ilya said something to her in Russian, but she realized she couldn't understand the language. Tara cursed out loud as she realized that they were no longer in the Otherworld and that meant that she wouldn't be able to communicate with the boy.

"He said he doesn't understand you," the dog said.

Tara stopped walking as she drew back in surprise. "You still understand him though? Okay, ask him what we're doing in this part of Russia, please."

The dog and Ilya chatted in Russian for a minute before Coyote looked back at her. "He said that in order to find his mother, he needed to return to the orphanage so he could find out her last known address," the dog said.

"Okay then," Tara said as she saluted them playfully. "Lead on."

Just as she said those words, Tara was instantly blinded as large searchlights were activated and were shown in their direction. Ilya cursed out in Russian as both of them were quickly set upon by over a dozen armed men wearing winter camouflage.

"What's going on?" Tara screamed as she was grabbed by two men. She tried to fight them off and run but they were too strong. "No, get away from me!"

Ilya also tried to get away, but they quickly picked him up and began to carry him to a nearby vehicle. The boy yelled out in frustration when they started to bind and gag him.

The little dog immediately started running into the forest as two of the men leveled their assault rifles and began shooting at it.

"Bibsy!" Tara screamed once more as someone placed a damp cloth over her nose and mouth. A pungent, bleach-like chemical smell suffocated her lungs and all she could think about before she finally lost consciousness was her little brother Timmy.

The Story Continues In:
Canticum Tenebris
Wrath of the Old Gods Book II
Now Available!

If you want a chance to get books for FREE as well as the latest news on this series and other exciting bargains, join John Triptych's mailing list. Joining the list is FREE and you can opt out at anytime.

Just copy and paste this link to your browser: http://eepurl.com/bK-xGn

Wrath of the Old Gods Series: The entire world is thrown into turmoil as the ancient gods of myth and legend return. An epic, post-apocalyptic series with multiple characters, mythical beings, and world spanning adventures.

> **The Glooming (Book 1)**
> **Canticum Tenebris (Book 2)**
> **A World Darkly (Book 3)**
> **And more on the way!**

Wrath of the Old Gods Young Adult Series: A complete and standalone series for young adults that ties in with the main Wrath of the Old Gods series. This trilogy centers on a young British boy and of his quest to save his country from supernatural forces.

> **Pagan Apocalypse (Book 1.5)** E-book version is FREE!
> **The Fomorians (Book 2.5)** E-book version is FREE for all mailing list subscribers!
> **Eye of Balor (Book 3.5)**

www.ingramcontent.com/pod-product-compliance
Lightning Source LLC
Chambersburg PA
CBHW021445240626
47153CB00001B/300